MATILDA

EMPRESS

LISE ARIN

MATILDA
EMPRESS

ARCHER • LOS ANGELES, CALIF.

A GENUINE ARCHER BOOK

ARCHER/RARE BIRD

453 South Spring Street · Suite 302 · Los Angeles · CA 90013
archerlit.com

Copyright © 2017 by Lise Arin

FIRST HARDCOVER EDITION

Set in Cochin
Printed in the United States

10 9 8 7 6 5 4 3 2 1

Publisher's Cataloging-in-Publication data

Names: Arin, Lise, author.
Title: Matilda Empress / Lise Arin.
Description: A Genuine Archer Book | First Hardcover Edition | Los Angeles, CA; New York, NY: Archer/Rare Bird Books, 2017.
Identifiers: ISBN 9781941729144
Subjects: LCSH Matilda, Empress, consort of Henry V, Holy Roman Emperor, 1102-1167—Fiction. | Great Britain—History—Henry I, 1100-1135—Fiction. | Great Britain—History—Stephen, 1135-1154—Fiction. | Princesses—Great Britain—Fiction. | Empresses—Great Britain—Fiction. | Queens—Great Britain—Fiction. | Fathers and daughters—Fiction. | Kings and rulers—Succession—Fiction. | Historical fiction. | BISAC FICTION / Historical
Classification: LCC PS3601.R5432 M38 2017 | DDC 813.6—dc23

The world stands out on either side
No wider than the heart is wide;
Above the world is stretched the sky, —
No higher than the soul is high.

—Edna St. Vincent Millay, "Renascence"

Foreword

atilda Empress is a book about a woman who does not get what she wants. Early on, she debates the merits of acceding to the restrictions imposed upon her by historical circumstances and patriarchal authorities beyond her control. Almost immediately, she considers an alternate path, one of resistance and self-empowerment. Because the Middle Ages were not a time when female self-actualization and daughterly rebellion were celebrated from the castle or hovel roof tops, Matilda's decisions to fight for her political rights and the man she loves are couched in heroic, mythic, and archetypal terms. When, ultimately, she faces multiple failures of love and ambition, her resignation and self-abnegation cannot be expressed in a way that we, as a modern audience, might expect. A woman of that period, even an empress, had to come to terms with grief and disappointment within the constructs of her time, and religion was the most available trope she could employ to express her abasement and resignation while still laying claim to public, social value.

In some ways, Matilda's career trajectory reminds me of my own. When I began to tell her story, over twenty years ago, I had big dreams—and an inner conviction that I was meant to be a writer. Once I had a draft in hand, and, coincidentally, a new baby in my lap, I sent the manuscript out into the world with every intention of receiving congratulatory letters and phone calls. The Internet had not yet been invented, so all the bad news I received trickled in slowly, if the recipients of the book even bothered to respond. And there I was, not an author, but a mother, choosing to deal with the nullification of my dearest hopes by burying myself in this other, draining new job. Another writer, famous yet surprisingly bitter, told me that historical fiction was of no interest to the marketplace and insisted that I would be better off shelving my project. And so, like Matilda, I spent a period of my life sequestered in the domestic sphere, trying to forget that I had had another vision of myself.

As the years passed, ten years, I grew increasingly abject and thoroughly pissed about my own passivity and inertia. Very few people knew my secret ambition, but the failure to achieve it still rankled. I found that I could not accept the status quo, could not let my own plans evaporate into nothing more than a daydream. Somehow, somehow, I garnered the mental strength to lay claim to my own future. I opened the proverbial Pandora's box, in my case a dusty hanging-file cabinet, and sat down to read my novel.

I wish I could say that I found it a masterpiece, but this would be far from the truth. I was embarrassed by my own shallow understanding of motherhood, for one, and certainly by my emotional distance from the concepts of futility and despair. What had I known about those when I first wrote the book, flush as I was with youth and promise?

So I drafted it again, and again, as my daughter and later my son grew up in the rooms next door. Sometimes months passed between stretches of productive work, as my children needed me to force them to practice their instruments or grudgingly escort them to birthday parties. Finally, I had the wherewithal, the courage, to send off a new version, only to be faced with more rejections. The more forthright parties told me that they did not care enough about my heroine's fate, because they could not relate to the angst and anxieties of an empress, too haughty for their liking, or even their empathy.

How could I make people understand that queens have problems too, and are as human as the rest of us? How could I help my readers appreciate all the difference eight centuries make? "The past is a foreign country," as L. P. Hartley said, and "they do things differently there." When a medieval nobleman was unhappy, he did not consult with a therapist, he went out on a public crusade, and set to killing Infidels, for good measure. If his wife's life was not what it should be, she repented, in front of their friends and family, for not living up to their cultural ideals, and she swore to atone, by lighting candles, indulging in acts of self-mutilation, building churches, or kissing the sores of lepers. Every bit of it was ritualized, concretized into meaning, and was sure to be more effective because it was watched and on display. The most private acts of prayer and confession were observed and remade into legend, proof of the feudal nobility's worth and conducive to the stability of medieval society.

Still, I took my readers' professional advice. They wanted more of Matilda, from the inside out. There was no inside out, during the twelfth-century, so I gave them, and you, the outside in. When my empress itches to take revenge on her enemies, she casts a spell. When she lusts for her beloved, she puts on a kick-ass, extravagant gown, and perfumes herself with herbs. When she is bored, she feasts on spiced meats or wears out her slippers in the garden. When she is at peace, she communes with her God and her saints, and they bring her the consolation and serenity she has earned.

If you have bought this book, I hope that you will treasure it as a triumph of the will and the imagination over stagnation, dismissal, and rebuff. Matilda only reigned briefly, and she never won over her true love, but herewith she tells her story into history, over and against the objections of a famous troubadour who wanted to tell it for her. Twenty years after I started it, I insist on unscrolling for you my version of these historical events, not only reinterpreting and reestablishing a disempowered queen, but recreating myself in the process.

Read on, and be inspired to fight for your own dreams. Give them up only on your own terms, and exchange them only for something of greater value. Define yourself how you will; write your own narrative. Hang on tightly to your own crown, the one you were born to wear. You are Matilda Empress.

Prologue

Scroll: 1155

*H*earken to me, Bernard de Ventadour, for I sing to you the history of a beautiful queen of the English and the terrible wars and devastation that convulsed her mighty realm. Her celebrated comeliness ornamented her high lineage, and she married to complement her status. Yet her bold, fierce desires brought forth much trial and tribulation. Only when she learned to abase herself did the Lord lift up His countenance upon her, and grant peace to her and to her people. Be it known unto you that she was Matilda, daughter of King Henry I of England.

†

WOE UNTO THAT OBSTINATE minstrel! Son of a kitchen maid, who is he to recite my chronicle, and make his art of my fate? His poem distorts the truth, so that I am reduced to a shallow figure of sin and suffering, almost grotesque in my contorted passions, inexplicably drawn to the forces that would destroy me and my kingdom. He paints me as a gargoyle, a she-beast frozen in vice whose redemption seems miraculous, unmerited, unexplained. Retired from the world, at the priory of Notre-Dame-du-Pré, outside Rouen in the Duchy of Normandy, I still catch wind of his stilted, simplistic narrative. Worthy readers, listen to me, as well as to the versemaker; I am more than his opportunistic entertainment.

I have had plenty of time to record my own story. I did not dictate my recollections to a clerk, but wrote down my memories in the years of quiet hours that I whiled away in my solar. My script is not elegant, like that of a monk; my letters are often cramped and ill-formed and never seem to stretch out evenly across my page. But what I recalled was too private, at the time, for the assistance of a secretary. I submit to you simple strips of parchment, rolled up and tagged with my imperial seal.

Authentic copies, meticulously replicated by the trusted scribes of this priory, and signed in my own hand, have been transported in ironbound oaken coffers to the courts of those of highest birth and consequence. Each chest has three locked compartments, to separate the scrolls into chronological periods, for my archive unspools at length. Those parchments on the left, the Treasury of the Lion, begin the tale; those in the center, the Matter of the Crown, continue it; those on the right, the Mirror of the Plantagenet, bring my tumultuous biography to completion.

You, who are so illustrious as to have received my gift, must disseminate it among your foremost vassals. Call a festival! My testament shall serve as its centerpiece. Let it divert your crowd of barons, in the idle days away from their fields of war. Rely on it to amuse your gaggle of baronesses, lessening the boredom of exchanging stale pleasantries and calculating the cost of each other's jewels.

See to it that you hire only the most polished player to relate my legend. But remember: my epic is not merely a jongleur's stylized performance, improvised and evolving, shifty and sly. Do not allow your man to strum lightly on a harp, or bat his limpid eyes at you, to weaken your discrimination or befuddle your taste. He may sing for his supper, as that fool Bernard does, washing your roast meat down with your spiced wine, but the words that fall from his mouth will be nothing but the truth.

Bernard's confabulations have been constructed to keep your interest through the lull of an evening, and if, in the light of the day, my reputation suffers for his creativity, his honor is none the worse for it. To each of my texts, I append de Ventadour's version of events. If you, noble gentlemen of distinction and discernment, princes all, are not inclined to credit my side of the story, I will pray for the salvation of your understanding, along with that of your soul. Courtly ladies, I have undertaken to recount my saga in your name, for I trust to your generosity of spirit and refinement of judgment.

As my history unfolds, you will find romance aplenty, for love always transforms the adventures of a woman, whatever her destiny. Fear not — as my account unravels, ultimately there will be redemption in faith. If I sank into the abyss of sin, I also crawled toward the oasis of virtue. If I plumbed the depths of suffering, I also climbed the mountains of joy. If I fought under the banner of love, it was in fealty to two different empires, one of the spirit and one of the flesh. Be it known unto you that I was the Empress of the Romans, the queen of England, the Duchess of Normandy, and the Countess of Anjou, who yet never ruled over the territory of her chosen knight's heart. Be it known unto you that I myself arose to conquer the largest fief, achieving the most sumptuous reward, the blessing of heaven.

†

BEFORE YOU CAN BEGIN to unwind the annals of Matilda Empress, and compare them to that arse of a minstrel's adaptation, I must describe what came to pass in 1110, when I was still Princess Alice Ethelric, the eight-year-old daughter of King Henry I of England. Before the year was out, I fulfilled the ambitions of my most august father, departing my homeland as the betrothed of Henry V, king of Germany and Italy and the Holy Roman emperor.

That summer, I prepared to take leave of my family and country. I was but weakly attached to my younger brother, Prince William, presumptive successor to the English throne, nor did he value me. An anxious youth, he was devoted only to our half-sister Maud, blonde and placid, born to one of our father's mistresses. I did regret the coming separation from my half-brother Robert, Earl of Gloucester, the only illegitimate sibling for whom I had any respect. More regal than Prince William, he had inherited Henry I's talents, and would have made a fine king. But Robert refused to be bitter about his birth, for he surpassed all of the court in manners as well as in accomplishments. He cared for me, who saw his true worth.

My royal father was wont to ignore such a weasel as I. Now that I was to be Holy Roman empress, he boasted of me, of my position in our dynasty. My fiancé was the most powerful king in Christendom. I was acknowledged as Maud's superior, William's foremost sister, and England's preeminent daughter. My willfulness was forgotten. Never again was I to be trussed up and plunged into a filthy moat to cure me of my disobedient humor. As the affianced of Henry V, I no longer had to submit to chastisement. I pledged to display, heretofore, a proper and feminine softness, but this was a vow that I made to myself.

Attention, how I courted it as a girl! My Uncle David always obliged me, and was heard to prophecy that Henry V would fall down on his knees in approval and thanksgiving when he saw me bedecked in nuptial jewels and draperies. Busybodies speculated that Uncle David hankered to wed me himself. His brother, Alexander king of Scotland, had married one of my bastard sisters, Sybil. I was quite fond of David, but it was much more to my liking to be an empress at the center of Europe than a lady-in-waiting in a cold, northern keep. The one time Uncle embraced me, catching me alone in a damp alley of Westminster castle and pressing me against a mossy wall with his legs, I squirmed out of his hot grip and scampered away. David laughed and let me go, for he would not force himself upon a royal kinswoman.

The scandalmongers who whispered about every couple entangled in the dark passages of our palaces thought me too young to be the subject of their talk, yet I knew all about men's appetites — the daughter of King Henry could not be ignorant. Unbeknownst to them, I also kissed my cousin Stephen, King Henry's favorite nephew, the younger son of his sister, the Countess of Blois. His Majesty had gifted the boy with many royal estates, such as the Counties of Mortain and Lancaster. Close to me in age, the redheaded youth often made one of our family parties. And one day, while exploring the shadowy corners of a brew house, evading its cobwebs and mouse droppings, we tumbled over one another. I enjoyed the taste of his soft lips and the pressure of his warm tongue in my mouth. After a moment, my cousin pushed me off and swore me to secrecy.

Before my betrothal, I had hoped to be plighted to Stephen, as my father seemed to intend him for a great match. Later, promised to the Holy Roman emperor, I was content. An ambitious princess, I scorned the status of countess. To a child, life stretched wider than love.

Resplendent in their continental finery, the German envoys sent to collect me from the provincial English court were relieved to find me very willing to depart. They praised my newly dignified demeanor, judging me well suited to rule over Germany, Denmark, Holland, Belgium, Italy, Poland, and Hungary. With my ancestry and education, and dark-haired, dark-eyed budding beauty, they declared that I should make the emperor a fine wife. It was foreseen that I would bear Henry V many sons. Yet "Ethelric," so purely Anglo-Saxon, dismayed the ambassadors; "Alice" bored them. My name was changed to match the future that awaited me. Born a princess, I stood ready to be lifted higher, transformed into the fabled Matilda Empress.

†

DESPITE MY FEELINGS OF anticipation, the sea voyage to Boulogne sickened me. Traveling overland was no better than sailing, and I suffered from bruises and chafing instead of nausea. We were quite a long, unwieldy procession of carts and pack animals, all laden with my dowry of magnificent treasures. Each endless day, we rose at dawn to recite mass. At midday, we halted briefly to eat, then drove on until dusk. Although I could dispense with my fear of sea monsters and drowning, I was constantly on the lookout for trolls, giants, and bandits along the unfamiliar highways and desolate byways.

Sometimes we sought harbor at a monastery, but those accommodations were rarely amenable. Unwilling to permit visitors any novelty or luxury, the religious guesthouses were often littered with heels of rotting bread, heaps of gnawed bones, and scraps of soiled linen. The monks seldom bothered to launder the blankets, and my retinue set to shaking and sunning them, in an almost futile attempt to eradicate their lice and fleas. In accordance with my station, I was usually allotted a private cell, but even my grate sat empty of firewood. If there was a basin or tub, it was invariably filled with the dirty water of its last occupant. No one suggested that I bathe my feet, nor was I tempted to do so. I slept fitfully in my filthy hose, clutching my arms against the cold.

On better days, I warmed myself in front of a blazing hearth, washed my extremities, and slept deeply in a featherbed at commodious, pleasant castles belonging to obsequious barons. In return for their hospitality, they plied me with questions about the state of the roads and the health and welfare of their neighbors and relatives. Eager to gossip, the baronesses squawked about the personal charms of my affianced husband. Tall, thin, and blond, with a nose like a hawk's beak, he had ignited a flame in the breast of many a German damsel, but had not wished to serve and honor any of them. Certain noble ladies insisted that he had escaped the wounds of passion's arrows; others claimed that he had a black stone instead of a heart and thus could not love any woman.

Along the inhabited routes, burghers and peasants clamored for a glimpse of me, although I fear they saw little beneath my mud covered mantle and my generous veil. I proceeded slowly among them, keeping my white, Hungarian palfrey well in check, so that they might have some small chance of prostrating themselves before their queen-to-be. The swell of their commentary washed over me; many marveled at my beauty, but some made jokes at my expense.

When our path wound through a forest, the gloom and cold unnerved us. It was a difficult thing to laugh when the sky had been hidden from view for the whole day. If we saw the scattered remains of a fire, we hoped that it was the former campsite of hunters, hermits, or wax gatherers, and not of fugitive serfs. Usually, however, we went hours without noticing the evidence of any habitation. The trees were a shadowy wilderness that emphasized our isolation. It was hard to credit my relevance to European affairs, my fame and significance, in the vast, uncultivated stretches of road. When we emerged, to travel through mountains and valleys, I was glad to see and feel the sun. Even then, the vastness of the landscape dwarfed the pretensions of our cortege.

I had ceased childish games; my dolls and knucklebones remained behind me in England. Every day, from the saddle, I mastered German with the gaggle of imperial clerks, repeating verbs and mimicking phrases. With the German chaplain, I recited scripture and discoursed upon the wondrous grace of our most Holy Mother, the Virgin Mary, swearing myself to Her service, beyond the mere commemoration of Her feast days. Thus, I prepared myself to be an avid pillar of the German church, and a true daughter of Germany.

I blush to admit that my juvenile oaths to Our Blessed Lady were those of convenience, and that every one of my pledges to Her was made with a puerile heart. When I spoke of the Virgin's Five Joys, I thought more of my own recent annunciation, the announcement of my impending eminence, and my own imminent assumption of imperial glory. When I piously listed Her miracles, and venerated Her name, I considered Her as merely the most distinguished of my vassals, whose powers were at my disposal, and whose reputation was to be at the service of my own ambition.

As the end of the journey approached, I sat taller atop my prancing white horse, and began to feel myself almost divine. At Liège, to honor my arrival, Henry V commanded so much fanfare that my head spun. The bells and trumpets rang out all day long. During the celebration, dancers tossed colorful flowers at my feet. My intended held my hand in welcome, yet his fingers felt cold and his gaze indifferent. Speaking from a dais, sitting alongside me, the emperor proclaimed the rights and duties of his consort. In front of the numerous assembly of courtiers and imperial administrators, he accorded me varied German lands and properties. Finally, he presented me with an enormous engraved seal for my official documents. Inscribed along the circumference were the words "Matilda, by the grace of God, queen of the Romans."

Despite my position, Henry rapidly dismissed all the women I had transported to form an English household. For my personal maid and companion, the emperor chose his milk-sister, Gerta, a commoner closely tied to him by affection. She was not uncomely, but she frightened me with her prominent brow, heavy features, broad shoulders, and capacious bosom. It was clear that she had been appointed the overseer of all my private occupations and ministrations. I was to be watched over, as I had been at home.

Adapting with alacrity to her new role, Gerta became my familiar, harassing and haranguing me. In order to be a credit the to Holy Roman Empire, I had to be ruled by her advice. The woman insisted that I always act as if guided by the seven gifts of the Holy Spirit: four for the mind — rationality, understanding, wisdom, and good counsel; three for the heart — piety, courage, and fear of the Lord.

We traveled to Mainz; a short while thereafter, my coronation took place on the Feast of Saint James, the first martyr of the Apostles. During the lengthy proceedings in the royal chapel, Gerta stood beside me, attending to my dress and behavior, ensuring that I did not mar Henry's dignity. The imperial crown was enormous, and we both were at some pains to keep it on my brow. My legs shuddered in fatigue, under my copious robes, but I was not permitted to take my seat on the throne.

After the sacred rites, in which I was anointed by God, I was allowed to brush my lips against the preserved hand of the blessed saint whose name day it was. This trembling kiss consecrated my change of rank more than any of the *Te Deums* tolling above my weary head. In the chaos and jubilation that followed, Gerta somehow purloined the relic, hiding it first in her sleeves, and then secreting it in a lovely blue enamel casket that safeguarded my jewels. The Apostle, cherished, stalwart, and glorious, would gird my spirit during the ensuing years of marriage, fortify my soul to serve the empire wisely, and soften my heart to love the emperor, as well.

The Treasury of the Lion

Scroll One: 1126

o I command your interest? When the time was ripe, destiny approached the lovely empress in the guise of joy and sadness. A certain nobleman earned her devotion, but there are no earthly attachments that cannot give occasion to some evil. Matilda was not to be dissuaded from her whim, although the man himself thought the better of it. From this strong and somewhat unrequited affection arose many tragedies.

†

Summer

I AM THE DOWAGER Empress Matilda, twenty-four years old and a widow. I travel on a ship bound for England, my homeland. I enjoy the sensation of speed, and relish the early morning fog that surrounds me like a cloak. I always stand upwind from the crew's stench and stretch my face into the gusts of fresh air that swell our sails and tangle my veil and braids. I inhale deeply of the brisk breeze, for it is the breath of our Heavenly Father. To keep my mind occupied, I chant the blessings of Christ: "Tranquility, amour, purity, discipline, strength, form, rule, custom, terminus, road, counsellor, foundation, heart, blaze, majesty, essence, lion of creation. Amen."

Each day I scan the sky for the sea birds that will herald the coastline, as vultures are the harbingers of a corpse. Death and upheaval are two faces of the same coin. Cancer defeated my husband at Utrecht, revoking my whole future. If I had had a son, I would have reigned in his stead, during his minority. Instead, the Duke of Saxony is elevated to the throne of the Holy Roman Empire. Having turned over most of the imperial regalia, all but one seal, I am put forth on the ocean, to a new beginning. Although many forget my English origins, I do not aspire to wed any of the minor German princes who compete for my hand, as a means to remain in my adopted country. Neither do I wish to immure myself in any European convent, to spend the rest of my days outside the ebb and flow of all the world's affairs.

As empress, I was praised for my lineage, my appearance, and my virtue. My marriage was celebrated lavishly at Worms; the highborn attendants who carried my train included five archbishops and five dukes. There were minstrels, jesters, and dancers without number; the elaborate feasting and novel entertainments lasted days on end. Our gifts glittered with costly gems. I myself marveled at the enormous size and elaborate rituals of our assembly. Only Gerta worried that the unruly flock of barons, prelates, and townsfolk, amassed at Worms to eat and drink and make merry, consorted purely for their own benefit.

Henry, a reserved but respectful husband, rarely asserted his conjugal rights. My one pregnancy resulted in a stillborn child. Without a successor, his throne would either fall to his enemies or be subject to election. Our courtiers prayed for an heir, but the emperor was preoccupied with raising taxes, contesting the pope's appointments, and crushing the insubordination of mutinous vassals. Henry sired several illegitimate children, but his aloofness to me did not portend a grand affair; politics consumed his spirit.

The German nobility grieved over my empty cradle, but blamed our sterility on the emperor's disobedience to the pontiff. I prayed for Our Mother Mary's intercession, and was never named the culprit, but was instead esteemed and favored. Many of the meddling sycophants attached to our household muttered against their supreme emperor's impassive demeanor toward me, and several of his advisors, those with the least to lose or the most to gain from the birth of a prince, went so far as to encourage him to attend more closely to his nubile wife.

Despite his impartiality, I ruled alongside Henry, and together we vigilantly solidified our vast empire. From time to time, as was the queen's privilege, I interceded with the emperor, either to gain his pardon or patronage. Those whose petitions and grants I sponsored were generous to me thereafter, winning me many friends and allies. Their accolades were many; I came to be known as "Matilda the Good." First hearing myself referred to in this way, I flushed with pride and some discomfiture, but I gradually became accustomed to thinking of myself as a great lady, gracious in her charity.

We had no set capitol, but traveled continuously with our court, a cast of many hundreds. Those fortresses chosen to house and feed us along our route were given six weeks notice to ensure that we received a proper welcome and suitable nourishment, amid appropriately august surroundings. For two years, we journeyed on a magnificent military progress across the Alps and throughout Italy, at the head of a column of fifteen thousand knights, easily securing many lands and towns. We conquered as far south as Rome, where I was again anointed and crowned Holy Roman empress in the St. Gregory chapel of Saint Peter's cathedral. Another Great Seal was commissioned, inscribed "Matilda, Holy Roman Empress." My husband returned to Germany, to put down various treasonous rebellions, but I was left to preside over Italy, as regent. It was wonderful to be always surrounded by pomp and circumstance. I thoroughly enjoyed my duties, formally dispensing the law and meting out justice, and was judged more than able to reign in my own name.

In 1120, a royal messenger brought tragic tidings from England. My brother, Prince William, had drowned in the Channel, in a disastrous shipwreck that destroyed his vessel, the White Ship. The accident decimated the young aristocracy of my homeland, for the craft had been overly laden with more than a hundred knights, all relatives of kings and earls, and eighteen noblewomen. Every one of them perished in the water, to be devoured by ocean beasts.

Many jongleurs now sing of the drunken carousing that preceded the debacle. The boat had been packed with William's wine, and his courtiers were celebrating the imminent crossing with much abandon. Likewise, the crew had imbibed from the prince's barrels. Due to their incapacity, the ship foundered on a great rock, concealed by the high tide.

I envisioned Prince William, perhaps as petulant a man as he was a boy, struggling to swim in the currents that did not recognize his importance, shouting for the fates to justify this perversion of history. A Rouen butcher, the sole survivor, swears to a horrible tale. My brother, safely aboard a lifeboat, and departing the scene, heard the cries of our half-sister Maud. He turned back, in an attempt to deliver his favorite. The wench dragged and pulled at his frail vessel, so that it sank them both beneath the waves. William sacrificed himself for the sister he always preferred, even above his wife, the heiress of Maine. Now, his widow entombs herself in the convent of Fontevraud, to forget that she might have been the English queen. Minstrels declaim the destruction of the White Ship to be a punishment for the unnatural relationship between Maud and William, which, in their inebriation, had blossomed incestuously. What the Lord does not sanction, He casts down.

Cousin Stephen and his wife, known as the Count and Countess of Boulogne, also planned to be part of the doomed voyage, but somehow disembarked from the ship before its passage. I have listened to the accounts of many poets, but whose version best approximates what really transpired? One narrative has it that Stephen distrusted the crew's state of insobriety. Another troubadour imagines my cousin so sick with wassail that he stumbled down the gangplank, not choosing to remain aboard the rocking boat. A third chronicle declares that priests, on hand to bless the proceedings, departed in disgust at the intoxicated behavior of the passengers. The knights aboard tossed drunken taunts at their receding figures; this sacrilege prompted my cousin's party to follow in their footsteps.

My father's letters keep me better informed about the present affairs of his court. Long-widowed, His Majesty remarried in 1121, in the hope of siring another legitimate boy to replace William. Unfortunately, in the five years since, his second queen has not born any offspring. Lately, the king sleepwalks, troubled by nightmares. He dreams that his peasants desert their furrows and his barons their fortresses, part of some violent revolt; he alone takes the field to reclaim the peace. In truth, his power is well established, yet fears for the future security of his empire plague him.

His Majesty never hints that he might endow his throne upon Robert of Gloucester, his most promising and loyal natural son, although he dreads that the crown could devolve upon William Clito, his hated nephew. Clito is the legitimate child of Robert, Duke of Normandy, Henry's elder brother, who was away on the First Crusade at the time of their brother King William Rufus's accidental death. My father ascended to sovereignty in the duke's absence, and was acknowledged king. Defeated and blinded by his brother at the battle of Tinchebrai, the duke languishes in His Majesty's prison. England and Normandy are one realm under God.

Despite the demotion of this branch of the family, some of the English magnates favor Clito as my father's heir. It is enough for them that he is the eldest son of the eldest son of the conqueror. They remember an old hag's fortune telling, and circulating the witch's prediction: no boy of Henry's will rule England and Normandy, for heaven cannot forgive his usurpation of the throne and Duke Robert's life-long incarceration.

Now that I return to my native land, His Majesty determines that I shall be queen of England and Normandy, instead of Clito. The English and Norman barons must accept my father's daughter, if he is to have no son. This new destiny suits my aspiring spirit. Educated to reign, I am well used to wielding authority. I will serve my father's family, as I did my husband's. I will be a splendid queen, worthy of praise.

Often, I am spellbound by the waves breaking tumultuously around the prow of the ship. Do their force and crash echo my inner strength? Will I be able to sail into my father's kingdom, and claim my due? Behind the stern of our vessel, the sea has been flattened so that a white trail of foam stretches out behind us. Need I fear that I am not the boat, but the water, deflated, suppressed, made quiet again?

†

BELOW THE DECK, IN my cabin, Gerta ably guards my precious chattel and my foremost treasure, Saint James's hand. Although the new emperor confiscated much of my wealth, I will not relinquish so holy and royal an object while my own holiness and royalty are in abeyance. It no longer lies among my jewels, in my blue casket, but is nestled in its own silver filigree box, set with a luminous toadstone, dislodged from the banks of the Rhine. Somehow, the sailors are aware that the sacred relic is in my keeping, on their vessel, and they rejoice that we are thus immune from pirate attack, fatal storms, and navigational error.

This morning, I gently lifted the withered hand from its case, wondering at its fragility and its ugliness. How marvelous that it is no more than a desiccated, shriveled, deposed piece of flesh, and yet, in my mind's eye, it blossoms and expands, quivering with its own power. With infinite care, I washed it in watered wine, reserving the liquid in a goblet, and then restored it to its safe haven. Gerta and I dipped our index fingers into the cup, and wiped some wine into our hair and faces, before drinking down the remainder with heady gulps. Side by side among the stacks of luggage, we bent our knees in prayer to the Apostle, and allowed the swaying of the waves to raise our souls out of the cramped chamber, toward the light of paradise. "Most blessed James, risen above sinful, suffering humankind, welcomed into the shining infinity of heaven, be our guide and our salvation."

For good measure, we also addressed ourselves to Mother Mary, Star of the Sea.

†

GERTA DOES NOT MALINGER, nor evade her service to me, but she sometimes seems a bit woebegone to be so far from her native land. She is most content when bustling through our belongings in search of her utensils and tools, her mind set on a new project aimed at my advantage. She berates her own ignorance of astrology, examining the stars in the wide sky above us, but unable to decipher the meaning of the patterns in the firmament. Instead, she counts the calls of the swooping gulls, prognosticating my future wealth and fertility. She studies the glistening entrails of netted fish presented to her by the rough deck hands, and smacks her hands together in satisfaction, interpreting therein my glorious ascendance to the throne.

I do not share her complete confidence in what is to come. For who am I? What is my worth? I am the Holy Roman empress; there is none who sits higher, or comes between me and the throne of heaven. But I am my father's unmarried daughter, to be disposed of according to his will. I can walk among the English court with my head held aloft, with none daring to meet my eyes, and yet I resume my place as an ivory pawn upon King Henry's chess set. On the other side of Europe, I dispensed the law with an iron fist. And now I shall be forced to sheath my mail in silk and manipulation. My face is struck from the imperial coinage. I have lost my currency.

I am the Holy Roman empress, but my greatness tumbles overboard, into the abyss of the ocean. To the world, I am no one, a child, a head without a crown. I must remember that I am stripped of my honors. It will serve me no purpose to cling to my former status, to remember with pride that I was divine. This will be a hard lesson, that of renunciation. How swiftly shall I learn it?

†

THE ROYAL COURT GATHERS at Windsor Castle. The stairways, wards, and ramparts of the keep bustle with servants and soldiers. Its great halls and elegant chambers clog with nobles, whiling away the days. In keeping with my formerly imperial dignity, I am accorded two rooms, a bedchamber and a solar, as many as the king reserves for his own use. They are a great respite to Gerta, still lonely among a foreign people, and to me, also a bit uneasy among the English.

There was ample spectacle to mark my arrival. Swarms of knights, fully armed, had lined the last portion of our route, stimulating my optimism, and I felt suitably welcomed. His Majesty himself greeted me at the castle gates. My father's colors were everywhere, on pennants and shields, for they are mine, too. A band of gaily-dressed musicians romped through the swarms of spectators. Festive burghers pelted me with flowers. Windsor's bells pealed out the melodies of my childhood.

Many chevaliers complained that Henry refused to permit a celebratory tournament, or even a military parade, to mark the occasion. The Europeans among my escort were astonished to be denied their war games. But I knew that there was no insult couched in His Majesty's distaste for martial exhibition. He is too frugal to award any trophies, and prefers to keep his Arabian stallions and purses of gold for other purposes.

My father's sober demeanor masks the leonine bearing that terrified me as a child. Henry I is an old man now; perhaps it will be impossible for him to beget a boy upon his young wife, Adeliza, daughter of the Duke of Lorraine. The queen is most kind to me. She is one year my junior and an ideal beauty, with tight braids of golden hair and straight, small features. The tips of her ears, nose, and lips blush pink against the ivory of her skin. Her lithe figure swells round where it should. The versemakers call her the "Fair Maid of Brabant." For once, they do not pander, and some of their songs even rise to Her Majesty's dignity and grace. However, in their cups, the idiots cannot be trusted to remember the respect due to their sovereign consort, and a number of their odes are little more than insulting presumptions upon her choice proportions and symmetrical countenance.

The gentle Adeliza presumes that I equal her in charm. Does she judge me too gullible or too vain to understand that I lack what men clamor for? I have neither yellow locks, nor light, sparkling eyes, nor a modest serenity that promises the rewards of Elysium. I have grown into a woman too much of this world. My black hair hangs thick, and my shadowy gaze flashes without restraint. I often sulk intemperately or argue without caution. My piety and wisdom are often a surprise to shallow courtiers who judge from first impressions.

Laughing at my self-appraisal, Adeliza calls it nonsense. She claims that my allure is regal, that I am dark as the sapphire is dark, perhaps cold, but still glowing from within. She insists that my lips curve like rose petals, and that my skin is perfection: pale, clear, and radiant. I suppose I am well enough. My hair is long enough to be worn proudly; my over-large teeth stand out, whiter than snow against the darkness of my tresses.

I have reason to hope that Adeliza judges fairly of my personal appeal. Among my father's principle lords here at Windsor, I discover my cousin, Stephen of Blois—now, through marriage, the Count of Boulogne. He is reputed to be the handsomest man in Europe; many admire his russet locks and gray eyes. Indeed, the feelings that I had in my youth are as nothing to the unexpectedly intense emotion that overcomes me in the presence of his elegant face and copper hair. His countenance makes my insides ache, as if I have eaten something that upsets the balance of my humors. My head buzzes, as if I have indulged in too much wine. I speak phrases empty of meaning or wit. I move without purpose or grace. When he gives me a kiss of greeting, I feel at once better and worse.

His wife is a woman whom I cannot abide. The Countess of Boulogne, also a blonde, carries herself with none of Adeliza's poise. She exudes the musty scent of matted fur. Her lips are engorged, as are her voluptuous breasts, and her very nose flares out. Her hair curls around her like a snake. Her name is Maud, the vulgar version of my own, so close to my own, but not my own.

†

Fall

TODAY, THE COURT MINGLED in the castle orchard to savor one of the last fine days outdoors before the onset of the cold season. The fruit trees have already been harvested, and most of their gnarled branches are bare, but the grass underfoot is a blessed respite from the mud-covered wards and the crisp air smells free of smoke and dung.

The group wandering in the naked rows included the Count and Countess of Boulogne and my uncle, now himself king of Scotland, at Windsor to welcome me back to my native land. Guiding me apart from the rest of the entourage, His Majesty flattered me. "Your attractions are all that we predicted. You shimmer, luminous in the firmament of the English court. You are well placed at the head of an assembly that boasts so many comely men and women." David's own features are irregular, but his tanned, bony face suggests fortitude, his blue eyes flash with common sense, and his smile testifies to his mild manner.

I lingered beside him. "Your chivalry and wit are much appreciated, Uncle. After all this time, I find you unchanged. Your hair curls upon your shoulders in much the same jaunty style. You are still able to wear the refined, form-fitting tunics preferred by young, noble knights. How right it is that the Lord has blessed you with a throne."

Stephen slipped through the depleted branches of the tree before us, breaking off one of its boughs. He bowed to me with proper deference. "My lady, God give you health and glory."

Looking at his smooth face and his uncreased brow, my mouth filled with saliva. I bent down to retrieve the twist of wood, swallowing with what I hoped was discretion. I arose with as much elegance as I could muster. "God give you peace and prosperity, cousin."

Stephen held out his arm, inspecting his crystalline fingernails, but then glanced at my face. "I hope that you have rid yourself of sadness. When we were playmates, yours was a bonny, blithe presence."

Clasping the branch behind my back, I resisted the urge to examine my own hands. Although I massage my palms every evening with an ointment concocted of sour sorrel, pork grease, and butter, certain calluses linger. I would not have him notice them. "Flowers fade and bloom once more. My pain is past, though my sorrow lingers."

Maud, stepping up to us, did not seem content that I should monopolize her husband. She cleared her throat. "I hear from my people in Boulogne that you may well cease your lamenting. There is talk that your lord lives, wandering the Continent as a hermit, in penance for his sins." Her plump cheeks moved up and down as she chewed out her phrases.

I had a strange urge to set them in motion once more. "What sins might those be, madame?"

Maud spoke loudly, apparently eager to debate. "Patricide and excommunication."

My fascination evaporated, in my annoyance at the cheek of her conjecture. "The Holy Roman emperor died in my arms, shriven by the church. His Imperial Majesty was buried beside his father, in the cathedral at Speyer."

Maud pursed her overabundant lips. "He feigned death and is now a monk at Cluny."

Here, Stephen interjected. "Now, now, my love, it cannot be right that you should sully the empress's ears with such talk."

At this, Maud's nostrils widened.

My own face was no model of decorum. That she should brazenly dishonor Henry V in my presence — that a mere countess should dare to be discourteous to me! Her provocation was almost too much for me to endure quietly.

King David gave her a look of royal displeasure, and helped me to my revenge by dismissing her from the barren orchard. I watched her sashay away from us, in a parti-colored fur mantle of quite dubious taste. The pattern of white and black pelts resembled a checkerboard, and did her curvaceous figure no favors.

As the rest of the court and our various retainers meandered back to the keep, I loitered with Stephen. "I would speak with my cousin alone. Do tarry with me in the grove. The mellow air shall keep us in health."

The Count of Boulogne paused before me.

I considered his sumptuous garments. "I was relieved to hear that we did not lose you on the White Ship, my lord. I heard with joy of His Majesty's further gifts to you, fiefs rich in manors and vassals. After my father, you are perhaps the grandest magnate in the land." Now I flung the stick to the ground and extended my hands.

Negligently, Stephen appropriated them. "Of all the things that heaven has spread before me, there are none better than my buxom wife and her plenteous county of Boulogne." He squeezed my fingers, as if to emphasize his affection for her.

I dropped his hands. Certainly this conversation coursed in the wrong direction. "She leaves a sour taste in my mouth."

"She is an astute woman, a bit drawn to gossip, but I need not tell you how indispensable scandal is to a courtier. My helpmeet, she discerns every intrigue, well before I do." Stephen's gray eyes grew distant.

What would it take to set them alight? "You are unwisely tied to a frivolous, troublemaking chatterbox. I pity you."

"No, you are mistaken. The countess is an enticing mistress. I hope that you discover as much corporeal delight in your next match."

"To what do you refer, cousin?" My tone appeared harsh to my own ears.

"I pass on only what Maud ferrets out. She gathers that His Majesty plans for you to wed and bear sons, so that the succession might be assured according to his authority, and in defiance of Clito's."

"And whom does Maud think that I shall espouse?" My fists were clenched; I released them.

The count nodded. "My lady, it behooves you to know as early as possible what is being said. Forgive her indiscretion today, and make her your ally."

"Which prince?" I made no promise to overlook that cat's faults, but I would lief know what she tattled.

"Geoffrey of Anjou, Count Fulk's son."

"Count Fulk? He who created the fashion for long, pointed toes, curled like scorpions, on a man's boots, so as to hide his own bunions?"

"The very same. His son is not reputed to be as frivolous or as vain."

"An empress to marry a count's son? The countess surely intends to insult me." I looked down at my elaborate gown, fine wool in a rich umber shade, embroidered at the hems with golden cornucopias.

My cousin soldiered on, oblivious to my splendor. "Maud thought me a suitable mate; I am sure she had no thought of affront."

"I am your wife's superior! You are a nephew of King Henry and a grandson of William the Conqueror, besides being a count in your own right. You stand very high, my lord. It would not be amiss for you to annul your alliance with Maud, and rise even higher." I held my breath, somewhat surprised by my own forwardness. My heart thumped in my chest. Goosebumps rose up along my arms.

The Count of Boulogne's mouth twitched, and I understood that he inferred the offer I made him, the boon that I would bestow upon him. But he did not bow down to me, and instead stepped away. "Surely, you jest. I could not give up Maud. Our exquisite sexual congress enslaves my manhood. And I am proud to have wed her, a descendant of Charlemagne. Two of her uncles were Kings of Jerusalem!"

I waved him back to the palace, so that I stood alone among the naked trees. Although the wind was mild, my humiliation was a cold draft, whipping against my hot cheeks and lapping against the lump in my throat.

†

DISAPPOINTMENT STIRS MY COMPETITIVE nature. Suddenly awash in fantasies of what could be, I pay more heed to my appearance. Yesterday, feeling itchy at the top of my neck, under my heavy tresses, I insisted that Gerta delouse me. Her medicinal remedies were in high demand at all the German courts, but her fame as an herbalist has not preceded her to England. Her pharmacia remains at my sole disposal.

For most of the afternoon, I had to rise above my prickling impatience, for my maid disappeared for quite a long spell of time, gathering her ingredients, the aloe, lead, bacon grease, and ashes necessary to a strong ointment. At her return, she thickly slathered my head, and had me sit before the fire, verily stinking up the room.

Eventually, she began to comb out the preparation, making long strokes from my scalp to my roots. As she found each egg, she sliced it between her fingernails, before dropping its pulp into the rushes. "My lady, if you would cease to entertain absurd and impure fancies, then you would rid yourself of these vermin."

"Of what unclean delusions do you accuse me?"

Gerta pinched one especially large nit, pulling it along a shaft of my hair. "Forgive my impertinence, but these larvae are certain proof that you are polluting yourself with an unworthy infatuation."

I tried not to scratch. "Nothing is beneath an empress that she elevates with her notice."

My maid snorted. "He plays a deep game. Do not let him tame you, as he would a newly purchased falcon, the better to chain you to his wrist and pull a hood over your eyes. To what use will he put you, once you are his pet? Who knows what he hunts for?"

"No more prattle! There has been nothing between my cousin and me but a kiss of greeting."

Gerta set aside her task, and sat still, with an almost exaggerated gravity. "I fear you enter Venus's army, as her newest, most witless recruit."

I averted my eyes and admitted it. "Despite my widowed status, I am unused to the hardships and cruelties that await me."

†

I OFTEN RESORT TO the library or the chapel, retreats only of those in a contemplative mood, congenial to my dissatisfied, distracted humor. Some days ago, in the otherwise empty reading room, I came across my brother, the Earl of Gloucester, hunched over a wooden lectern, studying a copy of the *Aeneid*.

Virgil! Some consider him the devil's servant. It is said that he once freed twelve demons from a bottle; grateful, they taught him their occult arts. What did my brother hope to learn from the ancient sorcerer?

Disturbing him, I touched his shoulder. Would he talk to the king, on my behalf?

Chuckling, he pointed at the first passage, and read out: "For what transgression did the Queen of Heaven begin to molest so valorous, so righteous a man?"

I smiled back. "It is not your offense, Robert. My ears ring with talk of my impending doom, some marriage to a mere boy on the continent. Such comments are most displeasing to me. Privately, I had been considering the Count of Boulogne. He would suffice for a husband."

Gloucester's face grew blank. "I will suggest the match to our father."

I was grateful, for if he did me such a favor, it was purely out of amity. I know that the earl dislikes my proposal, for he has long been jealous of Stephen's prominence. If our cousin were to share my throne, it would be an affront to my brother's royal blood.

A few days later, again in the same place, I interrupted Gloucester, immersed at a reading table.

In a hushed voice, Robert verified Maud's chatter. "His Majesty insists that you wed. He will not hear of Stephen's separation from the Lady of Boulogne. Boulogne must belong to a loyal man, a faithful vassal such as our cousin. Through its ports, the town controls most of the traffic on the English Channel, and he trusts Count Stephen to safeguard our economic interests. All the English wool passes through Boulogne, the gateway to the Flemish cloth towns. Our father can depend on his nephew not to levy steep tolls."

I had no tolerance for the king's priorities. "He guarantees the safety of his trade routes, but impairs his daughter's consequence." My fervid tone was most unfeminine, and certainly unbecoming.

The earl maintained a mild expression. "He justly weighs your importance. You are to be espoused to Geoffrey, the son of Count Fulk of Anjou. The late Prince William's wife, the heiress of Maine, was one of Fulk's daughters. Our father is preoccupied with the idea of an Angevin alliance, for the province of Anjou conjoins Normandy. At His Majesty's death, you and Geoffrey shall rule an even more enormous empire than we presently compose. A few years ago, Clito plighted his troth to another daughter of Fulk, with an eye to the Angevin inheritance, but English diplomacy persuaded the pope to annul the match. You are to be the means through which we will assemble a colossal realm."

Dismayed, I stamped my foot. "I know my geography! Geoffrey is untitled and a mere boy. Apparently, the Angevin counts plume their battle helmets with flowering twigs, *genista*, and are thus nicknamed the Plantagenets. Quite ridiculous and unmanly."

Ignoring my objections, Robert continued in quiet tones. "You are ill-informed. I hear that the youth is most severe and masculine. A groom has been chosen who will be able to buffer your throne with continental military prowess. A foreign match will better stem the rivalries between the English noble houses than a marriage made from among them. Of course, Geoffrey is young; the engagement will be long. But, for now, the king commands that the English and Norman magnates swear allegiance to you, as his heir."

I pounded the smooth surface of the wooden table. "The fishwives tattle about foreign policy and my father thinks it unnecessary to inform me?"

The earl started at the sound. "If the gossip is widely bandied about, the barons surely understand that they shall pledge an oath to you, your intended husband, and your unborn children."

Three traveling monks entered the library, so our private conversation was at an end. Gloucester withdrew, but I dawdled, curious to see what book had engrossed him this time. The text was the Book of Job; the illumination on the page portrayed a dragon, the "King of Pride." The monstrous beast wore a crown of vice, and the knots and coils of its tail wound around a poor soul, naked and twisted.

†

MY FRIENDSHIP WITH ADELIZA and dependence on Gerta grow apace. We three often fritter away the cold autumn hours in my solar, plying our needles within while the men hunt for game without.

Today, we debated who among us was the Sanguine Woman, artful and cunning, inclined to fleshiness, with a healthy womb. We easily settled upon Maud, that warm and wet creature of the air. I was named the Phlegmatic Woman, cold and wet, belonging to the water, recognized by my severe physiognomy, unbridled vigor, masculine manners, and charismatic allure. The queen we labeled the Choleric Woman, warm and dry, born from fire, in keeping with her delicate pallor and her benevolent, prudent, chaste, and loyal nature. Gerta could be none other than the Melancholic Woman, cold and dry as the earth, gaunt of figure, gray, moody, impulsive, sterile.

At some point, I steered the conversation to the Count of Boulogne. Her Majesty does not encourage my infatuation. The queen's youth and beauty ill reflect her opinions, which are those of an old woman, long past the days of romance. Her petite, rosy mouth puckered in concentration, as she stitched slowly at a complex pattern that she embroiders on the decorative bands of one of my father's tunics. "Only after many an hour do two people gently meld their wills and minds as one. It was not a few months before I properly understood your father. Now I can truly offer him my heart."

I regarded her seraphic coloring. "Your Majesty, you feel the reverence and affection due a husband, as I did for the emperor. In Germany, the duties of the conjugal bed seemed no especial burden to me, but I did not experience any of the incitements that the jongleurs ascribe to passion. Yet, when I dwell on the image of my cousin, I fall victim to irrefutable temptation."

Adeliza chose her words as carefully as she drew out her silken threads. "Empress, forego this madness. Do you respect the man whom you covet? You cannot adore truly where you cannot admire fully. Only an irreproachable man deserves your acclaim and your attentions."

I shrugged, as if to ward off embarrassment. "I must have inherited such a hazardous propensity, and it blinds my inner eye. I am incapable of measuring the true worth of my chosen hero, for all I feel is my need for him."

"The minstrels' sing of a bond that is pure and coupled with honorable service. Count Stephen cannot be both your knight and Maud's." My friend reached into her sleeve and brought forth a lustrous pearl, which she balanced precisely between two fingers.

The jewel glinted at me in the waning light. "The attraction is both carnal and spiritual. It is the union of both sorts of desire, the sacred and the profane. The versemakers depict a devotion that uplifts us; looking at the Count of Boulogne, I soar upon the clouds. The priests vilify a connection that debases us; I know that my sordid lusts are unworthy in the eyes of God."

†

Winter

CHRISTMAS WAS THE DAY chosen for the ceremonial vows. The great hall at Windsor was strewn with fresh rushes and hung with King Henry's most valuable tapestries. At his most imperious, my father compelled obedience, thundering at length to his assembled archbishops, bishops, abbots, earls, and lesser nobles. He expounded upon my claims to the throne: first, my birth to a reigning king and queen; second, my mother's ancestors, fourteen kings in the times of the Anglo-Saxons; third, my father's line—his father, his brother, and himself, all three Norman kings; fourth, my unification of Norman and Saxon blood, guaranteeing a future reign of civil unity and peace. His Majesty demanded an oath from all the men present. In front of the assembly and without delay or hesitation, they must swear to accept me and my legitimate sons as his heirs to England and Normandy. Each promise was to be accompanied by the kiss of fidelity, symbolizing their deference to my will and my reciprocal good faith.

The archbishop of Canterbury gave the first pledge to uphold my rights to the succession. The other church leaders followed, with murmured affirmations and cold lips. Some of the clerics failed to wipe the spittle from their mouths before approaching me; I struggled to mask my aversion. Henry of Blois, Stephen's brother and bishop of Winchester, smugly delivered his assurance, but fumbled over my face.

I heard several smothered giggles; His Grace is known to be lecherous, but is said to prefer the company of young men.

Then King David, the preeminent layman, emphatically guaranteed to be my vassal. After his booming declaration of service, his buss was sturdy, not quite the lover's, but I remembered our other embrace.

Unfortunately, squabbles marred the holy day. Robert and Stephen disagreed over who should be the next to give me his vow and kiss. The earl stepped forward as the king's son, but my cousin's supporters grumbled against an illegitimate coming first among the royal kin.

My brother interjected, "My grandfather, William the Conqueror, was once known as William the Bastard."

The Count of Boulogne flushed. "Our grandfather battled his way to the throne. Do you scheme to do the same?"

His Majesty put an end to this ugliness. "I hope and intend that neither of you will put on armor to usurp what is to be Matilda's by your oath. You are to be allies, in her defense and in her sons'."

Well-mannered Gloucester backed down, courteously waiving the argument that threatened to spoil the proceedings. So it was Stephen who next swore his fealty to me, offering an indifferent peck. Maud, whose smiles had greeted her husband's precedence over Robert, now seemed less gratified that he should be among the first to worship me as his sovereign. My brother offered his testimony and embrace with an air of affection.

All the court magnates followed, some honoring me with zeal and others with thinly concealed uncertainty. Perhaps they reassure themselves that an unsatisfactory queen may be deposed more easily than a troublesome king. Yet they gave their word in my favor, as my father ordains.

†

LAST NIGHT, GERTA AND I lay abed, huddled together for warmth, with the ornately stitched hangings drawn closed against the chill of my chamber. The muslin sheets were pulled taut to our jaws, under a coverlet lined in sable, but still we suffered from the cold.

Despite our apparent solitude, my maid whispered, for fear of prying ears. "Maud of Boulogne hires a jongleur to recite her bloodline, and that of your cousin, reminding the court that her mother is your mother's sister and that Stephen's mother is your father's sister; their sons will also unite Anglo-Saxon and Norman blood."

I murmured, "Go to sleep."

"Hear the worst! Her poet does not venture to discount your lineage, but calls you to account for your barren womb, and paints you as a forlorn and calamitous offshoot of the family tree, dissipating its nobility."

I shivered, but my breath was hot with frustration. "Their son Baldwin was too sickly to thrive, dying in his cradle. That harlot wastes my cousin's seed."

Gerta slapped my shoulder. "You are addled by jealousy. Maud threatens more than the satisfaction of your lusts! If you let her, that fox may come between you and your political destiny." My maid rested her cool hands on my back, to warm them.

I squirmed against her icy palms. "Yes, Gerta the Wise. Yesterday, I was Empress of Germany, Italy, Hungary, Poland, Denmark, Holland, and Belgium. Tomorrow, I am queen of England and Normandy. Today, I control nothing and possess no one, certainly not the man whose face saps me of my grit."

"Extinguish this mistaken flame before it is too late, my lady."

"I am the lady of naught but sorrow. Oh yes, I rule a faithful waiting woman who desecrates cathedrals to gather sacred relics for my keeping, but disapproves of my passion for another woman's husband. Gerta, let me be."

The Treasury of the Lion

Scroll Two: 1127

ear ye, hear ye: the angels blessed Matilda with a shining allure. Her loveliness reassured many of her loyal friends, for comely charm reflects the Almighty's glory. Indeed, the knight who would have withstood the enticements of an empress found that he was unable to defend himself against a face and form made irresistible by heaven. Celestial beauty may bewilder demons, but it likewise confounds mortal men.

†

Spring

I AM MY FATHER'S daughter. Now that the barons pledge themselves to my inheritance, I can do without the boy chosen for my husband. I stood as Henry V's regent in Italy and in Germany; I might rule singly or choose my own consort. Geoffrey Plantagenet, still fourteen years of age, cannot possibly lead armies for me, or give me a son. I seek supporters for myself alone.

Since the oaths of succession have reestablished my divine authority, I feel almost reborn, confident enough to bequeath the hand of Saint James. I have donated the silver filigree feretory, toadstone and all, to the abbey of Reading, whose felicity at this piece of good fortune has been gratifying. The monks celebrate its coming translation to their keeping, and foresee that their hostel will overflow with eager pilgrims, ready to admire the prestigious fragment, and disperse their coins into the collection box. They promise to pray for the success of all my endeavors.

On my last evening as the relic's private guardian, I was ensconced in my solar, burning down three fat candles in the Apostle's honor, and offering up my own pleas for his continued protection and blessing. "First martyr of the Saints! Your enemies had assassinated our Lord, Jesus Christ, and you lost hope in his eternal flame, even as you preached his Gospel, fanned the fire of his teachings and redoubled its strength. The Virgin Mary appeared before you, to encourage you when you doubted, entrusted you with a pillar of jasper and instructed you to build her a temple. So let it be, that I entrust you to a House of God, that shall enshrine you likewise in a sanctuary for the faithful. So let it be, that you shall be my pillar. Let me dominate over mine own antagonists and prevail, even onto my own throne, which they would deny me, against all of the laws of the land and of heaven."

Unfortunately, my standing with the king is not what it was at Christmas. He is angry that I withstand the arranged Angevin marriage. My arguments with him gain me nothing; my imprecations chafe against his authority.

This morning, in my chamber, I was brooding in a warm patch of sunlight. My father entered, wearing a mantle of deep red, the color of empire, festooned all over with lions, his heraldic symbols. He donned such a garment to cow me, as he often awed petty magnates, fresh to court. It ill befits His Majesty to think me as impressionable as a rustic.

"It is necessary, daughter, that you bow to my will."

"To you, I will kneel, but not to a scrap of a child ten years my junior!" I bent my legs under my heavy gown, glad that its thick material buffered my knees from the sharp rushes and hard stone floor underneath them.

The king shook his head, exasperated. "He is on the cusp of manhood. The minstrels name him Geoffrey the Fair, because he is handsome and all that a fastidious woman might find pleasing."

"Sire, he is no match for an empress." I straightened up to my full height, untucking the points of my sleeves so that they extended to their regal length.

His Majesty rolled his eyes, lucid and clear in his leathery face. "He is a descendant of Charlemagne. I acknowledge that Your Imperial Highness cannot wed where there is no title; I shall dub him myself."

I shuffled in place, sending up a small cloud of dust. "I love another, a full-grown, noble lord, ready and able to protect and defend your realm."

The king set his moth in a straight line, wide across his jaw. "That is enough, Matilda. Your wanton whimsy is nothing to me. My nephew, whom I trust to serve me, could not inspire accord and fidelity throughout England and Normandy. He riles up many other men besides your brother Gloucester. Mischievous lewdness between a man and a woman is naught in comparison with the security of the empire that your grandfather united. You will marry where I see fit."

I am shut up in my rooms until I agree to be disposed of according to his dictate.

†

OUR ENTIRE RETINUE HEARS tell that I refuse to espouse Geoffrey Plantagenet, but not why. Those who wish to comfort me, advise me, or shame me visit my solar.

Stephen's unpleasant brother, the bishop of Winchester, brought his sour face and frigid exhortations to my chamber, and urged me to submit to my father in all things.

I measured him more a slavish crown courtier than a bishop. "You preach worldly advice, Your Grace. Have you no wish for me to rest abstinent, the better to dedicate myself to Christ?"

"Ah, Empress, seasoned widows do not usually find celibacy to be possible. In that case, as the Scriptures say, 'let them wed, for it is better to marry than to burn.'" His eyes, hooded by their heavy lids, flashed at the mention of diabolical fire.

I folded my arms in front of my chest, to keep myself from slapping him. "Do you foretell that I shall be cast out of paradise?"

Sneering, Winchester rumbled on. "Let the Lord doff you with the mantle of humility. If you disavow this offering, if you refuse His munificence, you make Him your enemy. Allow Him to adorn you with the robe of meekness and you will also be encircled with His love." Bowing, he swept out of my room. I could see the flush on his cheeks.

Oddly curious, I pressed my ear against the wooden thickness of my door. His Grace was mumbling about St. Paul, but it was no benediction. "Who transposed the Lord's truth into a falsehood, and idolized the creature, forgetting his Creator?"

Despite such admonitions as these, my soul resists compulsion. My mind wanders often to Count Stephen. I almost swoon when I conjure up my cousin's face and amber tresses or imagine his long, slender fingers touching my cheeks. Indeed, I ruminate so much upon him that perhaps I will be denied salvation.

My arrogance falters. In faith, I do appeal to Mother Mary, for guidance and for self-abasement. I am a dry patch of garden, parched, thirsting for renewal. May the gentle Virgin rain down Her sweet tears upon me, as fresh as dewdrops, and bring forth my refreshment. As I blossom, so shall I rejoice and praise Her.

†

To Gerta's vexation, Stephen also called upon me. Seeing him step across my threshold, I tingled; my very nature thrilled to his presence.

The Count of Boulogne hesitated, ill at ease among my domestic belongings. As he spoke, his gray eyes avoided my gaze. "Fare thee well, Empress?"

I tried to catch his glance. "No, my lord, not when an alliance is formulated against my wishes."

Resolutely, my cousin evaded my regard. "Our fates are not always to our liking. When my son Baldwin was snatched from me, I railed against heaven, until I saw that I was as a stalk of wheat ranting against the harvest. Now that I have accepted the power and the glory of the Lord, he has given me the hope of another boy."

I inhaled a short breath. "Do you mean to say that Maud is pregnant?"

Such a direct question brought his eyes to mine. "She is. If you accept Geoffrey, in time you too will know the joy of an heir."

"I might marry where I like and bear many children." I held his look. Surely such a hint was within Stephen's understanding.

But again he averted his face. His eyes darted about my room, searching for some object on which to settle his attention, finally choosing my blue enamel casket. He strode across the floor to study it, then ran his fingers over its patchwork surface. "My mother, the Countess of Blois and Chartres, always surrounds herself with objects of stupendous beauty and value. The walls of her castle are covered with precious tapestries, woven under her personal supervision and to her design. Each boasts threads of gold, and trim of opals and pearls. Her ceilings are elegantly painted with all the signs of the zodiac. Her marble floors depict enormous maps of the known world."

The blue box seemed dearer to me, now that he had handled it. I hankered to cradle it. I felt sure that he admired it; I wished to compliment him in return. "Her refined taste does her credit. And to think she bore your father five sons!"

The count traced the outline of a large sapphire, affixed to its lock. "You are generous, Empress. Some measure her worldly, and speak of her valuable art with disdain."

"I have heard that she is an unfeeling woman, who set aside her feminine charm after the death of your father." I blushed, to my great annoyance. "Why did the Countess of Blois disinherit your eldest brother, and endow the second son of your house with what should have been the patrimony of the first?"

The count massaged his delicate jaw. "The first-born is disfigured, a heretic and a fool. She, as regent, was right to disavow him, promoting Theobald, austere and capable, to be protector of the county in his stead."

I focused on his tunic, made of a fine, gray wool, festooned with stitched sunflowers and columbines. Did he not know that columbines represent folly and sunflowers arrogance?

Stephen continued his tale. "The men of the House of Blois must distinguish ourselves to earn my mother's respect. The countess compares us to her illustrious father, William the Conqueror, and the sort of courage that captures a throne. Maud shares her shrewdness and her charisma, but she lavishes affection on me in a way that my mother never does."

I would not permit him to discourse upon the virtues of that witch. "Any noble lady would admire such a man as you, unless she were unwomanly. Be sustained by an empress's approval."

The Count of Boulogne bent his knee to me, but spoke of her. "I would be great and daring, my grandfather's seed. Maud charitably overlooks the limits of my ability. Indeed, she stokes my ambition. Just so, Geoffrey Plantagenet will serve as your backbone. Let him bring England, Normandy, and Anjou to you, and help you keep them."

Now my cousin arose and inched toward my hearth, though its dying embers offered little interest. I walked toward the fire, putting myself in his way. "Am I so soon to be another man's chattel, without ever knowing the joys of love?" Would he judge me a lascivious strumpet?

Stephen made for the door, scattering the floor rushes, dirty with the soil of so many extra visitors. "Your husband will take you in his arms with gladness. Despite the grandeur of your position among us, your dark grace haunts many at Windsor castle. You must excuse me, my lady."

With a sigh, I dismissed him, wondering whether he felt the pull of an attraction. Was he agitated by my presence, or did he merely play a courtly game?

†

SEVERAL DAYS PASSED WITHOUT my capitulation. Then, today, the sly king sent his queen to represent him. I am clear-sighted enough to understand that Adeliza's affection for me is surpassed by the importance she ascribes to her royal duty.

Finding me with my maid, sorting my gems, she took up one especially large brooch, a cluster of cabochon rubies. She marveled at it with a question in her eyes.

I am not as proud of it as I once was. "Henry V presented it to me on our wedding day. Its seven stones symbolize the seven gifts of God. The emperor graced me with all of heaven's bounty."

Gerta snorted at my first husband's munificence. "An empress may flaunt her lovely white throat, her shining white cheeks, and her slender white fingers, but she must hide everything else of note beneath a tightly pinned mantle."

Her Majesty caught her pink upper lip between two small ivory teeth. "Empress, I regret that my barrenness will keep you from another contented union."

I turned my gaze to the queen. "His Majesty has transferred valuable fiefs to his nephew. How is it that he does not approve of him?"

My friend relaxed her pinched expression. "There are worthier knights than Stephen of Boulogne. Very few truly esteem the man that you prefer. Envious of his rapid advance in power and wealth, many of the barons doubt his capabilities. They would not wish to bow down to him as their superior."

I smiled to speak on his behalf, to defend him. "His fairness and his gregariousness have established his reputation as one of the lights of our court."

Adeliza scoffed. "Oh, yes, he is vastly pleasing, quite the gallant chevalier! I do not doubt that he has been tutored in the seven liberal arts, or that he has memorized the seven wise precepts and mastered the seven knightly skills. But the other magnates rightly distrust his smooth manners." Here the queen paused. "The church's commandments are clear: thou shalt not covet another's husband. Whatever the poets claim, your cousin should know better than to cast his eyes upon you."

I began to fasten the ornament to the leather of my girdle. It took some effort to work the point through, as I did not wish to force it, so marring the belt. "Since we were children, Stephen and I have regarded each other warmly. The depth of my current passion for him disconcerts me. I am not even certain that he returns my feelings." I had established the brooch somewhat crookedly and would have to redo it.

Her Majesty stayed my hand. "As always, he makes too much of himself. But, my dearest dear, you will have to give him up. Henry's authority must not be questioned. You shall travel to Anjou, and be the ideal wife, ravishing Geoffrey's senses, but remaining chaste, discreet, and pious."

Although averse to control, my mutinous spirit faltered. The queen saw that she had breached the tower. She laid down her womanly arms, coming forward to embrace her defeated foe. I consented to be comforted, although her arms were no substitute for those of the Count of Boulogne.

I am morose to be exiled to a boy's bed in Anjou, just as my desire for a man awakens. Maud remains at the center of England's affairs, frolicking with my Stephen. If only the king would banish the inconvenient bitch to a convent, and leave me mistress of the field.

†

HIS MAJESTY IS PLEASED with my surrender, for Clito's star rises again. Some villain assassinated Charles the Good, Count of Flanders, as he prayed at the altar of the church of Saint Donatian, in Bruges. The king of France, feudal overlord of the region, claims the right to appoint his Flemish successor, choosing Clito. Whenever possible, Louis VI works against my father's interests. Of course the English sovereign thinks to baffle this scheme.

A frenzy of preparation engulfs Windsor castle. My wedding cortege departs posthaste, so that the soldiers who accompany us to the Continent can then go on to fight for Flanders. Stephen is to lead the armies against Clito, as his wife's county of Boulogne borders the Flemish principality. Haphazard in his anxiety to see his general set off on the road, His Majesty sends my beloved in my train. Stephen seems gratified to be part of our procession; Adeliza hints that he yearns to prove his mettle in battle. The king travels separately, in his own caravan, and will join me in Normandy for my wedding.

Despite my impending nuptials, I can scarcely understand my good luck. Maud is furious to be apart from her husband as she awaits her confinement, and barely appeased by the honor that falls to him.

Gerta admits to conniving on my behalf, sewing Maud's initials onto a scrap of linen, setting the fabric alight, and dropping the ashes into the castle moat. So it is that the slut has been compelled to remain behind as we set off on our adventure.

†

MY OWN WEALTH IS depleted now, my widow's dower spent, and I am reduced to selling off precious stones to augment the small annual incomes from my few German estates. With these reduced monies, I somehow maintain the knights and servants of my household.

Fortunately, my father's gratitude loosens his purse strings. With gold from the crown coffers, I order bolts of fabric from London, to make up into new gowns and cloaks, suitably sumptuous for my nuptial celebrations and my new life in Anjou. Gerta and I sew busily indoors, as the earth renews itself outdoors. With the change of season, the wind of fashion blows, necessitating that we redo my wardrobe, almost from scratch. The most elegant women suddenly decry their simple woolen gowns, preferring floor length, crinkled chemises, known as bliauts, layered under more elaborate, short, sleeveless jackets, termed corsages. The costumes are finished with ornamented girdles. Thankfully, the new style continues to permit tight waists and wide, trailing sleeves, both of which set off my slender figure to advantage.

Today, running her needle through the embroidered trim of a new bliaut, Gerta whispered the name, "Geoffrey the Fair," searching for rhymes. Too quick for her, I proposed "Knight of Despair," and "Lord of Nowhere." Stitching a honeycomb of fancywork onto a corsage, the queen seconded my maid's attempts, suggesting "The Ladies' Snare," and "Enemies Beware!" Yet, as I draped luminescent Turkish and Spanish silks over my shoulder in admiration, I thought only of the effect that they might have on my cousin. I will not wait until marriage to wear such magnificence.

†

Summer

MY BROTHER ROBERT AND another of my sworn vassals, Brian FitzCount, also accompany me to the Continent. The illegitimate son of the Count of Brittany, Brian spent long stretches of time at our court when we were children. I remember him playing at war with William. Physical games were always second nature to Brian, and his rangy athleticism would have brought him effortless victories, but somehow he arranged it so that my less able brother won most of their footraces and mock jousts. I see now that FitzCount is no mere toady; his mild, loyal nature ensures his popularity among the warrior earls and their retainers.

Brian has grown into a handsome man, but retains much of the puppy about him. To my taste, his features loom too large for his face, but many noble ladies and several serving girls moon over him. They judge him the perfect specimen of knight, heroic on the battlefield and unfailingly polite at the high table.

Gloucester's wife, Amabel, grieves over her beloved's impending absence. A pretty heiress, she endowed the earl with her fortune and her fertility. She is extremely distinguished in appearance, with a high forehead, wide cheeks, and delicate features. Yet I cannot make peace with her, for she resents Robert's allegiance to my claim to the throne, believing a king's natural son to be a more suitable heir than a legitimate daughter. Although my brother wishes us to be friends, she is stilted and uncomfortable in my presence. Her cold expressions wear out my patience. I no longer endeavor to win her over, and I am not sorry that she is left behind.

†

TODAY, FOR OUR DEPARTURE, I wore one of my new pleated chemises, trimmed with elegant bouquets of bluebells at the neck, wrists, and hem, underneath a blue corsage, laced vigorously to mold itself to my torso. Gerta questions the wisdom of subjecting such fine silken garments to the sun and the rain, but I overruled her objections and Adeliza's, who came to bid me farewell in private.

The queen and I swore to be eternally devoted and faithful to one another; she is the one soul in England whom I leave with any sorrow.

Her Majesty's own eyes brimmed with tears. "With the five fingers of my right hand, and the five fingers of my left hand, I send fifty-five angels after you, so that they festoon and trumpet your arrival at the Gate of Happiness."

Is it so? Do the fifty-five angels who bolster celestial paradise now hold aloft King Henry's plan for the English succession? Are we everything, on earth as it is in heaven? In Germany, I never doubted my divine rights. Despite the oaths given to me, my supreme confidence sometimes falters. Will I ever feel wholly myself again?

As our traveling procession assembled in the outer ward of the castle, I maneuvered my mount near to the Count of Boulogne's, wanting to witness his final embrace with Maud. Preoccupied, he hurried through their adieus. The countess soon quit the raucous scene, the stomping animals and packed carts jostling for space in the crowded enclosure.

As I fussed with my horse's trappings, I tried to let my cousin have a glimpse of my ankles. The minstrels assure us that ladies' ankles are irresistible, and mine are quite fine. I would give my general something more to think on than his upcoming military campaign. I wished there was a way to show him my knees, but such disarray could not have escaped the glances of the others in my retinue.

†

THE DAYS ON HORSEBACK energize me. I feel more in health than I have in a long while. I am young, and on a voyage. I wear an amulet of rosemary, which shields me from the malfeasance of evil spirits. The knight who sets my heart aflutter is always in my sights. I sit tall atop my prancing steed, unfazed by the droppings of manure, the swarm of flies, the raw skin between my fingers and the bruising of my posterior.

Southern England is in full flower. I am surprised at how much the beauty of the countryside invigorates me. I breathe deeply of the grasses, waving tall in the wind. The grazing livestock, the sturdy wildflowers, and the swarms of buzzing insects enchant me. Ah, the glory of Christ's largesse! Drinking in the landscape, I am suffused with His grace.

As we progress, Stephen ignores me, but Brian FitzCount grows especially courteous. I purposely avoid riding alongside him. He is sure to compliment the trappings of my mount or my own refined apparel. I smother a smile each time that he commends its indigo hues, for it is fast fading, just as Gerta predicted. Adeliza's charming embroideries are stained with my sweat. Now, my maid insists that I wear this ensemble for the rest of our sojourn, so that I do not spoil any other precious clothing.

†

THE TALK AMONG OUR party is all of the military engagements to come in Flanders and the future of our empire. The Flemish accept William Clito as their ruler. Now that he commands port towns on the Channel, he could easily invade our island. English barons who, a generation ago, supported his father, the Duke of Normandy, and whose lands were therefore forfeited to the crown, would be on hand to join Clito's marauding armies. If he prevailed, he could return their lost patrimonies. Other nobles who favored my father, and have prospered under his reign, might not fight against Clito's succession, and risk disinheritance.

The newly great and the once great are all motivated by avarice, hungry for wealth and honor. Few of our adherents speak of personal fidelity to His Majesty or to me, despite their recent oaths. Henry I cemented his alliances with rich gifts, but also created a class of landless men who have nothing to lose and everything to gain from allegiance to another cause.

Stephen's own counties were assembled from those who stood for the Duke of Normandy at the battle of Tinchebrai. Therefore, like the king, he is an intractable enemy of the incubus Clito.

†

My cousin begins to forget the family that he left behind, and I have long been ready to deny the marriage that I travel toward. Our horses keep pace, ostensibly so that we might discuss our mutual foe.

Today, whatever my words, I thought more of love than war. "I trust that you do not rank Clito too highly. The Flemish themselves have already trounced him. In Bruges, the townspeople barricaded their city, until he granted them a charter that promised to eradicate road tolls and property tariffs. In Saint-Omer, the burghers negotiated for similar liberties and even spoke of your powers to tax their cloth at your ports in Boulogne. Clito had to promise that if he fell, their privileges would not be overturned."

The count's tone remained neutral. "It is no shame to parry with townsmen. Their satisfaction ensures prosperity. The wealth of cities strengthens counties, and the men who rule them."

Despite my ardor for him, I disagree with his politics. "The fathers of many freemen tilled the land as serfs, and bowed down to their overlords in gratitude. You forget your place in God's hierarchy."

Stephen shook his russet locks out of his eyes. "Power can be won with influence, just as easily as with brutality."

I smacked at a gnat that harassed my neck. "Patronage and favors are the arms of women, and women rarely dominate. Aggression and ferocity are the weapons of men, and men do triumph."

My cousin grinned at this assessment.

In silence, we rode on for a few moments, long enough for his good humor to recede. He turned his destrier aside from mine. "I doubt not that you will master the man to whom you grant license."

I kept to the highway, mystified again by his flirtation. Had he divulged an interest in me? Or did his flattery mean as little as a troubadour's compliments?

†

WE TRAVERSE THE CHANNEL, from Romney to Boulogne, on a small fleet of vessels. Traveling on my boat, Stephen boasts to me of his city and castle, and the welcome that he will offer our entourage. Neither one of us mentions Maud's name, though it is her childhood home that will shelter and restore us. Falling in with our serenity, the water is as calm as a stagnant pond. There is no sickness for anyone on board. Even Gerta forgets to chasten me, as she enjoys the placid trip.

Just now, my cousin and I stood alongside the wooden railing, enjoying the view, sipping ale ladled from a barrel. Robert crosses with us on the same ship, the better to spy upon our trifling, and all the while he darted reproving glances in our direction.

Stephen withdrew below, and Gloucester and I remained alone on the deck. I tried to tease him, not to offend him, but to overthrow the pall that he casts on our merrymaking. "Your long face is out of sorts with the high humor of our band."

The earl did not smile. "The climate is indeed temperate, but the somber purpose of our journey should not be forgotten."

Why must he depress my own spirits, titillated by the clean air, the gentle breeze, and Stephen so near to me? "These past days, I have been counting my blessings."

Robert's light eyes were clouded. "I had hoped that this pilgrimage would renew your strength of purpose as our Lady of the English. Make these days of reflection."

I stretched my arms out, arching my back. "I prefer to look neither forward, nor back, but to live in the moment. I am not yet ready to resign myself to the injustice of my royal duty."

Gloucester put his back to the wind and to the expanse of the sea and sky. "How can you resent your fate, one that I would have embraced so willingly? I cannot help but notice, Empress, that you have been given so much, yet you still ask for more."

The serious earl darkened my mood. I sighed. "I will try to adapt myself to circumstances. But today you cannot dissuade me from bliss. Do you not know what it is to pine for the caresses of another?"

"Lust and obsession do not come well recommended, not even in the *Song of Songs*."

I shrugged my shoulders at his prudery. "Express your affection to your countess; your worthy passion will honor and please her."

"A wife is not the usual partner in such foolery, or the source of such misery."

If Robert had hoped to take divert my thoughts, he has succeeded. I wonder with whom such a courtly knight might be entranced. Gossip always places Gloucester above suspicion. Amabel's beauty and her husband's probity seem to guarantee connubial bliss. My brother is handsome; his lank, dark locks, shrewd green eyes, and small mouth assemble together harmoniously. His regal features are too fine and his hands are too small for my taste, but he personifies distinction. Could the earl be infatuated with Queen Adeliza? Both are models of virtue; I assume that their stateliness has never been sullied by wrongdoing.

†

THIS MORNING, ON OUR way to Stephen's fortress, we wended our way through the town of Boulogne. I admired its noisy spectacle and its teeming market stalls, all vending assorted delights. Like some naïve girl, sick with her first crush, I purchased unnecessary adornments, haggling with a crone whose booth displayed ribbons dyed every imaginable shade. I held various strips of silk against the back of my hand, enjoying their rippling shimmer of color against my skin. I could not settle on what hues I wanted or needed, and ended up purchasing red, green, blue, silver, and gold, undeterred by Gerta's pout at my heedless expenditure.

Maud's birthplace is a splendid structure, sweet smelling and cool, despite the heat of the summer. Gerta and I have been assigned a most agreeable chamber. Our comfortable surroundings speak of a woman's hand. I suspect that my bedroom is Maud's.

With admirable efficiency, my cousin's servants delivered water, so that we could wash away the dirt of the journey. His retainers filled a bathing basin, stirring in fragrant orange rinds. I exhaled as my maid peeled my worn and stinking chemise from my body.

As I sat in my rival's tub, her husband strode into the apartment, no longer shy around me, but quite the reverse. "You are welcome here, Empress. I hope that I will be able to amuse you."

Biting her lip, Gerta washed my hair with a vengeance.

I pulled my neck out of her way, eager to be gracious in my turn. "Your castle will fortify me for the rest of our travels."

The count laughed. "Tonight I shall offer you a banquet. The wine will flow more freely than the currents of the Channel did."

Gerta grunted in displeasure and yanked my locks. As my idol bowed out of the room, she could not contain herself. "He will ruin you, Empress. His eyes were where they should not have been! For him to speak of drink and glance at you so brazenly!"

"A nobleman attends the bath of all his guests of high rank."

My maid spit on the floor. "An honorable knight would not have entered here."

I lectured Gerta, who usually enlightened me. "To have disregarded my ablutions would have been a disreputable omission of hospitality. Stephen withdraws to attend upon the Earl of Gloucester, Brian FitzCount, and the other barons. He will speak of tonight's celebrations with them all." I rubbed my feet under the water and the clear bath began to cloud. I churned the liquid, to refresh its aroma.

Frowning, my maid watched me. "My lady, do not partake of too much wassail this night. Although, it twinkles at us through the glass, it is no better than poison. We have often heard it compared to penitents' tears, but wiser men have named it snakes venom."

I scraped the dirt out from under my toenails. "Ah, but Aristotle tells us that women are unlikely sots. What shall I wear to this devil's feast? Perhaps my green silk bliaut, with the short chartreuse jacket, embellished with golden leaves? I shall leave my tresses hanging loose, with my golden circlet atop my head."

Roughly, Gerta began to work a scrap of cloth along my neck and shoulders. "Green is the color of seduction. It is clear that you have not overcome your weakness for this man. The purity of gold will not be enough to protect you against yourself."

I stuck out my tongue and reached out onto the floor for a vial of olive oil. When I poured it into the bath, the color of the water changed to a gilded verdigris.

Gerta sucked in her breath. "Heretics transform the color of liquids!"

An iridescent glaze coated my skin. "Do not the angels hold golden censors in their hands, to waft the scent of spices into the presence of the Holy Father? I shall green myself, and be born again, moist and whole, pure and wet."

"You shall not be reborn without atonement, and you are in no wise reformed. Do not rate the arts of poetry more highly than the blessings of virtue, my lady."

†

LAST NIGHT, BOULOGNE CASTLE'S great hall felt crowded and overly warm. The royal visitors at the high table sat under an extravagant baldachin, woven by Maud's mother. The lower tables were loaded with lesser guests, as the Count of Boulogne had invited many of the town's leading citizens to join in the rejoicing of my entourage. There were delicacies without number; we gorged ourselves on saffron starlings, mustard venison, and even lemons, lately unknown in the West. The white wine, infused with honey, was the only source of cool refreshment. The pages of the high table galloped back and forth to refill our goblets, downed with both enjoyment and haste.

My cousin, my dining partner, shared my trencher of bread. Gloucester and Brian FitzCount supped to our left. Robert ate heartily, but absentmindedly, provoked by the suggestive way that Stephen and I sated our appetites. As my chosen knight sliced up a pear for me, and popped it onto my tongue, Robert glowered.

Even FitzCount, unaware of the tension, looked dubious. "The Infidels consider pears to be aphrodisiacs."

My cousin laughed. "This evening, my keep is a bower of every delight."

FitzCount's mouth grew smaller. "To dabble in pleasure, on occasion, may be permitted among friends."

Stephen clapped his hands twice, calling his vassals to order. "Empress, allow me to introduce the entertainers."

As a hush fell over the party, a minstrel asked my leave to recite a song of love, composed in the time of Rome. Pleased at the theme, I nodded my acquiescence, and expected to be held rapt by his verse. Instead, his words washed over me in a jumble: "binds, changes, seed, reins, clash, smash, motions, souls." The Count of Boulogne appeared to listen with a polite intensity, but I was incapable of following the sense of the performance. At that moment, I was ready to experience love with my body, not my mind.

After the performance, I found that I had drunk more than was wise. The earl rose from the dais, offering to aid me to my chamber. Gerta, seeing my brother chaperone me from the hall, stayed behind to enjoy the tumblers and contortionists. I passed her at a trestle table, smiling broadly among the merchants and men-at-arms, basking in those attentions that she is so anxious that I despise.

The excess of honied liquor dizzied my steps; crookedly, I advanced. Gloucester helped me up the circular staircase, steering me by the elbow. When we arrived at my room, he strode over to the hearth to stoke the fire.

Watching the earl fuss with the blaze, I swayed a bit, winced at the onset of a headache and itched to be in my bed. I untangled my girdle and it slid to the floor. "Robert, unlace the back of my corsage; I do not wish to sleep in my new things."

His eyes were unreadable. "It is not seemly."

"I would not roust my maid from her pleasure. You must undo the knots."

Finally, he loosened and tugged at the jacket. When I stood before him in my crimped bliaut, he exited without another word.

I drew its fine material over my head. Unclothed, I lay down on my mattress. The room whirled gently around me. I could hear the festivities, echoing in the inner ward. Bursts of laughter punctuated the music. I wondered whether I should rejoin the merriment in order to dance with Stephen.

A door in the wall creaked open, startling me. It occurred to me then that if I lay in Maud's bed, her spouse's chamber must not be far off.

His face swam above me. "I hope that I do not trespass upon you, Empress. My solar is connected to your room by this private entrance." Quite openly, he glanced at my naked form.

I shivered, but did not attempt to cover myself. "Your guests will surely miss you."

"The cavorting and gambling are well under way. Most of the revelers are so inebriated that they think only of their own affairs."

"Gerta's return is imminent, then." I struggled to sit upright.

"Your maid has fallen asleep in the outer ward, alongside many soldiers, burghers, and pages."

I did not know whether to rise or recline. "I cannot imagine that Gerta would do such a thing; to collapse among the dogs and guards would be beneath her."

He snickered. "Many of my people and yours were quite overcome by the wine."

My cousin's confidence perplexed me. "Gerta is not fond of excess."

"Did not she sip the ale? It was particularly potent this evening. My brewer attempted a special recipe, steeping many Oriental herbs into the lager. Shall I bar the outside door to your chamber, so that no drunken oaf mistakenly disturbs us?"

A warmth spreading through my limbs annulled the rest of my objections. There was nothing to stop us from acting upon on mutual desire. He was soon entwined in my arms.

I could not help but speak my happiness. "I thrill to you, Stephen of Boulogne, and will give you felicity in return."

I placed my hands on his abdomen, testing its firmness. His wiry arms and legs, his taut torso: nothing was exactly as I had dreamed it. Was my body likewise a mystery to him? I floated in a daze, unaware of the time.

As our perspiration dried, the count brushed my black hair down over my shoulders. He nibbled my ear lobe. "I have clipped the lily that stood out, faultless, from among the tangled stalks."

Delighting in his tender touch, I rediscovered the purpose of poetry. "If the noble scythe did not swing and topple the proud stalks of wheat, there would be no yield, no bread in our mouths, no regeneration."

Stephen kissed my mouth and then my forearms. "I have tasted nothing sweeter than your lips and limbs."

Enchanted by his wit, I ruffled his auburn curls. "We are together in our enclosed garden, encircled with high, impregnable walls. I banish time and decrepitude, dissatisfaction and envy, shame and sorrow, or any sort of hypocrisy from its precincts."

I had said the wrong thing. Suddenly, my cousin ceased to play the gallant. "I am apprehensive, Matilda, that we are transported to a new Eden. Shall what we share here be soured by the knowledge that comes after? I thank heaven for the high honor of holding you in my arms, but I sense that it is a short-lived joy."

My glee evaporated. "Take courage from my embrace! A lover is at liberty to be candid and gay, carefree." I ransacked the bed coverings for his hands.

They were cool and lay limply at his side. His voice rang flat and cold. "Tonight, I wantonly succumbed to temptation, and forgot what I owe to myself."

The fog in my head dissipated, but the throbbing persisted. "Put aside doubt. The night stars hide themselves during the day. We might do the same with our affair; no one will guess at our amour."

Stephen smiled ruefully. "I have many failures to conceal, Empress."

"You are too severe on yourself. Whose path runs straight and narrow?"

"If it were not for my insufficiencies, you might be free from your misalliance."

"What can you mean?" I sat up. The fire was nothing, the chamber almost completely dark.

"Almost ten years ago, King Henry ventured to subdue Normandy, believing the region to be a royal jurisdiction, not a duchy. He would owe no fealty to any overlord, especially not the French king."

In the inky dim, I could not see my cousin's face. "We fought and won that great war against France; my father's realm, comprising England and Normandy, is his and his alone."

"His Majesty allowed your brother, Prince William, to do homage to Louis the Fat, in return for the Frankish acknowledgment of the boy's eventual rights in Normandy."

"No, the kiss between my brother and Louis was an offering of peace, not of service. My father's military triumphs and his bribes completely conquered the Continent."

The count twitched, and seemed to speak as if from far away. "Henry needed to pay Louis because his victories at arms were inconclusive. Your father faced the combined forces of France, Anjou, and Flanders. All ranged against him, and his eminent barons were not all able commanders. Count Fulk, Geoffrey's father, routed me at Alençon; vassals from my Norman fief took the field against me, alongside Fulk. Only the English king's intervention ransomed my honors there. He paid Anjou to join our cause and united Prince William to Fulk's daughter. Now, with your brother dead, you will reestablish the relationship, dividing Anjou from France. If I had vanquished Fulk, such friendship would come more cheaply. I have no admiration for the Angevins, but I recognize that we stand with them now."

"Ten years ago, you were a young man, unready to lead. Now, you are great, in land and in wisdom. Let us be in league with one another, against Fulk and Geoffrey." I reclined in the bed, wrapping my legs around his middle.

Stephen shrugged. "You are even more sympathetic than my Maud. At least she berates me for my shortcomings before pressing herself against me. Above all, she encourages my staunch defense of your father's schemes."

I inhaled his scent, seeking it out under the odors of smoke, sweat, and olive oil. "I do not scold you; I take your part. His Majesty will have to give up his idea of an association with the Angevins. Many of our noblemen must be skeptical of our détente. I cannot marry a man whom my barons will distrust, or my kingdom will be less secure."

The Count of Boulogne did not make any move to caress me. "My wife advises me not to waver from my steadfast dedication to Henry I. My lasciviousness here makes me a sinner thrice over, before Christ, king, and family."

"My passion waxes; Maud's wanes. Plight your troth to me, who cherishes you."

"I am wed to love and duty."

Our lips met, but both our minds were elsewhere.

†

AWAKENING AMIDST HER FELLOWS in the courtyard, Gerta immediately suspected that the savory ale had been laced with a sleeping potion. By the time she returned to my chamber, I was alone. But Stephen had forgotten to unbar my door, so she found the solar locked against her.

Once I had let her in, I dove back under the coverlet, but she easily intuited her mistress's secrets. "Empress, you were once charming, yet blameless. Mother Mary's guidance kept you righteous."

I cowered under the blanket, flushing under her searching words. "I have fallen under the spell of a man's splendor and misplaced my own modesty."

Gerta's eyes were deeply critical. "Comeliness is a mark of the Lord's favor, and should be thus a badge of godliness and docility to the teachings of Christ." She whipped the shroud off my body. "Would that this were an enchanted rug woven by the fairies, able to ward off your guilty thoughts, or repel any night visitors."

I snatched at a pillow, before my maid could dash it away. "Stop preaching chastity to me; I will not hear these monkish exhortations. The empress thinks of her hair now and commands you to arrange it becomingly, more in the manner of a courtesan than an abbess."

The Treasury of the Lion

Scroll Three: 1128

$\dagger$

ircumstances now conspired to separate the two sinners. The noble knight regretted his transgressions and wished to atone for them. But the willful empress did not repent the loss of her virtue, and languished without her favorite. Innocent in the eyes of the world, Matilda declined to labor against her lust. She obscured her shame, yet she was disgraced, unworthy of her honorable standing.

†

Winter

MUCH TO MY DISAPPOINTMENT, the count never crept into my solar a second time. My cortege moved on to Normandy, to await the king. My cousin still abides in Boulogne, for Clito sacks the neighboring countryside, razing barns overflowing with the bounty of the recent harvest. Stephen abandons his charge of me, preferring to defend his territory from further incursions. By the time that we parted, exchanging a ritual kiss, my lover had evolved into a stranger, busy conferring with his soldiers and exchanging messages with his wife. He stood by my side, but we were flat figures, trapped in stained glass. My illicit affair brings me no joy. Have I triumphed over Maud, my own enemy?

We took to the sea to ensure against an ambush by Clito's forces. Our ship passed quietly from Boulogne to Dieppe, despite an infestation of rats among our provisions. From Dieppe, safely in Normandy, we continue overland to Rouen. Here in the duchy, there is nothing to fear. We sleep under the stars. From the comfort of my feather pallet, warm enough under a rabbit coverlet, I enjoy the black sky, but my health is not what it was. I slumber fitfully.

I miss my chosen knight; I dread my upcoming marriage. Gerta, satisfied that the adulterous connection is severed, grows ill at ease with my wan cheeks and intermittent nausea. She begins to suspect what I cannot imagine to be true, after one night of bliss.

This afternoon, we forded a rocky stream. On the strength of her misgivings, Gerta drove her mule hard against my horse. As she had hoped, I fell off the saddle, into the chilly water and sharp stones.

I understood her motive, although Brian FitzCount, riding behind us, challenged her. "Woman, look to your beast! The empress might have been trampled underfoot, or perhaps drowned in the river!" The forthright vassal dismounted near my prone form and held out his arm.

I grabbed onto his mail. The cold metal mesh burned through my sopping leather mittens. He pulled me upright, but my drenched skirts made it difficult to step out of the moving rivulet and onto the marshy bank. Brian wrapped his other arm around my waist, steering me out of the water, up to dry land.

I shivered and chattered, but sought to assuage his concern. "I am unhurt. Gerta's animal cannot be rebuked. Let my maid attend to my wet garments."

Gerta slid off her mount and began to wipe off the mud.

FitzCount moved off out of hearing, but others of our escort loitered nearby. Fortuitously, the noisy splashing of hooves and general cacophony of the guards engulfed my words. "Heaven blesses me with this infant, who will assure my marriage to my cousin. Our boy will inherit England and Normandy."

Swabbing at my clothing, my maid jostled and slapped my sides and rump. "No! The Count of Boulogne will not be divided from his lady, whose next baby will be born well before yours. If you are with child, your alliance with Geoffrey may be thwarted, but you will be undesirable to every other Christian prince. Most likely, you will be bundled off to a nunnery for the rest of your days, with me alongside you. Do not ask me to waste my life sequestered in a cloister!"

My confidence evaporated, under her pessimism.

Gerta pinched my side. "We must find a way to conceal or annihilate the fruit of your sin. You must wed Geoffrey before your lasciviousness endangers your chances of obtaining any husband."

†

RUMORS WASH OVER ROUEN. Clito's battalions defeat those of the Count of Boulogne, and my lover settles with the enemy upon a three-year truce, contemptibly betraying my father's ambitions. Joining us, His Majesty rages to hear of my cousin's mishaps and misdemeanors. The king will be apoplectic when he discovers his nephew's other achievement, impregnating his affianced daughter.

Gerta schemes to be rid of the fetus whose existence is no longer in doubt, brewing me tisanes of jasper stone. The situation endangers my future, but I cannot help but cherish Stephen's seed. Today, I pricked my finger, dripping my blood into a bowl of pure spring water, to reassure myself that the baby that I carry is a son. Some of the red drops floated in the clear liquid and some sank, an omen of nothing. Still, I waddle slowly, and my eyes appear hollow, sure signs of a male heir. Even Gerta must admit that my face is unswollen, and my energy sapped. Nothing augurs a daughter.

I remember growing great with the emperor's child. Oh, the courtesies that were lavished on me in Germany! I was cosseted by the whole court; my every whim was law. Now I enjoin to hide my discomforts, and only Gerta sees to my needs. Luckily, my father and his barons are so wrapped up in the struggle for Flanders that they notice no evidence of my alteration. They do not foresee the birth of the boy who will save me.

†

To plague Clito, Henry and his advisors sponsor rebellions among the Flemish burghers. They funnel money and men into the principle towns, fermenting dissatisfaction and starting trouble of every sort. Further, His Majesty levies an embargo against English trade with Flanders. No more of our wool feeds their cloth mills. Adeliza's father, the Duke of Lorraine, also forbids his populace to buy or sell with those who suffer Clito's rule. Our economic stranglehold upon the good citizens of Flanders will surely turn them against a prince who cannot guarantee prosperity.

The king commands my cousin's presence in Rouen. He charges my lover to close his Boulogne ports to the Flemish. He decrees that the truce with Clito be broken, and presses Stephen to go back on his word as a knight.

I have as much to demand of him as the crown does. I intend that he shall renege on his vows to Maud.

†

It was not a simple matter to catch the disgraced Count of Boulogne alone in Rouen castle. I had to spy upon all his movements from the small aperture in my solar. Today, seeing him enter the steward's tower on the far side of the bailey, I hurriedly climbed up to the parapet. I circled over to a small terrace on the other side of the keep, hoping that Stephen would find it necessary to take in the view. Men-at-arms came and went along the crenellated precipice.

At last my cousin emerged into the bitterly cold afternoon. "Ah, Empress, are you here?" He glanced nervously to the right and left, as if afraid to be alone with me, or to be observed meeting privately with me. He stepped over to the far wall of the landing and leaned over the edge.

I complained to his back. "How can you be so careless with the woman who has given you all that she has to offer? Your apathy pains me. Do not suppress your affection! You do yourself and me a great disservice by denying what has come between us."

Stephen kept his face turned outward, over the moat. "What we shared, my lady, lasted only one night. Our euphoria is best forgotten. We each owe allegiance elsewhere." His unruly amber hair stood out against the drab stonework.

I inched toward him. I could not see his hands, as the sleeves of his tunic dripped low for warmth. I placed my glove on his heavy mantle, gathering up a thick fold of fine brown wool. "Can you not call me by some term of endearment?"

The count swiveled his neck to meet my eyes. "That would be very unwise and unseemly. We had best deny that we ever were more to one another than intimate kin." He twisted about, tossed back his sleeves and firmly undid my grasp on his clothing. Then he stalked away, only to pause, searching for some polite way to quit my presence without my permission.

The truth would prolong our encounter. "You shall not foreswear me! My honor is at stake. I am pregnant."

My cousin blanched.

I thrilled to see his face register an emotion of which I was the cause. But his frigidity stymied me; I could have been jubilant by his side. "I will proclaim my unchastity from the rooftops, if it will keep you close at hand. I shall be a creature of unbridled wantonness, if it will please you."

"Hush, Matilda! If anyone guesses that there has been some connection between us, we will both be the worse for it. Geoffrey will not accept another man's leman as his wife."

My heat thumped. Could Stephen hear it? "Always call me by my name."

He blushed. "I shall retire, to think hard upon our dilemma. Perhaps you will miscarry, and this great difficulty will be resolved." With this excuse, the Count of Boulogne darted down the stone stairwell.

I listened to his footsteps fade away, then turned out, toward the frozen landscape, over the snowy city of Rouen. Considering the panorama of life spread before me, I marveled that anyone should question my fitness to rule. I will not permit this pregnancy to undermine my birthright. Why should I not be queen, with this son and heir to rule after me?

†

FOR SEVERAL DAYS THEREAFTER, Stephen continued to slight me in the great hall of the castle. Then he and his retinue slunk away, back to Boulogne. At the last moment, Gerta cornered my cousin's page in the kitchens, in order to formulate a plan for exchanging secret messages between master and mistress. I am to append the name "Dameta" to my letters. If Maud becomes leery, and inquires into her husband's infidelity, she will presume his paramour to be an unknown Norman commoner. He will sign his replies as "Arthur." Gerta disparages these hasty arrangements, improvised rather than deftly arranged.

This evening, my maid and I washed and readied a corpse, that of a young squire accidently killed during a mock battle engagement among the Rouen garrison. The victim had been armed only with a thick staff, and when he clubbed at the legs of two mounted knights from the opposing team, they whirled about and trapped him between their horses' flanks. The boy was unable to escape the flat blows of their two blunted swords. Although he wore suitable cloth padding, and his skin was unpunctured, he must have sustained fatal internal injuries. The men of the castle are somber tonight, to have unnecessarily lost one of their number. It shall fall to me, perhaps, to send the ill news to his noble parents, who entrusted his education to our royal household.

It was almost the hour of compline, when the godly retire to reflect on the fragility of life and the hope of salvation, but Gerta's mind was not on our task, or eternity. "To dub your scoundrel with the alias of our ancient king! His page rates him too highly!" She sprinkled an extract of chamomile along the adolescent's torso, which had not yet begun to putrefy.

I dribbled an ointment with the odor of thyme. "I am grateful that my beloved agrees to correspond."

"Do not ask that rake for advice, or rely on him to unravel this knot. We will adopt other tactics so that you lose the baby."

"Why should I disdain the child that mingles my royal blood with my cousin's?"

"The higher the rank of any person, the more perfect should be his or her obedience to heaven's authority." Gerta's words were swallowed up in the ringing of bells.

Several servants straggled into the room, bringing with them a newly sewn, linen winding sheet. The women were in low spirits, for the winter boredom had come upon them and the night was dark and frosty. They chattered dolefully. Some of them attempted, surreptitiously, to kiss the feet of the slain youth, thinking to come by some miracle cure, without having to leave an offering in a parish collection box. Gerta swatted them away from the corpse.

The eldest housemaid terrified the others. "When the late Count of Flanders was murdered, his assassins feasted on the very altar of the church where they had killed him. The body still lay warm, yet they sat down to banquet!"

Gerta silenced the old fool. "Ultimately, the sinners were cast from a tall tower onto the ground, so that their bodies shattered to pieces." She glared at the lazy ignoramuses. Huffing at their inutility, she placed the shroud under and over the dead body, before dispatching them on further errands.

Alone once more, we waited for the monks who would recite the mourning dirge.

Gerta could not resist another gibe. "Reflect, Empress; your exalted stature will not preclude you from the end we all face."

†

MY MAID CONVINCED ME to douche with lead, in the latest of her stratagems to evacuate my womb. There is a privy chamber located in the castle's inner wall, whose excrement collects in a cesspit in the ward, but there is another toilet in the outer defense works, whose waste drops into the moat. If I could expel a fetus there, it would be camouflaged by the muck and debris that clog the water.

This morning, before dawn, Gerta escorted me to this farther garderobe. We glided through the frigid dark. The fortress was silent, except for the occasional whinny and lower from the stables and barns. The extreme cold kept all the inhabitants of the keep to their beds; even the guards on the ramparts had fled their posts for the interior.

My maid had compounded a reeking abortifacient. She held out a flask. "Splash this medicine between your legs; try to ladle it into your womanly cavity. I shall watch the door, to ensure that you are unmolested."

I rolled my eyes. "The smell from this shit hole is noxious."

Yet I did as I was told. After several minutes, it was apparent that the vile concoction had had no effect. I felt no stirring or cramping of any kind. Relieved, I stepped out onto the crenellated corridor.

Gerta palpitated my abdomen, visibly enlarged, and scowled.

†

Spring

ALL WINTER LONG, MY maid infested my food with coriander, but eventually she lost confidence that I would be able to rid myself of the child. We successfully hid my protuberant belly under the fur-lined mantles necessary to the weather. As the chill of the season lessened, we cast about for some escape from our conundrum.

Ultimately, I petitioned my father for permission to visit the convent of Jumièges, ostensibly to retreat from the court and prepare myself for my new wedded life in Anjou. His Majesty agreed that solitude and the shelter of the church would be right and fitting for the bride-to-be.

In truth, I shall abide there for the spring and summer, giving birth with the connivance of a Rouen midwife. Left at the nunnery, the baby will be raised by the holy sisters. Through fasting and prayer, and well considering the possibility of a large donation, the abbess of Jumièges came to the conclusion that it would be expedient to shield the infant and foster it.

Dameta sent off a letter, bursting with passion and contrivance, relating the plot to secrete Arthur's heir among the brides of Christ. She begged him for some mark of his solicitude.

> *You never promised me your future, but I plead with you for some sign that the undeniable attraction between us will not be forgotten. I do not believe that you deceived me when you embraced me. Aid me, dearest heart, in my plans for this babe, who will pull down the barriers that keep us apart. Come to me at the convent, or send to him such items as will signify his heritage. Entrust to us your sword, or a ring or a manuscript with your seal. My lover you have been; my knight you must be.*

The response devastates my spirit.

> *I grieve that both my honor and yours are lost. I dare not reveal the truth to any layman, but my attendants comment upon my solemn demeanor. Even my wife hears tell of my melancholia. Her messages to me are full of remedies. I confide only in my confessor, who advises me how to proceed, so as to ensure the salvation of my soul and my political prospects.*
>
> *I forbid you to publicize our iniquity. I will not abet such a disgrace by sending any token of mine. Once our error has been erased by the passage of time, we will meet without any recourse to our previous intimacy.*
>
> *Your time in the nunnery will be well spent. I imagine that you will profit from your removal from the temptations of the world.*

Is it too much to hope that this rebuff was entirely penned by Stephen's chaplain, or composed by the Count of Boulogne in a fit of compunction toward Maud? I do not admire the rhetoric, the language, or the style of his epistle. And it is missing some of its requisite parts. Where does he essay to secure my goodwill?

Gerta consoles me, calling my cousin a poor writer and a weak creature, easily swayed by the influence of the moment: sometimes lust, sometimes faith, sometimes a king, sometimes a bishop, sometimes an empress, sometime a wife. Virgil claimed that women are the most fickle of His creation, but a man with a pen in his hand is never to be trusted.

†

JUMIÈGES IS SITUATED ON the Seine and constantly refreshed by the breezes that come off the river. The convent is a large village of stone structures, including a chapel, hall, infirmary, dormitory, and kitchen. There are farms and barns, a mill and a vineyard. The hushed tranquility that I expected is nowhere to be found, for the complex resounds with the clanging of bells, the braying of animals and the comings and goings of the sick and the poor. The holy women sing and chant as they work and pray.

For the most part, the nuns, born to aristocratic families, comport themselves respectably. Their abbess is a practical woman whose piety is none too evident. She runs her establishment with a firm, orderly hand.

Now that I am growing fat and lazy, I spend my days much as I like: sewing, writing, and napping. Frequently, I receive word of the outside world. Adeliza finds nothing odd about my stay here. She assumes that seclusion will increase my humility and my serenity, judging me in need of both if I am to be a proper wife to Geoffrey of Anjou.

The English queen reports that Maud has born a son, christening him Eustace, a name traditional among the counts of Boulogne. I am thankful that my own confinement approaches nigh. I do not quake before the coming torments, which will deliver unto me my beloved's child.

Gerta is quite taken with one mystical sister, Helewise, and often strolls with her around the cloister. Beaten and abandoned by her father and brothers when she refused to marry a neighboring landowner, Helewise preferred to preserve her chastity for Christ. My maid finds inspiration in this tale of forsaken carnality, but I see nothing to emulate.

Helewise is prone to inane babble, imagined illness, and ecstatic rapture. I judge her no better than a drunken dairymaid at harvest fair, overeager for enjoyment. Deprived of the outside world's ease and pleasures, she is rapacious for sensual gratification of any sort.

Have I have consorted with my cousin, indulged in hedonism, merely to compensate for my own thwarted ambition?

†

Summer

MY LABORS BEGAN AT matins, in the long hours of the night. Gerta sent quickly for the midwife. I called for the abbess to witness my travails, so that she can later testify to the baby's identity. Uninvited, Helewise appeared, crowding my chamber with her disordered gown and disheveled hair.

Wincing with discomfort, I tried to be rid of her. "Such a scene as this is no place for a virgin."

"You are right, Lady. The wickedness of childbirth is greater than all the other evils of the world. Out of your womb will come red ants and black spiders, and a torment of poisonous stings." The mystic began to prod erratically at her own rib cage.

From the passage outside, a chorus of nuns began to chant soothing and melodious music.

In contrast, Helewise's foolish, sinister words exacerbated my malaise. "Empress, surrender your body to holiness: to Christ, our king, and the Virgin, our queen!" She stretched her arms toward the ceiling.

I thought to sigh, but a moan came out of my throat. "The king is my father; I am your queen. Be gone with you."

"What you are, you are, but by the grace of God." Helewise exited the room, her eyes darting erratically around her face.

The midwife guffawed. "Such ranting does no good at such a time. You will have anguish enough."

A sharp pain cut through me, so that I cried out.

The abbess began to fidget, and inched toward the door.

I motioned her toward a trunk in the far corner. "Mother, remain through my troubles. Your time and attention will be well recompensed; your convent will soon have a new refectory."

Stiffly, she complied.

I yielded to the ministrations of the midwife, an old woman, well versed in the indecencies of this crisis. After rubbing her hands with grease, she stretched opened the mouth of my pelvis. I whimpered, but did not resist, remembering what was to come.

Gerta compelled me to drink from a flask stashed among the folds of her jacket. I swallowed some combination of breast milk, olive oil, and foul physic that did not assuage my misery. Gagging upon its bitterness, I sneezed, startling everyone. Immediately the midwife pinched my nostrils closed, so that my strength did not escape me.

As the night wore on, my difficulties increased, until my screams were so constant that they drowned out the hymns of the holy women.

✝

As Stephen's son lay swaddled in a cradle before the hearth, I dictated to the abbess a manuscript attesting to his parentage. At the bottom of the document, Gerta dripped a pool of red wax, and I impressed it with my imperial seal. My maid and the nun witnessed the parchment with their signatures; the midwife affixed her mark.

I rolled up the parchment with crimson ribbons, then presented it formally to the abbess. "Preserve this scroll; vow to me that this will be done. And send for a priest. He must baptize the boy, this very day." I would wash my heir clean of all sin.

The nun knelt before me, to swear, then kissed me in fealty. She hurried from my room, with its dank smells and gutted candles.

Presenting a purse of gold, Gerta dismissed the midwife, and dispatched her to procure the wet nurse. "She had better be big-boned and bonny, with a rosy complexion. Give her vinegar syrup to drink, and hurry her back here."

Alone, we dabbed honey on the infant's lips, to whet its appetite. Unmoved, my prince seemed to prefer sleep to sustenance.

I considered his mute form. "Shall I call him Arthur, after his sire, and in reference to his future greatness?"

Gerta looked askance. "Do not attract attention to him! His safety, and yours, depend upon disguise. Choose something more nondescript, appropriate for a convent foundling."

In Germany, despite all my exertions, I could only present my husband with a dead fetus. Had I forgotten to thank Holy Mary for her gift to me? "I am grateful for our deliverance tonight from death. I humble myself before heaven, and defer my aspirations. In return for the blessings of life and a robust child, I conceal his birthright under the guise of a noble but undistinguished name."

"Warin, Ingram, Gervase, Hubert—it does not matter, my lady."

"Gervase, then. I see in him that which has germinated from my passion. I feel for him all that I feel for his father, the flower of masculine perfection."

"The infant is yours, Empress, so he will rank high in beauty and talent. I say nothing of the Count of Boulogne. The measure of a man has never owed more to the delusions of love."

†

I MAY HAVE VERY little time to recover from my ordeal, no protracted period of recuperation. I will essay to stay here for the forty days of my pollution, until I can be churched and purified, but cannot be sure of the length of my reprise.

My son, Gervase, is a miracle. I wrap his long, delicate fingers around my own pinky, and marvel at how they remain perfectly curled as he sleeps. Overcome with his ginger beauty, I am momentarily tempted to renounce the world and all its royal trappings, refuse my contracted marriage, brave my father's wrath, and slink away with my child to a modest life of oblivion. I could appoint Gervase my ward, as if I had come across an orphan foundling at the convent, and taken a shine to him. And yet, I know myself incapable of such motherly sacrifice. I cannot turn my back on society, and relinquish wealth and status for the sake of this one heavenly gift.

To avoid the scrutiny of the nuns, I pray alone in my solar. I abase myself before my lady Mary, obliged to Her for Her intercession, contrite before Her purity and glory. She has permitted me a grievous error, and endowed me with a most precious treasure. The Holy Mother is the portal through which I reenter the fray. She will not refuse me Her grace, as I go forth into the world.

The Treasury of the Lion

Scroll Four: 1129

lind to the depravity of her soul, the empress would not redress her error. She remained true to her false knight, although married to another, in obeisance to her father's authority. Her young husband, likewise corrupt, cherished a woman without heaven's sanction. Many rejoiced at their wedding, but neither the bride nor the groom came to the nuptial couch in chastity and grace, and their union began in bitterness and grief.

✝

Winter

FOR THE LAST THREE months, I have been ensconced in Rouen, waiting aimlessly to be disposed of. No one questions my late absence or discovers my misadventure. Slim again and full of energy, I chafe at the infernal boredom of my passivity. Additions to my wardrobe long finished, Gerta and I have very little to do but speak in whispers of the infant and its imagined development. I dream of baby Gervase, his warm, milky, wrinkled little face, his shock of red hair. Yet I no longer dread the upcoming arrival of my intended, his knighting ceremony, or even my nuptials, as these rites and feasts shall herald my departure from this stultifying existence.

We are sorely in need of continental endorsement and assistance. Clito amasses troops at one of our frontier castles in the duchy of Normandy, making his first formal claim on our imperial territories. Thus my marriage, put off for so long, is now to be rushed, so that Angevin soldiers can swell our ranks. Geoffrey's father, Count Fulk of Anjou and Maine, sets out for the Holy Land, endowing Geoffrey with his European territories and titles, raising my betrothed to the dignity of count. Yet, despite what the troubadours declaim before the high table, it is my condescension that most honors my insignificant groom.

†

GEOFFREY PLANTAGENET HAS ARRIVED. Just at midday, his destrier clattered into the inner bailey, at the head of a goodly sized company of Angevin men-at-arms. I peeped at him from a slit of a window in the circular stairwell that descends from my solar. My abdomen tightened in anticipation and misgiving. To what sort of man must I give myself, body and soul?

Removing his coif, Geoffrey ruffled his close-cropped white hair, and wiped his dusty, perspiring face. His prominent bone structure and sinewy cheeks unnerved me. Appraising him through his surcoat and chain mail, I judged his torso to be narrow, but well molded. My stomach settled. At least he is no dwarf or bear! Then he lifted his eyes, somehow aware that he was under my scrutiny. His thin mouth contorted in a mocking smile. I gritted my teeth at his presumption. Does this scamp consider himself equal to my hand?

We met at none, in the great hall. Delivered from the dirt of the road, the Angevin's pale skin set off his finely wrought features, so sharply conspicuous that his expressions seem etched in stone. His first words were: "Welcome, first to God and then to me."

I pinched my lips shut. I knew that my father waited for me to offer him the kiss of greeting. Sighing, I presented my face toward him. His mouth was rough. Fortunately, he did not linger over the embrace, nor genuflect before me, like some ass of a courtier, false compliments oozing from his lips.

On the contrary, Geoffrey's arrogance and critical opinion, couched in his frown and icy blue eyes, were easily legible. With dubious tact, he exhaled to indicate his aggrieved tolerance of my portion of feminine charm. He inspected me in an orderly fashion, as the philosophers advise, from the crown of head to the soles of my feet. Clearly, I pass muster, but in no way approach the required excellence.

†

GEOFFREY'S EDUCATION HAS BEEN more thorough than is to be expected. His conversational and rhetorical talents, in French and in Latin, delight the king. The two hold wide-ranging discussions of history and the arts. Gerta is all smiles to see what Mother Mary blesses me with, in return for my sacrifices. Yet the Angevin is no hero to challenge Stephen's sway over the fief of my heart. My fiancé is indisputably beautiful, intelligent, and charismatic, yet I find the youth repellent.

†

YESTERDAY, IN THE CHAPEL of Rouen castle, my father bestowed the arms of war upon Geoffrey, with all the ritual appropriate to such a sacrament. Acting as his military patron, the king became his second sire. Accepting his honors from the English crown, the Angevin vowed to use his weapons to serve it in fealty.

Geoffrey wore a golden tunic under a purple mantle. His stockings were silk. My intended seemed somewhat ill at ease in such colorful, majestic finery, and I noticed that he frowned whenever he adjusted the folds of his bright cloak.

At the proscribed moment, the Angevin fell to his knees. His Majesty dubbed him a knight, calling upon the Holy Spirit to guide Geoffrey's might in accordance with the principles of chivalry, and to channel his thoughts in accordance with the rules of wisdom. Henry presented him with a golden sword from our royal treasury, with a white enamel pommel and a mother of pearl handle. My father blessed the blade, and he who would wield it. The king concluded with a benediction: "May you be distinguished among us, unto preeminence, and may your reputation for faith and courage surpass all others whose names fall from our lips."

Then Henry lifted the Angevin up, kissed both his cheeks and hung around his neck a shield displaying his new coat of arms. The heraldic device is an azure field, emblazoned with many small lions, the beasts common to the charges of our family. The blue background signifies an allegiance to the ideal of purity.

Receiving his accolade, Sir Geoffrey arose, elevated, reborn as the Count of Anjou and Maine. To me, it was a bitter moment, as I reflected that my rank would soon sink, to that of his countess.

Our party exited the cathedral, and stood in the public square. A sizable gathering of townspeople, farmers, serfs and prelates cheered the day. My groom's expression lightened when he was presented with an enormous Spanish stallion, hung with golden trappings. My father's squires attached golden spurs to his boots, and fitted him with a gem-encrusted helmet. Without stepping into the stirrups, the Count of Anjou vaulted astride his mount, to the pleasure of the crowd. He exhibited complete control over the animal, although he had never ridden it before. Even the meanest paupers and pickpockets roared their approval of his skill. Their palpable enthusiasm and my father's evident good humor were infectious.

Even I must try to open my heart to this capable boy, worthy of the world's admiration. If his fate equals his merit, perhaps together we shall bend the king's empire to our pleasure, and write history according to our will.

†

THIS MORNING, MY SECOND wedding took place in Le Mans, at the open door of its St Julian Cathedral. In the presence of His Majesty, two bishops consecrated the sacrament. A throng of local barons crowded the porch on which we stood. Swarms of curious burghers massed in the plaza before us.

Numb with cold, I wore a silver bliaut of the thinnest, pleated silk. My corsage, richly embellished with cabochon opals and moonstones, lacked sleeves. I had foresworn a mantle, preferring to parade myself draped in the color of chastity. I did not shiver, but stood rigidly to Geoffrey's left side, as Eve was formed out of Adam's left rib.

During the ceremony, the priests lectured me at length about my wifely duties, hardly mentioning the mysteries of heaven. "Empress, be subject to your spouse; lose Your Imperial Highness in his marital supremacy. He will value you, but you must revere him, just as you stand awe struck before the altar of the church. Count, foster your wife for the sake of her weaknesses, as Christ loves humanity, in spite of its sins."

This was the blessing that was to sanctify my union! During the Mass that followed, I found it difficult to remain composed and humble before the prating officiants. How can I stand it, to lose what gives me glory and grace? If I am not Empress Matilda, I am no one.

Geoffrey's face was smug as he took my hand for the rites of the ring. He slid the nuptial band upon my thumb, in the name of the Father, upon my second finger, in the name of the Son, upon my third, in the name of the Holy Ghost, and finally upon my fourth, as an Amen.

I turned my head, so that I could look inside the vast interior of the cathedral. Wan light streamed in through its windows, illuminating motes of dust in the air. My dissatisfaction must surely be as dirt in the eyes of Mother Mary. My anger dissipated, and I found it easier to bear myself with decorum. As proscribed, I sank down before Geoffrey Plantagenet, lying on the frigid stone floor at his feet, prostrating myself before my earthly authority.

I presume that this charade will serve to gladden my husband's spirit, and incline him to soften his demeanor toward me. Perhaps, in our sexual congress, ill feelings will be swept away by carnal pleasures.

†

YESTERDAY'S LENGTHY FESTIVITIES, AT a palace belonging to the house of Anjou, far outlasted my resigned humor. After the feasting, the wedding night was decidedly inauspicious.

I was uneasy in the unfamiliar bedchamber. By the light of the hearth, Gerta helped me to undress, tugging off my sumptuous jacket and under gown, then removing the braids and gems from my elaborate coiffure. I lifted my arms; over my head she placed a perfumed linen smock, long stored in a satchel of dried violets and lavender. She began to brush my hair, and her firm strokes tingled my scalp, mitigating some of my tension. With silk ribbons, we tied a small leather pouch around my upper left thigh, containing a yellow flower of henbane. My maid had done the same before I laid down with the emperor, and I had successfully conceived of a boy.

One of the bishops and several drunken earls ushered Geoffrey into the room. His Grace mumbled a traditional prayer: "Watch over these Thy servants, keeping guard over their slumber, shielding them from the manipulations of the devil. Defend them, protect them, as they live forever after by Thy commandments. Amen."

Throughout, the inebriated, mocking courtiers snickered and made bawdy gestures. One of them invited my maid to see to his pleasure.

Geoffrey gave them a look, which did not manage to turn them to stone, but which I would not have wanted to see pointed in my direction.

At long last, the priest sprinkled holy water upon the bed and backed out of the solar. Too soon, they all bustled out, Gerta included. I bolted the door after them.

Wearing only a nightshirt, with his short, white hair slightly tousled, my handsome husband stood before me. In the firelight, his youthful face flickered, sometimes up lit, then plunged into shadow. Just then, I noticed that he carried a small bundle. I imagined it a gift, some bauble to endear himself to me.

The Angevin held out what appeared to be a garment. "We will fulfill our duties to one another, but we will comport ourselves without voluptuousness."

I registered the weight and stiff texture of the cloth. "As you see, my lord, I am already suitably attired."

The boy huffed. "Wear this instead. It is a chemise cajoule, which I am surprised is unexpected to you, a princess educated at a convent, and just returned from a holy retreat. Our fornication must not include wanton delights. While the consummation of our marriage is a political necessity, I will not dally with you in an unseemly or impious manner." He turned his back to me.

I wriggled out of my scented nightgown. Eager to cover my nakedness, I slipped on the copious tunic. It had a small rent in the lower front, through which he could penetrate me. I hesitated, repelled by the obligation to copulate without enjoyment. Such a thing was possible for a woman, but certainly pitiable. "I am ready, Geoffrey."

The Angevin spun on his heel and peered at me through narrowed eyes. He patrolled the chamber, snuffing out candles. Finally, he gestured me toward our pallet.

Without any preliminary embraces, he lowered himself down, directly on top of me, and began to shove himself through the aperture in the cloth. "It is unfortunate that your dark locks smell so sweet."

"I readied myself to entice you, husband. Men generally appreciate such seductions."

Geoffrey grunted and pushed more roughly. "The arts of witchcraft! The nuptial couch is not the place for romance. We exert ourselves solely to beget an heir."

I whimpered. The wounds of childbirth had healed, but my body had been long untouched, although not as long he might estimate. "Cannot you be more gentle?"

The fireplace embers glowed, unextinguished, so I could see that he stared resolutely at the wall behind our bed. "The wave of history does not unfurl without force. I besiege a citadel that rightfully belongs to me, storming its walls with a battering ram. I take no immoderate pleasure in the destruction of my own tower." Explicating his principles of war, Geoffrey slid methodically inside me.

I squirmed, putting my hands on his chest to check his movement and lessen his thrust. "According to the rules of courtliness, man and wife are bound to satisfy each other. I have read of this marital debt in my father's library."

"You interpret incorrectly material wisely hidden from the eyes of women. You and I are merely required to perform perfunctorily. Only lovers have license to transport themselves merrily." The count shuddered; the deed was done.

Splayed under his prone figure, I wondered aloud at his callousness. "How can this be a true espousal? We cannot merge into one flesh, if we remain our separate selves at the moment of sexual intercourse."

Gingerly, Geoffrey withdrew from me, as if he was unwilling for our skin to come into any unnecessary contact. "Joseph was the husband of Mary, without touching her in lust. You too will deliver unto me a son to inherit the earth, a son whose generation has not been undertaken in a depraved frame of mind."

†

Spring

AT THE CASTLE OF Alost, on the border of Flanders, Clito's armies confronted our divisions. We give thanks to God on high, for He decreed that victory should be ours. Most miraculously, the Lord guided the arm of a common foot soldier, who wounded Clito to the quick. Our most dangerous and despised enemy has died from the infestations of this injury!

By the authority of the English crown and the consent of the burghers of Bruges, who are impatient for a cessation to conflict, the Flemish welcome our generous peace, and a propitious Anglo-Flemish treaty of trade and friendship. Our empire on the Continent rests, almost unassailable. With all speed, my father heads home.

I do not participate in the general jubilation. I am irrevocably tied to the Count of Anjou, and all for nothing. My only rival for the imperial throne of England and Normandy lies interred in a stone sarcophagus, yet I am forever saddled to a man whose spirit is as impervious and inert as marble.

†

TRAVELING SOUTH FROM LE Mans into my husband's territory, I heard no cheers of welcome from the laborers and villagers along the route. Despite the mellowing temperature, only a pretense of celebration marked my arrival in Angers, Anjou's foremost city. The tocsins rang out, but no festival obstructed the narrow streets. A procession of monks, holding lit candles and singing hymns, heralded us into the castle, but then quickly disbanded as we dismounted. Expecting speeches, I nodded as Geoffrey's vassals saluted us, and then was confused to see them turning their attention to tankards of ale. Overall, the atmosphere was as indifferent as the Angevin's deportment toward me.

†

WITHIN HIS KEEP, MY husband assigns me a second-rate solar, located in an inner ward, downwind of the kitchens and stables. Nasty odors constantly harass my solitude. Insects swarm interminably through my window. I smoke bundles of hay in my hearth to ward off the infuriating mosquitoes. I tuck alder leaves under my pallet, to attract and eliminate its fleas. A tattered, stained tapestry adorns my wall. There are no poles or hooks for my substantial wardrobe. All of my precious chattel remains folded in trunks and caskets, so crowding my ignominious chamber that there is very little space in which to maneuver.

Despite this and other evidence of the Angevin's dislike, Gerta blames Stephen for my continued disenchantment. Today, as we ransacked my boxes for garments suitable to the warming weather, she refused to credit my complaints. "The count is nothing to you only because you measure him against another man. Cease to dream of your cousin, and seek to be the most contented of queens. Virile Geoffrey will soon endow you with a child."

I slammed shut the lid of one of my coffers. "The Angevin imp does not even provide me with proper rooms, in which to spend my leisure hours in fitting comfort. Do not reckon that he will present me with a boy."

Gerta unearthed a bliaut of thin blond wool, trimmed with daffodils of Queen Adeliza's embroidery. She exhibited its cascade of sleeves. "Ah, daffodils to incite his chivalry."

I snorted and waved the dress away.

My maid persisted. "Angers Castle is not a royal residence boasting innumerable private accommodations to divide among the household." Despite my disparagement, she pulled the dress over my head, and smoothed its delicate weave over my hips.

I stroked the creamy, crimped fabric. "If Geoffrey were to divest himself of his fatuous concubine, her very luxurious solar would revert to me."

Gerta wound a wide yellow belt over the gown, showcasing my willowy waist. "Your count is very young, Empress."

I picked up the dripping wrists of the bliaut, tying them into knots to make them more manageable. "He examines the applicable code, and would have us live together unpolluted, in a 'white marriage.' His philosophy will withstand your meddling!"

Standing back to admire my ensemble, my maid dismissed my instruction. "Do not be taken in by his reserve. He preens over his new prerogatives as a knight and an earl. He is aflame with his adulterous romance. He will outgrow this woman, this Denise."

I shook my head. "I only begrudge him his love, for I have had to sacrifice mine."

†

SLIGHTED, I RESENT THE preference Geoffrey consistently shows to his mistress. The girl is an enticing creature, with knee length red curls, pink cheeks, and a high bosom. Her mouth forms a small, suggestive posy. She often has a love bite on her neck or a bruise on her arm, trophies of the night that she does not bother to conceal. Consumed by her, the Angevin's natural iciness melts away. I no longer puzzle over the chemise cajoule, surely my rival's scheme to frustrate her paramour's conjugal embraces. Geoffrey's pious obligation to me is no match for his sacrilegious devotion to his leman.

Sitting beside his harlot, my husband is the model of chivalry. He composes poetry in her honor, which he recites at length from the dais. Even I am expected to compliment the slut on the sentimental verses that her pulchritude has inspired. Most of them are exceedingly well-crafted, although Geoffrey sorely overuses the rhyme "pearl" and "earl."

Denise is the daughter of a petty nobleman, one of the Count of Anjou's lesser vassals. They met some years ago, when her father brought her to Fulk's court, so that he might offer her virginity in exchange for tax relief. Geoffrey took one look and burned to deflower her. Accepting the wench in payment, Fulk then sold her to his son, at a price equal to the fees and tolls owed. My husband may have violated the damsel, and exercised his *droit de seigneur*, but she insinuated herself into his heart. What a Greek tragedy! It is no wonder that an aging, secondhand widow, foisted upon him by political circumstance, cannot compete with this fixation.

†

Fall

FOR MANY MONTHS, I have resided under his roof, yet it was only last night that the Count of Anjou again availed himself of his connubial rights. Quite late, he burst into my inconvenient chamber. I stood, wrapped in a blanket before a small fire, miffed at Gerta's absence, which he must have ensured.

For some reason, the Angevin seemed less distressed by my dishabille than he had been on our wedding night. Indeed, he would tutor me, emphasizing the greatness of Clito and my nothingness. "My spies in England inform me of an enormous groundswell of grief at the untimely loss of the only legitimate male heir to the throne. With Clito gone, who deserves allegiance? Even your father mourns his worthy nephew, and casts about for a successor." Geoffrey sat his spare, well-shaped frame down on one of my trunks.

A chill had worked its way up from my feet to my shoulders. "His Majesty laments the death of the true prince, my brother William, your own sister's husband."

"That girl, long immured in a nunnery, is much better off serving Holy Mother Mary than sullying herself in the vice-ridden world. You overlook another of my sisters, who espoused Clito himself." The Angevin had made no move to disrobe.

I braved the drafts, drifting so close to him that I could feel his breath on my face. "Henry annulled that marriage."

The count did not flinch. "As easily as he assassinated his brother, King William Rufus."

I pulled my blanket more securely around my back. "His Majesty was killed accidentally, during a hunt, by an arrow gone awry."

"The shaft hit its target, guided by an ill star." My lord stood up, brushed past me and kicked off his pointed leather shoes. In clipped movements, he flung off a jeweled brooch and peeled off his bliaut. Did he ever require the service of his pages?

The rippling muscles of his narrow back jarred me. I tossed my hair off my neck, in order to clear my head. "Someday, I shall wear the English crown, by divine right."

Geoffrey stood naked in the low light. I looked into his eyes, avoiding the sight of his body. "Our union was solemnized so that you would defend my accession."

The Angevin stepped over to my bed and patted it. "On your behalf, I shall rule for you, and as regent for the boy who will be born to us."

Dismayed, I did not move. "Your role is to protect my inheritance. I shall reign, and my sons after me. There is no question of a regency. You must adhere to my interests and be content with your own county."

Geoffrey slapped the mattress. "Some man shall come to dominate the empire. Why should I not seize it for myself, as William the Conqueror, your own grandfather, did, as King Henry, your own father, did? They were not born to be kings of the realm."

I hooted at his vanity. "My vassals pledged an oath of fealty to *me*! Your body does not run with the blood of majesty. Anjou is an alien land; you would not be to any knight's taste. Do not think me ignorant of your military history. Your family raised its sword many times against my Norman nobility." In my agitation, my covering slipped, exposing me.

The count snarled. "Someday, I will press Normandy under my thumb."

"You will have to wrest it from me, you rapacious villain!"

Geoffrey shrugged, insouciant. "Verily, the continent shall sate my appetite. I leave England to you; leave Normandy to me." Here he paused. "Come, wife. I am ready enough to furnish you with a son, even though my captivating mistress lies abed very near."

I complied, but with bad grace. "Your mania for that woman is something to behold."

In the dim chamber, his expression warped. "You belong to me, despite all your manifold sins, your pride, envy, and anger." He smacked my leg and shoved me down.

This I could not permit to go unremarked. "Does it irk you when I inventory your transgressions against me, against my father, and against the holy church?"

With more vigor, the brute slapped me again, on my shoulder. "Carping bitch! Prating whore! You disturb my peace. I doubt that you would be to any knight's taste, but somehow I have the burdensome job of mortifying your flesh." Using his forearms to pin me beneath him, he drove himself inside me.

I readied myself to withstand a trial by ordeal. I separated my thoughts from my body, letting them drift away, to Stephen. He is under Maud's thrall. I doubt he subjects her to such loutish company.

†

THE ENGLISH QUEEN WRITES me, to report that Brian FitzCount, long one of the king's favorites, grows more prominent at court. Having completed an audit of the crown treasury, he is named a royal constable, and will preside over legal disputes in Henry's name. Now Brian is to wed the heiress of Wallingford, greatly enlarging his wealth and standing.

Her Majesty surprises me with her cynicism, her doubts that FitzCount is enamored of his bride. His behavior toward her is impeccable, but impassive, and she judges that FitzCount unites himself to the Lady Basilia merely because she casts some sweet glances his way, and he is too noble to decline her advances. In private, he confesses to my friend how proud he is of his vassalage to me, of the oath that he swore in my defense.

Once, reminiscing in this way, he broke off in the middle of speaking, and grew mute, completely forgetting the courtesy owed to Adeliza. When he remembered what was due to her, he blushed. "Please excuse my waywardness. My vows of service to a fair princess should not prohibit my attentions to a charming queen."

†

FOR ALL HIS VENERATION of the holy church, my husband resolves that it has no business intruding in his domestic arrangements. His zeal for Denise convinces him that adultery and marriage are morally equivalent. His ardor for his leman renders his affair with her just as venerable as his affiliation to his wife.

Today, my lord interrupted me, as I worked on a tapestry to enliven my solar. Colorful skeins of thread lay in heaps on the furniture and floor of my homely surroundings.

Geoffrey wore only the cloth doublet that underpins his suit of armor. He must have shrugged off his squires before they had finished attending to him. Over my shoulder, he examined my weaving. "Woman, I find myself incapable of continuing in bigamy."

Incredulous, I glanced up at his luminous eyes. "So Denise is to be sent packing?"

"You are befuddled! It is you who are to be discarded. Only the consent of a willing heart constitutes a genuine tie. Our connection is fraudulent." The Angevin paced away from me and picked up the lid of one of my coffers, as if to commence my preparations for decamping from his keep.

I arose and crossed the room to exhume my silver silk wedding gown. I held out the shimmering cloth. "It suited you to ally yourself to one of high birth. The Church sanctifies our bond. You cannot deny these things."

Dismissing my remarks, and dispensing with my evidence, the count waved his hand. "If both persons are noble, gradations of status are irrelevant. Religious institutions are unfit to legislate over the private organization of a family."

I still clenched the sumptuous bliaut. "You speak heresy."

"I do not mingle the carnal and the holy. I defend the purity of faith."

My husband's piety seemed none too stringent. "Your hussy persuades you to forswear our licit liaison, so that you can abide in heinous lechery? She must tamper with your wine, and infiltrate her menstrual blood into your goblet. Does she knead the dough of your bread with her derrière? I do not resort to such devilry. With me, you can fashion a spotless life."

Unconstrained, Geoffrey kicked at the corner of my trunk. "No knight can be sworn to two women. Irresistibly, my soul warms to her; she transports my spirit. The inauthentic chains that bind us must be unfastened."

"Very well. I do not choose to be held fixed by a contract that you do not respect, in your turn. You whore in bad faith, but expect me to cleave to you, and be content with the scraps of your affection. I shall choose another husband, more suited to my dignity and virtue."

†

EJECTED FROM ANGERS CASTLE, I am delivered to Normandy with a small retinue more appropriate to an ascetic pilgrimage. As our military escort is so woefully inadequate, Gerta and I pray that we meet no thieves on our way. Humiliated and fearful, I am consoled to be heading for the sanctuary of Jumièges. After my extraordinary largesse, I expect a hospitable reception from the abbess. I smile, in remembrance of my winsome baby. Of course, Gervase will be no longer the infant that I relinquished, but a toddler with no recollection of his mother.

The Angevin writes to King Henry, demanding an annulment on the grounds that there has been no heir. Like my father, Geoffrey is adept at diplomatic evasion. To His Majesty, I compose my own letter, unsparing of my husband's reputation, explicitly divulging his unjustified behavior, his flaunted ladylove and his beatings. But the response is clear; my father blames me for the failure of the match. The king needs a successor, and he worries that my separation delays its conception. It is His Majesty's opinion that if I had been more ladylike and accommodating, Geoffrey would have embraced me and ousted Denise.

†

LIFE AT THE CONVENT rolls on, with very little quietude, but many blank hours. Our retreat is bombarded with tenant peasants, come to tithe their portion of the harvest. Yesterday, I tripped over a sack of squash, which had not yet been stored in the cool cellars. It is but small compensation, yet I do relish the local cheese, and the abundance of fresh sage, delivered daily to the gatehouse.

I take pride in Gervase's antics and crooked smiles. I beam at his responsiveness to my fond kisses. As he drums his tiny fists upon my leg, I imagine him felling an enemy in hand-to-hand combat. He is the gift of my beloved; dandling him on my lap, I imagine what could be.

Gerta also dotes upon the little one, but she is usually absorbed with the absurdities of Helewise. What can she see in that erratic fool, who regularly refuses the sisterhood's plentiful and tasty nourishment, until she has starved herself into a euphoric trance? Blood streams from her nostrils, and she smears her cheeks with it, in a bewildering folly of madness.

While I resided in Angers, an elaborately dressed nobleman materialized at the convent, eager to see Gervase. In lieu of his name, he proffered a purse of gold. The abbess cannot identify him, beyond noting his ginger hair. For two hours, the anonymous visitor lingered in her cloister, bouncing the babe on his knee, distracting the sisters from their daily occupations. After their glimpse of him, the nuns least content with their worldly sacrifices have been most unmanageable. The "red-haired prince," they call him! Acknowledging that this mysterious man is the boy's sire, I urged her to foster and condone such intrusions.

I am eager to obliterate my interlude in Anjou, and the ludicrous notion that Geoffrey buttresses my political ambitions. I shall soon return to England, to safeguard my prospects. I ruminate much upon the future. If my marriage unravels so easily, why should not my father's authority disentangle the Count of Boulogne's?

My heart still stands Stephen's. Closing my eyes, I picture his perfections. No other knight stirs my innermost self. I am his; he must be mine. Gervase is the proof that heaven intends for us to commit ourselves to one another. As we have one son, so we shall have another, born in the purple.

Mother Mary shall guide me. I finally apprehend that She is not my vassal; rather, I am Her apprentice. Love for Her must be my uppermost passion. For Her sake, no man should trouble my peace.

Indeed, I am Her first acolyte, for who is higher among Her servants? When I am queen, I shall remain Her apostle, and herald Her great glory throughout the empire. In return, She shall protect my throne and my love. I submit myself to Her teachings and Her solace, and receive from Her my honors and my happiness.

The Treasury of the Lion

Scroll Five: 1131

*N**ever docile, the empress undertook to reverse the course of her wavering fortune. The fair lady did not acknowledge the resplendent power of heaven. Yet even the highest cannot thwart its designs. The princess who knelt before the holy altar would not be excused her presumption. Matilda's romance was nothing to the glorious force of the Lord. Ignorant before the onslaught of fate, she thought to find pleasure to equal her pain, but she was much mistaken.*

✝

Summer

I SPENT ALMOST TWO years, months empty of all adventure, sequestered at the convent of Jumièges. Retired from the world, my emotions cooled and congealed. I smothered my hot temper, my jealous spite, my unrequited passion, and my political obsession, masking my imperfect temperament with an apathetic expression adopted for the benefit of the good sisters. The wheedling abbess managed to extract all sorts of gifts from me; I underwrote the purchase of a chalice and a banner for the chapel, and even of curtains for her personal solar.

I grew intimate with my son, but the Count of Boulogne remained distant, unable or unwilling to visit us. From Arthur, Dameta received one conciliatory letter, full of praise for Gervase's russet curls and wide-eyed curiosity. My response, filled with news of the boy's small achievements, went unanswered.

Geoffrey sent word, as he set off on a pilgrimage to the holy city of Compostela and its cathedral, built in honor of St. James. I admit to a tinge of regret. Reconciled, we might have voyaged south together. The relic of St. James's hand had suffused me with piety and confidence just when I first set out alone to reestablish myself, after the death of the emperor. I would have been happy to accompany the Angevin, if only to pay my respects to the "Jewel of the Apostles." I wonder if Denise rode beside her lover to Northern Spain, or whether my husband's journey was one of introspection, meant to lead to the repudiation of his sins.

But it is no matter at present, for I have returned, one month ago, to the English court. I have done with stasis. I am all aboil, bubbling and seething with ire, envy, arousal, and ambition. Exchanging surreptitious, lingering looks with Stephen, I discover that he is more necessary to me than ever, and that I am no longer repugnant to him. It pleases me to woo him with my glances, but the seeming resumption of his infatuation confuses me. Does he smile at the mother of his child, or the strumpet he fancies?

Most of my subjects reproach me for my ruined alliance. None of the noble courtiers pity a woman rejected by her spouse. Their wives are especially insolent. I suspect that Maud's venom fuels the whispers against me. The countess, that bloodhound, immediately sniffed out my interest in her husband, and its reciprocation.

My brother Robert lectures me about this "little strife" in my marriage, as he calls it, and the necessity of my reinstatement into the good graces of a man so important to the secure future of our empire. Such discussions fatigue me, but I see that there is no avoiding the issue. Somehow my ambiguous tie to the Angevin must be clarified.

And now, amidst the stifling heat, the northern sky over Windsor Castle looms a lurid orange, as if a great bonfire lays waste to the land. Court astrologers argue and speculate, but the mystery of this ominous portent cannot be deciphered. It must foretell some "orange" calamity, perhaps conflagration or drought. Concurrently, a disease among the livestock escalates to dangerous proportions. None of the farmers have any oxen to pull their ploughs; our abundant fields lie unharvested. Corpses of pigs and chickens litter the countryside. The peasants foresee a winter starvation, deprived of their stores of meat, milk, and eggs. On the brink of some frenzy, the people fear that the end is near.

†

BY THE GRACE OF heaven, I still have allies here. Paying his respects to my father, King David of Scotland resides at Windsor. Bemused to see me, my uncle acknowledges that I cannot submit myself to a clod. Adeliza endeavors to reprimand me, but she is overjoyed to have the company of an equal during these long, hot days.

Today, in the fields, the queen and I reclined under a white tent. Gerta stood on the lookout for the approach of nosy idlers. Before us, King Henry's younger knights wrestled, to retain and improve their fighting skills. They wore only light padding, given the weather, and no mail. Whenever a bout ended, squires on the outskirts of the makeshift arena roared their approval. There were minutes of protracted calm, but only until the shouts of encouragement and disparagement resumed.

Adeliza had heard tell of Geoffrey's fine looks. She finds it difficult to credit that I did not fall prey to his attractions.

I shook my head. "Imagine pure, nascent manliness, but devoid of all warmth. The count's blond hair is shorn of all its grace; he considers long locks to be a sign of immodesty and feminine weakness." A forcible bellow from the field emphasized my remark.

Her Majesty has always admired masculinity. "Short locks better festoon the beauty of the male face."

I inhaled the hot air, trapped under our awning. "My knees go weak when I study the brush of Stephen's amber tresses against the curve of his shoulders."

Adeliza looked cooler than I felt. "If you still direct your thoughts inappropriately, it is no wonder that your marriage disintegrated."

"Oh, do be a friend to me, Your Majesty. So close to my beloved, I burst forth into bloom."

She smiled, but ruefully. "It ill behooves me to incite your recklessness, despite my sympathy."

In front of our pavilion, one knight straddled another, and began to strike him about the neck and shoulders. An older, more seasoned member of the royal garrison cried out some remonstrance, but the victorious wrestler did not cease to punch his weaker comrade. Finally, he stood, but gave one last kick of his boot to the other's temple, smirking to have distinguished himself as a warrior. He strode off, to the consternation of his peers, having violated the elaborate code of conduct for this sort of martial game.

My maid scurried to side of the defeated fellow, then knelt to smooth his brow as he moaned.

I swallowed against my thirst. "My husband's perversions undercut any chance we had at happiness."

Adeliza cocked her neck to the side. "Empress, it takes enormous, daily efforts to be a fond, but seemly wife." We both imagined her crushed under the weight of my father, the old goat. The queen flushed. "You did not strive hard enough to please your young, randy earl."

I noted that blood stained Gerta's sleeves, and stood out red against her pale crinkled linen. I shrugged my shoulders. "I will no longer prostrate myself before that Plantagenet ruffian! It excites him to hit me, and supplant me with a slut, both at his table and in his bed. Would that I were a witch, to cast a spell over his member, and make it disappear."

Gerta resumed her position by our side, in time to hear this vulgar outburst. She wagged her finger at my intransigence. "Ah, Empress, you must be the gaily painted shield, and his hard wood the lance that cannot shatter. Permit him to unseat you with the force of his thrust."

"I refuse to allow him to dominate me."

The queen squinted at me in the bright light. "Dearest! It cannot be so awful, to be overpowered by a virile husband. And, even so, your tie is not thereby expunged in the sight of God. The match was consummated. And it is not merely sexual congress that makes a union valid, but whether or not the marriage was undertaken in good faith, and with the consent of both parties."

Her disbelief nettled. "His intentions were never gallant or virtuous. He is the ideal knight, 'Geoffrey the Fair,' for everyone but me."

†

HERE AT WINDSOR, A newly fashioned maze much intrigues me. Just at vespers, when the cowardly lock their doors and windows against the coming of evil spirits, I slink away to the labyrinth. Making sense of the puzzle placates my frustrations. I enjoy the privacy of these dusk forays; I parade through the green lanes without the irritating presence of busybodies or snivelers.

At my insistence, Gerta murmured this secret to my cousin's page. Last night, Stephen waylaid me at the center of the garden.

Though the evening rapidly closed in, I could see his copper hair etched against the lavender sky. "Ah, Count. You have found an opportunity for us to speak discreetly." This was disingenuous; I rather hoped to entice some indiscretions from him.

Stephen inclined his head at my condescension. "Indeed, Empress, the maze grants us magical protection."

How I wished that it might be so! "Here we escape the confinements of the castle. The entanglements of the labyrinth permit more liberty of action."

Accepting my blatant invitation, my cousin embraced me, pressing my lips with his own. Almost at once, he pushed the veil off of my head, uncovering my braids. He began to tug at my girdle, attempting to unwind it from my waist. "Behold the slender sapling of your waist, the fulsome swell of your peaches above, the cooing of your voice, the starlight in your eyes."

What coarse, indiscriminate verse! The haste of his overtures disturbed me. I had returned his kisses, but now I stiffened. "I willingly offer myself to you, but you must swear to me that you will not cruelly neglect me afterward."

"I am deeply enamored of you, my sweetheart. Cannot you measure the extent of my delirium?" He handled me roughly, rubbing himself against me, so that I should verify the magnitude of his lust.

I ached to believe him, and allowed him to ravish me. At the touch of his fingers, the blood coursed through my veins. My tears welled up, for I was in the arms of my chosen knight, whatever the nature of his feelings for me. Love begins with such demonstrations, but how does it end?

†

Fall

THE COURT RELOCATES TO Northampton. On my account, the English king commands the presence of all his major vassals, convening a great council meeting to address the dissolution of my marriage and the threat that this poses to our empire. My father remains unsympathetic to my grievances against Geoffrey and my plea to be free of him. The need for a legitimate heir directs his policy in all things. Thinking little of my rights to his throne, he insists that I fulfill my responsibilities to the crown in childbirth.

I apprehend that someone, perhaps Maud, has divulged my adultery to His Majesty. Neither Adeliza nor Gerta would betray me, but my cousin and I trysted brazenly, out of doors. Surely, Maud's spies inform her of his duplicity. Or perhaps she has fed her husband a slice of bread, discreetly etched with my initials. If he had any difficulty swallowing it, she ascertains his guilt.

Tears of frustration watering her fleshy cheeks, she must have thrown herself at the king's feet. I imagine the countess wore her tightest, skimpiest corsage and her flimsiest, most diaphanous bliaut, with a scrap of a veil that did not fully conceal her golden tresses. My father, admiring her abundant favors, must have promised the despairing damsel to put an end to a relationship that threatens them both.

This morning, I awoke to find, among the twists of bedding, a lodestone, a magnet to test my chastity! My maid rested beside me, and her fury at such a sneaking attack is even greater than my own. Although Gerta judges me impure, it ill suits her to be bested in the womanly crafts. She plots to invade the countess's solar, and smuggle in some insult, in return. She waffles between various repugnant ingredients, which she might encase in an amulet: a piece of human feces, some timber from a gallows, the carcass of a black mouse. Let it not be said that an empress and her familiar are incapable of intrigue and soothsaying.

†

LAST SUNDAY, THE COURT attended Mass at an abbey just outside Northampton town. The sanctity of the church recalled my wedding to Geoffrey and the farce he has made of our religious vows. My mood grew heavy and resentful. The chants of the monks could not appease my ill humor. My father, stiff and authoritarian, stood beside me. I found it difficult to regret my own sins, stewing instead over the misdeeds of others.

A bishop intoned the words of the service: "I believe, therefore, I know."

I believe, but still I question the wisdom of heaven's arrangements, and strive to reshape them. I believe, but no longer only in what old men tell me. I believe, but trust most in the purity and goodness of my Holy Mother. Who else but Mary is fit to be my model and my interlocutor?

My cousin and his kin were positioned just next to us. Throughout the liturgy, I suffered the sight of the Lady of Boulogne, fussing with an impatient Eustace. Bile rose in my throat as I observed Stephen's outsized pride in his son. Maud preened in her extravagant costume, a gaudy yellow jacket, embroidered at the trim with green leaves. It shone as bright as the stained glass window above us, depicting a magnificent peacock, meant to be read as a radiant Christ.

The countess's garishness and simpering also distracted His Grace from his sermonizing. He launched out in a familiar diatribe against female whorishness. "She who is wont to decorate her lustrous curls with lace and ribbons, she who stains her comely face with pigments, she who rings her fingers with gems and hangs her neck likewise with sumptuous chains, will yet putrefy, nothing more than food for worms and vipers."

Maud blushed and settled down considerably.

I felt surer, then, that the Virgin witnessed my suffering, and struck this blow for me. I closed my eyes, focusing on this sense of Holy Communion with She whom I adore above all.

At last, the bishop dismissed the congregation. "May you, even the greatest of princes, go forth in fear of hell's fire and in hope of the cool waters of paradise."

†

NOT ONE TO PROCRASTINATE, Gerta coiled a dead, black snake, representing vicious sexuality, under Maud's bedcovers. This evening, sometimes betwixt compline and midnight, the countess's shrieks echoed throughout the keep. We chortled as quietly as we could.

I suppose it must be conceded that my triumph over that bitch is incomplete. Finding the lodestone, I had only my maid to succor me, while the countess has Stephen's endearments and reassurances. My beloved is sequestered in his wife's keeping. It is small comfort to know that he belongs properly to me, when he remains at her daily disposal.

†

TODAY, THE COUNCIL ASSEMBLED in the stark, forbidding great hall of Northampton Castle. I presented myself in a resplendent, bejeweled bliaut of dark red, the color of English royalty. The intensity of the carmine jolted the eye in the spare, somber, monochromatic chamber. I felt buoyed by its forceful color, empowered by its symbolic blazon.

Supposing that I would receive a daughter's welcome, I was aggrieved by my father's cold mien. His rebuff set the tone, encouraging the severity of his ministers and vassals. I was asked for my testimony, and told to plead my case. Losing courage, I became anxious lest the men assembled there should hear the thumping of my heart inside my ribs.

I reminded myself that I was properly Matilda Empress, for all that I was once and again a mere girl, unadorned with the protection of a husband or a crown. Mistletoe was tucked under my girdle, so shielding me from false condemnation in court. Swallowing my fear, I looked about me. "Marriage cannot be considered a sacrament when its stability is undermined. Although my match has been consummated, there has been no commingling of the soul between the parties concerned. There was unity by consent, but now there is separation by consent. What should be sacred and permanent, but cannot be, is most properly annulled." I felt some satisfaction as I projected my voice across the vast room.

Several church elders then spoke about the nature of the nuptial tie, including my cousin's malevolent brother, the bishop of Winchester. "Marriage is a bond of charity, a generous condescension on the part of the husband toward his wife. Just so, the link between Christ and his bride, the holy church, is not to be understood as love, but as a spiritual oversight on the part of the exalted, the saved, for the welfare of the lowly, the blind."

Such well-worn phrases, sermons threadbare from over usage! My retort was firm. "The count was indifferent to my well-being. His devotion to me was extremely sporadic." I assumed that such euphemisms were necessary to the solemnity of the occasion.

His Grace turned down the corners of his mouth, as if to suggest that my words were indecent. "An upright man looks to limit his conjugal carnality. The Lord unleashed the Flood in response to man's sinful excess."

I stood taller, lifting my chin. I would not be cowed. "The Angevin forsook me for the pleasures of a harlot. Should I have genuflected before him, in submission?"

King Henry grimaced. "A man acts as befits him; a woman is merely a woman, as is proper. You have had your chance to advocate, Matilda, and must cede the floor."

The bishop of Winchester could not resist tormenting me further. "A wife is not prohibited from taking the veil, if she finds herself too entwined in the paths of immorality to return to her spouse in goodness. Let me remind you of the hierarchy of feminine perfection, in which every woman aspires to the purity of a virgin, or a holy sister. Widows may wash their flesh clean of stain, but wives must tiptoe among the temptations of marital obligation, so as not to fall into defilement."

At least His Majesty did not permit him to sully my reputation. "There has been no misbehavior on the part of the Countess of Anjou. My daughter has been an exemplary wife. But although Geoffrey may have strayed from the paths of righteousness, their bond of matrimony cannot be effaced on this account. Fornication, whether here, there, or anywhere, is not the issue. Mary and Joseph were wed, and yet without knowledge of one another."

Then, to my shock, I was instructed to retire from the hall, so that the council could deliberate further. Despite my fury at the general tenor of the discussion, and my abrupt dismissal, I swept slowly out of the chamber in my gorgeous scarlet gown. Perhaps a white mantle, as Adeliza had suggested, should have completed the costume. Would the assorted barons and clerics measure me innocent and true?

I passed the next several hours in my solar, with Gerta and the queen at my side. Finally, FitzCount arrived to report on the outcome of the convocation. As he entered my chamber, his sobriety told the tale against me. "The king rules that the empress must return to Anjou."

I was more distraught than incredulous. "Did no one speak for me?"

Brian brightened. "Your brother of Gloucester suggested that perhaps you might find another partner, better suited to you, but the idea was quickly discarded."

"No one found such a notion reasonable?"

"I would not offend you, my lady, by repeating all of their affronts."

I waved my permission, and FitzCount continued. "Many persons are under a delusion with regard to you, and denounce you as a notorious harpy. They worry that the Angevin will not agree to reconcile with such a shrew."

Adeliza defended me. "How can they have found Matilda in the wrong, for fleeing from a house of iniquity?"

Brian blushed. "Empress, whatever your husband's errors, the English want to be rid of you. They find it difficult to accept your formidable character. They think of their queens more softly."

I clutched my ruby skirts. "A gentle queen would weaken their peace."

Brian knelt before me, hanging his head in obeisance. "It is my continual honor to protect the throne of the Lady of the English. All my strength, fervor, and prudence are yours to command." The knight's eyes mounted to mine. What I would give to see his expression in my cousin's face!

Turning on my heel, I began to pace. I noticed that FitzCount stayed on the ground. Some of my frustration subsided. "I am reassured by your adherence to your word of fidelity. How is it that the others disown so easily the princess that they have sworn to hold dear?"

"Your father decrees that his vassals are to undertake a second oath of allegiance to you. This ceremony of fealty will follow on the morrow."

"That is some recompense for this ignominy and my mortification. I trust that Geoffrey's name is not to be mentioned; he will not usurp my rights. The vows of service will be to me and to my heirs, alone. "

At my prompting, Brian arose. "His Majesty does not mean to elevate a man in your place."

†

I ACCEPT THE RENEWED promises of my people, in return for my banishment from their shores.

Unexpectedly, my husband concurs with the English. There is some disorder among the Angevin's barons, who disapprove of the ousting of a royal wife and the promotion of the daughter of a minor nobleman. He finds that the consolidation of his local power depends upon his having married well. Denise slakes his lust, but she cannot stoke his ambition. The trollop has born him bastard twins, a girl called Marie and a son, Hamelin, but Geoffrey's messengers guarantee that I will be received with all the dignities that are my due, including a spacious solar.

To signal his good faith, the count delivers a regal present, an enormous, handsome, honking swan. From around its snowy neck, I unfasten a sealed scroll, and the creature ruffles its feathers, content to be liberated from its burdensome collar.

Finally, the knave composes a poem for me. It begins: "Staunch despite Fortuna's wiles, noble still without her smiles, my queen inhabits majesty…" I give no weight to such newfound admiration, but his pledge, this magnificent bird, delights me.

Greedily, my father urges me to hand it over to the castle cook. Will the Angevin's courtly deference be as short-lived? The minstrels aver that there is no chivalry that does not spring from love, but my husband's heart has long been given over to another.

With the help of Mother Mary, ruminating on Her humility and strength, I steel myself to remember what recommends my husband to my notice. Certainly, his body is harmoniously formed, and he conducts himself with caution and good sense, even when he sins. He is indisputably literate and vastly intelligent; he spends his resources with prudence. He is steadfast and dependable in his opinions. He is an able horseman, a talented warrior, and a respected military commander. He appreciates the arts and values the companionship of women; he is a master of the hunt and excels at falconry. He has a reputation as a knight of distinction.

Why am I so loathe to resume my place by his side? The law has joined us, and our bond is found to be inflexible and irrevocable. I consider the example of the Holy Virgin. Where does Her mercy direct me? Can it steer me all the way from one the arms of one man to another? I find, in prayer, that She dries my tears. I cling to my love, but I attempt to separate it from my dynastic arrangements.

†

MY TRUNKS ARE PACKED and I willingly depart for the Continent. Much to my consternation, and still more to my joy, I am full once more with my cousin's seed.

I commanded Gerta to bring the Count of Boulogne to my chamber. I cannot exile myself without revealing what lies between us, even though it might mean alienating him once more.

As the bells chimed matins, Stephen stole into my room.

I longed to throw myself into his arms, but held back. "My darling, I am trembling to tell you something, for three years ago the like revelation cost me your attentions."

He twisted his nose out of joint, for a moment, but did not appear to be very much disheartened. "Do you intend to present me with a second son of the night?"

"I will hurry to the Angevin's bed, so that he will think the babe his own. I will be as false to my count as you are to your countess."

"Not so, Empress. My various amours are all worthy of me. I freely worship Maud, as I do you. My affection for my wife is genuine and steady. I find release in her rounded, delectable flesh, just as I find bliss in your strong, finely made form. I am nowise unable to keep from enjoying your favors; I am likewise incapable of neglecting Maud's." The blackguard approached me, for the depiction of his harem had excited him.

I would not sate desire stoked even in part by my rival. "You want everything; your passion alights everywhere. You will not make any sacrifices."

My cousin tossed his copper curls. "Why should I? Neither shall you. Bear our second infant as if it is Geoffrey's. Our secret rests inviolate. On occasion, we will enjoy mutual delights. Divided by happenstance, we will please others." He reached out for my hand.

I pulled it away. "I cherish you so strongly that I can neither mimic apathy nor overlook yours."

"You have no choice. If you are to retain your credit in the eyes of the world, we must part as ordained. Do not despair; our lips will meet once again." Perfectly content, the count exited my solar.

I was certain that he went to stuff Maud full of what I had refused, and a great rage swelled up in me. Setting my pen to paper, I scratched out my ire and dismay. Does destiny put forth into the field an army marching under my colors, or the pennants of mine enemies?

The Treasury of the Lion

Scroll Six: 1135

*R*emember, worthy ladies and noble gentlemen, that poetry is a heavenly science transmitted from heaven, a divine bequest. I hope that it pleases you to give me your full attention! It came to pass that the empress returned to the land of her husband, to serve him as she had undertaken to do before God. This period of her history brought peace, if not happiness, in the fulfillment of her duties. Still, hidden beneath the calm of her life, a deep tempest roared within her nature. Matilda was not scorched by the flames of perdition, but her soul smoldered, tainted by lust and pride.

†

Fall

IN ANGERS, I SPEND my days chasing after three-year-old Henry and one-year-old Geoffrey, abandoning the cultivated pastimes of my station for the peasant enjoyments of my boys. The Count, sufficiently satisfied with his brood, presides ever more assuredly over his vassals, but I think as much of my sons' obedience as of my political preeminence. Indeed, I enjoy the antics of my children more than I should. It was one thing to frolic with Gervase in the exile of a convent. To stoop to play with my infants amidst the life of a court is a great condescension on my part.

The birth of Geoffrey, my husband's son and namesake, almost carried me to my grave, despite the assistance of several experienced midwives. In their anxiety at the unusually slow progression of events, they bathed me in a soup of chickpeas, flaxseed, and barley. Still the fetus would not come. With closed faces, they rubbed my flanks roughly with oil of violets. They poured a mixture of vinegar and sugar down my throat, and then a dram of absinthe. They resorted to waving ground pepper under my nose, so that I sneezed, but without dislodging the recalcitrant babe. Only my prayers to the Virgin made any difference. Despite my exhaustion and anxiety, I directed several bishops in attendance to sprinkle me with holy water, in Her Name, to purge me of whatever evil spirit hindered the coming of this child. Finally, I pushed him out.

The equilibrium of my humors must have been disarranged by so much ineffectual intervention at my confinement. For several weeks thereafter, I burned with fever and convulsed with pain. Night and day, candles blazed within my chamber, and smoldering incense choked the air. Wretched, recumbent upon my pallet, I struggled to breathe and to speak.

Many of those inhabiting our court at Rouen presumed that I underwent my final agonies, and gossiped accordingly. I received many notes of condolence, and none so dear as the one from my beloved Arthur to his Dameta:

> *O blissful angel, do not lose courage as you crawl toward paradise, like the parched, aching deer stumbling toward the babbling stream. Cling to your fortitude and your faith, for your path leads to eternal blessedness.*

The Angevin's elation at the healthy birth of another boy softened his feelings toward me. I recall him, at the foot of my bed, cradling the swaddled creature, and thanking me for my pains. "This infant redeems your suffering. You have laid down your life to bring forth my blood."

His arrogance was enough to spur me on to health. My sudden restoration baffled most of our circle. The archbishop of Rouen proclaimed that I had been touched with the Lord's grace, and that my two living sons were His seraphs.

My father's joy in the elder, in Henry Plantagenet, his long-awaited male heir, knows no bounds. Of course, despite Henry's assumed Angevin ancestry, and his place as my husband's first-born, this precious child is the Count of Boulogne's.

Numerous miracles accompanied his arrival in Le Mans, and my corporal tribulations were few. My first cramps elicited a vivid dream of annunciation: a shining Holy Mary heralding the hero's appearance among us, and heaven's bequest to him of a great throne. A talented crone mixed potent unguents; the baby slid out into her hands. Cutting Henry's cord, she massaged him with salt and crushed petals. He roared with vitality, and every one present broke out into smiles. Even my husband's face was clear of malice. As word of the successful conclusion to my troubles spread, a flaming star coursed through the sky over the town. Several monks, praying near the altar of the cathedral, witnessed a bright burst of light and heard strains of a celestial music.

Alleluia! I am overjoyed to have secured the succession. But, behind my public satisfaction, I have immured my private jubilation. A son of my perverse love, somehow declared legitimate, is positioned to rule after me. Norman, English, and Angevin barons have sworn to protect and keep the Plantagenet, the future king of the collective empire.

†

I LEARN TO TOLERATE the continued presence of my husband's mistress and her two children, the four-year-old twins Hamelin and Marie, who remain among our ménage. The Angevin, distant but respectful toward me, does not reinstate his leman to her previous status in our household.

Gerta snickers into her hands, and admits that she has lodged a broken candle between Denise's mattress and its frame. Three white, stiff stalks of the count's hair are concealed within its wax; his name is stroked onto the side of the taper with the blood of a cocksparrow. My maid was at some pains to sneak her charm into the slut's solar, without being seen, but there is no one more cunning and adept than Gerta.

Lately, Geoffrey's whore endeavors to reestablish his passion. To her credit, he still warms to her various seductions. Whenever my lord retires "to be bled privately," he most certainly sports with his paramour. Yet I am grateful to be released from the penance of his amours. My husband's nocturnal visits are rare; we fornicate infrequently. On these occasions, he abstains from abusing me, but I willingly dispense with such dutiful coupling. My dreams are all of my cousin's touch.

†

DENISE PERSISTS IN DETESTING me, although I see the futility of our antagonism. Gerta is sure that the wench suspects Henry's paternity and worries that she will poison Geoffrey's mind against his supposed heir.

This morning, in the town that presses close against Anger Castle's outer wall, a traveling puppeteer perched on the back of his wagon, entertaining a crowd of children, courtier and burgher alike. Standing back from the crush, my maid heard the harlot humoring some town matrons with a yarn of her own.

> *A young noblewoman, oppressed with sadness, trekked south through the cold, jagged mountains that separated a northern country of sorrow and discord from its neighbor, a region of joy and peace. On her way to this Elysium, climbing high and hiking low, she was overcome with a great thirst. She broke off icicles from the boughs of enormous, gnarled trees, and allowed them to melt in her mouth. In this way, she drank her fill, only to find her belly swollen to a great degree. The weight compressing her soul was not lifted when she was brought to bed of a snow child, although she had been made welcome in the new land of felicity and harmony.*

Gerta scanned the faces of the local women; they had registered the message. A child of nature is foisted upon some unsuspecting lineage. An infant generated in a northern territory bodes ill for a southern kingdom.

Unsure of what Denise knows, I keep my countenance. Graciously, I allow my husband to retain his concubine. For now, she refrains from overthrowing my hopes. For my own part, I do not tell tales, although everyone has surely heard about the woman whose twins were the result of her concurrent affairs with two different men.

†

DESPITE MY DIFFICULTIES WITH the leman, I feel some affinity for her daughter, Marie. Defying her youth, the girl spouts verse. Sometimes she comes to my solar, to wait upon me, and I encourage her to recite. Her rhymes usually concern events that transpire at a fantastical court of knights and ladies. Today, as she brushed out my hair, she warbled out: "In what castle does your heart live? Its walls and hearth are hid, and your eyes, masked by their lids, forbid."

Unlike the other little ones, who cower at Gerta's ghost tales, the child refuses to believe that demons swoop down in the night to dine upon the flesh of naughty toddlers. In her high-pitched voice, she reassures my maid that she is safe from harm, for it is grown-up ladies who are at risk of nocturnal beatings and feastings.

Some in our retinue whisper against Marie and her precocity, considering her a changeling, an imp substituted by the devil, come to work evil among us. But Geoffrey adores his darling poetess. He will not banish her to a convent, merely to appease his underlings and hangers-on. My esteem for her talents and defense of her purity win me his gratitude. I will be on my guard, however, lest her clear-sightedness becomes inconvenient.

†

ALL THIS AUTUMN, GERTA has constantly nagged me to visit Avera, a witch who lives outside Angers, on the banks of the river Maine. County talk exaggerates her powers and embellishes her potions. Court innuendo has it that Denise patronizes Avera for salves, to secure her youthful charm, and brewing herbs, to enslave the count's desire. My maid proposed that we journey to the sorceress's magical lair, in order to benefit from her sagacity. I acquiesced, mostly out of curiosity and ennui. Geoffrey allocated us the protection of three men-at-arms, for what he assumed was a pilgrimage to a local "holy woman." His mistress did not dare to enlighten him as to Avera's true character.

Yesterday, on one of the milder days before the onset of winter, we traveled down the Maine. The enchantress is no haggard, loathsome crone, but a young peasant woman. Her dirty person is well-formed, underneath her torn clothes, remnants of once luxurious garments. Her face is grotesque or voluptuous, depending on the angle from which it is observed. I discounted the smeared face paint and the tangled mats of her yellow hair and judged her beautiful.

Avera's one-room cottage of wattle and daub is thatched with reeds. Fumes from her hearth thicken the air above the mud floor. A wooden shutter bars the one small window, so that the only light comes from the smoldering twigs that emit so much smoke. Discomfited by the hovel, Gerta and I waited for the witch to greet us.

With one long finger and jagged nail, she indicated a grimy, lumpen bench.

Settling down, I was glad of my crudely fashioned traveling mantle, worn to conceal my identity. Yet I felt only distaste, not trepidation. "Woman, I have come to you for I know not what."

Avera looked at me through wide eyes, circled with black powder. "Empress, you have many questions."

Gerta coughed in annoyance at her indelicacy. Would all of Anjou come to know of the visit?

The sorceress twisted her lip, and dropped the shadow of a curtsy. "I am honored to serve you. Your companion may be assured of my reticence."

This raised my waiting woman's hackles. "You would do well to be mute about her business. You are fortunate that the Church does not forbid you to practice your dark arts."

Avera smiled at me, revealing large, brown teeth. "Your bulging purse encourages me to respect your disguise."

Quite unexpectedly, the girl threw back her head and arched her back. "The sight of your brother floods over me. The prince, battered by brutal waves, tosses aside a golden mantle, and sinks naked below the swells. He is ensnared in the weeds of the sea, rotting, consumed by the fishes." Under the black and green striped fabric of her jacket, her huge bosom thrust forward.

Gerta laughed aloud. "There is no magic in that, serf. You speak of what is commonly known."

I was not as quick to dismiss her eloquence. "The White Ship smashed itself upon the rocks. Will my future be likewise run aground?"

Avera's lids drooped and she began to sway. The fire sizzled and emitted dirty steam. "I behold three kings, all tied to you in lust. The heat of one begot you, your own yearnings brought forth another, and the third lives for you in his sex."

I reddened. "I am concerned with my own accession to the throne."

The witch's voice sank. "Many men will die so that you might be the Lady of the English."

My heart unfolded, but the crown was not all that I needed. "There is a soul for whom my spirit longs."

"In his service, you have made a human sacrifice, offering up the flesh of an infant to conceal your own sin."

Now Gerta burst out. "Evil strumpet, you will burn at the stake! How dare you heedlessly accuse the empress of crime?"

I put my hand on my maid's arm to forestall her ire. "I do not choose to admonish her allusion, or disregard her hallucinations."

Avera stood up straight, opening her eyes. "I do not convict you, my lady."

†

LATELY, MY FATHER'S RELATIONSHIP with my husband grows cold, even discordant. Likewise, Geoffrey blusters against the English king. They dispute control over the Duchy of Normandy, which the count thought he had been promised when he wed me. His Majesty reneges on any such agreement, preferring to protect the interests of his Norman barons against the Angevin. The Normans remember the historic ties between Anjou and the French; they look fearfully to my husband's border county of Maine. In addition to my husband's voraciousness, the king suffers the fractious complaints of his Norman vassals, dissatisfied with my marriage and Angevin expectations.

Geoffrey contends that our marriage decides the Angevin-Norman rivalry in his favor. The future Henry II of England is a Plantagenet. Yet my father dissents, refusing to trust any Norman castles to the Count of Anjou's keeping, not even those that were pledged as part of my dowry. His Majesty distrusts Geoffrey's continental ambition, and looks to preserve the empire entire for his grandson.

Denise, distraught that anyone should trouble the peace of her knight, burns frankincense and saffron in the hearth of the great hall, invoking the angels to reestablish the concord between the English king and his matchless vassal.

†

UNDER THE PRESSURE OF this political friction, Geoffrey and I rediscover some of our enmity.

Today he spotted me in the castle pantries, where I stood overseeing a clerk's accounting of the strings of dried mushrooms, jars of honey, and other stores. The count dismissed his servant, waving me down among the barrels and sacks.

I knew better than to anger him with a refusal. Fortunately, I wore one of my least favorite bliauts. I sat against a crate of onions. My eyes watered at their strong scent. "Noble lords do not usually linger in the bowels of their fortresses where the provisions are safeguarded, but in their towers where the arms are kept."

Geoffrey lowered himself beside me. "Wife, I am glad to see you spend your days so productively, looking after the needs of our community. I am sure that you will do as I require to ensure its continued prosperity."

Did the Angevin aim to copulate amidst his stocks? His carnal pleasures are always odd. From my forehead, I untied the leather band that fastened my long veil.

"I would prefer that you remain modestly dressed in my presence, while I tell you how you may abet my plans. It is no secret that your father's death would be a boon, remitting to us the Duchy of Normandy."

In my shock, I dropped my coif. "You speak treason against the great king to whom you have sworn fealty. Normandy will be your son's."

"Certainly it will, but the sooner it comes under my power, the better I can protect it for the boy." The count ran his thumb along the rind of a cheese, pushing against its crust, attempting to bruise it. It was a perfect specimen, yellow not white, firm not runny, weighty and scaled.

Why would he spoil it? "His Majesty engages to preserve the realm intact. At his death, it is I, and not you, who will safeguard it for Henry Plantagenet. The magnates' oaths of allegiance were to me, and to my line."

My husband held up the cheese, sniffed, and winced at its pungency. "I can better shield our child's birthright. You are no warrior earl."

I picked up my veil from the floor and began to beat off the dust that clung to it. "Heave your sword aloft, but for me, not against me. We share a stake in our son's future. He bears my father's name, and your own."

My lord scanned my somewhat disheveled appearance. "Why should you be enslaved by His Majesty's designs upon you? You have married out of his house."

"I serve my prince, not my king." Nor my husband.

The Angevin spoke harshly. "Accommodate my wishes, before any other man's!"

My stomach fluttered, as he rose and strode out of the kitchen. Does Geoffrey plot to conquer Normandy for himself or does he intrigue to defy the aggrandizement of Stephen's boy?

†

RUMORS FLY THROUGH ANGERS, blaming "the virago" for the dissonance between the Count of Anjou and the English crown. Supposedly, it is my craft that stirs up their antagonism. Now that the two men are enemies, it is believed that my allegiance is to my spouse. Who is the source of this foolishness? Why are my husband's faults held to my account?

Gerta and I spend our idle hours debating these political developments and the meaning of our adventure with Avera. We puzzle at length over the mystery of the three kings.

Anything covert is beneath the honor of an empress; I embroider clusters of three intertwined crowns on several of my corsages and on the borders of some of my mantles. Flattering my husband's burghers, I purchase quantities of gold thread from various stalls in Angers town. This delicate work is well underway, despite our imperfect translation of the witch's vision.

This afternoon, as my maid made her neat, glinting stitches, she picked apart the sorceress's conundrum. "The three kings are the three Henrys: your father Henry, your son Henry, and your first husband, Henry of Germany. Your father's ardor sired you. Your misplaced passion gave birth to your son. You were the emperor's bedfellow."

I threaded a glimmering strand. "What if that rogue of an Angevin wrests Normandy from me, then schemes to be elevated to the throne of England, in my place? Geoffrey could be the third king."

Gerta worked her needle much faster than I plied mine. "Preposterous! His family is descended from a she-devil!"

I dropped my sewing onto the rushes. "There is only one man who 'lives for me in his sex,' and he is no king." I fished about on the ground, so that she could not see me flush at the mere mention of Stephen's embraces.

Fingers flying, Gerta peered hard at me. "Do not reduce your life to a riddle of depravity."

†

AS THE WEATHER SHARPENS, my eldest and I often play together before the roaring fire in the great hall. Today, the boy recited a ditty, overheard in the town. "Pope, emp'ror, king, cardinal! Prince with jeweled, royal ball! Duke, archbishop in his pall! All these sit high, 'bove us all."

I laughed. "Where am I in this wonderful song?"

Henry's eyes grew round. He put his hand in mine.

I enjoyed the tingle of his tiny fingers. "I am empress, wife of an emperor, and someday will be queen, which is a woman king. Before my first marriage, I was princess." Tightly, I hugged him to me, before he wriggled free.

With pursed lips, the Plantagenet murmured. "I am prince. One day I will be the king of many lands. Princes are sons of kings."

My mirth evaporated. "Or queens."

My son shrugged. "Is Father a king, Mother?"

I sighed. "No, you will be a king of my territories, not of your father's."

"Which title is his?"

I looked at his face, so suggestive of my beloved's. "None of them. Your father is count, standing beneath all the persons in the song."

Henry ambled away. "I do not think that he would like to hear me sing it."

†

DAMETA FOUND HERSELF IMPATIENT, and unable to withstand temptation. Hadn't Arthur written, when he thought Dameta lost to him for all eternity?

> *I preserve entire the whole of my precious love. I blush to recollect you, but instead of losing strength, I grow sure that our connection is sanctioned by heaven. Joyousness will be ours once more, perhaps forever.*

Arthur returned a letter, a model of circumspection, despite its affectionate tone. My cousin reports that he has cut off his superfluous amber curls, the red ringlets of my nightly reveries. I almost wept to suppose them swept into the countess's hearth, but gasped in glee when I discovered a small, wound circlet of hair enclosed within the scrolled note. I placed the lock in my blue casket, among my other riches. Each evening, at my retirement, I kiss the silky tress, and pray to the Virgin that I will soon be enmeshed in Stephen's arms.

Gerta strongly discourages me from presenting a similar token to my beloved. "Empress, such a wild deed will do your obsession no good."

"I wish him to compare my coal black mane to that yellow mop of Maud's. Are all my actions to be dictated to me by my servants?"

"Think of your son's future. Bend your own will, to serve the boy who is son to the man."

Once more I follow Gerta's advice, despite my aches and longings. I offer him nothing but my intangible devotion. Have I gifted my heart to a worthy knight, likely to treasure it?

The Matter of the Crown

Scroll Seven: 1136

*T*he high merit of my subject, and my comprehensive account of it, must certainly be worthy of your patience, and your continued consideration. For in this momentous year, what was once fixed ceased to be. Heaven struck down one king and raised up another in his place. The empress was betrayed by her false idol; he stole from her that which she would have gladly bestowed upon him. His triumph over her was a blow of the worst sort, for it smote down her love as well as her ambition.

†

Winter

LATE IN THE AUTUMN, the bells tolled until my head rang with their peals, announcing the death of King Henry I. Although my father had treated me harshly, I was shocked, then despondent at the news. With corroded spirits, I observed the frisson that convulsed the politicians and philosophers among my retinue, as England's throne fell vacant for the first time in thirty-five years.

His Majesty had hunted all day in the Wood of the Lions, near Rouen castle, and returned home to feast heartily upon his favorite dish, eels baked in cloves and fennel. Alas, the lampreys had been too long from the sea and were spoiled with age. Their succulent sauce masked any taste of their taint. My father was ever paranoid about the threat of assassination, and always equipped with his own utensils, previously blessed by his chaplain. He never neglected to sprinkle dried rose petals on his food, so as to ward off demonic influence. But this time, all his usual precautions were for naught, and he expired of a raging fever.

His prolonged torments gave him ample time to make his confession to the archbishop of Rouen. He recited his sins and gave instructions for his burial, coming at last to a Christian end. At his deathbed were my brother and several prominent barons.

In front of these assembled magnates, the recumbent, anguished sovereign again declared me to be his legitimate heir. In his final moments, he delegated Robert to ensure that I inherited the realm; Gloucester vowed to do so. His Majesty ascribed to me all his dominions, on both sides of the Channel, without mentioning the Count of Anjou. If he had ever previously intended that Geoffrey and I rule jointly, he did so no longer.

And yet, and yet! Almost immediately after the king succumbed, the Count and Countess of Boulogne crossed the Channel to Dover, a quick wind in their favor. At Christmas, before my father had been dead a month, my cousin was crowned his successor in Westminster Abbey. The archbishop of Canterbury anointed the entire family, all three of them, husband, wife, and son. It is generally hypothesized that Stephen acted on the advice of both Maud and his brother, Henry bishop of Winchester, the wealthiest prelate in England. Whatever or whoever inspired him, the speed of the pretender's assumption of power was decisive. The count snatched his chance, and sat upon his usurped throne, before anyone knew what treason he intended against his generous benefactor.

Apprehending my beloved's betrayal, cut to the heart, I have been wild with fury, then mute with hatred. I refuse to leave my solar, unable to shake either my shame or my loathing. Gerta avoids my indiscriminate ire, leaving me to mourn and rage in solitude. My jaw aches from the gnashing of my teeth; my heels throb from the stomping of my feet; my scalp tingles from the pulling of my hair. I shriek erratically, or whirl in a circle, before collapsing on the floor, dizzy and sick, unmoored. The days pass, but I do not emerge from under the stolid, dense cloud of my anger, which expands until it darkens every waking hour.

†

DID HE EVER LOVE me? What he was to me—what he is to me—was I ever so necessary to him? He has been lodged in my mind, a great mass, but I must float through his thoughts, without weight or measure. And still he put his bare leg across my marriage bed, and planted his seed into the heart of my dynasty. Was this all he wanted? Was his name always his destiny—*Stephanus*, crown? Did he play at chivalry, masking his avarice under his armor?

Demon, your face was the face of an angel! And I gave myself to you, body and spirit. But your soul lies in a locked tower, and I was pushed from the rungs of the golden ladder I set alongside it.

†

MY SWORN SUBJECTS, ALL repeatedly pledged to my cause, ceded the empire of England and Normandy to a blackguard, an imposter. Was it because they want no woman above them, or no Angevin? Where am I now, who stood poised between her first empire and her second? Dispossessed, who am I now? Holy Roman empress, I let my imperial garments slip from my shoulder, but stood naked and erect, ready to be draped in the mantles of England and Normandy. Bowing to circumstance, I graciously delivered the regalia of Germany and Italy to rapacious old men, eager to strip me of my power. Now, my future glory, my crown, and my puissance are thieved by an eager young man. Did none of them, old or young, see the purity of my white flesh, shivering without its royal cloak, waiting patiently to redeem it? Did none of them feel that I have been chosen by the Holy Virgin to lead?

†

GERTA SCAVENGES THE BLACK root of a green hellebore, and presents me with a narcotic capable of calming the deranged. Ravished, I lie on my side, and she drips it into my ear, until I feel the iron band around my lungs release its cinch. Dark flecks compromise my vision, but my mind rests. The specks please me, for if they mar its mirror, they expose the imperfections of the world. The spots themselves are faultless points, indivisible, a beginning and an end in themselves.

Under the influence of the hellebore, I spend hours chanting a rhythmic incantation, clapping the beat, oblivious to the listening ears at my door. "Mountain peaks do not tremble; towering, immobile, holy dominion. Mountain peaks do not tremble; towering, immobile, holy dominion." How long will it take me to believe that I am strong enough to withstand his duplicity?

†

I HAVE DISPENSED WITH Gerta's attentions, calculated as they are to gag my complaints and deaden my outrage and anguish. I would feel more, not less, of the cruel treatment that he metes out to me, and my own abhorrence. I am foul, malodorous, rotten, guilty of sins of the flesh, and I must make amends by some sacrament.

I hold my hand within the bright flame of a taper until a searing, streaming pain echoes and gives voice to my woe. And still I hold my palm over the fire, enthralled by the immediacy and simplicity of my suffering. I am luminous in my distress, incandescent in my agony. I am lustrous, noble, divine. He cannot touch me, for my affliction is no longer his crime. He cannot mark me, for I mark myself with stigmata, recording his infamy. I glow with misery, and yet I am washed clean, and shine. I burn like the sun and the moon and the stars in the firmament, shimmering in the heavens, praiseworthy.

Wretched, but farsighted, desolate but full of clarity of purpose and pure penetration, I reach an ecstasy of understanding, and pull my arm back from its torment. Despite the black scars on my skin, and the feverish blisters, I am incorruptible, and suffused with a flowing, harmonious sweetness. I am transfigured, inside and out, gloriously transported by the mystery of mortification.

I am honed, as the blade of a mighty sword is whetted and polished in the fire. I am unsoiled, resplendent, radiant with faith, and ready to cleave through the ambition of my transgressor.

†

I EMERGE FROM MY solar, only to be frustrated by the inactivity and passivity of those who might have been expected to fight for my rights. I exchange vehement words with Geoffrey, and the castle seethes with the tension between us. Still my warrior earl remains at his leisure, neglecting to organize his cache of weapons or strategize over his maps.

Today I was particularly incensed to find my husband in his chamber with his lector, discussing some fine point of the trivium. "You are dismissed, Master. Now is not the time for the count to ponder questions of grammar."

The wiry man had a neutral expression, as dry as his curriculum. He nodded and began to collect his slate and parchments.

"Stay." Geoffrey looked me over. "My lady rudely interrupts our disputation. I would talk further with you. The empress herself might profit from a lesson in rhetoric. Her words lack any elegance and hence any persuasiveness."

The Angevin's disapproving glance and insults gave me pause. Perhaps my influence would be more sizable if I employed the female arts. "You are right, my lord. I did speak too harshly, too hastily. But I would parley with you privately about a matter that concerns me deeply. I hope that your tutor will forgive me if I ask him to retire."

The count lifted his eyebrows, perplexed at my submissive tone. "You change your tune mightily, but its new melody does ring more sweetly." With a slash of his hand, he signaled the lector to quit us. "What is it, Matilda?"

I inhaled, essaying to compose my features into a mask of gentility. "I am confounded by your delay in the defense of my kingdom."

Sighing, Geoffrey picked up his blackboard and chalk. He scribbled a list, then held out the slate. "The components of rhetoric. The first part: *historia*. Your speech lacks historia, literal sense. Take in the view; it is the winter. No wise commander begins a campaign in the cold months."

The window in his solar gave out onto the Sarthe River, winding its way northward toward the Angevin city of Le Mans, then on into Normandy. I saw nothing of the weather, only the currents flowing in the direction that I wanted to go. Why was I still? I would surge through the landscape, as the water did. "The pretender perpetrated his black deeds in this season. Last year, in the short, dark days, you warred with my father, and schemed to revolt. Indeed, it was your late rebellion against King Henry that lost me my throne. Your hunger for a few Norman castles has cost us an empire. Now you must rekindle the flame of your military ambition, but in my service."

My husband underlined the next item: *allegory*. "Do not attempt to indoctrinate me in your political cause; I am inured to your metaphors. It is Stephen who deserves your shrewishness. He grabbed for himself what was left to you."

I fought the urge to smash the chalkboard. "You alienated the Norman barons, so that they preferred my cousin to be their overlord. Your designs upon the dukedom have been as dangerous to me as the usurper's greed. Which one of you has been more my enemy?"

The Angevin brandished the next trope. "Your argument is especially weak in its *sententia*, or moral implications."

"I will be more clear. You poisoned the eels—you murdered my father."

Geoffrey dashed his tablet onto the floor. I suspected that he would have liked to smack me with the same force. "Watch what you accuse me of, bitch! I am justified in my wrath against His Majesty; he did not turn over to me the promised dowry castles. But I had no hand in his passing, which was the working of divine authority. Heaven corrupted the food brought to the old man's table."

What could I say to stave off his violence? "The king's dismay at your rebelliousness conquered his natural strength, promoting the potency of the polluted eels. My own husband vanquished the lion of wisdom and justice."

The count resumed his discourse. "We should move on from rhetoric to dialectic, since you are especially deaf to my opposing point of view."

I rubbed my temples. "On your behalf, I shall pray to Our Lady to forgive you your shame."

Geoffrey shook his white head. "Logic, my dear, logic! You jumble the victims and the villain. You conveniently forget that Henry I was a rapacious wanton, a cruel tyrant, who arranged his coronation before the properly designated heir, his brother Robert Curthose, could return from the Crusade. Plundering your kingdom, Stephen of Boulogne merely follows his example. Possession is the law."

With slow, steady pressure, the Angevin pushed me to the ground. The rushes smelled stale. I tried to sit up, but he pinned his knee against my stomach. "You are quick to blame me, instead of your cousin. How can you overvalue that devious fool?"

Although prone, I did not quail before him. "Let us march together on England! Let us retaliate against Stephen's affront! Let us force from him a renewal of the homage that he swore to me."

Geoffrey straddled my waist, one shin to my left side and the other to my right. "I will not permit you to navigate the Channel in winter, or to journey anywhere, while you harbor my seed."

From under the weight of him, I interjected. "What is this baby to you?"

The count lowered himself upon me. "I will take you ferociously. Rough intercourse expels any ill humors from the womb."

I managed shallow breaths. "You violate me, to safeguard the infant? Now, it is your logic that eludes me."

Geoffrey shoved up my bliaut. For good measure, he placed his palm on my throat. "Such a shame, Wife, that you do not set my senses to throb."

I put my hands at my neck, to pull off his fingers. "Then it will not be possible for you to come to bliss." I could not get enough air.

"I will undertake to make the best of your slight attractions." The Angevin pinched my breast.

I yelped. "Do not handle me as you would your whore!"

I should not have said that.

†

I AM EXILED IN Anjou, while Stephen rules in my stead. My belly stretches with child, despite my husband's ministrations and the shivering cold of his keep. Again, I foretell a son; this fifth pregnancy unravels much like the others. My letters link me to the world, although they are of very little solace.

I hear from the royal widow that the preponderance of my father's corpse, embalmed with salt and wrapped in a bull's hide, lately arrived in England. His Majesty's bowels, brains, and eyes had already been removed in the cathedral church at Rouen, to be inhumed there. What remained of him was buried, as he had wished, in the Royal Abbey at Reading, where Adeliza endows a fund to keep a lamp burning in perpetuity before the tomb. The dowager queen had grieved much at the long delay between her husband's death and the receipt of his body from the Continent. A month of bad weather meant that it was long after the pretender's Christmas coronation before Henry I was shipped across the Channel.

The sea tempests that kept the king from his grave are also to blame for my political tragedy. Those loyal men who witnessed my father's death swore to one another not to abandon his exalted corpse before its interment. This oath held them fast in Normandy, while the usurper acted against us in Britain. The very barons who could have proved my appointment as heir were far away from the scene of my cousin's treachery.

In comparison, Stephen's swift appearance in London served his purpose. The Count of Boulogne vowed to uphold peace and promote trade; the freemen guaranteed him money and weapons. Received enthusiastically, my cousin promised preferment to the leading citizens, who then "elected" him king. The London burghers dared to vote him onto a throne rightfully dispensed only by God and his divine representatives. This unlawful compact between commoners and traitor was no great council of state, but a travesty of the proper workings of the succession.

After the pretender parried with the Londoners and assured them that they were the most vital part of the realm, he went on to Winchester Castle to claim the royal regalia and treasury, overflowing with the proceeds of the late king's efficient rule. Winchester, capitol city of our ancient Anglo-Saxon sovereigns, has stood a safe repository of English gold and crown. But it could not withstand its corrupt bishop, plotting to enrich his brother and stake his false claim. The snake bribed the collusion of his parish, the desertion of my father's constable and treasurers, and even, somehow, the perjury of the archbishop of Canterbury. Each and every one of these knaves had sworn his allegiance to me, and kissed me in fealty, whilst my father lived.

Winchester claims that all previous oaths made to me, by anyone whomsoever, were given under duress, and were therefore not binding. But His Grace of Canterbury must have given most attention to the bishop of Winchester's insistence that his brother's treatment of the church would be exemplary, protecting and expanding its liberties at the expense of royal authority. Quickly thereafter, in Westminster Abbey, the archbishop anointed my cousin, precipitously spreading the church's divine sanction over his heretical intrigue. The ceremony was a paltry affair, escorted by few of note, but the sacred rituals elevated the usurper, validated the citizens' false election, and cemented the hasty decisions of some disloyal barons to violate their consciences and their promises. Any subsequent evaluation of the legitimacy of events unfolds during King Stephen I's reign.

Can I have expected Winchester to stall the promotion of his kin, in my name, for my benefit? The House of Blois and the House of Anjou are rivals on the continent; married to Geoffrey, how could I hope to enlist His Grace's support? Whatever affection or esteem he felt for His late Majesty, the primary bond of family obligation undermines his service to the legitimate crown. Winchester's cunning and energy most likely allay fears that Stephen will prove to lack the mettle required to rule well. I remember how Stephen's beauty and easy amiability were disparaged by the other earls; his brother Henry's sober mask reassures them.

Five sons were born to Adele of Blois, a mother who cherished only courage and achievement. The first weakling she dispensed with, the second was given his father's county to rule, and the third, my errant beloved, was sent to the English court to rake up whatever preferment should drift down upon him. He purloins what did not fall in his way. Her last two sons, Adele raised up in the church. Henry, admitted as a child to the abbey of Cluny, advances into the center of the world's affairs, despite being brought up sequestered from court life. How long he must have schemed to achieve importance among us.

With regret, Adeliza alerts me that Henry of Blois removes St. James's hand from the abbey of Reading, installing it in his private treasury. This speck of news overwhelms me. Faced with Winchester's vice, my courage falters, until I remember that the righteous will triumph over the sinner, for the wisdom of the lord is true, worth more than the purest gold, sweeter than the amber juice dripping from the honeycomb.

†

Spring

I FEEL MY BABY quickening in my belly, and I fear that my wrath and sorrow may deform the child into a monster of evil inclinations. I resort to the chapel in Angers castle, to pray for its safety. Will I be able to ward off the demons that tempt the inconsolable? I need to find some peace, for my infant's sake, and for my own.

Our little place of worship is built into the wall of the inner courtyard. It is far from kitchen noise and odor, but near the gate and fortified bridge that lead to the constable's tower and the outer ward. The guards' chatter and the workings of the winch often pervade the room, interfering with my concentration. Sometimes I encounter priests or clerks, their eyes shut tight, their faces clenched in need.

My husband's religious artifacts, his precious chalices and Psalters, are stored elsewhere, under lock and key. The chapel's only decorations are a large wooden rood upon the wall and a rich altar cloth. I myself embroidered the white silk cover, glimmering with gold crosses and red-footed silver doves, representing the martyrs whose blood was spilled for Christ's sake.

Today, I had the sparse chamber to myself. In solitude, I attempted to focus my energy upon the ornate shroud, upon holy suffering. I recollected that the elegant stitches had cost me many hours of toil; I could not lift my thoughts from the material world. I appreciated only the beauty that perishes. My understanding was unequal to the spiritual perfections that subvert decay.

It came to me to lie face down, so that I might reach for a faith in what is outwardly hidden. I stretched out my arms to my sides, forming the shape of a cross. I shuddered on the frigid ground, and my nose ached, pressed against the rough floor. I could not help but notice mouse droppings and spittle that had not been properly swept away. Again, I was trapped by the material, unable to search for what was immaterial. I prayed then that my conceit might be lessened, so that I could find sanctuary in a higher plane.

Recollecting myself, I appealed to the Most Blessed Virgin. I called on Her, the gardener of the seeds of knowledge, the tender of the flowering of wisdom. I asked Her to bedew me, to bathe me with light. Mary consented to answer my pleas, for I am Her first, and most loving pupil. She welcomed me, She opened my ears, and I could hear the harmonies of truth. I felt my distress subsiding; a great ecstasy enveloped me.

I venerate the Father and the Son, but I am dependent upon the radiant Mother. She shall lessen my torments on earth and vouchsafe the salvation of my soul in paradise.

†

I REMEMBER THAT I am under the Virgin's special protection. Our Lady's pity and strength flow into my heart, conferring fortitude, reinvigorating me.

In secret, I write to my once adored friend, now my despised foe. I use an ink made from ammonia, which dries clear, so that my words are whitewashed upon the page. After a fortnight, they will darken into legibility.

With difficulty, Gerta seeks me a courier. Thieves prey upon itinerant merchants. We suspect every man's fidelity. But an insignificant friar traveling from Angers to London engages to carry a note to my cousin's household. The monk pledges to hide the tightly wound scroll in his copious beard, and agrees to personally deliver it, but only in return for several sordid favors. Gerta accedes to his proposition. Tonight, she endures the carnal embraces of a man who shirks his bath in the name of his piety.

We trust in the Virgin to hurry the friar's horse and dissuade him from prying. For my rash message jettisons pseudonyms. I will no longer be anything other than the pretender's overlord. His wicked, unjust usurpation of my throne has not transformed him into a king. He remains, to me and to heaven, the Count of Boulogne.

> *Where does your honor lie, in forsaking my father, and our amour, and the rightful inheritance, according to feudal custom, of our son Henry Plantagenet? It is useless to argue that my barons do not want a female above them, for at your coronation, it is said, the archbishop traced your right to the throne through the female line, through your mother. In truth, your path to power was paved with deceit and not the sacred blood of family. The speed with which you enacted your sin proves that you and your brother of Blois had long been planning to swindle the English royal*

house, which you purported to reverence. The treason against us began with your meaningless oaths.

You must have played me false every time that you took me in your arms. Under other circumstances I might have written to you about the career of our first boy, Gervase, now seven and at the age of reason. I think to dedicate him to the church, to guarantee his ultimate salvation, the hope of which you have overthrown for yourself. But such sweet domestic concerns are between us no longer, for you force your way into my house and shut the door against me. You put war instead of love between us.

You presume to take up heraldic arms like my father's, with your satyr in passing on a red field, so like his two lions walking on a gules ground. Your device fools no one. The firm justice and hard won peace that he stood for are no more. They are replaced with the rule of lawlessness and the evils of civil strife. As you disembarked from your ship in England, there rang forth a terrible peal of thunder and burst out the most horrible bolt of lightning, so that Judgment Day seemed upon the world. Your reign will bring no good to my empire.

✝

AS EASTER APPROACHES, THE six weeks of fasting required before the feast of the Resurrection sorely tries the vigor of my body and my spirit. Ravenously pregnant, I am obligated to suffice with one horrid repast of salted fish a day. Although I recognize the promise of grace and redemption couched within the austerity of Lent, I look forward to its conclusion.

Geoffrey's cook wails outright. In these Ember Days, he exhausts his repertoire of seafood sauce, and begins to experiment wildly, concocting mock eggs out of almonds and false meats out of crustaceans. My husband disapproves of his cheating and would dismiss him, but Denise is also fatigued by the period of penance and grateful for any relief from red herring and eel, however sacrilegious or imaginary. Our atonement suppers are often inedible, despite heaps of mustard. Gerta does not scruple to embezzle wig cakes and figs from the kitchen, for me to nibble on before retiring.

During these repugnant meals, the talk on the dais concerns the riots and disturbances that erupt across the contested realm. Geoffrey's heralds bring us tidings of violent skirmishes, truces broken, castles stripped from the keeping of loyal men, or fortresses withstanding my cousin's assault.

†

INCREASINGLY, HOWEVER, OUR FOES outnumber our friends. My envoy to the pope fails to enlist His Holiness among our supporters, lacking the skill to plead my case effectively. Apparently, my man was no match for my cousin's wily ambassador to the Vatican, who suggested severally that my birth was unlawful, that I was born to a nun, that my father kidnapped my mother from a convent and raped her. The Count of Boulogne's representative insisted that, given my marriage to a foreigner, Henry I repented of his decision to endow me with all his fiefs, disinherited me, and repealed both compelled kisses and oaths, releasing all his Norman and English barons from their extorted bonds. It was given as true, with false evidence, that the pretender was chosen by the late king as his successor.

A herald arrives with a copy of the pontiff's proclamation, approving the usurper's ascension, declaring that heaven answers the unanimous petitions of the prelates, magnates, and people of Britain. My beloved is named "the special son of the Blessed Peter." Will this engineer his subservience to Rome, and to the brotherly influence of the bishop of Winchester? The Holy Father seems to await the receipt of generous donations. Ah! Saint Peter's house is given over to moneychangers!

My envoy beseeches my pardon for representing my interests so poorly, but reminds me that the Holy See recognizes a new sovereign previously anointed by the archbishop of Canterbury. If the coronation were put aside, it would undermine the church's divine prerogative to create kings.

As news of the papal decision spreads, the usurper sets off on a triumphal progress through the English countryside. Accompanied by a large body of knights and decked out with the splendor of royal majesty, the Count of Boulogne receives the homage of towns and castles in return for the distribution of bounty.

†

SOMETIME BEFORE THE JOYOUS feast of Easter, Stephen reunited with Maud in London. In contrast to the sparsely attended coronation, the royal Easter Court boasts a populous assembly. Leading barons and clerics convene there to celebrate the newly exalted king of the realm. The pope's pronouncement in the pretender's favor makes up the mind of many who had wavered between our parties. They flock to London to compliment the usurper and wait upon him. In exchange, much is to be given to those plighting their faith.

At our own Easter banquet, we gorged ourselves on venison meatballs rolled in parsley, capon stewed in cinnamon, painted hard-boiled eggs, tansy omelets, and jellied beef broth in the shape of the Angevin's shield. All the while, minstrels sang to us of the great gathering over the Channel, of all the bold knights, meritorious priests, and fair ladies who accept Stephen as king. My ears burn at their repeated refrain: "As Christ conquers, Christ reigns, Christ commands."

My rival's sumptuous festivities roll onward, extended for more than a month. The Count of Boulogne insists upon the presence of the dowager queen among the multitude. From London, Adeliza assures me of her loyalty. She coldly observes the litanies chanted before the pretender, somehow raised above them all. With shock, she beholds the usurper touching those with leprosy and scrofula, as if to heal them.

The numerous jewels, rich furs, and widely embroidered mantles of the nobility likewise astound my father's widow. Henry I let lapse the custom of holding a magnificent, costly Easter Court, but my cousin rejoices without care for the state of his coffers, hoping that this immoderate inauguration shores up his stolen dignity. That tramp Maud hurries her husband on to each expense considered appropriate to their aggrandized status; Adeliza scoffs at her trumped up corsages. How I burn to hear of Stephen's prodigality, which ill becomes the English crown, so long the model of moderation.

†

Adeliza's undiplomatic correspondence startles me. The dowager dispenses with circumspect anagrams, secret alphabets, and the discreet use of initials, any of which might protect her letters from the accusation of disloyalty to her sovereign. Her innate dignity and reputation for virtue permit her the freedom to send and receive communications without fear of sabotage or reprisal.

And so I am awash in the infuriating details of my antagonist's presumption. At many of his royal feasts, a celebrated jongleur, one Bernard de Ventadour, regales the guests with verses from his newly completed *Histories of the Kings of England*. A copy of it has also made its way to our court, and it is a driveling cheat of a chronicle! Listening to its vapid hyperbole, the English baronesses and even some of their husbands applaud wildly, claiming to believe that the Count of Boulogne is another Arthur, reborn to bring the empire into a new golden age.

The former queen does not conceal from me the scores of highborn ladies pining for my beloved's handsome face beneath his golden diadem. Boulogne's delight in the gentle sex is well understood. The naïve fools dream of copulating all night long with their virile hero, whom they reckon immeasurably robust. Other devious beauties plot to exploit his affinities, once he is under the spell of their allure. Adeliza chastises their admiration, whether simpering or sly, for she would not cherish the token of any warrior who has not been three times victorious in battle.

The most seriously smitten take to displaying his colors, donning red silk jackets or weaving red and gold ribbons into their braids. No better than they, I have yearned for my chosen knight to drape himself in my pennant and adorn himself with my heraldic device. And now he does so, without me by his side.

Ignoring my father's longstanding prohibition against tournaments, which he disparagingly termed "French fighting," the pretender holds one, and on a massive scale. Colorful tents, to lodge all the participants, are erected in an enormous circle, around a vast parade ground and playing field. Wooden stands, built hastily and without proper attention to safety, hold the enthusiastic audiences that witness each day's assortment of martial exhibitions and games. The dowager cringes at the daily chanting of "Give chase, knight!" or "Thrust, stab, strike a blow!" or "Wound, maim, slay, slay!"

Magnificently equipped magnates and haphazardly armed minor knights, astride stupendous chargers or meager palfreys, demonstrate their valor, rashness, and vanity before the cheering crowds. No one gives thought to the Church's injunctions against such displays of pride, envy, anger, and greed. My rivals' adherents are hungry for the glory of the day, avid for the praise of the troubadours, and lusty for the appreciation of the court ladies. They are careless about the winning and losing of fortunes in ransoms, indifferent to the sometimes lethal wounds inflicted upon their fellows, and negligent of their own possible disgrace.

I will hold the English to a higher standard, when I regain the realm.

†

MY HUSBAND CONTINUES TO treat me with noticeable harshness. Lonely for a man's company, I am grateful for the amity of my brother, now lodging with us in Angers.

As today was bright and mild, he accompanied me and my two sons on a walk through the meadows near the castle. Young Geoffrey's short hair, the picture of his father's, shone yellow, almost white, resembling the patches of dead grass that rot among the new green sprouts. Henry's shouts rang out, as bright and insistent as a clanging bell. Robert smiled as the boys scampered around us, then sprinted past.

Hampered by my pregnant girth, I veritably waddled, despite Gerta's admonition that a lady of high station must never tread too heavily, nor take excessively wide or long strides. I carried a basket in which to garner fresh herbs and whatever else I might find of use. To increase their efficacy, it is best to pick herbs barefoot, and in silence, but at least I have been celibate for the previous week.

Gloucester steadied my swollen form through some particularly marshy ground. "Our new king bombards me with a torrent of messages, enjoining me to come to do him homage or forfeit my estates. My wife appeals to me, repeatedly urging me to submit to him. Amabel attended the Easter assembly, but her presence was no equivalent for mine, and Maud gave her many broad hints about the favorable reception that I would encounter at court. For my compliance, I am to obtain all that I wish. Of course, the queen also foreshadowed our coming impoverishment, if I did not soon swear myself to their new dynasty."

"Hussy! Queen of England, indeed! I am the queen of England." Sniffing, I sank awkwardly down to the ground to collect a pile of goose droppings. Geese manure cures baldness, and Gerta has begun to trade salves and ointment for scandal. I remembered to gather them with my left hand, so that they might operate with the most potency.

The earl pulled me upright. He opened up my hamper. "You remain Empress of the Romans. We have been outmaneuvered. Perhaps there is no point in isolating myself from the center of events. What good will it do our cause if I lose all my great fortune?"

I wrapped my handful of brown pellets carefully into a scrap of red cloth, and then placed the bundle in a corner of the basket. "Is your fidelity for sale?"

Robert slammed my case shut. "Without allies or resources, there is nothing to be gained by opposing the pretender. If I am to build up a party of our supporters, I must answer his call. I will abate his suspicions now and surprise him later."

I looked my brother in the eye. "You will give him the kiss of faith."

Gloucester kept my gaze. "I shall negotiate to serve him conditionally, for as long as he keeps the agreements between us, and protects my dignity entire. Trust to my diplomacy."

I flushed to remember how he had warned me against my cousin. "Ah, well. I am familiar enough with the traitor's disposition to prophecy that his vows to you will be worthless."

"Then it is no evil to offer empty assurances to him in return." The earl pinched a spider that was climbing up my gown.

I considered the creature. "Give it to me. I will stuff it into a plump raisin. Swallowed, it eliminates the ague."

Robert laughed low. "That medicine sounds worse than the ailment." He held out the bug, now curled defensively into a ball.

I quashed its round mass between my thumb and forefinger. "The Count and Countess of Boulogne will deeply value your recognition. They will think to have trampled on both my pretensions and yours. You were long his fervent rival for my father's favor. It will be painful for me to hear of my brother in obeisance to the man whom he has always hated. Some day you will bend your knee to me, who loves you in truth."

✝

Summer

The pretender received the scroll that our dunce of a lusty monk transported in his commodious beard. He response traveled in the saddlebags of another journeyman priest, finally reaching me in the new season.

Following my lead, my unworthy lover discards our pseudonyms. In response to my charges, the knave chooses to forward his *Oxford Charter of Liberties of the Holy Roman Church*. It upbraids my defiance, commencing:

> *I, Stephen, by God's grace elected king of England, anointed by exalted archbishops, welcomed and applauded by worthy subjects, and afterward consecrated by the holiest of holies, the pope, out of piety and duty, vow that the Church shall be free, and confirm to it the fidelity and service that I owe.*

The usurper dares to affirm the privileges, revenues, and fiefs that the church held at the death of the conqueror. He shall not confiscate vacant sees, as His late Majesty saw fit to do. He envisions a glorious alliance between Church and State, as between himself and his brother, king and bishop. It is pronounced: the kingdom of England shall be one with the Kingdom of God.

Does he imagine that he impresses me with his imposition of regal authority? I discount these pledged concessions from a dishonorable knight who keeps none of his oaths to me. How can his brother trust him to uphold the validity of canon law when he dispenses with his honor and his word, subjugating them to his ambition? My mind is in an uproar at these alterations; my cousin disposes of what is mine to accord or to deny.

Tucked within the larger curl of parchment, I discover another scrap of paper. Hastily scribbled, it reads: *"I approve of the plans for Gervase."*

†

AT THE END OF the hot months, my pains brought me to bear of another son, whom the Angevin names William. Throughout my confinement, young Marie kept vigil at my side. Her interest in my shuddering disfigurement aggravated Gerta, but served to distract me.

As one of my torrid moans subsided, the girl marveled. "You resemble a gargoyle; you make deformed, obscene faces."

"If my nature is polluted, these pangs will cleanse it." Another cry escaped me.

The child's composure never wavered. "Now, I see. Your strength is the strength of stones."

The Matter of the Crown

Scroll Eight: 1137

What queen can cease to hunger for power, once she tastes it? What lady can desist from passion, once she commences to listen to her heart? Only bloodshed could abate the empress's ferocity after she tallied up the injuries that she had sustained at her enemy's hands. Then she reveled in the onslaught of civil war. Matilda had lost her grandeur; in vengeance, she would devastate the land. O, let us give thanks to the angels who put obstacles in the way of those who sin against them! A great conflagration would envelop the empire, but the first hostilities were short-lived. The empress ought to have rejoiced in peace, but instead she schemed to engulf her people in destruction.

†

Spring

LATELY, I ENJOY THE pleasures of the hunt with the Angevin and his favorites. My husband is bemused to see me relish his blood sport, for I have never been receptive to his brutality. Yet, after a long winter of preserved meats, I willingly brave the mud and damp for the chance to slaughter fresh game in the clean wind. In the chill of the dawn, I gladly depart our stuffy castle for the physical exertion of the chase.

In the hills and valleys outside Angers, the sun shines brightly over the splendid view of the winding Maine. The foxes and harts cast off caution, for they too are itching to be out in the open, foraging among the new foliage. Geoffrey's huntsman has an easy time of it, stalking the quarry with our dogs, and almost immediately sights the animals in a clearing. The greyhounds strain at their leashes, even before the horn sounds. Each of our resident vassals has had an opportunity to make a kill, either with a lance or an arrow.

The Count of Anjou dotes upon his falcon, Euphemia, and caresses her with calm affection, setting her bells to jingle. I have heard him laugh more often in the past month than I have in the eight years since our marriage. In this season, Denise does not figure first among his diversions.

This morning, we had a bracing run. At sunrise, we scurried to gulp down wine-sopped bread in preparation for a long day in the saddle. My husband spilled a few drops of claret upon his mantle, then brushed off the beads of red liquid. "It is quite a different matter to smear one's coat with Bordeaux, than to stain it with the blood of another knight."

I offered Geoffrey a flagon of drink, to replenish his cup. "Today, you may look to your coverts for amusement. Leave it to heaven to strike down our enemies in reproof. I have heard that the traitorous archbishop of Canterbury meets his death, in punishment for his broken vows to me and to my father."

Alert, Denise essayed to offend me. "No, it is His Majesty who falls ill, carousing alongside his subjects."

I scoffed at her information. "You rehash rumor, and rely too heavily on the nonsense of the jongleurs."

The Angevin had little patience for our bickering. "The story is widely accepted. Relying on His Majesty's demise, and the cessation of crown authority, many of his vassals presume upon anarchy, and look to strengthen their positions against their neighbors. In an infectious spirit of rebellion, barons raid and pillage all the fiefs within their vicinity."

Geoffrey rose from the table and pulled on his leather gauntlets, adjourning us to the stables. "Your fool of a cousin marches against some, compelling them to surrender, but then pardons them. Why does he vacillate, rather than forfeit their property? What worthy knight lets slip through his fingers that which he has taken by force? Castles will be held against him, again and again, if there is to be leniency for the defeated."

As we rode after our dogs, I considered the usurper's idiocy. If English men of birth are restless, and ready to resist the pretender, then the hour of my revenge is at hand.

A black spotted greyhound, leading the pack, caught the scent of a buck. Enmeshed in my thoughts, I trotted at the same slow pace, suddenly heedless of the chase. My destrier gradually dropped to the rear.

A hue and cry went up among the hunters, as the stag emerged from the woods. I did not swivel in my seat to watch the hounds close in. My mind was full of the adventures of my rogue cousin. How to disarm him? I felt full of daring do, but the energy I might have expended on the hunt flowed outward, up out of Europe, over the Channel, and down upon my island of England.

A cheer erupted, as Geoffrey thrust his spear into the wounded animal. The greyhounds only ceased their braying once the beast was skinned and their share of the meat had been laid out on its hide.

A lull had come over our party. I glanced up, and noticed a vulture making lazy circles in the air above us. I caught my husband's eye and pointed upward. He motioned to one of his men, an archer, who took down the raptor in one smooth shot. The large, ugly bird dropped to the earth with a thud. I trotted over to it, eager to lay claim to its carcass. Gerta and I can use its skull, brains, kidneys, and testicles. I instructed one of the squires to secure my portion and deliver it to my maid.

Slowly, I rejoined the mass of my husband's entourage, offering up my congratulations. The Count of Anjou, flushed in his success, aroused by his bloody, finishing stroke, vaulted from his great steed. He strode over to Denise's horse, and lowered his delighted mistress to the ground. Together they wandered into the thick underbrush. Our attendants disbanded, to stretch their legs while Geoffrey fornicated.

One of my husband's squires helped me to dismount. Noting that I perspired, the boy drew off my mantle, draping it over my saddle.

I set off on a stroll down a small hill, to a copse of trees. I dropped down upon a mossy log, and fussed with the trailing hem of my bliaut, to free it from dirt and twigs. Quite by happenstance, I scraped the toe of my boot into an anthill, alarming its colony. The ants swarmed over my foot, and I stood up to stamp them out.

Suffused, in a moment, in flashing red ire, verily trembling with fury, I smote them down. I chased after those who tried to escape me through the grass. I circled back around to their home, and scraped it flat with a stone. I scattered their small corpses to the wind.

Finally, my head cleared, and I ceased to plague them. I was drenched in a cold sweat, but was myself again. I scrambled up over the hill to the clearing.

†

IN THIS SEASON, GERTA and I proposed to pay another visit to Avera. Indifferently, Geoffrey accorded us his permission and a small company of knights. When Denise was informed that the Angevin had sanctioned our journey, she maneuvered to join us. Thus, a beautiful spring morning found us trotting next to one another, on our way down the river.

Beneath her veil, Denise's fiery curls burst out of their plaits. Unfortunately, her manners were just as ill composed. Her red mouth minced her words. "Are you yearning for news of Good King Stephen? Is this why you consult a soothsayer?"

Why must I continually spar with the wench? "The Count of Boulogne's transgressions are no secret. The minstrels cannot seem to find another topic for their wit. Again and again, he destroys the trust of those who pay him credence."

The slut bit her lip, in mock dismay. "Oh, Empress, I know how he repudiated all of his vows to you!"

That sally was easy to parry. "Why yes, he did. He swore to protect and defend my claims to my fiefdom. He pledged to fight for my rights to the throne."

The bitch snorted. "He is keeping your crown warm on his own head."

Irritated, I dismissed her to fall back and ride among my guards.

With envy, I had taken note of the trollop's pale skin. Was the sun browning my own complexion? I reached into my sleeve, withdrawing the distilled juice of pressed walnuts that my maid had given me to stave off freckles. I rubbed it onto my cheeks and nose.

At my behest, Denise took the first turn with the enchantress, while I poked about outside Avera's hovel. Was it possible to eavesdrop? Surprisingly, all was silent from within. From the harlot's sly smile and full basket, it was afterward clear that she had transacted her business successfully.

Without Gerta, I entered the fetid hut. Avera was thinly dressed, although heavily painted. She wore many rings, presumably bartered by women lacking ready money.

I could still see the youth in her face. "You need only give useless herbs to my husband's concubine. The Count of Anjou still clamors for her."

The witch raked her eyes up and down my figure. "The girl worships her valiant hero. She cannot be blamed for her jealousy. Your wars will take him from her arms. He will fight for your son instead of hers."

Suspicious of good tidings, I mulled this over. "Tell me something of importance, what cannot be guessed. Enlighten me with what is imperceptible."

Avera's expression clouded. "I am enslaved to an ecstasy that may wash over me, day or night. I cannot always command it."

How well I understood her. "When I pray to Our Mother Mary, Her knowledge permeates my soul, without the help of my five senses. I do not see Her figure with my eyes, or hear Her voice with my ears, or touch Her robe with my fingers, or smell Her perfume. She has no communion wafer, for me to taste."

"But you have left Her altar, to come to me, as if you were my disciple."

I blushed. Why had I fallen in with a witch? Had she transformed me into a golden ass?

The enchantress closed her large eyes. "I scan the skies, clear and stormy, hazy and starry. Under what conditions will you meet your destiny?"

Goosebumps rose on my forearms. "My destiny is the crown."

Avera exhaled, opening her lids. "Unwind your shroud; your lovely face is a death's head."

Did she accuse me of vanity, or of atrocity? "It is the Count of Boulogne who lays waste to the empire."

The hag stood mute. My heart thumped in my chest.

Her voice tolled in the silence. "You idolize this dark horseman of doom; you make with him two sons. You are in league with him, to bring evil to the world. Is this your fate?"

I stamped my foot. "I cannot choose whom I love."

"No, you are wise there, my lady."

†

Summer

IN THE TORRID HEAT, Geoffrey tolerates the shrieks and silliness of our three young boys more than I would have supposed, given his aloofness and his erratic temper. The state of our marriage swings with his moods, from hearty dislike and poisonous conflict to banal respect and a settled normalcy. I do not stoop to potions or coquetry, but I am capable of lessening my contempt for the Angevin when I see him encouraging my sons and paying them proper regard.

†

MY HOUR IS AT hand. My husband and I are united now in our crusade against the pretender; at last, the Count of Anjou prepares to abet his wife's reconquest of the Continent. The heralds' announcements hail down upon us; disorder plagues Normandy. Every one of its noble magnates endeavors to increase his influence and territory at the expense of the others, in advance of Angevin incursions.

Leaving England, the usurper lands in the duchy and is immediately consumed by the chaos. Stephen liberally grants castles and pensions, attempting to mollify the greed of his vassals. Luckily for my cousin, the Norman barons have as much to gain from the English royal treasury as they do from the spoils of battle. The Count of Boulogne even bribes his own elder brother to fight alongside him, paying Theobald of Blois two thousand marks of silver for his adherence.

In accord, Geoffrey and I abhor my rival's treaty of friendship with the French King. Stephen and Eustace kneel before Louis VI, in return for formal recognition as the once and future Dukes of Normandy. My husband's furor at the conniving pretender who undercuts his own dream of a dukedom matches my searing desperation that the young Plantagenet's rightful title and property are transferred to Maud's boy. The knave! No English king gives himself in fealty to the French crown. My father's many victories on the field proved that Normandy is rightfully a part of our own realm, no fief of the Franks. My beloved's deliberate and indecent negligence unravel Henry I's empire and clearly illustrate his unfitness for the throne.

†

WE RAISE AN ARMY of several thousand knights, bowmen, and foot soldiers. Each day more men pour into Angers to swear their allegiance. The townsmen make an easy profit, selling weapons and provisions to the throng. Glittering shields and stiff trappings of new leather litter our castle courtyards. I keep a close watch on young Henry and Geoffrey, who scuttle among the lances and swords. My sons thrill to see their father parading about in his gleaming armor, directing an extensive war enterprise.

Some vassals owing military service to the Angevin send unfit underlings in their stead. My husband willingly accepts gold, horses, or equipment as his due, but, most of all, he needs able-bodied fighters. He rants against the weak condition in which many men have arrived, the incongruity between their iron suits of armor and their soft bodies. The Count of Anjou forbids his troops to wear surcoats of silk over their coats of mail. All their long manes are to be shorn for the coming campaign. Geoffrey despises all the modern warrior's effeminacies, out of place in violent engagement.

Much to his disgust, some of the heedless newcomers would overlook the religious aspects of their calling, and are ignorant of the word of God. This will not do in Angers. Our bishop blesses our men-at-arms, who are expected to pray daily for the success of our offensive. They must swear to be sons of the Church, wielding their foils first and foremost for the honor of the Lord.

I am to gallop at the head of our battalions. My husband gifts me with a magnificent destrier of Oriental lineage. Despite the arduous journey ahead, I am keen on the coming adventure. Eager to see my enemies trampled, I do not quail at the thought of battle. The count perceives that my presence among his men imbues his territorial aggression with respectability. Although I know that the Angevin fights for himself, he needs it to be said that he fights for me. I intend that he shall.

†

THE NIGHT BEFORE WE commenced our great enterprise, the highest ranking among our forces gathered for a sacred ceremony in the great hall of Angers Castle. The room was packed full, over warm from the burning tapers and the press of so many bodies. All three of my sons peered wide-eyed at the bustle and din of the knights amassed before them.

Geoffrey lifted a silver sword, ornamented with garnets and rubies, above his blond head. An expectant hush filled the chamber. "Behold the symbol of the highest order, the Order of Chivalry. Let the two edges of the blade remind you that you serve two masters, on Earth as it is in heaven. When you face your foe, do not disgrace the suffering of Christ, nor my cause." These stirring phrases brought forth a murmur of approval.

Then, unexpectedly, I was the subject of the Angevin's rousing speech. "Our great glory will be shared by my royal wife, Empress Matilda. Before she leads us into eternal renown, she must be prepared for combat."

Concealing my shock, I held my head level.

The count waved a bishop to come forward for the ritual cleansing, the baptism that must precede my dubbing.

His Grace carried a water basin and a swatch of linen, used to soak the cloth and bedaub me in the shape of a cross. "Go forth, with God's blessing upon you!"

Geoffrey approached me, bearing a carmine wool mantle, embroidered with a profusion of golden roods, and lined in white ermine. It had a sable collar, tied with silk tassels. He placed it over my shoulders and then knelt before me, to fasten golden spurs onto my boots. Forthwith, he arose, and indicated that I should sink down in his place.

Shuddering, I knelt before him, but stared resolutely ahead, so as to appear righteous and bold.

"The empress is washed in linen, so that she is bright like the flower of the lily; she is covered in red, like a rose. In honor and piety, she is pure and white, but she will shed scarlet blood. As each man carries arms appropriate to him, so I entrust my wife with shining spurs and a consecrated sword. I dub her a knight in spirit." My husband placed the flat of the blade on one of my shoulders and then hoisted me up, to a roar of cheers.

Relieved, I sensed that our vassals did not rebel against such an unorthodox investiture. My sons sauntered about on the dais, proud that their mother had been metamorphosed into a soldier. This was not my coronation, elevating me to sovereign status, but I was honored to be lifted into the noble estate of knighthood.

Out of the corner of my eye, I noticed that Denise's mouth twisted downward, out of its usual bow. I pity her the lonely months that she will endure, as her lover and I preoccupy ourselves with civil war. My boys are left in her keeping, far from the lawlessness of Normandy. Although disconsolate, she will not abuse them, lest she run the risk of Geoffrey's displeasure and Gerta's malevolence.

✝

THE ENCLAVE OF EXMES spouts a river of blood, a sordid gash slit across its fortified pretensions. Yesterday, we successfully assaulted its tower and outbuildings. Our sabers, spears, and maces struck down the Normans; our thundering hooves mangled their corpses. Now the Count of Anjou and his troops rampage outside the walls, plundering livestock from peaceful fields and torching swards of healthy crops. A demon atop his foaming warhorse, Geoffrey eggs his soldiers on to further ruthlessness whenever their zeal flags.

I relish our victory, but the battle fatigued me. As it wound down, I loitered at the base of a broken outer work. I slumped on my destrier, leaning against the saddle cantle for support. My silver sword, glinting with rubies, hung heavy at my side. I could feel the mass of its blade, etched with my name, hard against my thigh. I perspired under my padded leather tunic, trimmed with metal links. Exhausted, careless, I dawdled, admiring my bright spurs.

An arrow whizzed by my ear, clattering against the stone behind me. Instinctively, I ducked down, and just in time, for another bolt whistled over my prone form. My escort shouted and gave chase to the archer. He evaded them, but my guards had foiled the assassination.

Hearing of my narrow escape, my husband exploded with wrath. As of today, a gauntlet of knights narrowly surrounds me at all times.

✝

WE HAVE ADVANCED TO a spot deeper within Normandy, ten miles from Caen Castle, where my brother has lately settled. On my arrival, I sent word to the earl, entreating him to throw over Stephen and declare his fidelity to me. Today, I received a return message from Robert, who regrets to inform me that he still chooses to respect his vows to the pretender. His garrison here remains faithful to the usurper, who raises an army at Lisieux, in an effort to drive back the Angevins. To swell its ranks, my cousin engages Flemish mercenaries, disorderly ruffians known for their barbarity, and unwelcome to Stephen's Norman barons. My enemy presumes that his various battalions will be able to overcome their mutual antipathy in his service.

I cannot fathom why Gloucester still bides his time. It is unlikely that he dreads or reveres the Count of Boulogne. Does he no longer support my claim to the contested throne? Why else does he refuse to join the royal circle?

And yet, disarmingly, Gloucester does not himself advance to meet Stephen at Lisieux, rebuffing my foe's entreaties as well as my own. Geoffrey stintingly acknowledges my brother's cleverness, his stalling, his absence from the field in this civil war for Normandy. Robert avoids the necessity of fighting either for me or against me, just managing to sustain the good will of both camps. Beyond my own anger and hurt, I try to comprehend his strategy. Is keeping faith with a father and a sister no longer enough for him?

†

YESTERDAY, THE ANGEVIN DIVISIONS approached the citadel of Lisieux. By afternoon, they were arrayed for an engagement, and ensconced only a few hills away from my cousin's units. Watching from a nearby hillside, I strained to hear the shouts and chants of the pretender's men-at-arms and the neighs and snorts of their horses. Drums from both sides beat their shrill, staccato rhythms. Tense, I pretended that my nerves signaled excitement rather than fear.

Among the ranks of our knights, my husband paced, rallying his supporters with the exploits of Saint George. I could only make out a few phrases. He concluded at a higher pitch: "Your patron slew a dragon to serve the cross and to save a kingdom from terror. So too will your valorous acts eradicate evil from the land. May Jesus Christ be your shield!"

Immediately, there was a loud thundering, as thousands of mounted warriors charged toward us. In that moment, amidst the noise, I envisioned all the wives who prayed for the safety of these rabid creatures, all the children that these men had sired in love. Their ties of amity and devotion mattered nothing. Their gallant endeavor commenced; all alike would kill or be killed.

My guard enveloped me, urging my destrier further up on the rise, beneath a large, misshapen oak. Here I was safe, but could still witness the hostilities. One or two of my escort, indolent men, seemed relieved to be exempt from danger. The pugnacious ones appeared frustrated to be so far from the center of the action.

The air resounded with turmoil; metal clashed against metal. I fingered the silver filigree hilt of my sword and silently entreated the Virgin that I would not have to swing it in my own defense. Geoffrey's gift is so ponderous that I am unable to handle it with agility.

I scanned the scene, but could not pick my husband out of the martial crowd, contorted in combat. The sunlight winked, reflecting off a helmet topped with a golden crown. My heart lurched. It was Stephen, whom I had not looked upon in six years.

For a long while my eyes clung, fascinated, to his form. Like me, the pretender waited safely on the fringes, tightly enclosed by an armed entourage. He caressed the neck of his steed, jumpy from the screams of men cut down before him. The hairs on the back of my neck rose. Here was the miscreant whose unlawful act was responsible for all this havoc. Gore coated everything spread out before us: men, animals, banners, pennants, devices, axes, hammers, ground. How can the Count of Boulogne suffer such a stain on his soul? I kept the usurper in my sights, forgetting to identify Geoffrey among the living and the fallen.

I was distracted from my fixation by the exclamations of my retinue. A large battalion of my cousin's Norman knights, shields descended, retired from the battle. It was later ascertained that these barons abruptly refused to continue to fight alongside Flemish bandits, against other, even Angevin, noblemen; they withdrew their support from the conflict. Boulogne's vassals disbanded without his permission, signaling their open rebellion from their overlord. Too late, the usurper set off in pursuit of the traitors, and his enfeebled army disintegrated.

Finally, my rival's herald sounded a horn. The remnants of the combatants separated and the field cleared. Our forces streamed toward the fortress of Lisieux. My escort nudged my mount out from under the safety of the tree. Prancing its way through the sea of the dead, my steed stumbled over a headless torso, almost throwing me down. We had to move slowly, until we were clear of the detritus.

Now I picked out the Angevin, bloody and belligerent, shouting at his troops to follow him to the citadel. By the time we caught up to him, fire engulfed the redoubt. Soot coated Geoffrey's face, but his chain mail, soaked red, had kept him from harm.

I stroked the sweating, smeared flank of his horse. "Is victory ours, my lord?"

The count grimaced, truculent. "The bastards set their own tower aflame. The blaze burns too hot to defy. We add only a pile of charred stones to our possessions."

The fog of smoke clogged my lungs. I pounded my chest.

Geoffrey's pale eyes simmered in the hot air. "I ride now to lay siege to the neighboring town. My Angevins will not be thwarted! My warriors shall burn and loot. We will rip their treasures from the walls of their dwellings. We will ravish their women in the aisles of their churches. We shall devour their flocks raw, without bread. No able-bodied foe will be left standing."

Despite all that I had seen, or because of it, I was shocked to hear of the greater desecration to come. "Lisieux falls to us; that is what matters. Such savagery is no longer required. Your assault will leave much bitterness behind us."

"My power must be unquestioned." With a vociferous bellow, my husband cantered away, rounding up the massing men to surge.

†

Fall

WE RESIDE IN CENTRAL Normandy, at the Castle of Argentan, one of my father's favorite hunting palaces. Argentan has long been an administrative center for the collection of taxes in the duchy. Henry I enjoyed his sojourns here, gathering revenue and stalking game. His castellan has faithfully protected the keep's vaults and storerooms. I am at leisure to enjoy a citadel and inventory a treasury that has never been out of our custody.

Recovering from a wound, Geoffrey tarries, cared for by Denise. To my displeasure, his final, gratuitous attack floundered. The townsfolk defended their property and families with more spirit than common people usually exhibit. One of them laid hold of a crossbow and managed to shoot my husband's foot. Injured, carried away from the scene in a litter, his moans destroyed the morale of his rampaging band. After many casualties, our troops abandoned the half-destroyed buildings and retreated. The Counts of Anjou and Boulogne finished the day equally content to regroup.

At Argentan, I preside as liege lady, promoting the illusion that I am mistress of all my inheritance. As His Majesty did before me, I issue charters from the castle's great chamber. One flustered notary scribbles them out, as fast as I draft them. I affix a seal to my dictates, "Matilda, empress, daughter of the king of the English."

Is it done, then? Have I come again to where I was? Am I reborn the queen, risen from the dead?

†

TO MY SHAME, THE resumption of my political power proves a delusion. In league against my interest, my husband and my beloved conclude a two-year truce in Normandy. Once again, Geoffrey puts off the achievement of my ambition. Revolts brew in Anjou; he hurries his return to the land of his fathers. He sacrifices my patrimony for the security of his own legacy.

For his part, Stephen loses heart at the defection of his Norman barons. I scorn his shortsightedness! Despite the recent fracas over the Fleming mercenaries, the Norman lords much prefer to kneel to him than to the Angevin, their rival in Europe. My husband cannot guarantee their English rights. The pretender departs the Continent, without decisively subduing Normandy and without repelling the Angevin threat.

In addition, my ass of a cousin pays Geoffrey two thousand marks of silver a year, in exchange for a promise not to invade the duchy. Wisely, my husband demands the first year's ransom in advance. The usurper's word means nothing; his royal fortune ebbs. The Angevin takes the money offered, and delays his onslaught for another time. Boulogne appoints two deputies to administer Normandy in his absence, but they cannot reestablish the rule of English law. King Henry's sovereignty here is no more. His two regents will be no match for Geoffrey when he forays north once again.

Yet, there is no denying or dampening my absurd fancy for the scoundrel. Since espying Stephen at the battle of Lisieux, my incorrigible passion for him sparks to light. My hatred does not subside, but coexists alongside my desire, each burning me up, in opposition.

†

LAST NIGHT, MY HUSBAND and my cousin signed their treaty and gave each other the kiss of peace. Afterward, we celebrated with a feast. I had dressed carefully, first bathing in scalding water seeped with dried orange blossoms and aromatic lavender. Eager to inhabit my own majesty, I wore a shimmering bliaut, a silvery corsage, and the carmine and ermine mantle presented to me before our military campaign.

Throughout the evening's festivities, I seemed to float, as if I were still in my bath, enveloped in an intoxicating steam. I chattered, with a voice muffled to my own ears. My vision swam; the Count of Boulogne's face dissolved before me. I had to concentrate on the wall tapestries, or the flickering firelight, in order to rein in my confusion. I hope that my demeanor at the banquet acquitted me of innuendo, but, within my breast, all was anarchy, as my outraged ambition tussled with my romantic yearning.

At the high table, I was installed between Stephen and Geoffrey, each the father of two of my boys. A silk canopy sheltered the three of us. Outside the baldachin, on the Angevin's other side, Denise lowered at us.

The court gorged itself on peacock, heron, blackbirds, rabbit, pheasant, and boar. In my besotted state, I overate and could not differentiate between the dishes that I sampled. At the conclusion of the meat courses, several pages bore a sugar carving into the hall and up onto the dais. The troubadours struck up a jaunty melody to accompany the passage of the elegant sculpture, which depicted a castle with four concentric towers.

The usurper admired the confection. "Here is a fortification that we might besiege together."

My husband stroked his chin in agreement. "On this day of rejoicing, we merely sharpen our words."

The two, both masters of repartee, flaunted their wit. There followed a long bout of verbal sparring, abetted by large quantities of alcohol. Neither my lawful spouse nor my knight errant deigned to notice me.

At some point, Stephen began to narrate the intrigues of the fat king of France to marry his second son, Louis Capet, to Eleanor, Duchess of Aquitaine and Poitou. "The duchess is a woman of prodigious learning, capable of the most beguiling conversation."

The Angevin straightened his back. "She inherits two great duchies, stretching from the Loire to the Pyrenees, from the Rhône to the Western Ocean. Her goodly territory is more enormous and more beautiful than Normandy, and richer in resources than either the realms of France or England."

The Count of Boulogne drowned his goblet of wine, then smacked his hand upon the board. "I do not know whether young Louis appreciates anything but his imperial gain. He is insensitive to the value of the lady herself. Eleanor's loveliness is fabled, but he was raised in the cloister of Notre Dame. The king's second boy, he was destined to be a pope, and has the quiet demeanor of a priest. He is no god for such a goddess." Cataloging the perfections of a woman he had never met, my cousin glowed with lust.

Denise giggled, amused by the Dauphin's fate. "Louis Capet will soon find out how to beget sons on his duchess."

Geoffrey's agitation surfaced. "The consolidation of France, Aquitaine, and Poitou brings me no pleasure, Your Majesty. Blois and Anjou are both less secure now that France's power magnifies. The Duke of Aquitaine must renege on this alliance for his daughter and entrust his vast holdings to another."

The pretender's expression grew hooded. "Whom else do you have in mind for the nubile Eleanor?"

My husband considered the case. "Unfortunately, I cannot lay claim to her." He motioned to our little Henry, wandering among the lower tables, and then to me. "Empress, is our first born too juvenile to be wed?"

The young Plantagenet hustled over and stood before us, gingerly admiring the sugar castle. His reddish hair, a paler version of my beloved's, told the truth of his paternity for all to see. Stephen, Geoffrey, Denise — not one of them could possibly miss the indisputable resemblance between the boy and his true parent.

My stomach cramped. "He is five, but I would approve of such a marriage."

Henry, oblivious, hopped on one foot. "May I have a piece of the candy fortress?"

My cousin arched his brows, up onto his gleaming forehead. "And who might you be, young warrior, with your eye on the prize?"

The Plantagenet swaggered. "I am Henry, son of the daughter of King Henry, rightful heir of England and Normandy."

A silence fell over the dais.

The usurper drummed his fingers on the high table.

The Plantagenet frowned, worried that he had said the wrong thing, and added, "My mother teaches me always to pray for my father's love."

My beloved smiled with his lips, but his glance remained cold. "Do you have a foot, you imp?"

The Plantagenet looked puzzled. "Yes, sire."

"Do you have two feet?"

"Yes, sire."

"What are one and two?"

"Three, sire."

"Do you thus have three feet?"

The boy, proud of his intelligence, was clearly crushed to have been bested before the adults, and shown to be deficient in logic. He raised brimming eyes to the Count of Anjou, who clucked his tongue in disapproval, and dismissed him from our presence.

Just at that moment, dancers began to form rings and cacophonous music filled the hall.

Wincing at the clash of cymbals and the clapping of the crowd, Stephen gestured to my mantle. "Ah, Matilda, your cloak boasts a rich dye."

How I yearned to hear my name on his lips! "Its wool has been stained with the blood of the murex, a rough, spiny creature common to the warm seas."

Boulogne murmured low, and shook his russet curls, but I could not decipher his words underneath the drums and shouts.

I dared a hint. "What say you to my red-crested hoopoe?" In every bestiary, the hoopoe bird represents the loving child.

My rival sighed. "I judge the Angevin's son to be a fine, hale young man. Of course, I dote on Eustace, my first-born, the legitimate successor to my English and Norman empire."

The Matter of the Crown

Scroll Nine: 1138

*A*gain in this year there were brutal upheavals, raging fire and uplifted swords. The empress wooed calamity, as she might have seduced her beloved, and rejoiced that territories should be ravaged for her own sake. Following her exalted example, all her noble vassals courted violence, in order to thrust themselves up above their fellows. Matilda's supporters had minor victories and major defeats, yet she continued to pin her hopes on the utility of war. Her adored foe also put his trust in mayhem and confusion. Doom came first to barbarians and thieves, but ruin soon spread to all the Christian souls in the realm.

✝

Spring

GEOFFREY BACKTRACKS TO ANJOU, in accordance with his treaty with the enemy, but I remain in Normandy. In this citadel, bequeathed to me by my father, I recover my birthright. In Argentan, I am Normandy's overlord; I do not retreat from my honors, nor entrust them to anyone else's care. I do not permit the usurper's regents to be masters here. Peace persists under my firm authority.

From this side of the Channel, I exult in the various rebellions against my rival that sprout all over the island of Britain, so many insurrections that my cousin does not know where to fight back first. Does he repress an uprising here, or reinforce a front there? He apparently progresses from one scene of carnage to the next, but is unable to combat every incursion. I imagine his frustration, and gloat. Thief, rascal, blackguard! None of it is his: not one stone tower, not one blossoming meadow, not one bustling village, not one barn bursting with seed.

But England's glories, my glory, is devastated; the countryside has been stripped of provisions. Populous counties, rich with resources, fall prey to his battalions, and those of barons either loyal to me or fighting on their own behalf. What is left to revel over, among the smoldering wreckage?

Some intrepid warriors, fermenting havoc in my name, are guilty of impious atrocities. My gut clenches to hear the jongleurs broadcast the terror of my people, the shrieks of the women, the laments of the old men, the groans of the dying and the acrimony of the living. Mother Mary, I do not condone gratuitous brutality. I bow my head in shame at their misdeeds, but I cannot do without these evil agents. There are beautiful sunsets suffused with the color of blood. To sit again upon the throne that heaven intends for me, I must foray out into the darkness, heaving a sword.

I hear lately that my rival mourns the passing of his mother, the Countess of Blois, who died a nun, at the Cluniac priory of Marcigny-sur-Loire, here on the Continent. Although beset by trouble, Stephen's anguish cannot equal my own.

†

Summer

CIVIL DISORDER ESCALATES IN England. Seeking advantage, my husband transplants Denise and our boys to Argentan, to my safekeeping, and begins to trespass in Normandy, breaking his truce with our antagonist. By the grace of God, he captures several important towns in the duchy, including Bayeux and Caen. The Count of Boulogne, busy at home, delegates, to his subordinates, the task of resisting the Angevin abroad.

From the heralds and troubadours, we hear much of Geoffrey's investitures. Every meal is accompanied by a narration of recent developments, whether inconsequential or more crucial. Denise is full of her brave warrior. At great expense, the leman commissions a Parisian monk to compose a paean to him, and transcribe it. As much as I hope that my husband trods upon my beloved's pretensions, I cannot abide her mooning.

Last night, just after vespers, the harlot came to my solar, to quiz me on the details of her idol's many glorious exploits.

Although dusk had settled upon the keep, the heat was intense, and I wore only a pleated bliaut, worn thin with age. I lingered by the window, hoping to catch any small breeze that might waft into my chamber. "You can recite better than I can the towns that Geoffrey has conquered. He is a competent soldier."

Without waiting for my leave, the strumpet sat down, fanning herself. "He is the ideal knight. His skin gleams as if it were sculpted from polished ivory, his legs stand sentry like pillars of marble, his poise is that of a majestic cedar tree."

My impatience festered in the warm air. "Slut! Must you presume to flaunt your passion before me, and rely so heavily upon King Solomon's metaphors?"

She did not even blush. "Surely, I am blameless. All the Christian world praises my sweetheart, verily engulfs him with acclaim. In every category, he is beyond censure."

I felt the moisture on my neck. "I see him with more clarity than you do."

There was a bead of sweat on the girl's upper lip, but she did not wipe it away. "The Count of Anjou enslaves my body and my spirit. I want only to be where he is, and to present him with sons. I look for no reward beyond our bond; I do not seek to satisfy my desires, but his. To be a wife may be more respectable, but I prefer to be called his whore. The more that I am debased on his account, the more that my life has been touched by him."

I sniffed. "I see that you have been reading Abelard's calamitous history, without drawing the proper conclusions. Do not model your amours on Heloise's." I stood up and moved toward her, reaching out to brush off the perspiration from her pink mouth. I rubbed the warm liquid between my fingers.

Denise winced, shrugging off my grazing touch. "Abelard's romance circulates among the noble courts of Europe!"

I was offended on my husband's behalf. "Do you compare the Count of Anjou to that castrato?"

The girl reddened. "No, no. Geoffrey's story will be magnificent, a radiant manuscript, glittering with gold, sparkling with jewel tones, rightly the centerpiece of the library at the castle of Angers. It shall be a bible for all of Anjou, read aloud at our annual festivals, and my personal treasure, inspiring my intimate devotion."

I felt all the allure of her bright hair. I took one copper lock in my hand, to examine its hue. "Abelard's extravagant avowals annoy many whose merit has not inspired such an outpouring of song."

The wench regarded me suspiciously.

I dropped her red curl. "It will be some consolation to hail the Frankish monk's achievement. Beauty is scarce enough."

†

I RECEIVE WORD OF a significant triumph. My brother of Gloucester finally decides to embrace my insurgence and serve as the mainstay of my party. With all proper form, the earl throws Stephen over, sending him a formal defiance according to ancient customs. He no longer recognizes the false king as his overlord, and will no longer carry out his feudal duties to him.

I cherish Robert's missive. It renews my hope that someday soon I will come to possess what is mine by right.

> *I renounce the friendship between Stephen and myself because he unlawfully claims the throne, defying all the homage that he himself swore to you, and thus leads me to betray my own oaths to my family. Indeed, for all his protestations of fidelity to me, our cousin plots against my life. With my priest's blessings, I determine to follow my conscience, so as not to risk my happiness in the hereafter and my reputation in the here and now.*
>
> *The news of my insubordination disseminates; sedition flourishes in all of my territories. My vassals immediately begin to provision Bristol castle, reinforce its defenses, and commence hostilities against our enemy's supporters. Bristol shall be our party's central outpost in England, for it is an impenetrable stone structure, surrounded on three sides by a wide waterway that flows into the sea. It basks in a strong tide and forms a good port, safe haven for a thousand ships.*
>
> *Indeed, Bristol keep becomes a meeting place for all the disaffected who wish to join us. Men from numerous districts attach themselves to our cause. Some of these, unfortunately, are no better than brigands, perpetrating hateful crimes for their own gain, stealing or destroying yokes of oxen, flocks of sheep, fields of grain, and gardens of vegetation. But garrison soldiers are being recruited and trained, and the king does not yet arrive to assert himself in the city.*
>
> *As I am your brother, I promise now to undertake to be the life and soul of your rebellion. I vow to support Geoffrey's endeavors in Normandy and will join your husband's army.*

Regrettably, Gloucester does not act entirely as I might wish. Despite his renewed adherence, and for all his talk of Bristol, he does not depart the continent. It is clear to me that until we cross the Channel, we can never regain what has been stolen. The earl is needed in southern and western England. He must return home, to secure me a port of entry. There will be no true peace on my native soil until it is liberated from the grasp of a villain.

†

I WHOOP WITH DELIGHT! The Count of Boulogne marched on Bristol, but when he surveyed my brother's citadel, he was dismayed by the difficulties before him. How could he starve out the resisters when they could be reprovisioned by boat?

Ever unsure, my cousin consulted his barons. One group advised him to take drastic measures. They suggested that he build a damn across the narrowest part of river, filling in the waterway with rocks, timber, beams, and earth. This obstruction would block the castle's access to the town, prohibiting its burghers from aiding the rebels and perhaps flooding Bristol itself.

Stephen did not listen to these sage counselors, but to another cabal, secretly partial to me. They spoke of the impossibility of thwarting ocean currents. They insisted that any man-made impediment would sink in the mud, or below the waves, or be swept away in the powerful undertow. They encouraged the pretender to give up the idea of redeeming Robert's stronghold, in favor of capturing less well-defended fortresses.

So the usurper slunk off, leaving Bristol city and citadel to be our headquarters. The dolt does not foresee their geographical significance. An incompetent military strategist, he again neglects to forfeit the property of a treasonous vassal, even the mightiest one of all, the Earl of Gloucester.

†

FOLLOWING ROBERT'S LEAD, BRIAN FitzCount resigns his supposed allegiance to the false king and travels to Argentan to abase himself before his true queen. Formally repledging himself to my cause, he presents me with a marvelous gift, a superb silk canopy in which I can enjoy the outdoors without sacrificing any domestic comforts. The grandiose red and gold pavilion, decorated with my father's coat of arms, well suits a royal retinue. But it is not of more value to me than his homage.

Today dawned hot and bright, a perfect opportunity to inaugurate the tent. At sext, my servants erected it outside the walls of the keep, spreading carpets upon the ground underneath. Pages carried out tables and chairs, heaping platters, and brimming goblets.

The household picnicked, and then lingered, bellies full, in the scorched atmosphere. Soon, we all set to yawning. Gerta and Denise advised exertion, and set off to stretch their legs upon the meadow. The children chased after them, screeching like cats, and began a game of Hoodman Blind.

I flicked my wrist to dispense with the attendance of the rest of our contingent. Brian and I remained within. The sunlight streaming through the crimson fabric cast a glow upon the table and pink shadows upon our cheeks.

Did I look as rosy as he did? "This demonstration of your faith gratifies me greatly."

Brian bowed low before me. I held out my hand, and he kissed my knuckles with warm, fervent lips. "I thank you for your notice, Empress. A virtuous knight cannot suffer to make false promises. Whatever my nominal status at the pretender's court, I was degraded by my lies and posturing. My very nobility was eroded by my groveling duplicity."

Basking in the warmth of the sun, sated with a stomach full of meat and mead, I found it easy to be forgiving. "I acknowledge the difficulty that you must have faced. I see that you are pure of heart." Scrutinizing FitzCount, I appraised his appeal, perhaps greater than I had bothered to notice.

He shot me an open, genuine smile. "You reared me as your falcon. You stained my feathers with gold leaf, and entwined red silk straps around my legs. I was tied down, and weighted down, but I felt free. My spirit still soared and my heart still pounded wild. I flew, perhaps higher than had I been let loose."

I nodded. "Charming verse."

"Now you purse your lips and whistle, and this music from your mouth expands throughout the heavens. I plunge back down through the clouds to settle upon your raised gauntlet."

For a moment, I shut my eyes. Would that I could call for my lover, as I would a dog, and command him to heel. I looked at Brian, but his attractions were no longer uppermost in my mind. "Indeed, I need your succor. God forsakes the usurper, who reigns without sagacity or decency. The sins of that rogue are legion."

"As you know, His Majesty relinquished Bristol, without eradicating your force there. I was one of the barons in his army who encouraged him to forgo his attack. Although he left Gloucester's keep intact, to dispense with the necessity of a long and fatiguing siege, he needlessly laid waste to the area surrounding the city, merely to assuage his sense of boredom and antipathy. The king's compensations have been in short supply since his coronation."

I chafed to recall how our affair had been one of those enjoyments. "The Count of Boulogne regrets stealing my throne then, finding the role overly taxing and wearisome?"

FitzCount spoke in measured tones. "He does not shirk every duty. On one rampage to the south, he found himself at Castle Cary, loyal to your brother. Stephen starved it to surrender, while the residents of the embattled tower prayed for help that never came."

I was not entirely ill pleased to hear that my beloved could master a citadel. "For once, he had more wit than his opponents?"

"His Majesty did not pine over the loss of Bristol when he had subdued Cary."

"If he had taken Bristol, small fortresses tied to Gloucester would have come to him without bloodshed."

FitzCount looked at me soberly. "You were born to ride at the head of an army, my lady." His arm jerked, almost touching me.

Immobile, I gazed away from him, so that he would not to attempt to encroach upon my eminence. "I shall best the illegitimate king, in everything."

With tact, Brian nipped his hands behind his back. "The usurper values himself highly enough."

I sighed. "Rebellion erupts everywhere; the pretender cannot resist us."

For all his fervid devotion to me, the baron did not avoid unpleasant truths. "Firm friends of yours fall, and not just in the south."

I snorted. "The Count of Boulogne pardons our allies as is his wont?"

FitzCount did not waver. "Queen Maud forbids her husband to be too lenient, for she recognizes that the magnates despise him for his gentleness. She begs her husband to treat every rebel as a dangerous foe; she warns him that every man he releases will have to be conquered a second time."

My voice was shrill. "Does my cousin continue to pander to the insolent caprices of his witch?" Suddenly, the tent's scarlet haze felt confining. Did Brian gauge my venom, and presume that it conveyed only political fury? "The plague of the house of Boulogne! Do they truly believe that they shall reign untroubled, as if Stephen were my father's rightful heir?" In disgust, I rose to walk toward the entrance of the pavilion. I paused in the opening, with the ruby light behind me and the white light before me, and did not venture out onto the plain.

FitzCount approached the threshold. "Several times, the king confided to me his dismay that these civil disturbances mushroom out of control. He grieves that treachery grows commonplace. He mourns the loss of confidence in the safety of the crown highways. He is concerned by the distrust that arises between neighbors. There is no baron who does not rebuild and resupply his keeps, to ward off the greed of the others."

I watched a hooded Hamelin chase my three sons and Marie through the grass. The five children ran in wide circles, sometimes tumbling to the ground. Their yelps echoed over the clearing. "May the usurper's troubles be like the many heads of Hercules' hydra."

"They are so, Empress. His Majesty is always on the move, always overwhelmed by a general's anxieties. Whenever he crushes a revolt, or quells an insurrection, another looms."

I saw young Henry stoop to help Marie where she had fallen. "Stephen's nature is unsuited to such a life. He will not be able to fortify himself to withstand each new adversity."

Brian dared to touch to my sleeve, which hung down between us. "For this, too, the king turns to the queen. He must take pleasure from a woman if he is to gird himself for what is to come."

†

FITZCOUNT STRIKES UP A relationship with my sons and Denise's Hamelin. In the exercise yard, he narrates battle histories and educates them in the arts of war. Brian wields his arms with agility, and wears his mail with insouciance, as if it weighed nothing and stretched fluidly to accommodate all his motions. The boys can feel how naturally he comes to the life of a soldier. He was born to lift his sword up over his head, born to fell his foes.

Today I came upon the children, entranced as my vassal explained the importance of a knight's armor of proof, the suit of metal that can withstand an arrow. In deference, FitzCount lowered his head to me, but continued his lecture.

Seven-year-old Hamelin modeled a chain coif. Henry wore an enormous, pointed, steel helmet with a nose guard, entirely covering his six-year-old face. How could he breathe?

I strode over to lift its weight from his red head. "Can you hear under there?"

"I listen through the slits!"

Brian picked up a long, kite-shaped shield, held it in front of his chest, and demonstrated the proper ways to balance it. Slowly, he swung it to and fro.

The eyes of his young troops were alight with martial zest. I looked carefully at my sons' expressions. Geoffrey, now four, was just as enthralled as his elder siblings.

FitzCount took a defensive stance. I picked up a lance from the ground and clung to it like staff. I wiggled my fingers at the children.

William, the toddler, laughed at my antics. I croaked, in the voice of a crone: "Where is the warrior powerful enough to engage me?"

Hamelin spoke up. "Sir Brian, vanquish this intruder!"

FitzCount lowered the shield. With my lance, I poked him in the chest. "I have insulted your honor, and you neglect to challenge me."

Ignoring my sally, he addressed the boys. "A well-trained warrior aims his lance between the four nails of the shield, or right where the lacings hold the helmet tight upon the head. These spots are the two most vulnerable targets."

The Plantagenet wondered aloud. "Is it possible to manage several weapons at once?"

"If the sword is held in the right hand, the dagger may be wielded by the left."

Hamelin thirsted for something to happen, even to me. "Repel the invader!"

Brian laughed. "Do you, young lord, absolve me from all burden of vice?" The knight took up a long pole with a crescent shaped blade at its end. The boys grimaced to imagine its power, as he waved over their heads.

Hamelin chortled.

I peered at Denise's son, and then at FitzCount. "Familiarity with bloodshed should not breed disdain for it."

Brian inclined himself to me, and took a different tone. "Take heed!"

Hamelin sulked. "Why are we denied any excitement?"

The Plantagenet tossed his amber head. "We will be men someday soon."

FitzCount waved at an adolescent squire, who shot over to collect the weapons and carry them away. In his haste, he stumbled over the ground.

With interest, Henry and Hamelin inspected the clumsy attendant, clearly new to his formal training. Inspired, the two scamps began pushing at each other.

I had not relinquished my lance, and now jabbed at the wrestlers. The Plantagenet stopped scuffling, but Hamelin moped to be kept from his own little war.

†

Fall

MY HUSBAND AND HIS diminished battalion retreat to Argentan Castle. Our Norman campaign halts once more.

While recuperating his strength, the Count of Anjou mollifies his temper by planning for the town fair. He spends untold hours with his leman and his stewards, while I am relegated to Gerta's company.

We waste the lush autumn days, walking outdoors among the farmers who are harvesting grapes and sowing wheat.

Today, we meandered for three hours. Replete with political talk, I digressed. "I cannot take heart from events. My mind drifts into bittersweet daydreams of what was and what may never be."

My wise woman would have none of it. "What is most reckless, but that which negates our virtue?"

I rolled my eyes, then considered an outcropping planted in Roman times. Outlined against the horizon, the crab apple trees boasted gnarled boughs heavy with misshapen fruit. I would have gathered some, but knew from experience that they would be sour and full of worms.

It seemed to me that the rough branches, delineated against the bright sky, were human arms, writhing in supplication. I shut my eyes against such a picture, a reflection in the devil's mirror, to be sure.

†

THE SEASONAL LABORS CEASE, and the weeklong festival market commences outside the castle gates. Merchants from all over the duchy man over a hundred stalls, peddling an enormous variety of goods to entice the steady flow of visitors. The tavern in Argentan is swept superficially clean. Peasant women from the surrounding countryside pour into the town to prostitute themselves. The count appoints thirty sergeants, to patrol against the forces of misrule and keep our peace.

No better than a rustic simpleton or vulgar burghess, I indulge my every whim. I purchase ornate ribbons, modish flared headbands, pointed leather slippers from Spain, and a copper mirror. I buy elegant cloths, wools and silks of scarlet, so that I might more often wear the English color. Gerta scrutinizes the bolts of fabric unrolled before me, checking for defects of workmanship and dye. Bargaining with the vendors, she saves me many coins. I heap my solar with my new, superfluous treasures. Geoffrey does not say a word against my profligacy, for he loads his mistress with countless presents.

The fair means much money, to my husband and to me. We collect stall rents, highway tolls, sales taxes, and a percentage of all fees levied during the carnival by inspectors and notaries. The Angevin is in high humor over the state of his coffers.

†

OF LATE, I GIVE much thought to my appearance. Thirty-six years old, I have lost both my lover and my husband to the beguilements of other women. My beauty must be completely faded, but I would be sure before despairing. The copper mirror is my new companion. I look into it each morning when I arise and each evening when I pull the hangings shut across my empty bed.

My hair rests dense and dark, long and straight. It is not to be compared with Denise's flaming ringlets or Maud's yellow curls. Yet, their countenances lack my distinction. Mine is a refined, handsome face, even without the attractions of a crown. If only I could lie beside my beloved for one more night, and bring him joy, perhaps I could regain his affection.

When my reflection does not satisfy my vanity, I fall to my knees before the mirror of eternity. I abase myself; I wash my soul in the brilliance and glory of heaven. I look upon myself, until my whole being disintegrates and reassembles as the mirror image of the Virgin. All at once, I feel what Mother Mary feels when she comes to know her love has been taken from her; I taste what She tastes as She swallows the hidden, honeyed syrup, which the Lord Himself has steeped, and poured into the throats of those who praise Him.

The Matter of the Crown

Scroll Ten: 1139

T t followed that the empress's rival disappointed the expectations of his associates, just as he had played her hopes false. When the usurper neglected to pay tribute to his collaborators, Matilda's partisans multiplied. Soon the doors of her homeland were open to her, and she returned to the sovereignty that she had inherited. Old friends welcomed her and even her foes smoothed her way.

†

Winter

DISSATISFACTION FLOWERS IN BRITAIN, brewing among my cousin's votaries as well as his enemies. Stephen does not fulfill his promises, even those made to his brother. The bishop of Winchester assumed that he would be elevated to the archbishopric of Canterbury, yet the pretender supports the election of another. The disloyal Boulogne undermines the partiality of his most able crony, his closest associate. My count is a rogue, yet so prone to make mistakes!

As the cold days fade to colder dusks, our household at Argentan gathers near the fire in the hall. It is difficult to remember that my husband is the youngest among us. Tonight his thoughtful discourse was entirely given over to English affairs, rather than Norman ones.

Seated upon a high backed bench, Geoffrey stretched his feet toward the great stone hearth, nudging one of his lazy hounds out of the way. "His Majesty defrauds his own blood. The snake of Winchester has the competence to lead the church, and the king owes him that mark of prestige! Henry already acts as his chief advisor, the prerogative of the See of Canterbury."

Denise, perched beside him on a small stool, placed her delicate hand on his well-turned forearm. Her face swelled in the heat of the blaze. Together, they gleamed like a miniature in an illuminated romance.

I shifted about on my wooden chair, adjusting the tapestry that cushioned its angles. "He must fear to further embellish his brother's pernicious influence. The bishop is cruel and unchristian. He thieves many of the holy church's treasures, going so far as to appropriate the hand of St. James, which I myself presented to the abbey of Reading. Wolvesey, his palace at Winchester, overflows with his ill-gotten spoils."

The leman looked up into her lover's chiseled face. "A great rood stands in His Grace's cathedral. It contains a fragment of the True Cross, a piece of wood from the manger, a wisp of Mother Mary's hair, and the ankle bone of Abraham."

I chuckled at her simplicity. "From me, the rogue steals an authentic relic."

The girl smoothed her curls. "Henry of Blois gives many alms to the poor."

I flipped one of my long braids over my shoulder. "He does not pray for them, but for himself."

The Angevin snorted at our quarreling. "Winchester ought to appeal to the Heavenly Host. What of the ecclesiastical liberties, which the crown engaged to uphold?"

I exhaled. "Boulogne is not as great a nonentity as you judge him."

A page materialized, presenting a dish of stag testicles. Had Denise orchestrated the menu, to stimulate my husband's libido? As the count popped one of the dainties into his mouth, a drip of its sweet and sour sauce splashed onto his mistress' wrist. Would the hussy wipe it away with her silken sleeve?

Clever Denise lapped it up with small darts of her tongue. "The pope favored Henry of Blois."

I could not recline on my stiff seat. "The prize goes to another man."

"The new archbishop is a cipher, without fame or learning." The count waved another sticky morsel in front of his harlot. Denise squealed.

"Therefore, Stephen will manipulate him without effort." I had a yen for the delicacy, but would not entreat one.

The young Plantagenet dashed into the hall, over to the warm corner where we huddled. He lingered near the fire, listening in on the adults' discussion.

I rifled his amber hair, although he is too old now for such foolery. "It is amusing how my cousin's accomplices wrangle among themselves." Belatedly, I snatched up one of the last testicles, careful not to stain my garments. I tasted smoke and honey.

The Angevin nodded. "They compete for his patronage, but His Majesty permits himself be controlled. You may find yourself queen yet."

My son brightened, but Denise's expression blackened.

†

Summer

MY STURDY HENRY, NOW a hardy seven years old, proves likely to live to adulthood. At last, Geoffrey invests more care in the development of his supposed first-born. My husband presents the delighted youth with a full complement of equipment: a horse, a light chain link overcoat, a quilted tunic and leggings, a helmet, a lance, and a shield. Every afternoon, the Plantagenet gallops to and fro below the castle walls while the Angevin shouts instruction. Despite the daily training, the boy still handles his weighty gear with awkwardness. He regularly flounders, and is thrown to the ground.

Today, from under the shade of a large tree, I watched the count dust him off after one particularly rough tumble. A morose Hamelin stood beside me, toying sullenly with Henry's lance, sometimes dashing it at his feet, sometimes throwing it like a javelin, all the while muttering insults at imaginary Infidels.

Geoffrey removed Henry's metal headgear. "At the same time, you must learn to be aware of both your own physical dexterity and the potential of your animal. With practice, you will become more facile and comfortable in the saddle, even underneath all these trappings."

Exhausted, the sweaty child nodded glumly.

My husband allowed the sheepish boy a short respite by my side, though haranguing him all the while. "These skills are critical to a warrior earl. When blame is spread, it is always the loser who is named the culprit." The Angevin rasped in the heat.

I handed my lord a flagon of water to soothe his parched throat. "My son, perk up your ears. Athleticism and soldierly prowess are means to very great ends."

Geoffrey relinquished the drink to the Plantagenet.

Hamelin sidled up to his half-brother and yanked at his mail, so that he choked up a mouthful of liquid.

The count punched Henry's shoulder. "Are you revived? Shall you try your lance?"

My precious boy, still drained and battered, stepped forward.

I intervened. "The prince has had enough for one hot day. Perhaps Hamelin might try the weapon."

Denise's son immediately lost his scowl, and looked up breathlessly for his father's assent. Then he helped Henry peel off his protective coverings, before donning them himself.

My husband settled his illegitimate brat upon the destrier, arranging the spear under the crook of his arm. "Hold the heavy ram steady, while you charge forward. Add the force of your mount to your own vigor. Hit your target stiffly, without cowardice or dread!"

Hamelin rode away from the tree, onto the open field. The Angevin sauntered after him.

With relief and some shame, my heir watched. "I am sorry that I lacked perseverance. Someday, I will be a gallant knight."

My chest contracted, as I gazed upon him, the dream of my beloved made flesh. "You will repulse treason and glorify your grandfather's throne, both for me and for yourself. I can guess by your proud bearing and your noble manner that you will be brave in battle. You cannot help but be our champion."

Henry's eyes shone. "When I go back to Angers, I shall study the siege techniques of the Romans, in Father's great library."

I disliked our coming separation. "The Count of Anjou has collected tomes of warfare aplenty. Indeed, while we are apart, I hope that you will make great strides in your education. When you grow up to be the king, you will need to best others in disputation as often as in battle. I have hired a tutor for you, to teach you grammar, logic, rhetoric and dialectic, mathematics, and languages. You will have your own confessor, to catechize you. All this shall leaven your day with letters, so that your time is not spent merely riding and wrestling."

My mind wandered to Gervase, now age ten and a budding scholar. Perhaps he shall be our archbishop of Canterbury, when the See is mine to ordain.

The Plantagenet turned around to scrutinize Hamelin's performance as he struggled to make passes at a quintain. Aiming for the center of a hanging shield, the boy managed to strike his lance against the target, but tumbled off the saddle when a rotating sack of straw pounded against his back. Henry howled his encouragement.

I took in the boy's scarlet cheeks. "I am glad to see that you root for his success. An honorable warrior stands faithfully behind his fellows, his Church, and his realm, serving all these in truth."

I settled down on the grass, taking the son of my love onto my lap. I caressed his copper locks so that he dozed. For those few moments, my troubles evaporated.

†

LAST NIGHT, SHORTLY AFTER I had fallen asleep by Gerta's side, Geoffrey appeared in my solar. Nudging me awake, he pointed at my maid's prone form. "Your waiting woman must search for another mattress."

I shook Gerta, who complained at the disturbance, but did not arise. I slapped her with more energy so that she sat up, grumbling. Discovering the Count of Anjou, she bundled herself out of bed, then hurried out of the room, pulling the door shut behind her with a bang.

Still half conscious, I did not censure myself. "Does Denise rebuff you?" I could see my husband's face by the light of the moon.

He grimaced at my sarcasm. "Why has heaven burdened me with a harpy for a wife?"

I sighed, remembering my nakedness. "Husband, is the castle under attack? Do you need to mount the battlements with your deadly crossbow?"

The Angevin stripped off his fine linen undershirt. "Shall I treat you as you deserve, and starve or imprison you into a better humor?" Geoffrey lay down atop me, so that I felt all of his weight.

It was not worth the effort to dissuade or repel his advances, and it had been too long since I last enjoyed a man's embrace. I wrapped my arms around his muscular torso.

Despite our proximity, the count's mind was on politics. "Wily dame! I am not the pretender, easily softened by a woman."

I moved my hands down over the Angevin's taut back. For a moment, admiring his perfect form, I forgot the strife between us.

He stroked my hair, spreading its dark mass upon the pillows.

Unbidden, ugly memories of his preferences washed over me. I froze, awaiting what was to come. Would Gerta's cosmetic art be enough to conceal the bruises I was likely to sustain?

The Angevin smacked my hip. "Your rival's laxity incapacitates him; we only conquer when we stiffen our resolve."

†

FINALLY, THE EARL OF Gloucester journeys to Argentan, to devise our invasion strategy. Everyone is in a celebratory frame of mind. My spirit illuminates with the thought that I may someday find myself the mother of my people. Robert believes that we will prevail against our hated, disloyal cousin. Geoffrey counts on his future importance in Normandy. Denise gives thanks for the promise of my impending absence. The serfs, cheering the likelihood of a plentiful harvest and the restoration of their common pasturage, fall in with our mood.

The holy season gives our court an excuse to express our optimism. Yesterday, Lammas Day, Argentan's baker prepared sumptuous loaves from the first ripened grains of this year's crop. At our feast, the breads presented far outnumbered the platters of viands. I stuffed myself on the flaky, buttery wastel, the pink saunders buns flavored with sandalwood, and the noble pandemayne, marked with the Lord's cross. Trumpets heralded the arrival of the Lamb's Wool, a deliciously spicy apple cider. Our thirsty retinue emptied barrel after barrel.

I did not hold myself aloof from the ritual games. Our entire entourage circumnavigated the great hall, flourishing loaves speared with lighted candles. Children wove in and out of the flickering ring. I heard many murmur their approval of the spectacle.

Later, the castle steward snuffed the tapers, and the more abandoned dancing commenced. As the musicians struck up a carole, my ladies and gentlemen joined hands to form a circle in the center of the cavernous chamber, and began to sing, while skipping round quickly. Next to my brother, I cavorted to the jaunty, whistling tune and the raucous clapping and stamping. At long last, Robert and I collapsed upon one of the benches lining the wall.

The earl panted, his cultivated features distorted by his labored breathing. "You must excuse me. I have not danced so heavily since I courted Amabel. Women hop and leap for what they want; men wield their arms."

I fluttered my skirts, trying to cool myself. "Gloucester, are you angling for a compliment? You dance masterfully, yet with grace. You must have been the cream of the usurper's court, floating above their swill approximation of royal manners."

Robert stretched his legs, as the laughing ring romped past us. "When at his leisure, the king's various talents are most evident."

Geoffrey and Denise, flush in their beauties, whirled by us. I sighed. "If I had married him, we might have ruled wisely and well."

The earl looked me full in the face. His eyes posed a question. "Very few make any claim for His Majesty's character."

My voice quavered. "Boulogne's errors of judgment are legion. I say nothing of the pretender's honor, which he discards, only of the knight that he might have been under other circumstances."

Gloucester clenched his knuckles. "So many men of our generation fling their integrity aside."

I nodded. "Gentle knights are unhorsed. Their steeds circle the field, with empty saddles and swinging stirrups." The chirping, galloping music began to grate on my nerves. I rose to retire to the dais.

Robert accompanied me, and settled me under the canopy.

I cast a glance over the rambunctious crowd. Henry, Hamelin, and Marie darted among the groaning boards of food. Geoffrey had collapsed onto the musicians' platform; Denise sprawled on top of him. He fondled her while she mopped his brow with her sleeves.

The earl reclined his arms on the back of my chair, and fingered my veil.

The touch of his small hands made me uncomfortable, and I stiffened. "How the vanities of this world differ from the simplicities of eternity."

Gloucester massaged the base of my neck, under my flowing hair, where I had perspired during the exertions of the festival. He wound damp strands between his fingers. "Sister, now is the time to overwhelm England." My brother's grasp supported my head. "I receive numerous messages, assuring me that the country will be ours, that the throne will by yours, within six months."

"Many who back us in southern England have been vanquished by Stephen."

The music wound down. The dancers cleared the floor, making room for the gymnasts and tumblers. The sun had set, but the torches on the walls were left unlit, to cool the room. I was glad that the dim light and the acrobatic performance accorded us more privacy.

Robert's words swirled around me. "His Majesty manages badly without his cunning brother as his chief advisor. More and more discontented subjects stand ready to fight for our dynasty. On our return, we shall carry with us only one hundred and forty adherents, a small army for so enormous an enterprise. But we are awaited with great expectation, by the high and the low."

The rhythmic thumping of the tumblers enlarged itself, and became for me the drumbeat announcing the arrival of our army. "Where shall we land our expedition and find welcome and safe haven?"

Gloucester knelt down beside me, so that his mouth was level with my ear. "Our enemies watch the southern harbors day and night, to intercept us upon our arrival."

I shuddered. My beloved would be apprised of my every move, from the very moment that I appeared on the other side of the Channel.

Now my brother whispered. "We cannot travel around Land's End to Bristol, for it is too long and dangerous a trip."

The pounding beat clarified my intention. "I have a better idea, which shall blindside them."

†

Fall

WE CAME ASHORE AT Portsmouth. I had not reckoned upon the banality of our homecoming. No crowds materialized to toss flowers or otherwise formalize my disembarkation; no multitude of glittering knights appeared to escort us to a place of security. With dispatch, we betook ourselves to Arundel Castle, Adeliza's dower gift from my father. My dear friend unlocked her doors to us, in shock as much as in support, for I had not wanted to compromise her, or risk refusal, by requesting hospitality in advance. Immediately, Robert and twelve of his men repaired to Bristol along rustic and unused byways. I stayed put at Arundel with Amabel of Gloucester and the rest of our excursion force.

Adeliza is remarried now, to William of Aubigny, Earl of Sussex, an intransigent promoter of the Count of Boulogne. Well-contented, the dowager cleaves to a knight worthy of her admiration. I notice her blushes, as she stands by the side of her virile, patrician husband. The earl's gray hair distinguishes him, while his full mouth and beaked nose suggest that the queen has been introduced to the pleasures that she once chastised.

Today, buffeted by a strong wind, we stood upon the battlements of their keep, searching for any signs of the pretender's auxiliaries. Chivalrous William commended his wife: "His Majesty does me a great service, wedding me to my fair and royal lady. Her superiority, which is yet without inflated grandeur, her noble speech, her agreeable company, the delight her sweet expressions bring me—all these I owe to your cousin."

I gazed out upon the countryside of Sussex, ablaze in the colors of the season. "Well should you praise and value her pure heart."

Antsy, Amabel adjusted the veil framing her widely spaced, cornflower blue eyes. "The dowager's modesty merits our approbation."

My friend's white cheeks mottled with pink. "I reject reverential regard, now that I am no longer England's queen." She stretched out her hand for Aubigny. "King Stephen also grants me a boon. Heaven blesses my new family, my husband and son."

I wondered at the handsome pair: Adeliza, wrapped in a light green wool mantle trimmed in fox fur, and William, gathered up in a darker green surcoat. Draped in her newly found happiness, the queen seemed remote. Did I still matter to her? "Beware the patronage of the usurper. All his promises are made in bad faith."

Amabel chewed her bottom lip. "Fortune smiles on those who sit atop of her revolving wheel, wallowing in their success. But she grows disgusted with them at last, sets it to spin, and knocks them off."

The earl slammed his palm down upon the rough wall of his ramparts. "I am His Majesty's satellite. My wife offers refuge to you dissidents, but I do not countenance her generosity. I earnestly desire to wish you 'God speed.'"

†

UNEXPECTEDLY, MY PERFIDIOUS LOVER encircles the fortress of Arundel. Demanding my surrender, he plants a large army of well-seasoned soldiers outside Aubigny's walls.

From the small window of my solar, I often catch a glimpse of his red hair beneath his chain mail coif. My stomach churns. I yearn to signal to him, even to prostrate myself before him. If he would greet me with kisses, I could submit to some compromise. I essay to stay out of sight, so that he does not have the satisfaction of seeing my liberty restrained by his might. Yet, again and again, I am drawn to his figure.

This afternoon, I loitered by the opening, mesmerized by his desultory movements.

The dowager entered my chamber, sitting down upon one of my wardrobe trunks. Her face displayed none of its usual serenity. "Empress, royal messengers urge your capitulation."

I dragged my gaze back inside. "Two years ago, the count and I met in amity. Does he not transmit to me some token of his regard, some private communication?"

Adeliza startled. "You cannot still worship your enemy?"

I thought of her potent earl. "Out of love he besets me, ignoring the greater threat at Bristol."

My friend shook her head. "Matilda, you pose a bigger danger to him than the Earl of Gloucester does."

"The castle at Bristol is impregnable. Some number of his counselors surely are sagacious enough to perceive the strategic importance of winning it. Under the sway of his passion, the pretender jettisons their foresight." If I could not convince myself of my cousin's devotion, how should I persuade Adeliza, or Stephen himself?

The queen argued carefully. "We stand such a small garrison here, despite the addition of your brother's unit. As of yet, His Majesty declines to bombard our tower, although he knows that it is not equal to the force that he brings to bear upon it. We, you, must come to terms with him. The king grants you safe conduct, back to Robert's custody."

In frustration, I kicked at my skirts. "Why do you speak for my despised rival, whom you never respected in the past?"

"I cannot defy the crown. I cannot sacrifice Arundel." Adeliza sank to her knees on the rushes. "Empress, I beg this favor of you."

I towered above her delicate form. "I return to England—I return home—to guarantee that King Henry's will be done."

The dowager's eyes filled with tears. "His Majesty swears to me that knights of high repute will guide you safely to your brother."

With chagrin, I understood that my lover's word of honor was more credible when it was directed to my father's widow than to me. "Do you deny our confidence in one another?"

The queen flushed, weeping. "Matilda, you do intrude upon me. I succor you, and His Majesty graciously ignores my treason, in return for my husband's unwavering allegiance."

"Against my claims!" I did not permit her to rise, but stalked back toward the aperture in the wall.

Without my leave, she did not presume to quit the floor. Her tone was wistful. "You weigh me a fickle comrade, another who plays you false."

I picked out the pretender, surrounded by his battalion, laughing uproariously at some joke. "Someday soon, you will no longer have to degrade yourself before the Count of Boulogne. I will sit upon the English throne, and he will fret in misery. He will come to know what it is to be abandoned."

†

STEWING, FURIOUS, I BALANCED atop my fidgety warhorse. Arundel's massive winch creaked round. The drawbridge slowly lowered over the moat, to the stone ramp on the far side of the water. Adeliza and William stood behind me in their outermost ward, ensuring that I decamped their custody. I could feel their relief between my shoulder blades.

Erect in the saddle, I spurred my horse forward, under the portcullis and onto the wooden planks. Traversing the bridge, Amabel rode beside me. The usurper and his mounted retinue came into focus. Henry of Winchester, appointed to guide us to Robert, sat adjacent to the false king.

My sister-in-law smoothed her gloves down over her wrists, although there were no wrinkles in the leathers. "We were wrong to suppose that His Majesty no longer confides in his bishop."

On the far side of the moat, we inched up the stone incline, reining in several paces from my rival and his entourage.

His Grace heaved himself off his horse and stepped slowly forward, to give me his ritual kiss of protection. I pulled off my gauntlet and extended my arm downward, stretching and elongating my fingers. Henry, surely aggravated to find that I did not dismount, and greet him as I would a spiritual father, pressed his rough lips against the back of my hand, signaling his promise to safeguard me to Gloucester's care. As soon as I dared, I drew on my glove. Relieved to be going home, Amabel smiled down upon the bishop, and received a much more distinguished ceremonial buss.

The Count of Boulogne's expression was sober. "Empress, let us parley alone, before I turn you over to the keeping of your contingent."

My breath caught in my throat. I forbore to assent.

We trotted some distance away. Impetuously, I yearned to gallop off with him, out into the wide world, but he came to a halt still within sight of our retainers.

His eyes matched the color of the sky on a cloudy day. "Those who care for us both do not know where to pledge their troth."

My emotion ran high; I dispensed with politeness. "I do not want the tribute of buffoons, but of honest men who hail their rightful queen. You were once my first vassal. Damn your apostasy!"

My cousin began to unfasten a tangled ribbon on the embellished mane of his stallion. He frowned, either at the complicated knot, or at my ill humor. "Do not lambaste me, Matilda!" The pretender raised his gaze to mine. For a moment, there was only silence between us. He exhaled, and shrugged his shoulders. "You should exalt me; in your arms, I am the master of joy."

I scoffed aloud, some guttural noise that was unintelligible, even to me.

"Or dread me, then; in the throes of combat, I am the master of pain."

I could have ripped off my cloak, baring myself. In the same moment, I burned to plunge a dagger into his corrupt heart. "What of our two sons? Henry Plantagenet begins his own military training. Would you have him grow to adulthood to ride against you on the field?"

Annoyed, the Count of Boulogne flounced his amber hair, long again, over his shoulders. "I have been elected, anointed, confirmed. Why do my subjects heinously desert me, or dare to raise their swords against me? By Christ, I will never be a fallen king!"

I glanced back at the restless swarm of courtiers, impatiently awaiting the end of our conference. "There are many who rally in my defense."

Regaining his composure, Stephen grinned. "The Lord in His mercy suffuses me with enough energy to overcome every trial."

His inflated self-regard sickened me. "Let heaven confound you with doubt and lamentation."

The pretender finished straightening his animal's plumage. "I have it on good authority that the Almighty has installed me upon the English throne. Who would presume to question the ways of the Lord? Who would dare to subvert the will of heaven?"

I clenched my fist, pulling the mane of my mount, which sidestepped, so that my lover's legs and my own were pinned together between our horses' flanks. I looked into his face, and poured out all my hate. "You are a false, debased monarch, tainted by wicked debauchery and stolen glory. Your crown is steeped in wanton vice and bloated with ungrateful pride. The Holy Mother is vexed to anger against your realm. Confusion and sorrow torment Britain. But I will wash England clean. Your vile sins, against my father, against me, against our sons, shall be expunged."

Engulfed by an immense hunger for him and a prodigious ire, I spun my destrier around and cantered back toward the keep.

†

WE TRAVERSE THE BISHOP'S diocese, and have stopped to rest at Wolvesey, his sumptuous palace in Winchester.

My grandiose accommodations stagger me; domestic luxury usually requires a woman's hand. Gerta whistles at the stately, brown silk bed hangings, the cushioned niches below the windows, and the rich, cultivated tapestries decorating each wall. Wolvesey is clearly a house of earthly, not spiritual, plenty.

After bathing, and some calculation, I dressed myself in a crimson silk bliaut and a gray corsage stitched with a honeycomb pattern of silver fancywork. My pointed sleeves dripped all the way to the hem of my skirt. My maid wound silver ribbons into my hair, left hanging down my back.

At supper, I inspected His Grace's nondescript, but displeasing visage, comparing it with his brother's elegant symmetries. In Henry's face I see my cousin transformed into a man who no longer holds any appeal. Lifeless orange strands replace rich russet tresses. A permanently astringent expression twists fine lips. Dark sacks beneath comely gray eyes rob them of all of their magnetism.

Repelled, I stared none the less at a pink rash that rose from the collar of his tunic. He should know to refrain from scratching until the sun had set, and then to spit three times upon his bloody fingers. Winchester was no friend to me; I would not advise him.

And yet, given our close proximity, I was forced to converse with him at length. Amabel flirted assiduously with some minor baron, and did not pay any attention to our remarks.

Enjoying a joint of meat, glistening in its own grease, His Grace discoursed upon the sin of gluttony. "It was an idle, nosy woman, ravenous of stomach, who ate the apple, and destroyed Eden."

I pressed my lips together, to hold back a vindictive retort. Despite the appetizing smell of the roast, my hunger evaporated.

I smothered my intense dislike, in an attempt to exhume the bishop's motivations. "So, you are still Boulogne's man?"

"The king lends me his ear, especially when my propositions fall in with his inclinations. I counsel him to permit your safe passage to your brother, thereby containing your revolution in one place. It does not suit us to allow Arundel to function as a second center of disaffection." His Grace took a deep swallow of wine from an excessively ornate goblet.

Verily, his intelligence was to my rival's credit. "Sussex is loyal to the pretender."

The bishop slowly lowered his cup. "I caution His Majesty to push all the rebels as far as possible from London." He slid the vessel toward me, presumably so that I should sample his fine vintage.

I wished to refuse; I would not soil my mouth with his spittle. But the queen cannot dispense with courtesies such as these. I wafted the drink under my nose; the alcohol was heavily spiced. Sipping as small a drop as I could, I tasted celery seed, cumin, mint, clove, cardamom, and ginger. I smothered back a laugh; this recipe was the usual remedy for flatulence. "Conferring freely with Gloucester, I will be at liberty to ferment trouble."

Henry inclined his face toward me, and lowered his tone. "Backed by the earl's battalions, Empress Matilda might launch a serious challenge to Stephen's royal authority. New recruits will surely flock to her party."

Did he speak of himself? "Many such are already making themselves known to Robert."

His Grace snorted softly. "I myself recently waylaid Gloucester on a little known road, a mere footpath, in a tiny hamlet outside Bristol. We had much talk together."

I made no response to the usurper's old watchdog, consumed with my own dilemma. Could I ever trust such a schemer? Did the bishop consider that it might be to his greater profit to incarcerate or to assassinate me?

Drenched with a cold fear, I rose to return to my chamber. Gerta and Amabel also stood up, so that we could pass back together to our solars, in the far reaches of the palace. None of us would wander alone in the dark, among so many who wished us ill.

Winchester made no remark upon our departure, for his attention had turned to a kitchen servant, a young, pretty boy only a few years older than the Plantagenet. The page's arm trembled under the heavy weight of a carved silver flagon, molded in the shape of toad. The bishop leered, undoubtedly plotting some heretical obscenity; his night would not be spent in pious supplication. No doubt, he considers his sins of the flesh, his infamous effeminacy, to be less criminal than his brother's adulterous fornication.

Undressing me quickly, Gerta folded herself into the bed and immediately dozed. Yet sleep would not release me. I have been awake all the night, recording my chronicle, scratching out my history.

I embark on a pilgrimage, to my destiny! Faith, ambition, and devotion send me onward. I quest for what will complete me. The Holy Mother promises to grant me the enlightenment of paradise, but for now I gaze into the abyss of war, and plumb the well of passion. As dawn breaks over the city, I pray to the Virgin to inherit true things: a true life, a true path, a true love, and a true mercy. Will I discover them to be irreconcilable?

The Matter of the Crown

Scroll Eleven: 1140

T he empress's stealthy reappearance convulsed Britain, impelling further chaos, savagery, and treachery. Matilda sat on a throne in the heart of her realm, and received the devotion of worthy subjects, yet the civil war did not subside. Englishmen persisted in their designs against their neighbors, and contested the imposition of royal authority. Calculating the cost of so much ungodliness, the new queen made overtures to her most despised rival. But he refused to seek tranquility, for he could not comprehend that the crown they disputed was the crown of woe.

†

Winter

I HOLD COURT AT Gloucester Castle, the favored stronghold of the first Norman kings, my grandfather, William I Conqueror, and my uncle,

William II Rufus. Gloucester befits me more than Bristol keep, the seat of my brother's earldom. Here, the village elders remember with respect the sovereign solemnities and royal display. This is all to the good, but I assume my throne without waiting for permission from any man, old or young, archbishop or burgher, brother or cousin.

Yesterday, in this keep's great hall, generously draped with banners and flooded with tapers, noblemen, freemen, and priests paid homage to me as their Lady of the English, rightful heir to my father's kingdom. Every knight present pledged his fealty and swore to be my liegeman, against all others. I clasped each vassal to my breast, demanding his obedience and extending my protection in return for his service. Likewise, the local citizenry and clerics knelt to me, offering up their fidelity. From the highest to the lowest, all persons present kissed my hand. Greedy for such ceremonies, I no longer wince at unwashed bodies and stinking mouths.

After the vows, I addressed the assembled, jostling throng of magnates, petty landholders, townsfolk, and divines. "The district of Gloucester, as far west as Wales, is the first to belong to me. I shall not soon forget such friendship." Disdaining female grace, I loudly regaled the crowd, adopting Henry I's imposing demeanor.

Flushed with gratification, I summoned a minstrel, who recited a poem to the Lion's memory. But, in the silence that followed the oration, my ears picked out some grumbling.

One voice called out. "Have you come among us to revive the spirit of a tyrant?" The faces surrounding me registered surprise and confusion at this challenge.

Robert stepped forward, but it was my place to suppress such insolence. I shouted my reply, not attempting to hide my anger. "With purpose, I abandon my womanly modesty. It is not fitting that your queen should quail. In these dangerous times, my valor and strength will avail you well."

The earl interjected. "Do not be amazed at her majestic grandeur! Do not think of her as a wife, daughter, sister, or mother. She is our right, our might, and our salvation."

The murmuring in the hall quieted. Many persons turned their attention to the pages bearing carafes of hot, seasoned cider.

†

I LIBERALLY DISTRIBUTE WHATEVER honors I can reasonably be thought to control. But there are not yet enough spoils to endow my entire entourage. I have naught to reward FitzCount's early good faith and his most recent feats on my behalf.

Currently, Brian serves as castellan of Wallingford Castle, strategically important on the route from London to Oxford and the West Country. With his loyal garrison, he has already rebuffed one ill-managed assault from the Count of Boulogne, safeguarding the tower, and wounding, killing, or imprisoning every one of the usurper's soldiers. My cousin will never subdue the west while Wallingford remains outside his dominion.

Other, less appealing knights swagger around my baileys and ramparts, boasting, spitting, and spouting obscenities, drunk on the very idea of rebellion. To my shame, I overlook their audacity and vice. In this great enterprise, I cannot dispense with these sinners; they eat heartily of my suppers and swear to despoil in my name.

I pray to the Virgin that the good deeds of my most able warriors will atone for the evil handiwork of the others. I rely upon my men of Christian spirit, by whose activities I need never be disgraced.

†

Spring

GLOUCESTER CASTLE POSSESSES A lovely, walled garden, situated next to its chapel. The warming sun sprinkles it with pale primroses and showy bloodroot, sturdy purple hyacinths and large, pink peonies, airy as clouds. It is a great pleasure to recline upon a stone bench between the flowerbeds, breathing in their fresh aroma. Cloistered, saturated with beauty, my spirit convalesces. I garner strength from the earth's blessings.

I permit my mind to wander, mesmerized by the sprouting colewort and ragwort, the greens that excite passion. Hypnotized by the erupting, blooming flora, I am nothing but a simple girl, dreaming of carnal oblivion. Perhaps Gerta should sow psyllium, whose seeds bring on frigidity, the remedy for my affliction.

Yesterday, FitzCount disturbed my private meditations. "Empress, despite the boldness of my interruption, the esteem in which I hold you makes me timid, so great is your distinction." Brian sounded winded, as if he had run a great distance.

"What boon do you seek, sir? I wish that I had manors and abbeys aplenty, to testify to duty such as yours." I balanced the heavy head of a peony in my hand, offering it to him, but misjudged the distance between us. Its delicate mass fell on the ground.

FitzCount gathered it up, then buried his nose in the wisps of its petals. He raised steady eyes to mine. "None shall mow you down. Dishonor to you or to me is an impossibility."

Could I discourage him from some rash avowal? "You are one of my most valued allies. The jongleur's epics will burst with your faithful triumphs."

"Will my deeds herald my message?" Brian's boyish face, strong and pure, crippled with distress.

I thought of my own sleepless nights and troubled dreams. I sighed. "You have my permission to speak, if you will."

FitzCount shuffled side to side, trampling a few blossoms. "I worship a perfect specimen of heaven's creation."

Must the sap make such an ado? I tried to head him off. "Your wife is a saintly creature."

Brian stood still. "She is not the flower that blooms in paradise."

I shook my head, dislodging my veil. "I am a dark lady, lacking a sweet heart."

"Do you despise me because I am illegitimate?"

Did he not consider my royal majesty to be a bar between us? Did he have no inkling of my relationship with the Count of Boulogne? "You are the complete lover, obtuse to everything but your own torments."

Disordered, the knight sank down, crushing more plants under his knees. "I intrude upon you only to throw myself at your feet, to offer my soul unto you. Strife storms around us, yet no adversity can divide me from you."

I paused, discomfited. "I admire your courtliness, but I cannot return your noble sentiments. I know that my rejection is abuse to you, who has been one of my most loyal acolytes."

Rising upright, Brian dashed off my headdress, uncovering my hair. Grief gutted his expression. "God is my witness, the sight of you is my only happiness. I ask nothing of you, or of your possessions, but that you retain me as your minion. I would be in bondage to you, all of my life."

†

Summer

DESPITE THE SEASON, THE English landscape displays no new vegetation or signs of domestication. Crops and flocks, systematically eradicated by castle garrisons so that enemy marauders will not be able to sustain themselves, are ravaged a second time by besiegers ensuring that blockaded communities cannot forage for new supplies. Roving bands of outlaws strip away any thing that remains. Our once proud wheat and corn, our sweet milk and honey—all are deflowered.

The grand keeps of the kingdom now serve merely as focal points of intemperate violence, from within and without. The good peace that England enjoyed under my father is vanquished. Britain, formerly the bed of tranquility and holiness, becomes the couch of misery and blasphemy.

Even our money is no longer sacred. Bandits pass counterfeit coins. The Count of Boulogne debases the currency to extend the life of his dwindling treasury, ordering the weight of the penny reduced from the standard of King Henry's time. My treasonous cousin liquidates the royal regalia, bequeathed to history by my predecessors. He openly puts property from the royal demesne up for sale, including churches and abbeys. It is everywhere known that the pretender scrounges for funds to wage his war in defense of his unlawful coup.

In retaliation, money is struck in my name, both at new mints that we establish at Cardiff, Wareham, and Oxford, and at the contested royal mint in Bristol. I have ordered that the silver used for my pennies be only of the best quality and unvarying in thickness. My image, in profile, fills up one side of each coin. The obverse is a Holy Cross, and reads "Empress."

My faith runs strong now, for heaven conspires to punish my beloved foe. Last night, a miraculous eclipse foretold the imminent collapse of his impious ambitions. The darkened sky portended my rival's damnation. May the Lord preserve the worthy, and hold us back from the apocalypse.

†

WE ENDURE UNREMITTING CIVIL strife. My friends supposed that six months of insurrection would see me anointed in Westminster Abbey. Instead, it has been a year of anarchy. Our military strategy, to hurry Stephen here and there in response to our various uprisings, siphons his strength, but does not crush him. His traveling battalions are usually superior to any local gathering of rebel forces. If he sometimes, through stupidity or slothfulness, does not triumph over our schemes, I have very little to show for his failures.

Winchester writes to me in the name of peace, eager to shape events. Will I consider coming to terms with my cousin, and free England from oppression? Robert and I agree to meet with the insufferable Maud, under Henry's aegis.

†

YESTERDAY, I FOUND MYSELF face to face with the Countess of Boulogne, just returned from France for the betrothal of her twelve-year-old Eustace to Constance, sister of the king of the French. Maud's blonde hair is grayer than it was nine years ago, but her lips turn down as much as they ever did. I found it difficult not to stare at her presumptuous pearl diadem, fastening her veil in place. I wore a circlet of rubies, more valuable than her pearls, but fewer in number. It matched my bliaut of red silk, worn under a white silk jacket embroidered all over with my father's golden lions. Maud's garish yellow bliaut was in keeping with her usual ostentation, and her irksome preference for England's second royal color.

Without any formal preliminaries, the false queen began to prate. "My son forms a wise alliance with the Franks, securing our empire in Normandy against the Angevins. In this regard, Louis VII is our natural friend; he also seeks to quell your husband's mutiny on the Continent."

I rarely thought of Geoffrey. "The Count of Boulogne's power on this side of the Channel is quite tenuous."

The harlot sucked in her breath. "Louis stands in favor of King Stephen's reign and of Eustace's future majesty. Once again, he confers the duchy of Normandy upon our boy, receiving homage for it. He does not measure the Countess of Anjou to be a serious threat to our royal position."

How dare that ninny boost herself above me! Sighing, I essayed to scrub my aggravation from my tone. "The Lord debases those who exalt themselves above their proper sphere, casting down many who felt sure of His love."

Maud smirked, adjusting her tiara. She rotated her neck right and left, to stretch out some kink, and smoothed her costume over her bosom. "His Majesty's right to the throne is not in doubt. We have proved it in combat. With the exception of the Earl of Gloucester, your military leaders are all barons of the second rank."

I itched to slap the strumpet, but held my arms stiffly at my side. "I appeal to the judgment of heaven. Christ's harmony will ring out, on England and Normandy both."

Here the bishop clapped his beringed hands. "His Holiness the pope prays for nothing more and nothing less than a cessation of the hostilities between your two camps."

Maud cast a disparaging glance over His Grace. Despite his decadent vestments, he appeared shriveled next to his sensual sister-in-law. "What are your motives, Winchester?" Henry stood silent, but the countess would have an answer. "Before which one of us do you prefer to humble yourself?"

The bishop smiled thinly. "Two queens must not palaver here in vain."

The bitch grimaced at his diplomacy; I frowned at the equation of our status. Neither one of us was gratified to be the other's double.

Maud kicked at her skirts, poised for attack. "There shall be no concord until you and yours are expelled from our realm."

I clamped my lips shut and strode from the room, refusing to acknowledge her gall.

†

Fall

UNRESIGNED, WINCHESTER SAILED TO France, to discuss with King Louis conditions in Normandy under which Stephen and I might reach some agreement. Returning to Britain, His Grace journeyed back to my court at Gloucester to present the possible terms of a détente.

After much prayer, I give my sanction to these proposals in which the usurper remains on the throne for his lifetime, to be succeeded by Henry Plantagenet, grandson of King Henry I. In the meantime, I am to rule Normandy, as regent for my son. The pretender is to be compensated for the duchy. The wedding of Eustace and Constance is to be called off. In all this, there is enough for me, for my heir, and for the Count of Boulogne. Can I persuade my brother of the validity of my decision?

I surmise that Maud and Geoffrey will find this plan unpalatable. But who are they to turn the tide of history?

†

I FOUND ROBERT IN the outer ward of Gloucester keep, welcoming a clutch of actors and settling upon the fees that would be paid for the presentation of *The Prophecy of Merlin*. The assorted performers, oddly dressed in cast-off theatrical garments, gestured grandly to their tattered wagon. The earl turned over a small pile of copper, before escorting me out of the public courtyard.

We climbed a narrow stone staircase to the battlements that overlook the main gate to the castle. All was secure. The drawbridge had been lowered to admit the troupe and once again raised safely. The moat appeared tranquil, although it admitted a sharp aroma of household waste. I noticed a rusty shield floating past, most likely dropped by a careless knave tussling in jest with his fellows along the crenellated walkway.

"Brother, I have consulted my heart and the Virgin. I accept what is tendered."

Gloucester's expression did not change, but his eyes lost some of their gentleness. "Why do you so willingly abdicate what we have fought and died for?"

I clutched at my mantle in the chilly air. "We have struggled, not only for me, but for my son. This proposition guarantees that the Plantagenet shall rule our father's empire entire, as well as Anjou. And I shall reign over Normandy in the meantime. To have wrested some control away from the traitors will be sufficient to sate my revenge. Indeed, retribution is not my primary motivation."

Robert massaged his feminine chin. "Geoffrey's seed inherits everything, including the duchy that he has always coveted."

I nestled further into my garments. "My husband will not be easy to appease. I am concerned that he will interfere with my regulation of Normandy. And he does not love Henry so very greatly."

The earl placed his arm around my shoulders, to warm me. "Why should the Angevin not rejoice in the future magnificence of his line?"

I raised my face, reddening. "He suspects that the Plantagenet is not his own son."

Gloucester exposed his small, white teeth. "How dare he…" His voice trailed off. "Do you mean to say…?" He glanced about him, but we were entirely alone upon a long stretch of parapet.

Flushing deeply, I admitted it. "Henry is Stephen's child, our second boy. The first has been raised as an orphan, within the Church."

My brother ceased to embrace me, and moved some distance away. "Ah. Then it is certain that the pretender will submit to the bishop's instructions, which now appear none too severe. At His Majesty's death, the crown reverts to his own son, whose blood unites every claim to the realm. There is a logic to it, greater than any objection that I might raise."

"The logic must rest a secret."

†

THIS EVENING, IN THE great hall of the fortress, the itinerant players put on their poem, supposedly the lost manuscript of a hermitic sage, found recently on the Cornish coast, and purportedly his prophetic vision of our civil war. Draining my liquor, I tried to suspend disbelief, but it was not so simple to look beyond the greasy skin, open sores, and hobbled gait of some of the troubadours.

The man in the role of the king of the Britons had only one eye, but his voice boomed out his verse.

> *I crouched upon the misty shore of an evaporated lake, and two dragons, one of which was white, the other red, appeared, stumbling from their cliffside caves. Staggering toward one another, they began to claw and bite and expel fire from their snouts. The red dragon had the greater strength, and the other took flight above my head. Then, roaring out its confusion and ire, the white dragon descended to recommence the terrible strife, this time forcing the red dragon to retreat.*

This narrative caught my attention. At first blush, I thought myself the royal red dragon, but I must be the white, and my amber-haired cousin the red.

The king's monologue unspooled.

> *In its ascendancy, the wings of the white dragon beat so furiously that the jagged cliffs convulsed, tumbling down into the dry lakebed. Quaking thunder cracked open the sky, and scarlet drops of blood showered down so furiously that the lake began to refill itself crimson.*
>
> *The red dragon, spent, slept through these plagues, but now awakened and began to terrorize the kingdom, razing what man had built and what*

the Lord had given, maiming himself in the process. And so, let us give
Praise, for the kingdom of the white dragon shall be resurrected, and the
red dragon shall soon be bound in chains.

The actor is no dimwit of a jester. If the red dragon had subdued the
white, I would have commanded Brian to smash the troupe's dilapidated
cart with his battle-axe. Given the white dragon's victory, I overload the
performers with presents.

†

THIS MORNING, THE DRAWBRIDGE of Gloucester Castle was let down to
admit a monk who claimed that he had urgent, private words for the
empress's ears alone. In Gerta's presence, I welcomed the man to my
solar, but he refused to deliver his message with my maid in attendance.
I looked at his tonsure, a white and pasty crown atop his bushy head. It
did not seem to have been recently shorn.

Dismissing the curious woman, I stood before him, holding
my breath.

"I have memorized a letter, my lady, which I beg leave to recite to
you." Holding himself erect, he commenced:

Still cherished one, what is the point of trying to keep dry in a
tempestuous storm? I must refuse the terms to which you have given
your accord. Those from whom I take advice continue to believe that
war assures my eventual and complete subjugation of your forces and
aspirations. Certainly, they speak to their own ends; my earls all have
fiefs and honors to gain and my queen has her son's patrimony to protect.

But I cannot abandon her love; she cleaves to me in faith. My amorous
desires are annihilated before her constancy, blessed by the Church. She
is no fool, understanding well enough her husband's failings. She finds
me changed from the chivalrous hero I once was. I must struggle now
to charm her again. I must empty my mind of other distractions. I need
her beauty, her virtue, and, above all, her intelligence. I need her mercy,
whatever it costs England.

The Matter of the Crown

Scroll Twelve: 1141

*W*rongly *supposing herself to be the Lord's anointed, the wretched princess charged into battle, commandeering the four horsemen of the apocalypse: conquest, war, famine, and death. Overrun, the empress's antagonist was deposed from his throne, but their contested kingdom sank further into perdition. In celebration, Matilda trusted her ardor to revive a golden age, and call forth the adulation of her people. Adorning herself in the soiled magnificence of her bliss, she was deaf to the voices of complaint and the spirit of contradiction.*

†

Winter

COLD DRIFTS OF SNOW and opalescent icicles shroud the landscape. We are shut up in Gloucester Castle, where the smoke and ashes of perpetual hearth fires and the excess disorder perpetrated by boredom pollute our solars.

Yet the news of another blow to the pretender gladdens our hearts. Our ally, Ranulf Earl of Chester, seizes Lincoln Castle, held for the crown. Ranulf, wed to my brother's daughter, had so far declined to unite his cause with ours; Geoffrey's territorial ambitions continually threaten his Norman holdings. But the ill-defended fortress tempted him to rebellion against the usurper.

Chester sent my niece to call upon the wife of the castellan of Lincoln keep. When its garrison filed outside to exercise the horses, he approached, as if to safeguard his lady's departure. Wearing no armor, and accompanied by only a small entourage of four men-at-arms, the earl did not excite suspicion. Once inside the castle, he and his band snatched up pieces of wood, bars of metal, anything that might be used as a weapon, and attacked what knights remained in the tower, driving them out of its gates. Supplementary troops faithful to him soon poured into the stronghold from the neighboring vicinity, and Lincoln was his.

Local bishops and burghers appealed to the Count of Boulogne. Mustering a regiment from London, my cousin surrounded the citadel. With sly dispatch, Ranulf fled back to Chesire, where he raises another battalion from among his Welsh allies. This newly assembled unit shall besiege the besiegers.

Chester urges Robert to be a part of the scheme to rescue my niece, left behind in Lincoln keep. In return, Ranulf agrees to pay me homage.

Gloucester and I rejoice, determined to make the liberation of his daughter the catalyst for an intensified military offensive. Stephen's callous refusal to cede his throne to the Plantagenet leaves me little choice but to escalate the hostilities, bringing matters to a conclusion on the field. Our righteousness guarantees us victory by ordeal.

†

THROUGH THE BITTER WEATHER, we march north to Lincoln, to combine our forces with Chester's. Waging war, I don a soldier's trappings. A padded wool gambeson, fashioned to fit my frame, keeps me warm.

However, the constant weight of my chain mail hauberk, although cut down to my size, gives me an ache in my neck and shoulders that will not subside. My gauntlets are my brother's; his hands are so small that they fit properly without any alteration. I wear my golden spurs and the red and silver sword with which Geoffrey dubbed me a knight. Altogether, I no longer resemble my lover's pliant mistress, but the rival who denies and thwarts his ambition.

✝

TODAY MARKS THE FESTIVAL of the Purification of the Virgin. Our battalions are mustered near the city of Lincoln; in a short while we will likely clash with the pretender's army, and, at long last, overthrow his pretensions. I see in this coincidence such an omen of the Holy Mother's beneficence and grace! At our dawn Mass, brightly burning consecrated candles symbolized the eternal transcendence of Her son, and the future marvel of mine. I pray equally for the strength to uphold Her celestial dignity and my own worldly honor.

✝

WE APPROACHED THE RIVER Witham. Our troops massed on its bank, awaiting the signal to charge. The narrow bridge was of no use to us, for Stephen's archers, posted on the far side, would have wiped us out as we funneled through it. We needed to ford the swollen waters.

I did not despair at the roaring current that coursed between us and our fate. Hoarsely, I shouted. "Once across the barrier, there will be no returning! We conquer the traitors, or die in the attempt!"

Inspired by my cry, Robert and Ranulf plunged their destriers into the churning river. Without pause, all of our mounted knights followed them across. Those in the forefront, already emerged, began to engage the enemy, and handily dispensed with their relatively sparse numbers.

In the rear, I traversed the channel. My horse's courage steadied my nerves. I did not draw my legs up, out of the frigid waves.

Wet through, but otherwise unimpaired, our regiments regrouped and surveyed the scene. Southwest of the walled town, downhill from

Lincoln Castle, the usurper's forces littered the plain. The minstrels had overstated the size of Boulogne's legions. My noble retinue began to murmur among themselves, gladdened by the sight of so few foes. The barons started to smile and preen.

As I prepared to rouse them to even greater assurance, the Earl of Chester smoothed his overgrown moustaches and rumbled his thanks. "I am grateful to you, Empress, for abetting me in my private quarrel with the king. You must allow me to be the first to hack a route through the center of his squadrons. Follow my lead! I feel it strong within me that His Majesty will be routed. Success will be mine!"

I opened my lips, but Gloucester responded to Ranulf's pretension. "I understand that you should desire the honor of being foremost among us. We do not question your valor, which is justly praised. But I am also awash in personal bile, anxious to free my daughter, ready to risk any hurt. If it were merely a question of rank, I should be at the head of our militia. But, at this moment of momentous endeavor, let us think of more than our own hatreds and our own reputations. As we emancipate one castle, we deliver all of the empire from the cretinous snake who stole my father's crown and broke his holy oaths to my family. I lay at Stephen's feet the death of thousands of our subjects and the destruction of the tranquility that once bathed England and Normandy."

I could finally assert myself among my barons. "When I am restored to my throne, I shall redress both of your grievances. For today, we will have two lines on the vanguard, one conducted by each of my daring earls."

I swiveled in my saddle. I could see the empty faces of my common soldiers. I maneuvered my steed atop a small outcropping, and projected my voice, so that my words rang out above their heads. "Be led by your swords! Depend upon your stout hearts and upon the protection of the Virgin. She will transform us into the harbingers of Her justice, the bringers of Her punishment. Lincoln will not be able to withstand Mother Mary! Fighting my battle, you may each take for yourselves a piece of holy glory. If you are united now, and wish to execute the divine will that I reign as your sovereign, lift up your weapons to heaven!"

A thunderous cheer rang over me. My men thrust their lances, bows, and axes into the air. Some swore that they would never succumb. Others commenced a chant: "Long live the queen!"

Robert grinned, and turned his destrier to guide the mounted line of attack. Ranulf, grim, vaulted off his horse, to command the infantry line; Brian FitzCount stood ready to follow him. Chester's rough Welsh pagans arranged themselves to one side, to operate as our flank.

I thrilled to the blast of our trumpets. Suddenly, we were all on the move, rushing to meet my cousin's battalions upon the plain. We gathered speed, but our formation remained orderly. The pounding of hooves overwhelmed me; the earth quaked beneath our rampage. Dislodged clumps of snow and mud flew up into the air. I rode in a position of safety, toward the back of my brother's troops, and closely hemmed in by my personal entourage. Yet I felt in the thick of it. Drenched with sweat, my heart thumping, I concentrated my energy on maintaining my balance as I galloped down the inclined ground.

Approaching our destination, I glimpsed my beloved, my despised knight-errant. He was swathed in armor, but his copper hair was exposed beneath his golden crown. He stood beside the royal standard, surrounded by guards, also on foot. He did not wince at the sight of my invading horde. The English flag flapped over him, sometimes obscuring him, sometimes unfurling behind him.

My escort drove me away from the Count of Boulogne, and likewise held me off from the clash between Robert's unit and the enemy cavalry. Gloucester soon dispersed them; they retreated rapidly, almost at the sight of our greater might. At the same time, our Welshmen careened into the fray, scattering many of our foes, who then began to retreat, turning their backs on the false king. Ranulf's line, running behind, swept through Stephen's infantry, and smashed its way toward the usurper.

My cousin made no attempt to evade the encounter. My entourage, forgetting my safety, or drawn in by bloodlust, closed in on him as well. Amazed, I perceived that my rival was surrounded only by lesser barons and common persons, armed haphazardly.

Chester's troops essayed to breach the circle protecting Boulogne. One of our warriors penetrated the ring, but Stephen himself fought back viciously, felling him. Under our onslaught, he never shirked. Lifting his glittering sword, he defended himself again and again, littering the ground with bodies. Entrails coated his mail; his upturned arm appeared to me to be a great red bolt of lightning.

Ranulf made for the false king, easily piercing his band of supporters. Chester and the usurper engaged one another.

My insides lurched as the earl's sturdier blade shattered his bejeweled rapier. In that moment, I thought that my darling would be eviscerated before my eyes. I would never be free of him; he was enormous to me in the moment of his death.

Then, before Ranulf could benefit from his deadly advantage, someone tossed a two-headed battle-axe to the pretender, who roared and pounded it down upon his antagonist's helmet. Chester sank to the mud, but was not killed.

I breathed again, full of loathing. My eyes were moist. I hated Stephen with all my soul.

I had a mace, tied to my saddle pommel. The Virgin invigorated my arm and my aim. I rotated the awful thing in the air, and flung it forward. The studded round glanced off the ground, at my cousin's feet, distracting him and causing him to stumble.

Brian FitzCount grabbed at Boulogne, wresting off his crown. He shouted: "Here, everyone, here! I have taken the king!"

†

WITHIN A TENT HASTILY erected between the castle and the river, I dismissed the squires and apothecaries, and tended in private to the wounded usurper. I removed his gory metal casings, which had swathed him in violence. Bathing his head, I had an excuse to comb out his matted hair. Dressing his injuries and soothing his hurts, I assumed the role of a nurse, but acted no better than a camp whore. Dazed and in pain, prone on a litter, he could not fend off my touch.

After some time, Stephen's focus returned. He did not seem astonished to be in my care. "It is too easy to surrender to a lady fair."

I flushed. "You have not yet heard my terms. I serve the Holy Mother, who has delivered unto me this great triumph." I adjusted one of his auburn locks, tucking it behind his ear.

Grimacing to shift position, he brushed the curl back onto his shoulder. "Somehow, I have offended the Virgin. At dawn, I held a mass for Her in the cathedral of Lincoln, but when I handed my sacred taper to the bishop, it dropped, splitting in two upon the stone floor. Such a mishap much disheartened my army. They put their faith in this bad omen and mislaid their courage."

"Before the Lord's altar, spurious kings cannot be as polished, nor as blithe, as true ones." Roughly, I wiped off a streak of blood from his cheek.

My cousin nudged me off. "I did not stand upon ceremony. I stooped to the ground to retrieve the damaged candle, mended its seam, and relit it. The renewed flame proved that, in the end, I will not lose my throne. I may have sinned, but after I atone for my errors, I will regain heaven's favor. Christ's glory will restore my realm to me."

I stared at the man who had ruined all my hopes. His beauty was poison to me. "You are my prisoner."

The pretender shook his head. "Although I am kept captive, I am your sovereign. As I was anointed, royal majesty clings to me, eternal."

I silenced him with my lips. For all his bluster, he kissed me back. In my passion, I found my power over him. "In my mind, you are called "Beloved." Put amour higher than hatred."

Just then, a sickening smell of burning flesh wafted over us. Leaving his side, I pulled open the flap of the pavilion and saw the city of Lincoln, aflame.

With difficulty, my rival raised himself up on his pallet, so that he too could view the conflagration. "Churches burn the most brilliantly. Their devastation is the most to be pitied."

"Treason immolates the innocent alongside the guilty." I held my breath, so as not to imbibe the aroma of hell.

Boulogne pointed at my armored chest. "It is your men who butcher yonder."

How I adored it when he regarded me! "We plunder Lincoln according to the laws of war. My battalions, serving their rightful queen, are justly rewarded for risking life and limb, and are not obligated to commiserate with their victims."

In the other direction, hundreds of burghers rushed pell-mell to the swollen Witham, crowding wildly onto small boats or attempting to swim, clawing at each other, clambering atop one another. Overborne crafts sank in the rapid current, drowning both those who clung to them and those who floundered in the waves.

The count lay back down. "O most puissant conqueror, in shedding blood, you have spilt the essence of the lamb."

I sucked in my breath. "My magnificence is my blessed reward. My slain subjects forfeit their earthly life, as Christ did, and are hallowed by the comparison."

Gloucester entered the loge, pulling off his gauntlets, discarding them upon the ground. His face was streaked with ashes, his green eyes haggard. His wrinkles had deepened; blood caked within their folds. "I have come to formally demand your submission, cousin, and to relieve you of your arms."

Stephen blushed. "My humiliation is complete. I need no longer be filled with dread, for I have come among you to scourge myself. My sins are not greater than the crimes of those fallen ones who rebel against me, their liege lord."

I could not abide his pride. "You are no longer the sire of England."

Robert sighed. "We cannot permit our kinsman to be harassed, even with words. In his person, in the body of the king, many of our people see the crown; its stateliness must not be sullied. Though I have vigorously assailed him as a usurper, I will preserve my noble prisoner from indignity."

†

THE FALSE MONARCH IS deposed! I am England. Each morning, I rise jubilant, suffused with spirit. I walk with more assurance and speak with more freedom, now that there is no authority above me but heaven.

The whole of the realm quivers with astonishment at the sudden change in the political reality. The jongleurs, those sycophants, herald and welcome the news of the pretender's downfall, a complete military conquest that promises the end of our civil strife. Little caring which one of us sits upon the throne, the farmers and villagers prefer whoever will stop the warring. Although most of the kingdom had been inclined to support Boulogne, now the majority surrenders to my rule. My cousin's more slavish barons transfer their allegiance without waiting for my invitation.

We sequester the scoundrel in Bristol Castle, the strongest fortification in our possession, and gather an enormous party of adherents under its roof. Herewith, my brother's lady deigns to approve of me, and I receive her polite attentions. All smiles to be reunited with her daughter, Amabel is suddenly willing to acknowledge my status.

In accordance with Robert's wish to be hospitable, his wife exerts all of her domestic charms to coddle her prestigious captive. His accommodations are garnished with a roaring blaze and sweet smelling floor rushes. The walls of his solar are festooned with rich arras tapestries, depicting the *ars amatoria*, the arts of love. The guards posted outside his chamber are not vigilant, allowing him to wander about at will, or entertain as many visitors as he pleases. Restrictions are tightened only at night, when Stephen is held under lock and key.

Still, after dark, it is not difficult to gain entrance to my beloved's room. Our castellan, fatherly and grizzled, sits each evening upon a bench outside the solar, but has the tact to stretch his legs in the inner bailey when I make an appearance.

Last night, I entered my cousin's chamber, pulled shut its heavy wooden door, and made it fast. Seated by the fire, washed all over in amber light, Boulogne looked more beautiful than ever. His thin fingers, his slender chin, his great forehead: I took in every detail. My innards melted. Straightaway, I sat down on his lap.

He wrapped one arm around my waist, and with the other gestured to the tapestry portraying the secrets of passion. He ran his thumb across a couple engaged in the act of intercourse. "Can the pleasures of the flesh indemnify us for the distress we have caused the kingdom?"

I clasped him to my breast. My head spun. "Tonight, do not think on ugly things, on all the venom unleashed in the land. Forget your anger in my eyes, in my hair, in my womanhood."

He nuzzled my neck and licked my collarbone. "I wish that I could refuse your delights, Empress. I will not be able to rinse my mouth of the acrid taste that taints your skin. When I take you, I take my sins to me. But I cannot do otherwise, avid as I am to keep despondency in abeyance."

My blood churned, in bitterness. I am no vicious siren, singing at the gates of hell. I am an angel of the Lord, come to console a weak fool and deliver him from error. But I could not find the will to remove myself from his mistaken embrace. Instead, all compliance, I joined him on his bed, lifted my skirt and burnished his ego. The tears that clouded my vision went unnoticed.

Immediately after our coupling, the pretender fell asleep. As I arranged the bedding to make him more comfortable in slumber, I considered how easy it would be to suffocate him with the silken coverlet. I hunger to punish his impudence and cripple his power over me. Why was I unable to bring myself to stop his breath?

†

THE CASTLE GOSSIPS GET wind of the usurper's furtive night visitor, supposedly endeavoring to plot his escape. Robert feels that he cannot ignore, or be thought to ignore, the rumors of this insidious intrigue. Thus the count is no longer permitted to exit his quarters. His hearth is no longer swept, nor is he delivered daily washing water. After dark, he is loosely fettered in chains.

However, in the late hours, the old castellan remains posted at Stephen's door. Tonight, he averted his gaze when I entered the makeshift gaol, but did not quit the corridor.

My adored one sat upon his pallet, and greeted me with a smile. "Ah, Empress, you are here to assuage my loneliness."

I thought of all the years that I have spent in desolate solitude, years in which my cousin enjoyed his wife's company, instead of my own. I felt grievous rage billowing up in me, alongside my wondrous rapture. "Do not complain to me. I do not come here to limit your discomfort, but to pander to my own."

His grin collapsed. He started to toss two pairs of dice upon his blankets, rattling his irons. "These manacles are nothing new. Ever since my coronation, I have been imprisoned by the greed of the barons. My throne was secure only as long as I kept purchasing their noble affections, for your rebellion stimulated their insubordination. Every magnate demanded more than he deserved."

I tried to hoist one of Stephen's chains, but could not. "As my subject, you would have been freed of so much heavy responsibility."

My cousin cast his dice, and I studied the numbers as they came up: a four, for the Evangelists; another four, for the letters in Adam; a five, for the wounds of Christ; and a ten, for our holy commandments.

Boulogne shook his head. "Even you insisted on more than I could spare. Why could you not adore me as Maud does, as a king out of legend? If you had abdicated your own claim, so that I might have reigned unmolested, I would have believed in your devotion."

"The countess's infatuations are nothing to me. The queen does not model her intimacies upon another's." I swept his ivories into the far corner of the room, where he could not get to them. I noticed that three came up sixes, alongside a two. I laughed, recalling a childhood ditty. "She who throws three sixes clear, will sate her fancy in this year."

The count demurred. "The two, my darling, means that adversity shall plague your plans." Stephen jerked at his restraints and succeeded in stretching himself out lengthwise. He reached toward me. "Let us come together without antipathy. Those who love well do not repine with chagrin."

I sat down upon the bedstead, permitting the pretender to run his hand along my thigh. "I am unable to allay my vexations. If your affections were true, you would have served me as my vassal, as you vowed to do. You might have married me, and found in our union all the preeminence that you lusted after. Even now, if you would designate our son as your successor, I could forgive you all that has come before."

The usurper ceased his caress. Then he lurched toward me, burying his face in my belly. "It is too late for any of it, Matilda, except for our bodily joy in one another." His expression was hidden in the folds of my bliaut.

Still he blocked me from my deepest desire. I could not touch him. "You radiate the light. I see in you an ideal that is still achievable. Accede to my dreams for us. If you dared to believe in our tie, we might undo the great wrong that we have done my father's empire."

The Count of Boulogne uncovered his gray eyes, which refuse to see the world as I do. "You are chafing against the will of God. If He curses me now, He will acquit me later. I do not need you to return me to my grandeur."

"Choose me, Stephen, or rot in purgatory for the rest of your life."

†

THE TROUBADOURS, THOSE BOOTLICKERS, aver that my husband has conquered Normandy, and is now titled its duke. In truth, hearing of my success over the Channel, many in the duchy immediately relinquished their fortresses and abbeys to Geoffrey. His control is almost absolute; his supremacy extends all the way to France.

As my wedded lord's influence grows, so my disloyal cousin's decreases. Lately, fearing that my nocturnal adventures compromise my restoration, Robert orders the usurper installed in the castle's dank dungeon. There, his fetters are affixed to iron rings on the stone walls. The only light to his small cell descends from above.

Despite his confinement, I allow my rival to receive and bless those who arrive here to renounce their allegiance to him. He absolves the visiting clerics and laymen from their previous oaths. The archbishop of Canterbury conscientiously consults his former king, and Stephen accepts his apologies. Although he squats in a shadowy and odiferous cage, Boulogne does not dispense with courtesy.

I had anticipated that Gerta would cease to chide, now that I no longer slip away in the frigid dark, but she continues to rebuke me. "How shall you gird yourself against the devil's blandishments, whilst he abides in your house, as your familiar?" She exults that Gloucester impounds the cad to the bowels of the keep, but insists that I hang him or behead him.

Yet, I cannot ruthlessly execute my rival. I cannot withdraw my adoration of my foe. He has never truly cherished me, but I cannot change my fate. My heart belongs to him.

†

Spring

I WISH TO INHERIT my father's throne, and rise to greatness, just as he did: first elected by a church council convened at Winchester, where the royal treasury and regalia are housed, then anointed in London's Westminster Abbey. To this end, Robert facilitates a rapprochement between Bishop Henry and our camp. His Grace proposes the terms of my succession. In exchange for my acquiescence to his demands, he hands over the keys to the royal coffers and encourages other important prelates to support my elevation.

This morning, the bishop and I met at Wherwell, near to Winchester, upon a level and open meadow, at the foot of a slope that rises above the river Test. The day was gloomy, damp and cold, overhung with the sort of black clouds that presage bad fortune. I refused to interpret the inky sky as an ill omen, and conducted myself as if the sun were shining all over Britain.

Eager to cow him, to impress upon him that I am England, I wore full state dress, including a saffron, pleated bliaut, embroidered at the sleeves, hem, and neck with thick, golden rope. An ornate girdle draped its tassels to my feet. My scarlet velvet mantle, scattered with Saxon knots and trimmed with needlepoint medallions — each the portrait of an individual saint—hung heavily across my shoulders. A short, white veil covered my hair, with the exception of two extensive, false double plaits, twisted with golden ribbons, which brushed the ground. Atop my veil, I balanced an enormous, heavy diadem emblazoned with topazes and striped jasper, the opaque red mineral that forestalls harm.

Henry, remembering his manners, did not refer to the unfortunate weather. "I greet you, Empress, as King Henry's daughter and England's queen."

I did not forget that the bishop's bloated eyes were shuttered windows. "You have sworn for me in the past, then seemingly regretted it."

His Grace did not lose his composure. "You loitered long in Normandy, Your Majesty, and the delay endangered the well-being of the realm. The monarchy decays into anarchy when the throne is vacant. And so my brother was permitted to transform himself into a king. Now that he languishes in your brother's dungeon, and you reside among us, I support your claim. It is futile to swim against the tide. Many a man has drowned trying."

As we parleyed, large raindrops splattered the ground and my skirts. "It was you, Winchester, who negotiated the pretender's unlawful transfiguration."

Henry fussed over the water sprinkling his own robes. "Indeed, I am ashamed. Forgive me, Your Majesty, for I thought too much of the needs of the holy church, which the Count of Boulogne undertook to protect. A weak liege, he failed to safeguard the ecclesiastical liberties or the security of the nation. He surrounded himself with evil agents, and threw off sage and honest associates."

I thought of Stephen, filthy now from his cramped quarters and harsh treatment, but still comely beyond measure. "You do not consider it your sacred duty to cherish your kin?"

His Grace rustled his garments, and smiled sourly. "My most pious obligations are to God, my immortal Father, who has seen fit to cast the king down from on high."

I rather enjoyed the glistening rain. If it soiled my gown, it washed my spirit clean. "The Holy Mother delivers unto you the true heir to England and Normandy."

Winchester knelt before me, despite the downpour, and the mud underfoot. "I am ready to vow fidelity to you, and to hand over your dominion. England's throne cannot rest empty, to rot and erode."

I remembered Robert's instructions and made the bargain. "I am prepared to agree that the Church retains its prerogatives, provided that they do not countermand customary crown powers." I paused, wondering if such a bribe might be enough.

The bishop stayed put, awaiting the rest of his payment.

There was nothing for it, but to swear to enrich and embellish the corrupt priest. "And I pledge that you, Henry of Blois, Dominus and Pater, shall be my chief counselor, advising me on all clerical affairs. Specifically, you shall oversee the appointment of prelates and the disposal of abbeys."

Smug, His Grace clucked his tongue. I held out my hand, to lift him up from his knees. We kissed each other's cheeks, in an embrace that warranted very little.

†

THE SKIES CLEARED. AT terce, the bishop admitted me and my entourage of barons and knights to Winchester. We progressed through the streets, cheered by his parishioners. I saw one woman faint away at the sight of me; my chest swelled with the hope that I was rising again to my former estate. A few buildings were draped with silk in my colors. Some locals carried swaying branches of palm; others held flickering tapers. I made out the jaunty scratch of a few fiddles, underneath the louder, raucous singing of a band of inebriates. How much had Henry paid for this display of fervor?

His Grace led me to the portals of his magnificent house of worship, in order to publicly acknowledge his change of party. We composed ourselves upon the steps of the fine cathedral. The watermarks and discolorations upon my mantle and bliaut were so faint as to be noticeable only to me. I doffed my precious coronet, and entrusted it to His Grace's keeping.

A crowd of ecclesiastics and laymen gathered in the square in front of us. Observing the plaza fill with exuberant burghers and men of the cloth, Gloucester relaxed his stance. The furrows around his eyes diminished. Although the bishop disputed and slighted my brother's precedence, the archbishop of Canterbury had joined us, and treated the earl with suitable deference, as son to the late king. Brian FitzCount stood among the group; his raw devotion reassured me. Hearing some lovely chanting, I took note of a clutch of nuns from the local convent. I nodded my head in their direction, to thank them for their song.

Before the great throng, Winchester raised his arm, for silence. He brandished my crown aloft, then placed it in my grasp.

I lifted the richly jeweled circlet high above me, then lowered it back into place upon my brow. I relished the weight of it, and extended my neck to balance it properly. I exulted to be recognized as their mainstay and their Mother.

Henry expounded: "All hail Her Majesty, Queen Matilda! Salute her!"

My subjects whooped and clapped, in approval. Across the square, the bells tolled the news. On the porch, the din was infernal.

As the peals receded, I proclaimed: "Let all those present, and all those with whom you speak, know that the daughter of King Henry is the Lady of the English." A satisfied roar rolled over me.

The bishop addressed his loyal flock. "As the pope's representative, I call upon the assembled divines to heed the sanction of heaven. Promise your fealty where the Church places its faith, or be hereby exiled from the community of Christians on earth. Any man who curses Her Majesty is accursed himself; any man who blesses Her is himself blessed."

†

PROLONGING MY VISIT, I remain behind in Winchester for its fair, while Robert advances to London. His letter apprises me of his doings on my behalf.

London grows like a weed, and is now a hydra of a metropolis, where I am jostled in the streets by a continual parade of philosophers, harlots, sailors, sheriffs, monks, dairymaids, urchins, barons, and guildsmen. After dark, the city's decadent, luxurious conviviality sometimes disintegrates into drunkenness, but not always into disorder.

Sister, I make headway with both the city's leading commoners and its aristocratic grandees. I commit to reinstating lost titles and treasures, and to reinstituting the rule of law. But travel in slow stages, so that I have opportunities enough to increase the number of your friends.

I remain your faithful vassal, in town as in all of your empire.

Gerta mumbles under her breath, dissatisfied with this missive. "An austere, upright man is often no match for the feckless citizens who clog the towns, like the refuse that obstructs its gutters."

†

THE PALACE OF WESTMINSTER sits just outside the gates to the English capitol. Its vastness inspires awe, although its stolidity cannot mask a sewage stench, which seeps into every corner. Despite the various enticements of the stinking city, I prefer to remain within this keep that I remember from my childhood. Here, I shape the plans for my coronation in Westminster Abbey, which I would commemorate with high solemnity.

I recline upon my throne in the castle's great hall, built in the time of William Rufus, and the largest chamber of its kind in Europe. There, at the king's high table, I confer honors and approve charters. I have commanded the engraving of a new Great Seal, emblazoned "Matilda, Daughter of King Henry and queen of the English," so as not to be a foreigner among my people. For the most part, I take pleasure in the queen's work.

Heralds forward a message from Geoffrey that pricks at my self-satisfaction.

Yours is the bloodline, the legacy of tyrants. Let your thirst to rule, your thirst for territory, be quenched at the deep well of wisdom, there where the

princess adorned both in modesty and majesty draws her water. Suppress
your self-will; purify yourself, if you would never more be ashamed.

†

TODAY, LONDON'S FOREMOST BURGHERS formally approached me, in answer to my recent tax levy. I sat upon my throne, surrounded by my cohorts, Gloucester, FitzCount, and that dog, Winchester. The great hall was full of toadies and pages, baronesses and minstrels, knights and dogs, minions who had come to ask favors and simpletons who had come to see me for themselves.

One wizened spokesman from the city stepped to the front of the assembly. Like all his compatriots, he wore a cap, which he now twisted out of shape. A gaudy brooch perched upon his green wool cloak. His tight sleeves, suitable for his business dealings, and his deep leather cuffs irritated my taste.

He bowed to me, but with an incomplete obeisance, and neglected to touch his lips or fingers to my mantle. "Lady, we embody the commune of London, dignified by King Stephen, and given privileges by him, as its overlord. Now, we ask to be treated by you with as much respect as any other of his tenants."

The hairs on my neck rose. "The Count of Boulogne has never been your rightful sovereign. Any corporation that the pretender recognized is nothing to me. My traitorous cousin wrongfully escalated the status of the people above its natural limit, threatening the order of society."

There was silence from the old man, but a furious whispering among his companions.

After a pause, the elder resumed his appeal. "His Majesty ascertained that freeborn Londoners are as the freeborn Romans, senators to the state."

"You covet the position enjoyed by my barons, the right to advise me."

The burgher shook his head. "We ask only to be subject to the reasonable laws of King Stephen, as opposed to the harsh edicts of King Henry."

The other townsfolk stuck up their middle fingers, as if to ward off my father's evil influence.

I bolted up from the throne. "How dare you make these obscene gestures? The Lion's dictates will stand. His taxes will stand. I insist that you pay the large sum that you owe the crown."

The citizens shuffled backward, looking nervously at one another.

Their leader, however, did not shift his stance. "The endless civil war has swallowed up our monies. We have donated generously to the church, to aid in the relief of our poor. We have gratified His Majesty, each time that he requisitioned our gold to equip his armies. Now, we are almost bankrupt."

The sight of him, upright before me when he should have been prostrate, increased my ire. "Where do you find the audacity to inform me that you have nothing for your true queen, because you have endowed everything upon her enemy?"

Winchester inserted himself. "My brother's courtesies toward you were intended to enlarge and hasten your disbursements."

The spokesman gravely adjusted his cloak upon his shoulders, and patted his ostentatious brooch. "Your Grace speaks true. King Stephen acted not proudly, but cheerfully, to all who kept the peace."

Henry nodded, then pursed his lips, waiting for the murmurs in the hall to fade away. "Those who curse she whom the Lord has elevated, this lady who is to sit above us by divine right, will be themselves accursed! But those who bless her name and person will be themselves blessed."

The citizen flushed at the cited threat. "We only request that Matilda, who now wishes to be queen, ask less of our limited resources and allow us a longer period of time to pay."

I grimaced, wrinkling my mouth and forehead, so that he should know my utter disapproval of all his presumption. "You, with your rich decorations and your love for my foe, have no right to ask for such capitulations on my part. You, who barely bow to me, will be made to bend under my demands."

The old burgher spit into the rushes. Inclining himself as little as possible, he and his cohorts withdrew from the vast chamber.

Many of my aristocratic courtiers jeered with disdain at the citizens' arrogance. Brian FitzCount swung his fist at their retreating backs.

But Robert's small mouth twisted right and left. He sighed. "Sister, you must sometimes court the favor of those beneath you."

Why did my brother not defend my dignity? "The Count of Boulogne found these townsmen eager to serve him."

The earl took my elbow. "You forget that Stephen trusted to his gifts to foster their devotion. Before your accession, you must bribe, not threaten. The Londoners have a certain power that cannot be contravened by a mere contestant to the throne. If you are to be anointed, you need their adherence and their patronage."

†

THIS AFTERNOON, AT NONE, Winchester came to my solar.

I had retreated from the court's scrutiny, eager to have Gerta's strong fingers massage out the kinks in my neck and the aches in my lower back. The throne is uncomfortable, and I sit continually erect, never willing to relax my posture.

His Grace did not have the tact to withdraw, despite my evident bodily fatigue. He wiggled his wrist at my maid, who scrambled out the door, without waiting for my leave.

"My queen, I come upon important business." Remembering himself, the bishop gave me a slight bow, but did not remove his head covering, as was customary.

"If you interrupt me without invitation, you must be bursting with news of the utmost interest."

Henry smiled thinly. "I am not come to broadcast some novelty. I speak of what is always true. You are required, at a minimum of once a year, to catalogue your sins to a priest. It has come to my attention that you have neglected this sacred duty. I will, of course, take on the duty of your confessor."

Was this what I had guaranteed him? Did Winchester have the audacity to assign me hours of public prayers or a stringent, debilitating fast? Surely, he scheme to dictate my almsgiving. Would he snicker as he lashed my flesh with a knotted cord, or force me to parade my welts before my barons?

The bishop pressed his palms together, and placed the tips of his long fingers against his lips. "I shall grant you absolution, once you have admitted all of your misdeeds, and made a credible show of atonement."

How little he believed in me. "What will be the form of this interrogation? I presume that you will begin with the common vices, and if I allude to these, you will push me to describe the more deviant ones."

His Grace flushed. "Those who are susceptible, and who affirm it, need not be ashamed. Your penance will be in keeping with the gravity of your error. Ultimately, you will be redeemed. You would not wish to suffer the consequences of your trespasses in purgatory."

"How often do you confess, Henry of Blois? None of us are free of peccadilloes." I remembered the young boy at Wolvesey Palace. Had Winchester made amends for his lechery? I have read that fornication by a father of the church requires ten years of penitence.

His Grace met my eyes, but his voice was cold. "Each and every person, having reached the age of reason, must avow their misconduct. If I permit myself some breach, my interior sorrow is enormous. I hunger for the temporal privations that scrub me clean before the Lord. I often pray to fortify the strength of my arm, to buttress my bishop's crook, so that when I plunge it into the neck of the dragon of enticement, I am victorious."

Surprised, my voice was not completely steady. "I cannot undertake to make you my confessor without further thought."

"If you refuse my pious counsel, you defer your entrance into the society of the holy. I am your invitation, your navigational chart, your key to the gates of heaven. Cannot you hear the blast of God's trumpets? Cannot you see the banners of Christ that wave from atop His tower?"

†

THIS AFTERNOON, ANOTHER SUPPLICANT sours the atmosphere at Westminster.

Maud, bedecked in a chartreuse gown verily wreathed with netted pearls, strode through the great hall, coming to a halt directly before my throne. She began to speak without curtsying. "The archbishop of Canterbury…"

I refused to allow her to address me so boldly, or even to stand before me. "I will not hear the Countess of Boulogne until she debases herself, according to precedent."

The wench snorted, but slowly lowered herself to her knees. Then, in a charade of compliance, she painstakingly arranged the pleats of her extravagant bliaut, shaking out the few sheaves of straw that clung to it.

I waited for her to finish the performance. "You are none too humble, Countess."

Maud's face tightened, pronouncing its plumpness. "You are none too gracious, Empress."

I gloried to see her sunk upon the hard floor. "I am the queen of England. I need not extend any politeness to you."

The bitch shuffled her weight from leg to leg. "I do not wish to be pampered while my husband undergoes your torments. I come here to denounce His Majesty's imprisonment and to demand his release from the nasty oubliette into which you have plunged him." Again, she ruffled her skirts. "I come also to broadcast the archbishop of Canterbury's proposal, that you restore Stephen's territories and possessions. In return, we will abdicate the throne."

I scoffed. Did she think me an idiot? "The pretender stole what was rightly mine. Once released, he will surely plot to deprive me of my patrimony."

Maud crossed herself, then turned her lips up, in a little smirk. "The king shall become a hermit, or a pilgrim. I shall part ways with him, and retire to a nunnery."

I laughed aloud, imagining the sultry countess burying her ambition in a cloister and my randy cousin transfigured into a wandering ascetic, indifferent to pleasure. "It will be difficult for you to bamboozle your husband into agreement."

The harlot flushed. "His Majesty pays much heed to my advice."

I stamped my boot against the ground. My voice resonated throughout the hall. "Damn the usurper!"

The countess seemed sure of herself. "As the king has disinherited some of your noble vassals, making enemies of them, so you will strip the honors from our allies, engendering their hatred. If you have not the stomach to enfeeble our friends, you will embellish their influence, only to wonder where lies their real faith. You will never be sure of them, nor they you."

With a stony stare, I dismissed the slut from my royal presence.

It is clear to me that my throne here is a Chair Perilous, merely the first stage in my hazardous quest for what is mine by right.

†

ALTHOUGH I HAVE LONG criticized my cousin's errors of policy, I made his mistake, and treated my enemy too leniently. To my shame, I underestimated Maud's prowess; instead of confining her to Westminster, I permitted her to depart. Immediately, the aggrandized whore began to ferment trouble.

Maud retreated to Kent, to connive with continental mercenaries employed by her friends in Boulogne. She gathered together an army, and, in order to pay them, bargained with moneylenders, sold off jewels, and mortgaged landed assets. The countess marched her hired warriors back here, drawing up on the south side of the Thames. From Southwark, her regiments raid the city, burning, looting, and slaying each night. The jongleurs conjecture that this villainy is Maud's vengeance against London, in return for its apparent acceptance of her nemesis.

From the safety of Westminster, I can see an orange haze in the black sky and hear the dull roar of screams. If only the citizens had paid homage to me; if only the burghers had sworn themselves my partisans! Then I would deploy my own troops to protect them from the ravages of my antagonist.

The townsmen named my father a despot, but it is their "Good Queen Maud" who attacks them now.

†

Last evening, we banqueted, in celebration of my upcoming coronation. The palace servants had adorned Westminster's great hall with flowers and foliage, enough to mask its usual odor. For the first course, the chefs outdid themselves, presenting us with boar's heads stuffed with eggs and chestnuts, swans baked with turnips, and eagles smothered with currants.

Needled by Gerta's paranoia, and enslaved by my appetite, I abjured her advice, and did not sprinkle salt upon my portions, so as to detect any pernicious tampering. Muttering at my insubordination, my maid presented me with a spoon fashioned from rosemary wood, another tool to protect me from any enemy interference.

Once the first tempting dishes were cleared, servants brought forth almond pies containing live songbirds. When the tarts were cut, the creatures escaped, and the chamber filled with their warbling. Finally, a page rode into the room on horseback, bearing onto the dais a masterpiece in aspic, a huge map of my empire.

At the high table, to my right, that parasite, Henry of Winchester, greedily partook of the confection. He dug his finger into the richly spiced jelly, and shoveled in a large trembling mound of it.

I caught his eye. "I welcome Your Grace to the pleasures of my court."

The bishop frowned, and waved over a laverer. He dipped his hand into the washbowl.

I could smell that its cool liquid was redolent of the sage and rosemary that had been boiled in it. I pointed to a heaping platter of candied fruit.

His Grace refused to sample it, and stood up from his chair. "I must attend to other business, church business. I cannot wait upon you further."

I guffawed. "It is difficult to please two masters. You will always be looking over your shoulder."

The words had hardly left my lips when, suddenly, all the bells of London were tolling the tocsin, the call to arms. One knight of my garrison dashed into the hall, from his post upon the battlements.

"A tremendous crowd runs out of the city gates, converging toward Westminster. They stampede like a herd of beasts!"

I jumped up and hastened out of the room, as the bishop scurried away, intent on his own welfare. I clambered up the curved stone staircase to my private apartment, where I snatched my blue enamel casket and my satchel of manuscript rolls. I would not, I could not, forfeit Stephen's lock of hair, my copper mirror and jewels, my letters and writings.

Suddenly, FitzCount entered my solar and pulled me to him. "Empress, abandon your chattel. Salvage your life."

I shook my head vehemently, clutching my treasures.

My vassal whisked us both back down the steps, through the keep to the stables.

Very few horses remained, but Gerta held onto two noble destriers. "I forbade any to touch them, in Your Majesty's name."

Brian settled me in front of him, on one steed; my maid mounted the other. Galloping out of the bailey, we heard a wild howling, as a hostile throng of our adversaries cavorted in the palace's hall, setting fire to the decorations and wolfing down the leavings from our feast.

We careened along the major thoroughfare, as fast as we thought our animals could bear. The many barons who had been present at the coronation banquet were nowhere to be seen. FitzCount guessed that they had sagaciously branched off onto various rural byways, the better to melt away into the night. To my relief, the Earl of Gloucester and several of his men waited for me at the crossroads to Oxford.

My brother pushed back his hair. "Our retreat has not been orderly. Many of our fawning followers have scrambled to their own safety, revealing their commitment to you to be shallow and canting. Without hesitation, they abandoned you to the mob. We will make our own escape, and outwit them all another day. Ride onward!"

The Matter of the Crown

Scroll Thirteen: 1141

And so I ask you, you who have been so courtly as to absorb yourself in my story: Who abhorred the empress most? Of course, it was not her falsehearted lover, but his tenacious wife, for the rancor of women is insatiable. The warriors in the service of the two rival queens relished their conflict, perpetrating much wickedness in their names. Now it came to pass that Matilda sank beneath the waves of trouble, and struggled to surface. In her panic, she relinquished her idol. Once again, her history resumed its perverse course, its unending cycle of requited violence and unrequited desire. It is well to remember that God our Father fashioned the night as well as the day.

†

Summer

MY BROTHER AND I ensconce ourselves in the royal castle of Winchester, hoping to conspire with Henry of Blois to regain the ground that we have lost. But the bishop barricades himself in his decadent palace of Wolvesey, on the other side of the city, refusing to grant us his company. As my political prospects stymie, His Grace apparently regrets my presence in his diocesan capitol.

The bishop begins to hire soldiers and fortify his sumptuous edifice, built more for pleasure than for war. He executes several infamous criminals in the market square, bolstering city business and swelling his tax receipts. How can we not suspect that Winchester worked against us in London? Each day that passes without his appearance before me indicates a reversal of his allegiance.

At the very least, I am now at liberty to ignore his interests.

†

OUR SPIES INFORM US that Winchester meets in secret with Maud, at Guilford. Reversing course, His Grace now pledges to staunchly support his brother. The sentence of excommunication lowered upon Stephen is lifted, falling instead upon me. While the pretender's fate rests unsure, the bishop and the countess agree that Prince Eustace shall be endowed immediately with his mother's personal fief, the County of Boulogne, and his father's hereditary territory, the County of Mortain.

The Earl of Gloucester urges me to consider providing for Eustace, so that Henry Plantagenet's eventual succession will have one less adversary. But my antipathy to the scheme persists, implacable; Boulogne and Mortain would make fine reward for Brian FitzCount or for other of the hungry barons who surround me. The usurpers thieve from my heir; I will do no right by theirs.

†

IF MY PRESTIGE SUFFERED a setback in London, my numerous battalions here belie my disappointment. This royal castle swarms with lackeys and adherents, lesser vassals and greater earls, among them Brian, Robert, and David of Scotland. Only Ranulf of Chester absents himself.

As in Westminster, I fill the hours dictating and signing charters. However, I grieve to find that my new Great Seal has been lost in the chaos of our hurried flight from London. Each evening, Gerta draws an eye on the wall of my solar, and drives one copper nail into its center. Still, we do not dream of the stamp's whereabouts, nor see any one of our retinue suffer some diminution of vision. With relief, we understand that the thief is not among our circle. In any event, I retain my other two insignia, and resume using the one emblazoned "Matilda Empress." For good measure, I always append my son's name, "as rightful scion of England and Normandy."

I do struggle to discriminate among the candidates for my notice and favor. Whose landholdings should I forfeit? On whom should I confer them? It is not enough, and sometimes too much, to arbitrarily disavow each of my beloved's decrees, to bankrupt every knight whom he enriched. It disquiets me to transfer to Henry Plantagenet an empire riddled with contested manors and fiefs.

With great complacence, I annul the vexatious Maud's right to the Queen Consort's property of Waltham in Essex, regranting the rich land to Adeliza.

My former friend acknowledges my gift with affectionate indifference.

> *I humbly acknowledge your continued favor, despite my unbreakable tie to your cousin's vassal. I pray that the Virgin's mercy shall be a blessing unto you, and shall enable you to redress your own transgressions and to fortify your own virtues.*

†

THE COUNTESS OF BOULOGNE, that she-witch, marched upon Winchester and besieges our stronghold. For the last six weeks, we have been well encircled by her malevolent army, a motley crew of Flemish mercenaries, awkwardly equipped London folk, and those barons partial to the House of Boulogne.

By the grace of God, and unanticipated by the villainous Maud, our fortress seethes with many brave warriors and numerous talented archers. In our daily skirmishes, entrenched as we are by our position, we inflict almost as much damage as we sustain. Indeed, my garrison thrives, gleeful at the many opportunities to prove its courage.

Every man at arms, on either side, dreams of burnishing his reputation. The soldiers of Matilda and Maud are full of one another's exploits. This extended blockade of Winchester, and the temperate season, permits the perpetration and publication of many acts of knightly daring and skill.

To my glee, Winchester's burghers turn in disgust from the countess, her rapacious foreigners, and her greedy Londoners, and now flock to my cause. I hear tell that the sisters of the neighboring convent, whose chapel butts up against up our outer wall, the same women who witnessed Bishop Henry's invocation in the town square, pray and sing for my triumph. The regular hail of stones and firebrands over our battlements and into our baileys prohibits me from spending many moments outside, but I sometimes make out fragments of their chants. Exasperated by the constant clanging din, my ears strain to decipher the murmur of their melodies.

†

NOT CONTENT WITH STASIS, the loathsome Maud razes the city, to liberate it from my influence. From the narrow windows of my solar, I count almost forty steeples on fire. Robert and Brian forbid me to walk the ramparts during the heightened crisis.

Just now, Gerta returned to my chamber, covered in soot from the billowing smoke. "The wretched bitch commits all of the seven deadly sins. In envy and avarice, she desecrates Winchester's churches; her impious band strips their priceless trappings. In gluttony, she lays waste to the convent; in lust, her scoundrels rape the brides of Christ. In anger, she licenses the slaughter of the women they have defiled. Full of pride, she has the audacity to wipe out all that is before her."

I stared at my maid, a dark incubus, a harbinger of devastation. "You neglect the seventh sin, moroseness."

"We shall mourn on her behalf, then, and on behalf of the holy sisters. Some of them mutilated their own faces, in an attempt to repel their attackers. We shall drain the cup of gloom and sorrow. It will take some care, Empress, not to cut our lips on its cracked rim."

I dismissed her, for even Gerta's presence is unwelcome to me when I need to convince myself that I am not to blame.

†

SULKY AND DEJECTED, CRAMPED and bored, I am eager to accomplish even the smallest of tasks. Today, despite our declining rations, Gerta and I stirred up a vat of mead. The vast kitchens are quiet, for there are few stores left to prepare for each meal.

From our meager cache of honey, I poured out half, combining it with a crushed knuckle of precious ginger root, before infusing them both in a barrel of boiling water.

As the mixture steeped, I sighed. "Perhaps Robert will find me too liberal with our dwindling supply of water."

"Your brother and the others are in sore need of some pleasure to reduce their tensions."

When the confection cooled, Gerta added the yeast, and we watched the drink leaven.

I shook out my arms and legs, unused to exertion after so many days of inactivity. "There are herbs that we might brew, if our suffering grows unendurable. In her last letter to me, Geoffrey's daughter Marie remits efficacious powders along with her greetings."

My maid looked over her shoulder, at a few idling pages who guarded the pantries. "Surely the girl did not urge such a sacrilege?"

I laughed. "She exhorts me to follow the commands of my heart! I am at some pains to decode her meaning. I think that she intends me to poison my cousin with a tisane. Of this idea you must approve."

Sealing the wooden container of mead, Gerta engaged the servants to transport it to a cool cellar. As they disappeared, she continued. "Marie, at ten, rates passion very highly. I do not imagine that she would have you serve the toxic brew to the ogre Boulogne, but rather to his countess. Widowing your captive, Marie fosters your romance, thereby encouraging the liaison between her own parents. She would legitimate herself if she could."

The boldness of the plan rattled me. "Dare I test the integrity of my beloved's devotion, by submitting it to the world?"

"Love is like mead, Your Majesty. In times of peace, the competent cook lets it ferment for the space of six months; in times of war, a week must suffice."

†

MAUD'S INVESTMENT OF WINCHESTER continues. During this unending bombardment, the members of my court struggle as much with ennui as with hunger. Brian's eyes track my movements. Robert studies FitzCount, as if his own scrutiny could undermine the knight's romantic obsession. Uncle David turns his charm upon one of the baronesses entrapped here; she seems willing enough to dally away the empty hours in his royal arms. Vice runs rampant, unfettered by concern for the morrow. When the household is sated with gambling, having only bones or kisses as tokens, they tell each other bawdy stories. One of the Scottish squires juggles quite proficiently. Brian, ever physically adept, easily picks up the skill.

Gerta's fortune telling is popular, although I worry that she broadcasts her abilities too widely. She swears to me that she will not invoke the help of spirits, or utter any incantation whatsoever, beyond the Lord's Prayer. Desperate for entertainment or solace, my people crowd about her when she takes out her polished basin, clamoring to see the future in its midst, and do not think to accuse her of heresy.

I am full of waiting: waiting to fight, waiting to die, waiting to be reunited with my adored one, waiting to punish him. I would live for my bliss, but it unravels, rolling ahead of me, nearly out of sight. The tender memories fade. I can no longer clearly envision Stephen's face.

†

AT DUSK, ELUDING GERTA'S companionship and Robert's authority, I swathed myself in a rude cloak and mounted the battlements of the fortress. In the low light, the ruined city still smoldered. I heard the swish of an arrow, but it jangled against the stone wall below me.

I willed something to occur, even a catastrophe. I was ready to take my leave of my beloved, my throne, and all the world. My anguish is already the agony of a spear through the heart. Death would resolve my political troubles and personal dilemmas. When will my destiny reveal itself to me?

When I returned to my solar, unscathed from my forbidden tour, Brian and Gerta awaited me. The knight's eyes shone, and my maid looked as if she had just popped a cube of sugar into her mouth.

I unwound myself from my coarse outer garment. "What excites you, FitzCount?"

He knelt before me, in obeisance. "I ask Your Majesty's permission to perform a worthy deed. I would defy every difficulty to serve you."

Gerta grinned, and put her hand to her heart. "He burns to carry out Marie's instructions."

Brian could not have understood my motivations. If he hoped to assassinate Maud, he did not do it to promote my affair. I noticed that his breath came fast and shallow. I peered at his ruddy cheeks and raised my eyebrows. "You seem alight with the fire of intention, sir. Do you so readily consign a woman to eternity?"

"Put my devotion to the proof."

From my blue casket, I removed the packet of deadly herbs and gingerly handed it over to him. Marie's spidery writing covered the small parcel, and she had drawn, with some talent, the picture of a hazel tree wound about with honeysuckle. "Your instrument is rather tame, ill-suited to a warrior's arsenal. But its power is nonetheless mortal."

FitzCount placed the small sack within his sleeve. "I do not scruple at poison. If you prefer, I will suffocate the countess with my bare hands, and hang for it. It will be an honor to give my life for you, as I have sworn."

"Sir Brian, sacred friend!" I bent over his head and kissed him, allowing him to taste me.

"The flavor of your lips is the hothouse citrus of the Orient and the wild berry of the Occident; the zest of both has been steeped in celestial steam."

Despite the gravity of the situation, I winced in irritation. Had he prepared his metaphors in advance?

Gerta, provoked, shooed FitzCount out of my chamber.

†

Fall

BRIAN HAS HAD TO bide his time. Finally, last evening, our antagonists permitted the entrance of a monk, supposedly come to shrive one of my noble ladies-in-waiting, likely to perish from undernourishment. After he had taken her last confession, Gerta directed him to an ill-frequented cellar, where FitzCount did away with him. My maid assisted the assassin as he costumed himself in the victim's clerical robes; it was she who razored a tonsure into his thick locks. Thus disguised, and aided by the night, Brian disappeared into Winchester.

My sly maid shaved the entire head of the corpse, before sewing it up into a coarse linen sack. She assures me that the body was disposed of in such a way that no one need be the wiser. Diligent Gerta! I would not exchange her for a lustrous pearl.

†

TONIGHT, CLOISTERED IN MY solar, we enjoyed the last dregs of the mead.

Uncle David, pared down, is all nose and cheekbones, giving him a haughty expression that his noblesse little merits. Gloucester's face, likewise thinner now, appears drawn. He is dirtier than I have ever seen him, for we waste no water on hygiene.

The earl swished the honied broth in his mouth, savoring its sweetness for as long as he might. "We have lost enough men to severely limit our capacity to thwart Maud's offensive. Our food supplies are completely exhausted, and in several days will be exactly nothing. Empress, it seems increasingly unlikely that our endurance will discourage the countess. I believe it to be expedient for us to escape, if we can."

His Majesty agreed with this assessment. "Although Winchester's citizens side with us, all of their resources have been stolen or burned. They starve, as surely as we do. Our enemies have completely cut off the route to the west. Neither Gloucester nor Bristol can afford us any relief."

Robert winced, at this mention of his own embattled keeps. "If we manage to leave here alive, our garrison might regroup, somewhere to the north. It is rumored that there they have food."

I sniffed, aware of my musky scent. "There is no shame in a shrewd flight."

Alone now, I examine myself in my mirror. My face has not sunk into itself, the way David's has, or resolved itself into a map of lines, like my brother's. I remain Matilda, pale and clear, surrounded by a halo of darkness.

†

On the Feast of the Exaltation of the Holy Cross, we were not to be found at our empty table. As plotted, we mounted the few horses still left alive in the stable, sitting two or three astride. I rode behind Robert on a once magnificent destrier, now little more than a skeletal hack. Under the black sky, we slunk out of the royal castle of Winchester, and through Maud's sleeping encampment.

Shame upon us, for we were unable to outwit our foes, and were immediately surrounded by a pandemonium of shouts and clanging weapons. We abandoned our tight line, and scattered, away from the tents, but large numbers of well-fed knights perched upon strong, able steeds charged after us.

Galloping through the darkness, into the neighboring meadows, my brother and I soon discovered Gerta, standing unhorsed.

Winded from running, she panted, "Our plan has been betrayed."

A horseman appeared and spurred his animal toward us.

My maid screeched. "O heaven, protect me!"

The Virgin must have had us in Her sights, for it was Brian, still robed as a monk, who had materialized.

"FitzCount! This is well met. Guard the empress; deliver her to safety. I will loiter here, blocking your retreat. Waylaid by my barricade, our adversaries will lose time."

I shook my head, and did not unwrap my arms from around his waist. "Brother, I cannot leave you to such a fate." Remembering his gentle touch and his wise advice, I forgot that he had ever kissed the mantle of my cousin.

He spun to face me.

Although there was no light beyond that of a wan moon, I could sense his green eyes on mine.

"Be off with you! I do not quail before the abyss. You will reign and elevate your son to reign after you."

Brian pulled me and my bundled valuables from Gloucester's saddle onto his own, so that I rode before him. Gerta was placed behind him, quite taxing the resilience of his destrier, who stumbled and whinnied at the weight of three. FitzCount smacked its rump with the flat of his sword, and it began to canter away.

Over my shoulder, I noted that the earl remained astride, while his stallion dangled its neck down into the grass.

Pieces of armor littered the ground over which we traveled. Racing past, FitzCount swiped a shield, which he added to his small store of gear.

After some miles, FitzCount vaulted off his steed and spoke urgently. "We are in danger both from Maud's battalions and from the local peasants, who will assail us for our belongings, or to ransom us to our opponents. Empress, toss aside your ornamental garments, anything that suggests your majesty."

Off came my fur-trimmed cloak, my ornate girdle, my gold-stitched corsage. I shivered in my white bliaut, while Gerta disentangled my braids, stripping them of their yellow ribbons. She wrapped me in her blue mantle, of less quality than my own, but Brian rejected it, as alike too fine. He insisted that we rend our remaining clothes to disguise their rich materials and sumptuous designs.

At last, we stood scantily clad. We made a lamentable sight: a warrior monk and two practically naked women.

I flinched, as my vassal put his hand on my shoulder.

"We must pass through yonder forest on foot, as commoners."

My maid groaned, but I was ready in a moment.

It was a hard journey to Bristol Castle. Here, I am confined to my bed, verily worn out. The excruciating pace, set by an anxious Brian, blistered my feet, until they bled through my thin leather boots. Twice, racked with fatigue and trembling, I collapsed and vomited onto my muddy skirts. Each time, FitzCount hauled me upright and urged me onward, as a mule driver does a recalcitrant beast.

My beloved lies beneath me, in the dungeon of this keep. My exhaustion is such that even his looming presence does not light my soul afire. I begin to consider him an abstraction, a courtly image, a knight who once equaled my whole world. I have loved him and hated him, with all my heart, but neither love nor hate can bring him near to me. My spirit yearns for equanimity, in the place of wretchedness.

Today, my copper mirror reflects pasty flesh and a deadened expression. Rumor has it that I was smuggled out of Winchester in a coffin, but I would, in that case, look somewhat more rested.

Indeed, the fortress stirs with gossip. From my chamber, I can hear the walls whispering. Gerta relates every bit of news. Maud's mercenaries thrice abducted Uncle David, but he thrice ransomed his own freedom. Ultimately, the Scottish king vanished back over the border, managing to evade the countess's regiments. The minstrels claim that he discarded all the emblems of his status, every royal accouterment, and sallied forth a beggar, until he reached safe haven.

Robert, captured, is the countess's prisoner. Those avid, sniveling jongleurs report that Gloucester, in good spirits, withstands tribulation as less chivalrous knights bear prosperity. To account for his sanguine temper, they describe in excruciating detail the kindnesses that Maud lavishes upon him. Unfettered, my brother is completely at liberty to navigate castle and town, and to see and speak with any one of his choosing. He has even been furnished with monies, a stallion, and extravagant clothing.

The bitch embellishes her reputation for gentle femininity, differentiating herself from my masculine ill treatment of the pretender. But if she thinks that her benignity will prompt the earl to throw me over, she is much mistaken. Robert's good humor is mere good manners. The countess's seductive mildness will not avail her of my vassal's faith.

With carmine cheeks, Gerta informs me that many at Bristol palaver at length over the relationship between FitzCount and their empress. Sir Brian's solicitude cannot be hidden. Our arrival together, his friar's costume, and my bare limbs, stimulates the invention of our retinue. Much is made of his being chosen to escort me in the hour of greatest danger. My supporters wonder why there has been no earldom created for him. They are sure his bloated passion for me robs his wife of her due. My own court scorns my negligent return of the knight's affections, thinking nothing of my foreign husband's rights.

I have asked my maid to bring FitzCount to my solar tonight, at midnight watch.

She blustered, not wishing to fuel the stories that circulate, yet must obey.

†

MY ARDENT DEVOTEE ARRIVED.

I was bathing, holding my torn feet up out of the water, so as not to wash away the stinging paste of mint coating my blisters.

Scrubbing my back and shoulders, Gerta adjusted her position, so that my admirer could see less of my form from the bench that he had chosen.

I turned my head. Brian was dressed as befits his position, but his tonsure has not yet grown in; the discrepancy between his noble tunic and his pious coiffure unsettled me. "Sir, the world notes the nature of your fervid attachment. As intimate as you are with me, you must realize what boon I demand of you."

FitzCount hung his head, and addressed the ground. "You have never asked me to account for my most despicable failure, Empress. I am grossly ashamed to have let you down in such an ignominious fashion."

I pushed my waiting woman to the side. "The risk that you took was immense. If you did not succeed, then the task was too great for any man."

Brian rose from his seat and approached. He lowered himself to his knees and clasped his hands on the ridge of the tub.

Gerta froze, incredulous.

The knight made his confession. "I befriended the ugliest of Maud's servants, the one least likely to have enjoyed a man's favors, and sullied myself with her ungainly flesh. In gratitude, the hussy agreed to brew Marie's herbs. She was to offer the potion to the queen, as a digestive drink, after the Feast of the Exaltation."

I reached up one wet hand, to stroke FitzCount's boyish face. "What terrible luck."

"The news of your decampment from Winchester cut short Her Majesty's dinner. Instead of whiling away the evening, she stormed furiously across the countryside in hot pursuit. Abandoning her entourage to come to your defense, I do not know what became of the packet of poison." His glance fell to what was clearly visible under the water.

"Gerta, the temperature falls. Perhaps you might retire to the hearth in the great hall. Sir Brian will help me to my pallet."

My maid nodded gravely, and spoke with as icy a tone as she had ever mustered. "As you wish, Empress."

After she quit us, FitzCount stroked my hair.

I trembled. "Do not lay a finger upon me. You told me once that all you needed was my regard. Is it no longer enough for you?"

The young man slid his palm onto my collarbone, and then along its ridge. Softly, he grunted.

"You must not allow everyone in my household to translate your fulsome sentiments. I cannot be the subject of so much lurid talk."

Brian plunged his hand lower, onto my belly. "Do not refuse my adoration!"

I shivered, but when I closed my eyes, I saw Stephen's face. I swept Brian's arm away from my thigh.

Just then he moaned aloud. "Oh God! An angel commands me to adorn myself with excrement."

I blushed. "I deny you the solace of my embrace, for I am the seraph whose virtue cannot be sullied."

†

IN THE HOUR BEFORE the dawn, I slid along dark passageways, gliding in stealth to the oubliette, in the basement of the marshal's tower, in the outer ward. I carried a candle, carefully sheltering its small flame. Holding the taper to the grill on the floor, I could barely pick out Stephen's prone form. Gradually, I discerned his red head and his emaciated body, curled up like an infant. I muffled a cry, for he was a shadow of himself.

My chest thudded. "Shall I trade your decrepit carcass for my brother's?"

The Count of Boulogne turned over onto his back. Mutely, he gazed up at me.

I gathered my thoughts in the silence. "On the other hand, I might send you, or what is left of you, to the wilderness of Ireland." Was he gone into the void?

Then his voice came out in a croak. "Ah, Matilda, my fair one. It would be something to cavort again in one another's arms. I would relish your hot touch in the cold of my prison."

How could he flirt with me now? "The Virgin herself deposed you; without Her favor, how can you ask for mine?"

Stephen rolled back onto his stomach.

A sharp pain coursed through me. Tears moistened my cheeks, but I dashed them away, and struggled to strangle my emotions, or, at the very least, to conceal them under the guise of sterile detachment. Had I fooled him, or myself, or the heavens above?

†

AT TERCE, AMABEL ACCOSTED me in the sewing room. I was at work upon a small tapestry, stitching two bodies intertwined, surrounded by serpents. "Queen Maud makes my husband a magnificent offer. If he swears affiliation to their party, he will stand the second lord of the land. After the king's, his will would be law."

I looked up from my needlework, into her pouting face. "Robert is no fool; he will never agree to such a patently absurd proposition. My brother knows what little trust to put in the promises of the House of Boulogne. He will be immune to the blandishments of that slut, the countess. He is not like most warrior earls."

Amabel's wide face registered surprise. Perhaps she had not thought to be jealous of Maud's bribes or allure. "Without Gloucester, your cause is lost. Trade him for His Majesty, and regain your respectability."

I pricked my finger and put it in my mouth to suck. "Robert would never advise me to unleash the pretender. With the usurper enslaved, the throne of England sits empty, ready to receive me."

The countess looked as if she would have spit upon floor, if she had been beside any person beneath her in rank. Her fury exploded. "Your own brother sacrificed himself, to guarantee that you lived! Would you let him die? The queen threatens to ship him off, to rot in Boulogne."

In my lap, the snakes harassed the lovers. "Gloucester would not want me to capitulate, merely because he is no longer his own master."

My sister-in-law fairly shouted. "You are a hard mistress, Lady!"

†

To be Empress of the Romans is nothing.

Loyal only to themselves, Amabel and Maud agree to barter their husbands. My birthright and all the oaths of fidelity sworn to me do not stop the Countesses of Gloucester and Boulogne from circumventing my authority. When Eustace arrived at Bristol Castle, as surety for my brother's safe conduct, Amabel's keys freed our prisoner. Accompanied by a splendid procession of his barons, my desiccated cousin trotted off to be reunited with his wife. His destrier gleamed, somehow sporting crimson trappings and brass fittings. Which lout of a groomsman in my stable washed and brushed the animal's mane? What disloyal page wound red ribbons into its tail?

Meanwhile, Henry of Blois and the archbishop of Canterbury safeguard the earl's return to us. Until then, my sullen hostage ill recompenses me for the loss of his father. Indignant at the threats to his succession, Eustace alienates everyone in my household. The resentful youth, still unbearded, has his mother's features. My Plantagenet inherits Stephen's beauty and charisma.

Discounting my disapproval, everyone, on both sides of the conflict, agrees that the civil war must revert to the time before the Battle of Lincoln. The gains and losses of this year shall be erased; Boulogne and I are to resume our rivalry from our previous positions. No one speaks of peace. Every corner of Britain remains at odds. All are blind to the horrors of continued disorder.

I pray to the Holy Mother for my own ambitions, and also for the plight of my subjects. In anarchy, nothing shelters them. In misery, they fester. When will the Lord lift up His countenance upon them?

†

At a festival court in Canterbury, the archbishop crowned and anointed Stephen and Maud for the second time. The minstrels swear that the spectators were more dazzled by the countess's comeliness than by her copious jewels. The ceremony renewed the pretender's solemnity and repaired his eminence, restoring him from obscurity to his status, his regalia, and his friends.

A great entourage assembled to celebrate the usurper's reinstatement. Bishop Henry was one of many who assured my rival of his renewed partiality. His Grace excused his brief flirtation with my cause, calling it the result of extreme necessity, not of zealous preference. The false king repaid this betrayal with amity, and humored his sibling by agreeing to enter into a pact of brotherhood. The jongleurs, pretending to have witnessed the ritual, describe the chalice into which they each dribbled a bit of their blood. They vowed not to divorce in times of trouble, then drank to one another's prosperity.

Oddly, my cousin's late sufferings reinforce the mildness of his demeanor. In his renewed glory, he is no harsher than he was before. Of course, those who adhered to him throughout his ordeal are well rewarded. Adeliza's husband, William, is granted the earldom of Lincoln, formally negating Ranulf of Chester's claim to this title.

†

IN PITY AND LONELINESS, I license Sir Brian to enjoy my beloved's carnal privileges. I blush now to record my shameless foolery. I have stooped so low as to dance lewdly before him, while strumming upon a little harp.

In gratitude, FitzCount pushes a scrap of parchment under the lintel of my solar door.

> *There is no man on earth, no king, no prince, no emperor, who could not be charmed by your dimpled navel, your lean flanks, the very soles of your feet.*

Gerta suspects that the knight has subjected me to some enchantment. She ransacks his quarters looking for evidence, and triumphantly presents me with a mangled broom, missing a chunk of its straw. She is sure that she saw him, at three consecutive Masses, clutching a bulging satchel. She declares that he has brewed the sheaths into some infusion, and drunk it, to have his way with his goddess.

In truth, I burn to consider that Stephen must have fornicated with me for the same reasons that I permit FitzCount's attentions, a charitable impulse and the promptings of a vicious nature. I take reasonable precaution, and swallow a hornet, so as to prevent the conception of a child, but still I allow Brian to caress me, and quiver under his touch. He is not my heart's idol, but I have consigned my beloved to the past.

If I am to recover my sanity and my worthiness, I must disavow the pretender everywhere, in everything. The corpse of a great passion decays in my heart; its effigy swings in my mind. I can no longer permit myself to feed this cadaverous yearning. My lust is infected, putrid; it saps my resolution, drains my vigor, and tarnishes me to the core. It offends Christ, and I would be spotless for Him, as before my own son.

The Matter of the Crown

Scroll Fourteen: 1142

*A*nd so Matilda found refuge, yet her spirit drowned in the waters of discord. She could boast of her freedom, but rage and misery contaminated her soul. Too soon, her supremacy melted away, inundated by the atmosphere of disharmony and contention. Her husband denied her his protection. Her lover stripped the pleasure from her flesh. In vain, the queen fought and trysted, but nothing tasted sweet. Her vision clouded; she could no longer distinguish between mastery and servitude.

†

Spring

I MOVE MY COURT to Oxford. My couriers relay my messages to all those fighting men bound to me in homage, enlisting their continued support. I hear tell of my cousin's similar attempts to gather battalions, and his success with many young knights, new to their mail, eager to dent their gleaming shields and to blunt their spotless blades.

Henry of Winchester, that forked-tongued serpent, essays to lure FitzCount away from my cause. Sir Brian refuses to show me the bishop's letter, but shares its substance. His Grace admits that his brother's captivity constrained him, for a time, to make one of my party. He intimates that FitzCount, poor man, is also driven by political realities to align himself with the Angevins. As I have broken faith with all my promises, Winchester is free to follow the dictates of his conscience. Disillusioned, but unchained, he renews his pledge to the blessed king of name. Brian must open his eyes, and see that my word is not to be trusted, whilst the pretender holds out his hand, in amity and generosity.

FitzCount permits me to read his response, hoping to counteract the pall that has fallen over my mood.

> *To His Grace, nephew of Henry the king, cousin to Empress Matilda. The holy church and the Lion of England have several times obliged me to kiss the hand and the skirts of their true daughter. I remain under oath to abet her in the contest against the Count of Boulogne. She shall not forfeit her legacy, or permit it to be stolen.*
>
> *Neither I, nor my vassals, choose to fight for Matilda in the hopes of accruing gold, or fiefdoms, but we do it solely because the empress is the rightful heir to the crown and throne. She remains the Lady of the English. I, Brian FitzCount, who received from Henry I and his daughter all his arms, titles, and honors, am ready to prove, either by battle or ordeal, where my fealty lies.*

†

THE JONGLEURS AVER THAT Stephen falls ill among his new recruits. He lies, they claim, on a sorry pallet, his army sent back home. Smirking with self-importance, they pronounce the pretender's imminent death. Many among my retinue believe the troubadours and begin to bow more deeply in my presence. But I cannot credit any honied news, so bitter does my fate lie on my tongue. Although my vitals boil with loathing, it cannot be denied that my heart still beats in time with the Count of Boulogne's. If he were no more, I would know it.

Wishing to make the most of my cousin's sickness, Robert advises me to appeal to Geoffrey. Tonight, among our entourage in the great hall, he tried to galvanize my enthusiasm for a new offensive. "It is the Count of Anjou's duty to maintain his wife and child's English inheritance. It is time for him to cooperate with us."

A frisson of excitement surged through the room. The barons and their ladies sat up to listen, and neglected their fèves—chocolate discs rolled in ginger syrup and granules of crystallized sugar. Despite their renewed animation, I hunched over the high table, my energy flagging.

With her usual peevish vehemence, Amabel pushed her venison ribs to the side. "The Angevin has conquered Lisieux and Falaise, indeed all the land in the neighborhood of Rouen."

I sneered. "Geoffrey was rebuffed from the city itself." Why could she not be silent? Had I given her leave to speak? My head ached; I could not remember.

Brian's voice was light. "It is a fine day for us in Normandy."

Suddenly ravenous, I waved over a page who brandished a frumenty pudding. I gulped down the dessert, tasting the wheat and the milk, thick and pasty. Then my belly cramped. "Send an envoy to Geoffrey, if you find it mete and fitting." All I wanted was to sleep.

✝

Presumably, the Angevin does not intend to participate in my English war. He regrets to disappoint the empress, but he rebuffs my emissaries. Instead, he invites Gloucester to his court, assiduously flattering the earl, engaging to draw him out of my sphere. He calls him "Brother," and professes to need his honorable, noble presence in order to weigh the costs and benefits of our proposal. He will parley only with the son of a king, not with mere messengers.

For now, Normandy, Geoffrey's hard won prize, takes precedence over my throne. Yet the Lord of Anjou will not be able to ignore forever the mutual suspicions and jealousies of the continental barons. To my aggrandizement, he rests indifferent, but he must understand that it is the Plantagenet who will come to ensure their ultimate surrender.

†

MY WOUNDED SPIRIT IS in need of balm. The castle plantations burst with renewal, and I hunger to commune with the glories of nature. Unfortunately, I am but seldom in solitude. I am vexed to be always under the surveillance of my bustling entourage, which further strains my bilious disposition.

This afternoon, I wandered with my closest associates in the Mary Garden that I have installed directly adjacent to Amabel's kitchen plot. The flowers, all named for the Virgin, are arranged in the shape of a cross. I would have preferred to give my attention to the brittle trills of the plump-bellied robins, but instead listened glumly as my retainers encouraged my brother to take his leave of my household.

Even FitzCount dispensed with Robert's presence. "Go to Normandy! We need Geoffrey's warriors to inflate our shrinking battalions. Foreign troops abet our enemies. We can no longer afford to shun the addition of mercenaries."

Despite the bright light, I saw his devotion; it emanated from him, as if he were the daytime moon, visible against the celestial blue of the sky.

Gloucester, strangely neutral, bent down before a bed of marigolds. "What a lovely sight, reminding us of the Holy Mother's love." Nearby, the Madonna lilies were fully opened, giving off a noxious, sugary scent. He gathered a nosegay of both, choosing each bloom as carefully as he parsed his words.

Brian grasped the earl's forearm. "Think hard on it."

Bright orange pollen stained Robert's fingers. "The journey that you propose entails traveling through enemy territory, on both sides of the Channel."

Where lay the seat of Gloucester's pride? "Our cause will languish without you to mastermind it, brother. Who else dissuades the adventurers and scofflaws from desertion?"

Brian reddened. "You have more than one trusted knight to stand by you, Majesty."

Robert considered. "I might take hostages from some of our barons, so that they cannot abandon you while I am away. Loyal magnates will furnish me with their sons, without complaint."

I stamped my foot on the path, but then caught the heel of my boot in the hem of my mantle. "Oxford will be left with a paltry garrison!"

FitzCount drew up his fists. "We will defend this keep with our lives. No one can penetrate the waters that encircle us, dismantle these outworks, or dismember our tower."

From the bower, I could see part of Oxford Castle's sturdy wooden palisade. The turgid flowers at our feet seemed more tangible than our defenses. "No fortress stands impregnable."

Gloucester paused. "Sister, you could withstand everything except a fire." He had come to a decision. "Stephen ails; now is the time for me to plumb the depth of your husband's fealty." He handed me the posy, and bowed over his pointed boots.

I received it with a curtsy, but tremble to think that I am no longer the object of my brother's chivalry.

†

Summer

THE EARL'S CONVOY SAILED from a harbor near Wareham Castle. Although a great storm racked the waters, so that some of my brother's ships were lost at sea, and others were pushed out of their path by the winds, Gloucester's own vessel landed without trouble.

In his saddlebag, Robert carries a gift from me to my husband, an enormous ring, set with five opals around a center diamond. On the interior of its gold band, it is inscribed, "The Word became Flesh," promising invincibility in combat. I mean the jewel less as a bribe than as a token of princely enrichment to come, the rewards I shall shower upon the fidelity of my closest confederates.

†

ROBERT TARRIES, WRITING TO me of Geoffrey's enormous learned charm and various elaborate military projects. Apparently, in this season, he aims to reduce all the rebel strongholds in southwest Normandy. Together, the earl and the Angevin have already invested, stormed, and defeated ten castles, including Stephen's Mortain.

No thanks are sent, and no credit is given, to my talisman.

I lag behind, nursing my sore and impassive purpose.

†

I HAVE NOT BEEN able to shake the malaise that haunts me. Eager to combat my cantankerous temper, Gerta seeks out various doctors. I deem them all fools in Phrygian caps, and bemoan their extortion of exorbitant fees, but my maid persuades me to submit to their arts.

Today's leech, misshapen, suffers from a curvature of the spine; his chin rests against his collarbone and his left arm curls up into a crook beside his jaw. It does not seem likely that he sees beyond his own two feet. Yet he is a creature of ceremony, presumably out of respect for his own university credentials.

He inched into my solar, then bowed many more times than the situation required. Without waiting for my permission, he lowered himself onto a stool.

The grotesque seemed certain of my symptoms, before he had been in my presence for a minute. I suspect he bribed one of my women to describe the irresolution and pique that perplex me.

He glanced at Gerta, as if to dismiss her. "In order to alleviate your despondency, Empress, I would taste your piss."

My maid grimaced.

Would he also insist sniffing the solid waste in my noisome chamber pot? I snorted, rather scandalized. "I do not wish to slake your curiosity."

The doctor frowned. "I examine Your Majesty's urine, merely in order to determine whether you suffer some imbalance of the humors. Are your humors a lion, roaring ferociously within you? Do they scatter forward and backward, like a crab? Do they canter, like a stag, or bleat as a sheep? Do they claw within you, like an angry bear?"

"The queen cannot allow you to investigate her water," Gerta interjected. "It is nefarious to suppose that she is possessed by animal spirits."

The physician coughed up some phlegm, spitting it out on my rushes. "If the empress is querulous and impaired, her illness may be the work of the devil." Then the cunning charlatan began to recite a mess of botched Latin, Greek, and cipher.

"No, no, I see now that you are a master of your profession. By all means, sample my malodorous pee." Hurriedly, I relieved myself, splashing my legs under my bliaut.

The quack swirled his finger in the pot, then licked it, smacking his lips. "Ah, you are much afflicted. However, if you drink only beer flavored with licorice, I can vouch for your recovery."

Gerta clucked at his diagnosis. "With what largesse can we repay such good news?"

†

THE PRETENDER ARISES FROM his sick bed and retakes the field against me. Aware that I lack Gloucester's protection, my cousin attempts to eradicate my rebellion, once and for all. He sacks Wareham, thwarting Robert's plans to land there on his return. Isolating me further, he bombards fortresses all over the west and southwest, scattering my battalions to the far corners of the island. I try to focus on the fact that Oxford Castle still dominates the Thames valley, commanding the north-south route from Northampton to Winchester.

In this hour of danger, I beg the earl to come back and succor me. I send off so many scrolls to the continent that I have expended all of my trusted couriers and exhausted all of my supplies of ink. Proud of my industry, I mix up a new batch, using rainwater, tree sap, and the larvae of caterpillars.

Ever assiduous, my maid submerges herself in the castle kitchen, busy with another recipe. She promises that this sweet water will lift me out of my doldrums. This will be an easy prescription to swallow, as I relish its taste: young, green licorice, figs, and crystallized sugar, all stewed with barley. The castle cook convinces Gerta to make a second pot, to fatten up the chickens for the royal table.

†

IN ADVANCE OF MY brother's long-awaited arrival, letters sail back to me across the Channel, alerting me to my husband's harebrained scheme. The Angevin packs off the Plantagenet, to accompany his uncle. My mind spins; is this stupidity or shrewdness? Does Geoffrey dispose of Henry, so that our second boy, his namesake, can inherit Normandy and Anjou? Has he understood that my russet haired son is not his own?

Robert values the youth as a figurehead; the lawful heir must boost morale among our adherents. Knowing my secret, does Gloucester intend to substitute his nephew for his sister upon the English throne? I begin to comprehend the appeal of abdication, but Henry is only ten years old, and does not belong in the eye of the storm. Deaf to my misgivings, the earl counsels the boy's presence among us, arguing that my son stands to acquire a more thorough knowledge of Britain, and should play a part in the fight to regain it.

How can a mere adolescent make a difference? So many of my vassals, seasoned warriors all, have been unable to turn the tide of civil war.

†

Fall

PUTTING ASIDE ALL OTHER things, Stephen marches against Oxford, at the head of a great battalion, one thousand knights strong. He arrives at the Thames, to our south, at the ancient ford of Saint Frideswide. Very deep, in the best of circumstances, it has flooded over with the summer rains. Still, he plunges his troops through the churning current.

We sound the tocsin, and my foot soldiers stream downriver to meet their adversaries. My loyal bowmen dash alongside, stumbling onto a muddy plain, ready to launch their arrows.

Just now, my valiant men-at-arms are driven back by the invaders, inside the walls of our stronghold.

†

I STAND ON THE castle battlements, engulfed by dissonant yells and cries. The pretender's force murders, pillages, and fires the town. Evading his bombardment, some of the burghers cling to our gates, clamoring for refuge. I smuggle a few of the more prominent ones inside the keep, although how I shall feed them during the siege to come is beyond my ken.

I do not doubt that my once beloved violates his share of unwilling women. Does he gnash his teeth at the thought of me?

†

THIS MORNING, AT DAWN, we lowered our drawbridge to admit my rival's heralds. Stephen's messengers stayed only long enough to demand that I return with them, as a prisoner of the crown. In return, His Majesty will pull back from the investiture of Oxford. Acknowledging my adamant refusal, nodding soberly, they remounted and cantered back across the wooden planks.

In the same moment, a few of the most scurrilous of our hangers-on scudded out of the fortress, to escape the hardships likely to follow.

†

IT HAS BEEN A month. Our foes still blockade the castle, pelting us with stones and debris, battering our walls with their war engines.

Today, I surveyed the damage to the outer bailey, under cover of FitzCount's protection. A small parcel thudded into the dust before me. I snatched it up, and saw that it was addressed to the Lady Dameta. Furtively, I tucked it up into my long, commodious sleeve.

Brian raised his eyebrows. "We have no Dameta here."

"You do not know her, sir. She is a local woman who cowers from men, still in shock after her abuse at the hands of Boulogne's militia." My mind raced; would this satisfy him?

My vassal did not look convinced. "Go within. The catapult extends its reach."

I listened to the patter of shrapnel streaming down upon the ward. FitzCount's shield dwarfed me; he held it close and stood very near. I might have stayed put, under the aegis of my stalwart champion, but I was anxious to open my letter in the solitude of my solar.

Still Stephen's dupe, I shivered to read of his derision and his perfidy.

> *I cannot forgive you my chains. I would subjugate you if I could, the better to revenge myself upon you, and have my way with you. I no longer admire you in any way that can make a difference, yet I flit about you, slighting other concerns. I despise you and crave you. I would mistreat you, even snuff you out, but I cannot desert you.*
>
> *I was young, whole, and pure, when I lay with you, before the time of my domination. You say that we might sustain our empire in righteous union and place the crown upon its fruit. This dream is not possible, after all that has come before. When I rid myself of you who have tainted me, I will find myself complete once more.*

Hastily scanning his message for the first time, I only perceived his indefatigable passion for me. My chest tightened; I shook all over, thrilled to have bewitched him, my supposed apathy all but forgotten. The second time through, parsing the note more carefully, I was overwhelmed by my cousin's odium, how he shuns the happiness that is ours for the taking.

I glory in his debilitating despair, for I have had more than my portion. I am outraged by his willful denial of our connection, yet understand that it behooves us both to travel down new and disparate roads, away from each other. These, then, are our separate fates. My reviled beloved sinks into hell, where sorrowing and gleeful beasts await him with open mouths, while I float upward, to Christ's kingdom.

†

WE STARVE, AS OUR supply of foodstuff dwindles under the depredations of our unmanageable guests from Oxford. Despite my angry protestations and the dire warnings of my knights, the burghers sneak into the storerooms to assuage their rumbling stomachs. They are unable to discipline themselves, not even through prayer.

The Count of Boulogne's army cuts off every avenue of approach to the city. We have no hope of reinforcements or provisions. From the aperture in my solar, I can see the paths running through the neighboring landscape; enemy regiments crowd the overland routes. The usurper's patrol boats clog the surrounding waters.

This evening, a royal herald deposited an odiferous package into my solar.

My maid, delighted, seized and ripped open the gift of viands. "Oh, Empress, your scoundrel repents."

I held my nose at the congealed fat, plastered to the flesh, and the unmistakable stench of high meat. "He endows me with scraps unfit for his hunting dogs."

"We cannot be so choosy in this hour."

"Eat it, if you must. I will not take his leavings."

Gerta tore into the food, unmindful of her smeared cheeks.

I closed my eyes, remembering the sacrifices of our Mother Mary. "Hail, Holy Virgin, Hail."

My maid finished off the nasty victuals. "Does She hear you, you who have so long neglected Her counsel? Does She forsake you, you who have only turned to Her so late?"

I said nothing, for what defense could I make?

Gerta laughed bitterly. "Your evil familiar does not forget you. He hopes for no other advantage than your notice, and fears no other loss than yours."

†

LAST NIGHT, AFTER ALL were asleep by the wan light of a crescent moon, my despicable cousin appeared in my chamber, fully disguised as one of my own guard. Had he struck a bargain with a demon, and traded his king's mantle for a cloak of invisibility?

Sighing, I thought he was a hallucination, born of my strangled desire. Only Gerta's gasp shook me out of my mistake.

Harshly, Stephen whispered. "Do not howl, woman, before you are sure that your lady wishes you to alert the garrison."

A wail formed itself at the back of my throat, but I snuffed it out. I quivered, and my voice choked. "Retire. Report nothing."

"For love of you, Empress, I will commit this sin." My maid rolled away from me, inching open the door to my solar. Its hinges squeaked. "But beware!"

In the darkness, the pretender disrobed, peeling off my colors and pieces of chain mail. "I have been sequestered under your pallet, cramped and miserable, for hours on end." He began to stretch, twisting his slender torso to the right and left. "Maud challenges the single-mindedness with which I invest your citadel. She will have noticed my absence from our tent, and I will have to apologize most abjectly."

Now Boulogne wore only a linen chemise, resembling the pilgrim's white shirt of atonement. His pale legs glowed faintly.

Titillated, furious, I clutched my pillow to my chest, hiding its emaciation. "Her acrimony matches my own; you have made us mirror images of one another."

Stephen tangled his fingers into my hair. "I cannot achieve a perfect rapport with her, or commune with my honor."

"One last time, I ask you to dispose of her."

"She is my family and my kingdom."

The count climbed over me.

Despite my long-standing enmity and my newborn renunciation, I returned his kisses more wildly than I ever had. The voluptuous blackness of the night cloaked our viciousness.

He spent little time on the preliminaries. Almost immediately, Boulogne was inside me, rutting ferociously. Suddenly, he pulled himself out of my depths, soiling my thighs.

Bereft, I placed the flat of my palm on the flat of his abdomen. "You have been enriched by our love, but I have been impoverished by it."

The usurper moved to my side. "I trespass against the Lord, driven on by some emptiness of spirit. But I have His promise. I may fall seven times and rise again, if I sink into contrition and righteousness. I shall not forfeit the name of a just man."

I laid hold of his manhood, shriveled and sticky. Had the Virgin interceded, and forbidden him to fill my belly with his seed?

Stephen inched away from me, and rose up from the bed. "Even a wicked man abhors the greatest wrongs. I am ready to grovel before my wife and heaven."

I knew then that we had exchanged our last caress. "When have you ever sated your appetites?"

†

BLESSED BE THE VIRGIN'S grace! My brother and son cruised smoothly over a waveless Channel. All fifty-two of their fleet came to shore safely. Robert marches at the head of four hundred knights, both English and Norman.

Advancing to Wareham stronghold, encamping before its walls, the earl oversaw the construction of siege weapons. Almost immediately, he received word that its royal battalion wished to forsake the false king.

How simple it can be to take a tower from the pretender!

†

IT IS CRUSHINGLY COLD. Snow covers the scorched city, and whitewashes the desecrated landscape. The spring that supplies our fresh water freezes solid, as does the river. We have no more wood for our hearths, having already chopped up and burned all of our furniture. The throbbing in my stomach seems less of a burden now that I can barely feel any sensation in my limbs.

All yesterday, I abased myself, prone upon the frigid floor of the chapel, in supplication to the Holy Mother. My jutting hip bones ached to be pressed against the icy stone. "Mary, have pity on the sorrowing sinner. Redeem me from this disgrace. I would be like you, a mother of wondrous fame."

The Virgin answers my beseeching call, suffusing me with valor and the germ of a devious plan to extricate myself from this fortress. Gerta, FitzCount, and I shall be robed in white, from head to toe. Our men-at-arms will let us down by a thick rope, over the stark wall, into the snowy landscape. Stealing across the Thames, we will creep through our opponent's camp, then slip into the surrounding woods.

†

TWO NIGHTS AGO, I wiggled out from under the usurper's thumb.

An enormous white cape and a copious white veil entirely masked my identity. I wore thick gauntlets, to buffer my hands from the rough cord that I gripped as I was lowered into the darkness. Safely delivered into Brian's grasp, I regarded Gerta's descent. Slung over her shoulder, a white satchel transported my blue casket and cache of parchment rolls. Tense with adrenaline, delirious with liberty, I perspired, although my breath formed clouds in front of my mouth.

In silence, the three of us padded over the frozen waterway.

FitzCount tightly clamped my upper arm, anxious that I not trip and split the ice beneath us. Once upon the further side, unseen in the snow banks, we shuffled past the edge of the royal pavilion, clearly marked with Stephen's heraldic device.

My ears pricked at the sound of Maud's squeals and giggles. I pawed at Gerta, to slow her steps. Reaching into her sack, I slid out my enamel box, opening it up to the night.

Urgently, Brian shook my shoulder.

Shrugging him off, I thrust my gloves at him.

From the casket, I pinched the amber lock of hair. For the last seven years, it has been my most cherished treasure and my most poisonous source of affliction. Anxious to set my soul free, I flung it down, very near to my cousin's tent. It stood out against the crystal ground cover, like a stain. Thus divesting myself of his relic, I discarded my enemy's worthless love.

Then, with my two faithful servants, I ran six miles to Abingdon, through high drifts and muddy ditches, hardening myself against the yelps of werewolves: savage, cannibal creatures, once men until the fury came upon them. At Abingdon, we claimed horses and galloped astride, nine miles east to the isolation of Wallingford, FitzCount's own castle.

†

FITZCOUNT'S STRONGHOLD REJOICES OVER our recovery; their sumptuous hospitality does not ebb. Still famished, we overstuff ourselves to nausea at every midday meal, then nap away the short afternoons.

The romantic imprudence of my loyal vassal annoys me. He is ever underfoot, and resists when I would shoo him away. "No one has the right to be indignant if I dedicate myself and my deeds to Your Majesty's service, and acknowledge you as my foremost mistress. On the contrary, I am bound to be extolled and avoid all stigma of wantonness."

But my heart is walled off, interred in an abyss of grief. Brian overflows with affection, but I cannot let him fill me up with his tenderness. I would leave my soul empty, colossal, titanic.

†

THE BEAUTY OF FITZCOUNT'S wife, Basilia, has been much exaggerated. With her cornflower hair and unlined face, she resembles a child, or a fairy. It bemuses me to see my knight hounded in turn by her unrequited infatuation. Her eyes, dark brown, very deep, dart after her husband as he dogs me, catering to my whims. As the days pass, she sours with the knowledge that he worships me with more than a political fervor. Contrary to his view of her prerogatives, she resents his ill-concealed desires and flaunted subservience to me.

Last evening, in the dusk of vespers, already retired to my guest quarters, I heard a sharp, hacking sound coming from the inner ward. Standing so that I could look out from the slit window in the wall, but not be seen to be spying, I watched a hooded Basilia hammering one rather large boulder against another, which lay embedded in a small depression on the ground. Holding my breath, I could make out the words of her spell: "I do not pound these stones together, but beat and smash the essence of him and her, whose names are etched upon them." I exhaled, and saw that she picked up a spade, to cover the rocks with mud.

Once the darkness of compline had fallen, and Brian's wife had evaporated back into the castle, Gerta ambled outside, accompanied by a Herculean soldier partial to her face and form. He had a battle-axe in the crook of his elbow. My maid simpered becomingly, presumably urging him to show off his purported strength. The warrior exhumed Basilia's fragments and further buffeted them to pieces, before kissing Gerta's hand. My maid picked up the shards and stuffed them in a leather satchel; her admirer slung it over his shoulder. Arm in arm they wandered off, so that she could reward his fortitude and his discretion.

Now these broken shreds of stone smolder among the embers of my fire. If anything is left of them, when we depart from this keep, I shall tumble what remains into the moat.

Does Basilia think that her pixie magic can sever the sworn bonds of fealty between a chivalrous knight and his lady?

†

MY BENIGHTED COUSIN TAKES Oxford. Within hours of my departure, the garrison and the townsfolk surrendered to the pretender. Generously, my cousin pardons my guards and courtiers, permitting them to disperse. But the main routes, from London to Gloucester and from Southampton to the Midlands, are his. Despite my trick, our adversary retains the upper hand.

Gloucester, apprised of my flight, marched his forces to Wallingford. Reunited with my brother, I am primed to share the burden of the resistance. The earl's praise for my daring exploit encourages my renewed sense of purpose.

Discovering the Plantagenet safe, grown tall and strong, I am glad beyond measure. Already, Blessed Mary rewards me for my sacrifice of the Count of Boulogne, and redirects me, toward my son and his future.

Tonight, at Brian's board, we feasted on piglet, stuffed with compote of nuts, scrambled eggs, bread, dates, and spices.

Seated next to my heir, I fluttered over his face and form. "This evening, it is almost possible to be negligent of the misery and discord that swirls around us."

Henry grinned exuberantly. "We are winning your war, Mother. Our armed campaigns are like waves, crashing repeatedly upon the helpless shore. The Lord's hand is visible in every one of our triumphs."

I considered the warmth in my belly. "My own escape is one of the Glorious Virgin's proven miracles."

The Plantagenet glowed, for I am no coward. "It is said to be so, by every minstrel in the land." His red head dipped down, as he stuffed his mouth full of fruit and meat.

I grinned, as I used to. "I have hired notaries to record my daring and Our Lady's wondrous support of me; they write it down in the annals of every church in Oxfordshire. Some of them embellish the historical account with details of their own invention. One claims that I adorned myself in Mary's most holy shift, which she wore to give birth to Our Savior. Only this robe was unspotted enough, white enough, to blend in with the snow, and pure enough to safeguard me among impious traitors."

The prince smiled, his lips red with juice. "The shift was smuggled out of Constantinople on the orders of Charlemagne! Your supposed tie to it will heighten our stateliness in times to come."

FitzCount arose to oversee the changing of the watch upon the battlements.

Once he was out of earshot, Basilia's opaque eyes pulsed. "Empress, your boy's red hair quite strikes my fancy. It puts me in mind of His Majesty."

I was careful to speak languidly. "We are cousins."

Brian's wife hissed.

I smelled her breath, acrid, like mustard. "Are you named for the evil basilisk, half fowl and half serpent?"

Basilia pursed her lips. "Very few disparage me without coming to regret it."

Henry Plantagenet shook his amber head. "Hold your sniping tongue, woman."

Whatever it takes, I shall depose the father and elevate the son. Hail Mary, Vindictive.

The Matter of the Crown

Scroll Fifteen: 1143

*D*o not suddenly rise up from your cushioned seat, and discount this history of conceit and deception, supposing it merely the work of the devil. Even worthy men took up arms in iniquity, so that bustling villages once celebrated stood desolate, and noble castles, once mighty, fell into decay. The empress's own tragedies hardened her to the miseries of her people. She frolicked in corruption, to ease her own burdens. Englishmen prayed in vain; in retribution for the sins of the ream, heaven withheld its mercy. Much was the wicked Matilda to blame.

†

Winter

MY BROTHER, MY HEIR, and all my most important vassals reestablish my court at Bristol. Despite his youth, the Plantagenet's presence facilitates the recruitment and retention of our partisans. Most are in good spirit, given the broad consensus that the true prince abides among us.

Adeliza sends me word; her letter flusters me, for its tone is less conciliatory toward me than I deserve, for all that she remains loyal to young Henry.

> *The king to come sets his foot on English soil, despite the hazards of a winter sailing and the swirling civil disruption. Neither could deter he whom I would honor as Jesus, son of Mary, he who will release his subjects from the evils of war. Your son rises; we must all unite to keep him clean of blood. In the time before, your anger oppressed the land, but now your zeal is righteous, for you are whole like the Virgin and Christ is God and man.*

†

THE WINTER SETTLES ITSELF down upon us. Hour after hour, we loiter in the great hall of the citadel, warming ourselves by the radiant hearth. When our conversation palls, we gloat over my boy's marvelous arrival.

Today, I bored him with more such talk. I cuffed him on the arm. "I have confidence in you, in the wonder of you."

Henry tossed his head with impatience. "The antlers of the stag would be miraculous, if they were not its natural crown." The pretender's son displayed Geoffrey's fine mind.

I tested the prince's logic. "But what of this? The flesh of a corpse is eaten by worms, but reconstituted whole in paradise."

"God can subvert the laws that order His creation." Snagging an earwig from among the floor rushes, he tossed it into the fire, snickering when it sizzled.

FitzCount sat with us; he has always been fond of my heir. "What news of your two brothers, long unseen?"

"I have been at Angers with young William, now six. We are seen to by Denise, my father's leman; we have been brought up with her twins, Hamelin and Marie, who are eleven. My brother Geoffrey, eight now, lives further south in Anjou, in Saumur."

I sniffed at the mention of that slut, once so much my rival. "Tell me about the young lady. Does she still compose fanciful poetry?"

The Plantagenet flushed. Was it from the heat of the blaze? "Marie's agitation at my departure was improper. She claimed that she could not exist without me, that I am her only joy."

My jaw hinged open. "Then it is fitting that you were banished from her side." I closed my mouth, remembering my first kisses.

Sir Brian coughed. "Denise should intervene, or counsel her daughter to be wary. A girl's heart is pure, and ready to love in the twelfth year; if she settles her faith upon you, she may remain constant to the end of her days. But this passion, this inner flame, will serve her ill. To an illegitimate wench, your royal smiles can only bring tears. She will never wear your coronet."

The prince turned toward me, anxious. "At night, she displays the signs of the frenzy. She moans, slaps her hands, bangs her head, grinds her teeth. In the daytime, she will not speak of this, but laughs and sings, until she ends by weeping."

The Earl of Gloucester pounded his fist in his lap. "It is not for you to bear witness to her insanity!"

Amabel piped up, quite satisfied to take my family to task. "Denise must snip three boughs of juniper, dousing each one three times in wine, whilst making the sign of the Trinity. If she sets the branches upon her daughter's pillow, while she sleeps, Marie will be freed from her torments. Of course, you could do these things, if you are in the girl's presence after compline." The bitch's cheeks reddened at the boldness of her implication.

Certainly Henry has my carnal weakness, his father's and his grandfather's. But I believe him innocent of the act of intercourse.

The Plantagenet frowned. "I am full of her troubles and choose to watch over her. When she rages, I know best how to soothe her. What you propose, Lady Aunt, is superstitious nonsense, if not heretical."

Now Amabel whitened, remembering that my heir is the king to come.

Robert scowled, discomfited. "Boy, you are not a physician. Your pity prolongs her madness."

FitzCount nodded. "Marie must be bound up and left in a dark place."

My son's voice deepened. "Mother, may I not marry her, when I ascend to my rightful throne? Shan't I do what I like, then?"

The conversation had run away from me, but now it flowed back. "The girl is your half-sister; you two cannot wed. But you have my leave to adore her, for it never serves to advise against love. Someday, when you are of age, you will outgrow her attractions."

The Plantagenet's teeth flashed white. "Every beauty is alive in Marie. Among all the other maidens, she has no peer. I will never know peace in the arms of another."

I laughed low, to hear Stephen's son vow to be true to one woman. "Dear child, pride of my loins! Your veins run with milk and honey."

Henry cared nothing for a mother's devotion. "Whatever admiration is paid to Marie is her due, for without question she is the finest, most amiable damsel in all the world."

Both Brian and Robert's expressions were glum. I pressed my own lips into a thin line. Groaning sorrow is the usual result of unbridled esteem.

†

OUR LORDS DART OFF from Bristol, once more to engage our adversaries. In their absence, we ladies rely on the minstrels' battle chronicles. I permit the castle garrison to cede entry to any and all troubadours who request shelter, in exchange for their news, gossip and verse.

Several sing of the Count of Boulogne's vile rampage through the southwestern countryside. To lessen the sting of my celebrated escape from his siege, my cousin attempts to retake Wareham. Finding it too strongly defended, his ire grows. Full of bestial fury, he pillages all the territories surrounding Oxford and even ravages further afield, meting out fire and the sword.

At Wilton, the pretender's forces swarm the nunnery of Saint Etheldreda the Virgin, transforming it into a fortified post, and forcing the good sisters to wait upon them at table, and in bed. The jongleurs insinuate that the lovely abbess is the usurper's willing concubine. Amabel shakes her head at Stephen's depravity.

†

THE EARL OF GLOUCESTER launched three divisions against the convent, and routed the usurper from Wilton. Robert's regiments looted the town, tossing firebrands onto every roof, dislodging the burghers from their hidey-holes. Our battalions stormed every church, granting no right of sanctuary. Finally, they burst into the nunnery of Saint Etheldreda, smashing the doors down, raping and terrorizing the same women who had been taken against their will once before, and whose voices were too hoarse to scream a second time. The troubadours recount, without equivocation, that the Earl of Gloucester violated the abbess, mingling his tears with her own. This Amabel does not credit, spitting at the scoundrels who repeat it.

†

ONE PARTICULAR JONGLEUR, BERNARD de Ventadour, skulks about me, ever ready to tell me what I do not wish to know. This afternoon he had the apish temerity to scratch his long nails against my oaken door, and creep into my solar, brushing past a confounded Gerta. When I nodded my permission, he smiled, flaunting his blackened incisors. "Ah, Lady, you are charity itself. Do be soft-hearted and mild, and send for some victuals."

I dismissed my maid on the errand, curious in spite of my misgivings.

Bernard is tall, but far too thin, and his sonorous voice booms out from a sunken chest. He has agreeable, symmetrical features, limp hair the color of an icicle, roguish brown eyes, and a dank odor. He is affable enough, when he remembers his place, but most often oversteps himself, to my continual irritation.

With great impertinence, Bernard scrutinized my belongings. "The king has spoken of your charms, but not of your gentleness."

I burned to hear that my once beloved bandied my name among his retainers. "How is it that traitors and commoners discuss their queen so freely?"

"His Majesty shares many of his private thoughts, when he is in his cups. I often sup with him, and his consort, to entertain and distract them from this ugly war."

Now I was alive with interest. "Surely the Count of Boulogne does not compliment my person in front of Maud?"

The troubadour demurred. "Indeed he does so. Her Majesty is sorely tried by his wandering eye. Lately, she sheds many tears over a lock of red hair that she found in the snow outside the royal pavilion, on the morning after your astounding departure from Oxford."

I rejoiced that my hated rival guessed at her husband's link to me. But I would not reveal my satisfaction to a minstrel. "Whosoever discarded it must have intended to mark her renunciation of him."

Bernard guffawed. "Yes, yes, but Maud is a woman, and a woman does not often see the distinction between an affair that is over and one that is not. Long ago, she granted her heart unconditionally to the king, thinking that he would always be hers to command."

For the moment, I forgot that the fool was a mendicant versemaker, loyal only to his belly and his purse. "Have you ever known such a bond that did not wither away?"

The minstrel did not flinch from telling me the countess's secrets. "The queen believes that His Majesty will not break faith with her again."

I smiled bitterly. "In lust, he has wronged that witch and in lust he will wound her again and again, no matter how they try to hide this from one another. Their match was an inopportune one."

Bernard would not agree. "Maud considers the wife of a handsome and virile sovereign to be entitled to share a great romance with him."

"The larcenous whore deals in stolen position and stolen emotion."

"Their embrace is an honest one. They couple as true lovers."

I let out an indiscreet bark, then stood up, remembering my place and his, and casting a shadow over him. I pointed to my door, and the oily, insubordinate man scuttled away without his supper.

†

Spring

MY BROTHER'S TALENT FOR war waxes full. Gloucester successfully invests the magnificent Castle of Devizes. Without complaint, the archbishop of Canterbury allows the superb structure to fall into our hands. We do not have Bishop Henry's Wolvesey, but Devizes is an even more splendid palace. Its taking is a credit to Robert's prowess.

Indeed, the earl wins a whole series of strongholds in the southwest. In victory, he shores up the defense works of each captured keep, requisitioning laborers from its surrounding countryside. Those who will not agree to work for us are made to do so, under duress. The jongleurs relay the growing resentment against my brother's impressment of manual workers. But I will not allow the songs of minstrels to curdle my high pleasure at Gloucester's achievements. As of now, we have smashed an open north-south line, from Gloucester to Bristol, to Devizes, to Wilton, to Wareham Castle on the Channel. This path shall stay clear, until the prince shall be old enough to travel it in triumph.

†

MUCH TO AMABEL'S PLEASURE, Gloucester returns to Bristol; she rarely leaves his side.

Oddly, he seems despondent, despite our gains. I presume that his malaise dates from his abuse of a holy sister. His eyes are shrouded, his conversation cheerless. Gerta presses my brother's pages for information and discovers that the earl is seldom able to sleep through the night.

Gloucester and I come into conflict over his methods of reinforcing our new strongholds, and I have been forced to debate with him in his wife's presence. I wish the peasants to toil for me, and for the Plantagenet, in duty and in devotion. But my brother reminds me that our revenues are sorely depleted, after our recent offensives. As we lack the funds to launch any new sorties, our defenses must be reinforced with the free labor of unwilling serfs.

†

THE SHADOW OF PEACE reigns over England. Despite the mild weather, there is no fighting, for so many are killed or exiled from their proper places that there are too few to stand the field. Our position in Gloucestershire and Wiltshire is now reputed to be invincible. Our court at Bristol begins to rival the false king's in magnitude and grandeur. It is commonly accepted that I am the master of half of England and that my laws hold sway in the southwest.

Bernard de Ventadour, the naysayer, does not see the good fortune in this stasis, but rather the reverse. "My lady empress, the sun must set on the day of doom before we awaken to the dawn of a new age. The conflagration to come will purify the nation, to be sure, but will surely be hot and uncomfortable to witness."

I consider evicting the lout from my keep. Why should he drink my mead and shelter his mule in my stable, if he is unwilling to sing me a song of resurrection?

†

FITZCOUNT HOVERS ABOUT ME; I have been unable to hold myself aloof from his repeated advances.

Disapproving Gerta castrates a weasel, and sews its testicles into a goose skin pouch. When I lie with Brian, I am to keep this small sack between our abdomens so as to prevent the conception of a child.

Today, he came to my solar at prime.

My long-suffering maid shuffled off to the kitchens.

In the light of daybreak, I could see that he was wearing knitted umber hose, the color of Stephen's hair. "Take off your braies, sir."

He complied, awkwardly untying the garters and peeling off the leggings. Then he stood up, unsure but aroused.

"Come here, man." Apparently, I had to direct his campaign against my virtue.

"Empress, I am in the thrall of my mania for you." Brian walked over to me and tried to pull his tunic off, but it had not been properly unlaced and stuck upon his head.

I sniggered. "Your ignoble lust demeans your noble grace." I entwined my fingers in the ties and freed them, then dragged off his robe and plucked at his chainse. The undertunic was of a very fine linen, embroidered all over with delicate foliage. This was Basilia's handiwork, I was sure.

In his eagerness to be naked, FitzCount almost ripped off his wife's souvenir. "I am only your servant. I have no other rank, no other name, no other center, no other purpose but to love you."

I began to discard my own clothes. "Before we succumb to our passions, we suppose that we will find happiness in physical pleasure; afterward, whatever the raptures of amorous sport, great is our consternation."

"My darling, for you I will gladly be ensnared by despondency!" Brian fumbled with the fabric of my pleated skirts.

I guided him to what he searched for. Why must I always have a man gasping for breath in my ear?

In his delirium, my vassal shouted out, "Oh! For this I willingly contaminate my flesh in wantonness and vice!"

I closed my eyes against my own memories.

FitzCount exhaled, and pressed his sweaty torso against me. "We recline in a wide meadow, under the boughs of an ancient elm. How tenderly a nightingale warbles out his song above us."

I adjusted the contraceptive pouch, which tickled my belly, and sighed at his earnestness. "You might kiss me again, sir, and see how warm my mouth is."

Brian looked toward the ceiling, but seemed to see the sky. His smile faded into an expression of deep seriousness. "I fear no more to die, for I have known true jubilation of the soul."

†

Summer

MORE TERRITORY FALLS TO the Count of Anjou, still fighting his own battles on the continent. Rouen is Geoffrey's next objective, and his last one, although the city has rebuffed him before. But he already controls all of the duchy south and west of the Seine. Now, the Angevin is generally referred to as the Duke of Normandy. Just as my perfidious lover snatched one half of my inheritance away from me, my ruffian of a husband steals the rest.

I have a message from Geoffrey, ebullient to have won the title to which he has long aspired.

> *I have put my trust in courage, mail, axes, and battlements, but not only in these. I give my most precious thanks to the Holy Virgin on high, my helpmeet, who interceded for me, and who saw that justice was served. Normandy has bled a red sea: Ave Maria. My Glorious Lady has done this, so I set my bell towers to peal the Te Deums.*
>
> *You, Matilda, are the Duchess of Normandy, as the Lion of England intended. Our son must return to my side. I will append him to all my grants and charters. He shall receive homage, as my heir.*
>
> *Your crown may never be his, and the English vassals who have sworn to him may pledge fealty to your cousin another day. Whatever his crimes, the Count of Boulogne remains the lawful sovereign.*

No! I shall prove that a daughter can transmit the right of succession. I never struck out against my sire. A mere child, I crossed the sea and passed over mountains, to dispose of myself according to his command. After a spotless marriage, I again obeyed his summons. I tied myself to a man of his choosing, even though I was the Holy Roman empress.

My son, the legitimate recipient of Henry I's imperial realm, will reunite our two provinces, so that English and Norman magnates can hold property on either side of the Channel. The Plantagenet shall rid this empire of the plague of divided allegiance.

†

Fall

ALL OF THE PLAINS surrounding Bristol keep gleam gold and white; a fulsome wheat harvest awaits the farmers' scythes. And yet the days pass without any cultivation of the grain, for the local peasants lie dead from famine and violence. In order to save some of nature's abundance from waste, the great families and the once prosperous burghers of Bristol come out in force, to labor in the fields. All this week, my brother, young Henry, FitzCount, and others of our noble retinue toil among the stalks, sewing our own crops.

Today, from the saddle, I watched my ill-conditioned courtiers struggle to cut down the sturdy sheaves. The Plantagenet's red head regularly bobbed up and down, as he did more than his share. Brian felled the wheat quickly and efficiently; he was lathered all over with sweat. Robert exerted himself turgidly, capable of less physical effort in the heat. The others, generally, had difficulty keeping pace even with the Earl of Gloucester. Unused to grinding away like serfs, their pride interfered with their ability to do what was needed.

Finally, tired of my passivity, I condescended to join them. Dismounting, I walked with the other women, gathering up the broken fronds that the scything had left behind. There was a buzz at my appearance, for my hair was completely uncovered and hung in one loose braid down my back. Feeling overly warm after only a few minutes of drudgery, I tied up the sleeves of my bliaut, then hiked my skirts up, into my girdle, exposing my legs in the blazing sun. Stooping again to participate, I noticed a greater resolve and industry on the part of my subjects.

†

AUTUMN HAS BEEN PRUNED of the glories usually associated with the gleaning and the hunt. I tarry at Bristol, sitting out my husband's continental preoccupations, my cousin's stalemate, and the provocations of Amabel's stilted hospitality.

Last night, in defiance of shortage and foreboding, I organized a feast to mark Henry's departure for the continent. Its centerpiece was a gleaming platter of lampreys, of the right sort, the variety with small heads and large bodies, white bellies and lustrous, sparkling skin. In my son's honor, I had spent several hours down in the kitchens, watching the scullions skin the serpents, remove their innards, and drain their blood. I supervised the roasting, and the careful reserving of the oil drippings. Under my tutelage, one of the cooks made the sauce, grinding together raisins, ginger root, and dried rose petals, combining them with breadcrumbs and vinegar, then the blood and the grease. To my delight, the galatyne recipe found much favor with my boy.

We sat long at the board, stuffing ourselves with more food than we needed. Alongside the lampreys, we devoured a blackmanger—a sweet chicken potpie flavored with licorice, lemon rice with almonds, and fritters of parsnip and apple. All the gluttonous freeloaders present complimented my opulence, but I cared only to gratify the Plantagenet.

Gleeful at the sight of so many delicacies, he chewed with gusto. "How eager I am to be off, Mother."

I savored the tart citrus of the rice pudding. "Go with my blessing. Recruit an army for the second Norman invasion of England!"

Brian sighed. "And none too soon. One can journey a whole day in Britain, without finding an inhabited churchyard or a tilled field. In every town, vagabonds swear that they were once men of substance."

The feeling at the high table grew somber. Our food turned to ashes in our mouths.

Sensing that I resented his remark, FitzCount drank deeply from his own goblet. "At Bristol, we do not repine. Your comeliness, Empress, creates its own utopia."

Why must he parade our affair? "My beauty has been of no utility."

Amabel grimaced. "A well-formed figure and a translucent complexion are still subject to worms and rot."

Brian would not cease his foolery. "A knight who woos a lovely mistress wants nothing more than the privilege of kneeling at her feet."

Bernard de Ventadour rudely interrupted his betters. "It would be best, sir, if you left the arts of poetry to the talents of the jongleurs. We will leave the arts of war to you."

And what of the arts of love? I no longer believe in them. Is there any difference between the smarting shame one feels to have encouraged an unrequited passion, and the aching nausea of falling victim to the same unsavory obsession?

I inhaled, satisfied at least with the fruit of my unworthy love, and how it has ripened.

The Matter of the Crown

Scroll Sixteen: 1144

he empress had long wandered in a meadow, drenched in the spirit of earthly love. But now she understood that she was lost to the Word, exiled from heaven, ignorant of celestial things. All about her, following her example, men affronted the Lord's goodness. When would Matilda rouse herself and begin to drink from the river of wisdom? Could she slake her thirst for adventure? Would she ever discover the road to paradise, and set her feet upon it, one after the other?

†

Winter

NO LONGER WILLING TO form one of my brother's household, I remove to Devizes, that massive, magical palace. In my solar, I am surrounded by luxury, for it is stocked with rich embroidered hangings and inlaid ivory furniture, under a ceiling fashioned from gleaming mosaics. The fireplace never smokes. Lovely stained glass windows filter the sunlight on the short, bright afternoons of the season. I sit, bathed in glowing bands of red, green, and blue, as if I were a brittle, illuminated saint.

Gerta grumbles at me. "Rainbows often bedeck dark and stormy skies."

Slothful, I neglect to regret the magnificent state of my current accommodations. Here I rest, warm and dry, while my husband busies himself on the continent. Despite the impediments of winter, the Count of Anjou completes his conquest of Normandy. In January, he crossed the Seine and marched northwest, advancing to Rouen. He pitched his camp close to the walls of the city. There followed a momentous storm; it felled many trees in the surrounding forest, and destroyed many neighboring farms. Yet this omen was interpreted in the Angevin's favor. Under the clearing sky, the Rouenais greeted Geoffrey with cheers. The burghers flung open their gates and proceeded with him to their cathedral. There, they solemnly turned over the city to his guardianship, and to our son's.

†

To enliven my day, I have a letter from Maud, delivered by a monk of lascivious expression. I imagine he consoles the Countess of Boulogne whenever her husband gambols outside the marital bed. Beads of sweat glistened on his tonsure and his hands trembled as he held out a parchment page, folded in three. I dismissed him forthwith, to read what jealousy had wrought.

> *May the Holy Mother grant me retribution!*
>
> *How many hours of blissful enjoyment have you purloined from me, how many amorous embraces have you stolen from me? Why does my own husband set aside a putrid, shadowy corner of his soul, wherein he stores up his moldering dreams of you?*
>
> *May some incubus poke out those impious black eyes of yours! Even the angels would sing his praises.*

If you were murdered, I would declare a festival.

The bitch cannot mar my calm. Her belligerence is nothing to my own sacrifice. Maud's antipathy cannot undermine the fortifications that I have erected around the ruins of my love.

†

GERTA AND I EXPLORE the palace, and, in a subterranean study, unearth unimaginable treasures, including my very own hand of St. James! That evil genius, Bishop Henry, had smuggled it here, from Wolvesey, the better to conceal its whereabouts, or to ensure its safety during the long weeks of warfare at Winchester. My silver reliquary, set with precious gems around a toadstone, remains in perfect condition. The bone itself glistens still with holy energy. It does not appear to have been sliced up, or ground down in any way. I weep to find it incorrupt, and restored to me.

The underground chamber holds much of interest. We discover a Bible, annotated in the margins. Essential passages are marked. I note His Grace's interest in the magic of the apostles, such as the power of St Peter's shadow to cure disease.

Next to his Bible, we disinter a copy of Aristotle's *Secret of Secrets*. My rudimentary knowledge of astronomy is not enough to unravel its riddles and formulas, but I itch to know what they mean.

As is to be expected, we find a notebook of diabolical arts, a *Quaternio Nigromantie*. Gerta and I will need to study its black spells, to see if we can improve upon our own white knowledge of the natural order of things. Winchester Magus was apparently captivated with one device, a sort of occult square. It is an anagram of the opening phrase of the Lord's Prayer, twisted into a box. Did he think to wield the power of heaven against me?

Finally, on our third visit below, we exhume another manuscript, a diary of vice, a penitential catalogue. Given its odor, it must have originally been written in onion juice, and been illegible, but the passage of time has darkened its text. The bishop was his own confessor.

I blush to take on his role, but I read with avidity the details of his infamous obscenities. So much of what men learn has been hidden from me, despite my literate education. Winchester quotes Plato; is it possible that Plato said, "Those who have earned the esteem of other great men ought to be free to frolic with any winsome boy that they choose"? Henry of Blois marshals the ancients in his defense, but reaches his own guilty verdict just the same, denying himself dispensation.

> *I do not forget that I am first and foremost a servant of the holy church. It is for me to set an example of chastity, and to be a stranger to all forms of unclean delight. I must keep my body unspotted for the Lord, since the Lord has granted me special nobility, the absolute privilege, with my own hand, to consecrate flesh and blood, and, with my own words, to absolve the offenses of sinners.*
>
> *And yet I plunged head first, again and again, into dark transgression, into what is clandestine, forbidden, and cannot be forgiven. To what murky depths of awful shame has my unbridled sodomy and unremitting heresy anchored me?*
>
> *I am to blame; I am profane; I will pay with my soul. I shall not inherit the kingdom of God.*

†

YESTERDAY, ROBERT MATERIALIZED AT Devizes, crossing the drawbridge with his retinue.

Under the portcullis, I stood to receive him.

Leaping off his stallion, he took me in his arms.

I was surprised at the earl's warmth. "Why, brother, what brings you from Bristol and Amabel?"

Gloucester hustled me into our spacious and clean outer courtyard. He pointed to the stables, dismissing his attendants to see to his horses. "This keep is as prodigious as I remember it." Without delay, Robert urgently propelled me across the fortified bridge, into the inner bailey.

I wondered what to make of his anxiety, but saw that I would get no answer until we were alone. I quickened my own pace as we headed for the tower. Mounting the spiral staircase, I could feel him brooding upon some question of importance.

Once we approached my solar, Gerta appeared on the stone steps, descending as we rose. My maid paused to curtsy, and made as if to turn back and join us upstairs.

But the earl said, "No, no, do not be bothered by my presence. Go on about your business."

Gerta's face was curiosity itself, but she obeyed his command and continued down.

By this point, I was fairly bursting to know what had brought Gloucester to me. I did not hesitate to bolt my chamber door. The light in the room was yellow, jaundiced from the sun streaming in through a golden pane of the window.

Just then, my brother roughly kissed me, muttering, "My sister, my bride! You have conquered the territory of my heart. After all these years of waiting, we can be as one."

Taken aback, I passively allowed his mouth to roam freely over my face. When his lips sank to my neck, I pushed him away. "What is this that you do?"

The earl stood back, frowning, but then his aspect softened. "My dearest, how is it that a lady of your great beauty and distinction lacks a knight of her own?"

I could not believe that Gloucester would commit incest. "Imprudence! Impudence!" I smoothed my hair and took a deep breath, to steady myself.

Robert grabbed at my posterior, clutching himself tight against my skirts. "Do not attempt to disembowel my passion. It is your face that is to blame."

I twisted in his powerful grasp. Troubled, I saw that his green eyes were dimmed. "I lament that you gift yourself to me; it is not right that I accept your bequest."

The earl held me immobile; his hands spanned my waist. "Be audacious enough to love me, for you will do us great harm if you will not."

I felt cold sweat gather at the nape of my neck. This was not what I wanted. "Brother, I cannot do what is horrible."

Gloucester pawed at my girdle. "A queen should dare what she wills; I will not think you base."

I started to struggle in earnest.

Robert ripped the neckline of my bliaut. "You have given yourself to many men; I want my turn with you. Take me; you have not had me inside you."

"You insult me, Brother, when you force yourself upon me!" I could not get through to him, past his desire.

The earl pulled my hair, so that I screeched. "Come to me, Matilda. Taste the forbidden fruit, the sweetest taboo."

I stamped my foot down upon his boot. "In your dementia, you are like a moth, drawn to the flame!"

Somehow, I had broken the spell. Gloucester released me, and I dashed to the other side of my solar, pulling my garments back into place.

Robert stood, desolate in the yellow glare. "You confound me, Empress. You are unwomanly, when you bar the gate to your garden of delights. O that my hands were sticky with your nectar!"

I kept a trunk between us. "You have fallen out of grace. You are not worthy of my compassion."

The earl ran his hands through his hair. "You were pleased enough to see me bow to you. Now I lie at your feet, and you tread upon me." He staggered to the door, unbarred it, and passed out of the chamber.

I lowered myself slowly onto the floor, and sat, staring at nothing. After a short while, I heard the creaking of the drawbridge and the shouts of my men-at-arms, as Gloucester and his mounted company rode off.

Now, over the shock, I am choleric at his violence, and his excuses. As if I myself am not forced to withstand solitude and hunger! My broken heart longs for what will never be, but vice cannot lessen misery, cannot be the ladder we lean against our walled keeps of grief.

†

Spring

I HAVE A MESSAGE from my errant sibling, written in cipher. I decode it with very little trouble. Gloucester merely replaces each vowel with the consonant that follows it in the alphabet. He must be too disordered to invent a puzzle more fitting to our shared intellectual talents.

> *For so long, I presumed upon my perseverance and strength of character. I expected to gallop through the pearly gates, while seraphim trumpeted my arrival into paradise. I have given up the idea of fanfare, but still hope to rise to heaven.*
>
> *In order to conquer my desire, and expiate my sins against you, I fast, deny myself the balm of sleep, and mortify my skin with hot irons, thick needles, and sharp thorns. My wounds drain my soul of its evil inclinations. In the midst of my pain, I float upward into bodily indifference and spiritual communion.*
>
> *But you, intolerable blackbird of temptation, still haunt my thoughts. Your claws scrape at my soul, your beak pecks at my heart; beneath my deadened flesh, you cause me further suffering. I have no net to snare you. I cannot lock you away in my dovecote.*
>
> *Nothing is left to me, but to throw myself upon burning coals, and engulf one fire with another.*

In return, I remind him of the well-known parable.

> *Lucifer was best loved, among the Lord's angels, and exalted by Him. But Lucifer, so eminent, so trusted, grew arrogant before his God, and defied His commandments. Then the Lord cast him out of the oasis of the celestial heavens, down into the deepest conflagrations of hell.*

†

IT IS THE SEASON of rebirth, but a great refusal swells within me. No man's caress can bring me spiritual ease. My dismissal of my own brother's advances, and his self-flagellation, solidify my resolve to dispense likewise with the carnal attentions of FitzCount. I have long been addled by lust, yet at my increasing age it is high time to renounce every physical pleasure. I will not be held to account, and punished. No one shall be able to defame me.

†

YESTERDAY BRIAN APPEARED AT Devizes, ostensibly to facilitate the return of the hand of St. James to the abbey of Reading, which lies very near his fortress at Wallingford. I yearn to restore it and the concomitant wealth and favor that will accrue from a steady stream of pilgrims, keen to be the first to worship the relic of the Apostle. I have ordered the fashioning of an enormous gold-plated feretory, ornamented with jewels, for the ceremonial translation to Reading. In addition, I propose to present the abbey with the royal manor of Blewbury, vast and fertile. I intend this endowment to honor FitzCount's longstanding adherence, and hope that it shall excuse and repay his garrison's raids and depredations in the neighborhood, perpetrated in my name.

Meeting me in my solar to discuss the details of this transaction, he would not talk business, without first slobbering all over my palm.

He repelled me; I could not bear his touch. "My wretchedness must be called wantonness, nothing more. Praise is due the Virgin, for my depraved craving has diminished now, into nothing. We remain tied by the bonds of fealty and deep affection, but nothing more."

Brian's sensual features, throbbing one moment ago, paled and went flaccid. "Empress, I have not begun to drink my fill of you!"

I foretold that it would not be a simple matter to divest myself of his attentions. "Whenever we fornicated, I knew that I defiled myself, and would bring you only sorrow." How could I soften the blow? "I lay with you, under some compulsion, but it was not love."

FitzCount paced away from me, pulling at the dark hair at his temples. "Matilda, have I not been true to you?"

The sound of my name, so familiar on his lips, so inappropriate coming from one of my vassals, was a dead weight in my stomach. I was nervous, lest he persuade me or entice me to restore his rights. "You must return to modest Basilia, who suffers on your behalf. Her delicate heart freely chooses you. Make a present to her of your dedication. Show her you regret your perversion, and take solace in her embrace."

Sir Brian walked about my chamber, denying my logic, opposing my dictate. "Why do you speak of her, who never did you a good deed? My distaste for her is just; her lumpen pallet is laid upon broken stones. Her flanks are rough with grit, and her spit tastes of sawdust."

I was full of impatience now, and went to warm my hands by my fire. The day was chilly, despite the budding foliage. "You are besotted, but it is better to be righteous! Today I deliver unto you the Holy Mother's mercy."

FitzCount followed me to the hearth and wrapped his arms around my back. His words were harsh. "I zealously fought for my queen, and took only this little reward. I never thought to experience such distress, when I pledged her my muscle and cunning." Resting his head upon my shoulder, he began to cry. "I never dreamt of sharing your throne, but only your bed. You are most unjust to me."

His tears moistened my neck. I was glad that I could not meet his eyes. "Indeed noble sir, I beg your pardon. You are a worthy knight, of great renown. In courtesy, you must find it possible to admire your wife, or conceal your apathy or disdain for her."

Brian's voice took on a deeper timbre. "I have already given myself to you. There is no other warrior who has a more single-minded determination to bend his knee before you. Your name is inscribed in the pommel of my sword. You will be my idol until the end of my life."

How well I empathize with his fate.

†

THERE IS NO CITADEL or hamlet in Normandy that does not belong to the Angevin. My husband has reached a détente with the French king; even Louis VII recognizes him as the duke. The sycophants who surround me profess their congratulations. They sense that my continued presence among them, combined with my husband's undisputed control over the Channel, gives our party the momentum needed to win the civil war. It is unfortunate that we have no money to prosecute our cause here with any sort of concerted effort. And so we sit and wait for heaven to accord us what we deserve.

†

Summer

UNBEARABLY TORRID WEATHER ROILS tempers all over my realm, on this island and on the Continent. The peasants and burghers are subject to religious frenzies, perceiving in every passing cloud and gust of wind some hint of the Lord's dissatisfaction with the state of our affairs.

I have had a message from Marie, similarly disturbed by vivid hallucinations, thought by her to pertain to me.

> *A comely lady, of the highest rank, sank into adultery, seduced by a nefarious demon, disguised as a crimson falcon. Outraged, and bereft, the upright husband ran the whore through with his lance. Publicly, he blamed her death on the depredations of a band of marauding brigands.*
>
> *At the ceremony of her entombment, when the man was surrounded by all his vassals and family, a horrible lamentation arose from the errant wife's corpse. A huge scarlet raptor had alit upon her body, straddling her torso, and was devouring her heart, all the while spreading wide its enormous tail feathers. Those present were terrified and distraught.*
>
> *The man was a pure Christian, so he stood battle with the red fiend. Yet the harlot arose from her coffin, dripping blood and gore, and began to toss sweetmeats to her falcon, caressing it around its neck.*

I can explicate Marie's perverse dream well enough. Her father, the Angevin, is the hero, pure and brave; the incubus is Stephen, with his inflated and erect tail feathers; I am the slut, accused of cajoling sin and entertaining evil. Pretending to inform me, does she taunt me? Does she not consider that the Mother of the Redeemer comes first among all the saints?

†

Fall

GERTA, ATTEMPTING TO COMFORT me now that I have "opened my eyes, closed my legs, and seen reason" stirs up a vat of Flemish broth. It would be a miracle if egg yolks and white wine, boiled with salt, were enough to make everything right.

In this time of civil sorrow, I too hang upon a cross, interred between my striving and my resignation. I discard lasciviousness, and affection, courting despair, yet still struggle to abandon my idol. My nostalgic heart reclaims him everywhere. I give him up, but my diseased mind still serves him. Without any hope of superficial joy, I cannot find the will to sever, conclusively, my ties to true love.

The Matter of the Crown

Scroll Seventeen: 1145

A ll you who would live to be worthy of salvation, attend closely to the empress's example. Answering the tearful supplication of her innocent subjects, Christ shone his light upon Matilda. Small shoots of virtue sprouted within the garden of her soul. Yet, in acknowledgment of her first bursts of repentance, she commanded a magnificent favor. She pledged to ignore the blandishments of her beloved's courtly invention, if she might be once more at his side. Heaven made the bargain, for the sake of her atonement, a sacrifice of more value than gold.

†

Winter

I LINGER AT ELEGANT Devizes, while, once more, my partisans take up their weapons in the northeast. Adroitly besieging a fortress loyal to

Boulogne, but becalmed in a protracted stalemate, the earl forward me these lines of repentance.

> *Most precious lady, defender of all those who bend their knees you, condescend to look gently upon me! Help me evade any suspicion of wrongdoing. Let no one have the right or the power to forbid me your fellowship. I depend upon you; you may depend upon me. Receive my soul into your blessed trust, and into the presence of your glorious son.*

Praise be to heaven! In my brother's eyes, I am reborn the Holy Virgin, an unseemly object of improper desire. In relief, I transmit to him a gift, a hare's foot to be bound to his left arm. It shall protect him from hazard, from the dangers posed by men. Will it solidify his remorse, and prevent his obligation to me from faltering?

†

DESPITE THE FREEZING TEMPERATURES, I pace the palace battlements, looking through its crenellations upon a sodden, muddy landscape. I gaze upon a river and its stone bridge, much traversed by persons of little consequence. They would be confounded that their empress has them in her sights, and envies their common lot, their ordinary cheer. My splendid birth assures me no concomitant bliss. Round and round the walls I go, considering the heavy ache in my chest, measuring it equal parts acquiescence and persistence.

My romantic liaison has been a farce, undeserving of me. I was a ninny of a girl, luckless, who gave her heart away without cause or effect. But yet amour abides, coursing, constant. I would, I have, withdrawn from the carnal life. I would entrust my soul to the Virgin's keeping, but my sinful obsession is tenacious.

The gusts of wind are cold, but when they blow over me I perspire underneath my fur-lined cloak. The frigid breeze sets me alight, for I imagine it originating in the northeast, where he marches out, on the offensive. I inhale the air he breathes, opening my mouth to take it in. How far I have strayed from ecstasy, how near to desperation! I have ploughed the way to a cold peace, yet the thought of my audacious hero still warms me. How can I lament my fondness, when it is, it was, sincere?

I stand agape, incapable of any solace, save my imaginary one. And this false dream must evaporate before the almighty truth, that the knight whom I adore is not to be mine. The boy born of our passion must destroy him, to recover that which he stole from us. We may make ourselves mighty only by feeding upon the hate that consumes love.

I have received the blessings of face and figure, mind and spirit, coffer and scepter. My thoughts have all been noble; my abdication from the seat of love is princely. But none of it has been enough to avert my punishment. Why, among kings, am I alone reproved? Are endurance and loss to be my only prize?

†

Spring

ANOTHER ONE OF MY allies defects to Stephen's court. This time it is the Earl of Chester who pledges himself to my cousin and kisses his royal mantle, admitting to encroachments upon His Majesty's favor and an inappropriate zeal for self-promotion. Ranulf and Stephen swear mutual oaths, vowing never to do each other harm. In return for his ceremonial humility, the earl is presented with Lincoln Castle.

I little think that the pretender welcomes him with any real trust. The usurper cannot have forgotten that Chester was the rebel who instigated the disastrous battle of Lincoln. Will one keep be compensation enough for the Norman fiefs that we will strip from him?

Only one year ago, I was thought to have the upper hand in this perpetual civil strife! All at once, the Count of Boulogne is in the ascendant.

The pretender and Chester launch an attack on Wallingford, perhaps cognizant of the growing distance between FitzCount and his patroness. With a newly recruited cavalry of three hundred horsemen, they approach his fortress. Finding my vassal still of a mind to stand by me, and his stronghold secure, they raid the neighboring districts.

I wonder whether Basilia realizes that I have cut my amorous ties to her husband. Perhaps she spends her days encouraging Sir Brian to plight his troth to Stephen.

†

TONIGHT MY STABLE OVERFLOWS with the mounts of heralds, messengers, and minstrels. The mules and the stallions must split their oats, and the attention of my overtaxed squires, grown fat and lazy from underwork.

I am presented with confidential letters from Brian and Basilia, apparently written and sent without the other's knowledge. Did their couriers smirk at each other along the road, and share a campfire?

Brian's lamentations are to be expected. I would be mortified to have inspired less, given his protestations of undying faith.

> *Oh, my empress, my Matilda! You are my lodestar, more resplendent than the summer sun, more brilliant than winter's glittering icicles!*
>
> *I quail before you, in unbearable agony. I stuff my mouth with the flowers of the willow and the poplar, but my ravenous appetite for you is not diminished.*
>
> *Many moons ago, on the eve of my dubbing, I lay prostrate before a high altar. In a cold stupor, I yearned to personify the chivalric code in the service of the crown and in the pursuit of a distinguished lady. In you, I unite both claims to my fealty, and my vassalage has been whole and entire.*
>
> *Now, I am of no use to you, or to your throne; I am the unfortunate one. My sword, my shield, my mail, my stallion: I no longer have the right to boast of them.*
>
> *Yet, according to the law of courtesy, you owe me your clemency. I beseech you, discard your cruel frigidity, which is of no profit to anyone. Though my wantonness is blameworthy, and my complaints unmanly, you must not refuse to succor me in love.*

Although I read his note with a cynicism born of my own despair, my heart flutters with remorse to have caused a fine man so much distress.

Basilia's scratchings and screechings, on the other hand, will make fine kindling for the fire in my solar.

> *Vile, selfish bitch! Hedonist! Degenerate! Burn all the oat straw that you will, soak your rotting limbs in your steaming witch's cauldron! Still you will be unable to rid yourself of maggots, for they are your familiars.*
>
> *I have measured myself with a thread, and coated it in wax, and burned it as a candle to the Blessed Virgin. Heaven chose me, me, to receive in Christian marriage the hand of a perfect knight. I have honored him, and his name, in word and deed. I have held him dear.*
>
> *But you, you, have spoiled and corrupted all that was true in him. He sinks into sloth of your making. He was formed to serve the Lord in joy, but now he refuses to do his duty, to me or to the world.*

†

MANY OF MY SUPPORTERS adamantly maintain that I must sue for a decisive peace. Robert adds his voice to the general call for a truce. Surprisingly, my rake of a cousin agrees to a cease in the hostilities. Would they all cede my inheritance, the better to divide my goods and chattel among themselves?

Everyone concurs upon the terms of a conference between the primary antagonists, empress and pretender. A propitious meeting day is chosen, by a committee of astrologers representing the interests of both parties to this civil war. Thus, after three years apart, we meet again.

I almost wish to deny my own consent. To parley with him will be to tear open all of my wounds, hardly scabbed over. Infected, they fester, giving off a great stench.

†

Summer

YESTERDAY, UPON A WIDE, green meadow, an hour on horseback from Devizes, my nemesis and I reconnoitered.

I wore a blue bliaut, in a mood to announce my fidelity to the memory of our bond. Gerta's frown dampened my boldness, so I covered it with a stiff white corsage, heavily embroidered with cabochon emeralds, for emeralds can be trusted to moderate lust.

Stephen's hair, jarringly red, preposterously red, stood out against the blue sky. The lines on his sharply boned face pronounced themselves along his brow.

My stomach lurched and my breathing became labored when I met his gray regard.

We stood alone, next to a white field pavilion. Some distance away, other tents sheltered our retainers. Closer at hand, Maud waited in an enclosure decorated with the royal blazon. I could smell the rot of her impatience.

The Count of Boulogne smiled down at me, taking my arm, and led me into our meeting place.

To stand with him, with no one's eyes upon us, was more than I had ever presumed to do again. Tears rolled down my cheeks.

The pretender held out his little finger, the finger that holds the secret of a man's life and death, and wiped it around the edge of my lashes, to stem the brimming tide. "I well recollect those times when we turned our back on our disagreements, when we thought only of trading delights."

I gathered up my elation. "I gave you three gifts: my heart and our two sons."

The usurper circled my waist, still narrow after five pregnancies. "How can it be that we are such dire foes?"

Until that moment, all was euphoria, but then the atmosphere curdled. I had to refuse what was offered, and repudiate what I wanted most. "I have cried out against my fortune, but now I accept what is written down for me in the Great Book. I will think and think on you, evermore, but never again know you. There is only one way for me to step, along the path of atonement. I entreat the Holy Virgin; She accepts me as Her penitent."

His expression did not change. "My sword cleaves you in half, but my manhood heals you, remakes you whole. I wield them both before you. It has always been my nature to hesitate between the gifts that have been showered upon me by the glory of God. You and Maud always demanded that I choose between my crown and my felicities, but I withstood both your blandishments and your recriminations."

I knew that I was the stronger one, the one who could forswear my longing. "In order to salvage my own sanity, I hold myself aloof from you."

Stephen mouth twisted. "I would be no more than a shadow of myself if I thought that I had truly lost you." My cousin still had his palms on my hips. Now he lowered his mouth over mine.

My eyes overflowed and my limbs shook, but I pulled sharply out of his embrace. I pinched the skin of my arm, and hard, so as to recall me to myself. My rival would have had me, there on the carpet that had been laid upon the ground; I knew that I had only to touch him again for it to be so. No one would dare to interrupt our two majesties.

Struggling to snuff out my own ardent need for him, my voice quavered. "Our mutual passion once enriched us, even as it humiliated us."

Boulogne gaped at me. My beloved could not fathom the abyss of my despair, nor plumb the depths of my denial. "Maud weeps before me, castigates me, terms my foibles a disgrace. Yet, untamed as I am, she is always willing to lie with me."

I inhaled my rage and my woe. I had no thought to spare for that shrew. "Her tempestuous nature is only one of her frailties. If she smarts upon her stolen throne, she would do best to remember that someday soon she will be bereft of everything that she has thieved from me."

The count bowed curtly and inched apart from me. He raised the flap of the white tent to survey the crowd of his subjects and mine, come together in the hope of ending the destruction of civil unrest.

He dropped the panel of the pavilion; we were hidden once more from spying glances. With a somber expression, he returned to my side. "I admit I am a villain. But essay, great lady, to bend as sweetly as my wife has done. I will never be free of the unbearable, parching thirst for gratification."

I stood my ground, poised to leap away from him. I struggled to keep my voice steady. "Your battle-axe cannot pierce my skin, but your prick wounds me to the quick."

The pretender had regret in his eyes. "Shall we talk of the treaty, Matilda?"

I covered my face with my hands and spoke into the darkness. "Will you turn over your crown to our son, Henry?" I envisioned it atop his father's red locks. In the hot darkness, I seemed to dream.

Stephen's voice washed over me. "I will devolve it upon my son, Eustace. His mother insists upon his accession."

Still I would not look at him. "That impertinent wench is not the heiress to England. You must concede the succession to the Plantagenet."

The count took my hands down, into his own grasp. "Although Normandy is yours, Britain remains mine."

I freed my fingers from his. "I shall never abjure my sovereignty on this side of the Channel."

Suddenly, the usurper pivoted on his boot, and strode back toward the entrance to the tent. "We are reduced to our former state of enmity."

Holy Mother Mary, you have taught me that he is no longer mine to caress, but I entreat your further intercession, for I have been an imperfect pupil.

†

Fall

IN THIS SEASON, MY sizable palace is swollen with my most prominent allies and their vacuous wives, triflers eager to amuse themselves at someone else's expense. My stairwells and baileys ring with their catty laughter and the clink of their jeweled ornaments.

Full of smirking spleen, the Countess of Gloucester and her attendant ladies convene a "court of love," trying the merits and demerits of a well-known affair, poring over the details of the case until they reach a verdict. The story presented is that of a highborn lady, properly wedded to a great warrior, renowned for his beauty and elegant verse. Separated from him by historical circumstance, she begins a relationship with another married knight, fine of face and famous for his pleasing manners. They ask the question: May the lady claim to be virtuous?

Gerta puts her ear to every door, and worms the rest of the truth from the least frivolous among our guests. Unsurprisingly, Amabel's court of love holds the accused to account, and names her wicked. One or two women, with no personal animosity toward me, insist that any two married persons who freely decide not to prefer one another should not be bound together forever. But the countess will not tolerate any dissension within her coven. My sister-in-law proclaims faith between spouses to be eternal, and wedded union evermore. How dare that bitch peer into my soul, rooting for Stephen's image?

Gerta detests Amabel and moans about her pernicious allusions. But she herself has continually disparaged my amorous adventures outside of Geoffrey's bed. She has always stood guard before my reputation, wishing to truss it up, unsullied.

Doing what she can, she winds my long hair and some linen strips into braids, then fashions the beribboned plaits into knobs on the back of my head. "I have a mind to misplace your copper mirror. You may take my word for it; you still sway the feeble minds of men. Indeed, none surpass you. But withhold yourself from amorous trouble! Live for your son, the king to come."

Is it not enough that I have suppressed my inclinations? Must I exorcise all my memories? "I fear that love is an incurable affliction. There are no quacks talented enough to lessen its influence. No leech can bleed it out of me, or drain me of lechery."

Gerta's capable hands yanked firmly at my tresses, vigorously pulling them into order. "You have had too many sexual relations, if I may be so bold as to say it. This has overtaxed your womb, which now wanders about your insides, unbalancing you."

I flashed pink. "I was long stymied by a lack of intercourse. This insufficiency damned up my uterus with the spinster's venom." I flushed again. Had I insulted Gerta, long my friend?

She did not stop twisting my locks around her fingers and pinning them close to my head, sparing me no jab or poke. "Speaking for myself, Empress, I can say that it is difficult to repose the forlorn spirit and refresh the corrupt humors, when the lonely scourge of nights stagger, one after another, on and on through the seasons."

I sat in silence, for she had foretold my future.

Gerta grunted. "When Christ is resurrected, you shall not be able to fool Him. Do not foreswear your prayers to the Holy Mother. Only She can whitewash your polluted soul."

The Matter of the Crown

Scroll Eighteen: 1147

*W*hy should the Almighty have rid the empress of her troubles? She had more courage than piety, more beauty than compassion, more zeal than humility. She knew that she sinned when she fought only for her earthly kingdom. Now, pained at the loss of her greatest vassal, she doubted that she would ever claim her due. To compound her woes, Matilda's errant lover judged their first-born son foreign in spirit. With their second, so much more illustrious, his soul vibrated in sympathy, but she knew not whether to exult in this ripening tie.

†

Winter

HERE AT THE PALACE of Devizes, a year passes without adventure. I have been too full of lassitude to record mundane events of court life;

even our war seems banal, as we grow used to an unending armed stalemate amid a barren landscape. The jongleurs do not cease their fear mongering, and yet, in the face of their reproofs, civil turmoil persists. Knights throughout the empire continue to launch their arrows and javelins against one another. The newer they are to the riot and unrest born of greed, the more eager they are to demolish and dismantle, and thumb their nose at the law. Scoundrels dream of lavish additions to their wealth and territories; their mutual pacts of fidelity are nullified again and again.

I pray fervidly for peace, but only my victory can ensure complete tranquility in England and Normandy.

†

THE MINSTRELS ARE FULL of a new story that raises my hackles and guarantees them a warm dinner.

The Earl of Chester traveled from his marcher fief to my cousin's court at Northampton. He petitioned the usurper to abet a campaign to put an end to Welsh harassment, the devastation of crops and the firing of villages. He insisted that a few battalions, under Boulogne's banner, would send the marauders fleeing back into their desolate fens. He further claimed that the royal presence could terrorize the looting hordes more effectively than the arrival of thousands of soldiers. Seeing the English king, the insurgents would scatter back across the border, never to recross it. Such a rout would burnish Stephen's already magnificent reputation as a strategist and a general.

Fascinated by this flattering invitation, my cousin ardently agreed to the earl's proposal. The counterfeit queen urged him to desist, calling the scheme wild and impracticable. The Welsh inhabit a region of mountainous forest, traversed only by narrow passes, unfamiliar to strangers. The crown counselors harped long on Ranulf's previous treacheries, and how reckless it would be to send the body of the king into an unknown territory, under Chester's power. But the pretender would be munificent.

Stymied, the Count of Boulogne's advisors required hostages from the earl, given that he had proved himself so unreliable a friend in times gone by. Arrogantly, Ranulf denied the request, claiming that he had not come to Northampton to satisfy such an enormous demand. Maud, oblivious to the obligations of the king's peace, shouted out at this supposed evidence of disloyalty, and immediately ordered her guards to clap Chester into chains. As they shuffled him away, she blessed the day that delivered his wickedness into their hands.

Those in league with the earl negotiated his release. Ranulf ceded the royal castle of Lincoln to my nemesis, and was given his liberty. Within a week, he hired a troop of miscreants, and set them alight with wild rebellion in the neighborhood surrounding the contested stronghold. The embattled keep held for my cousin; Chester ultimately retreated.

The pretender celebrates with lavish entertainments, honoring the fortress of Lincoln's endurance and faith. Unhampered by superstition, my cousin flaunts his crown, embellished with brilliants, so as to wash away the blot of his own previous captivity. The visiting courtiers are wary, thinking much of sudden imprisonments, and display only lukewarm enthusiasm.

†

WITH GREAT FLOURISH, HERALDS deliver unto me a papal bull, demanding the return of Devizes to the auspices of the church. The pope admonishes my disgraceful larceny; if I do not vacate his citadel, I shall be excommunicated.

Whose pride is so great that they would pilfer from the Lord?

For four years, I have lived within Devizes' splendor, and its stateliness no longer astounds me. Yet, I am ashamed to find its luxury necessary to my domestic comfort. In order to gain time, I have promised to compensate the pontiff, to bequeath in exchange other of my manors and lands, anything else but this keep.

I await the Holy Father's response.

†

CHESTER ARRIVES AT MY palace, asking to be readmitted to my favor, to be the flower of my support. In light of my recent fracas with the Vatican, I readily agree, asking Ranulf to oversee the reinforcement and resupplying of my castle. I hope that it can be rebuilt as a staunch fort, with the potential to withstand any attempt at investiture.

The earl introduces new recruits to my garrison; they crowd my ramparts, scattering their knives and maces along the walkway. The evening air fills with whoops, catcalls, and the clanging of tankards of cider. Short, powerful destriers and noxious, wizened baggage mules clog my once pristine outer ward with their dung and stench. The inner bailey chokes with a glut of bursting supply wains. Grandiose Devizes, my refuge, is a disorderly cesspit of mud, refuse, and noise.

Chester encourages me to be ready, at a moment's notice, to don a suit of armor. Gerta instructs the castle smith to fashion me a helmet, and to cut down a shirt of mail to my size. He lines it with hide, so as to give me a further layer of protection; my maid is adamant with the man that the skin be taken only from the breast of a deer. Resting against my solar wall, a new and extravagant sword awaits some extremity of circumstance. The pommel and hilt are bronze, inlaid with topaz. Our wily smith tempers its blade with an unknown chemical, so as to heighten its ability to slice through the thickest obstruction.

We must not cower before the threat, but gird ourselves to demolish it. Ranulf warns me of leather scaling ladders that will permit our adversaries to breach my crenellated walls. He arranges for the household attendants to stand sentry at the narrow windows of the tower, which he has provisioned with burlap sacks of rocks, weighty enough to crush heads. Will my army of servants gather up their wit and their will, or be useless, dazzled by the sight of waving pennants and the glint of metal shields?

†

TODAY, CHESTER EXERCISED OUR battalion, loading the men with heavy weapons, then jostling them up and down the stone staircases. He bellowed at them when they raised and lowered the drawbridge too slowly. He oversaw mock battles, crying our units on to more and more exertion.

This evening the earl's smell was so baneful that I offered him a bath, a hospitality overdue to him as my vassal. In keeping with his high birth, I honored him by consenting to be present during his ablutions.

A page kneaded his back with a cloth. Naked, Ranulf is ugly, shaped like a barrel and covered with coarse, matted hair, of the same blond as his oversized mustaches.

His broad shoulders reassure me of his vigor, but I could hardly keep my eyes steady upon his bloated, massive form. "My lord, I wish to acknowledge the thoroughness with which you have shored up Devizes."

Chester smiled, exposing his darkened teeth, irregularly spaced in his wide mouth. "As much as I appreciate this sign of your respect, Empress, I am no mincing pretty boy prone to frequent washing. If I stay too long undressed, my soul is likely to run off from my body, leaving the territory ill-protected from imps and demons."

I laughed aloud. "The steam will rehabilitate your spirit, sweating away the poison of overindulgence." His bath was less of an ordeal than I had foretold, for the infusion of spices in the water gave off a strong and pleasing scent of musk, cloves, nutmeg, and cardamom.

Ranulf sighed, shifting about as if he would rise. "I cannot abide all this womanly nonsense. Females may be moist creatures, but I prefer to be dry." He stood up, splashing the floor.

I averted my gaze from his nudity. To my relief, Chester kept his distance, stepping over the edge of the tub to his clean clothes. Then, I was annoyed to hear him dismiss the servant. A small sound of protest escaped my throat.

"You are a beauty, madame; there is no doubt that the fairies went to some effort to shape your face and form. Such a nice mouth you have; your nose is well enough too. There are barons who proclaim you the handsomest wench in the kingdom."

I sniffed with displeasure.

The earl grunted. "Do not alarm yourself. I have no wish to fornicate with you. Queens make dangerous paramours."

"Hah!" I said, and then stopped my mouth, for I would not argue the point with him.

Ranulf laced up his stockings. "A girl's embrace is nothing to me. No satisfactions are so complete as those of a hearty meal, a refreshing bout of sleep or the sound of a trumpet blaring out the call to arms. Ah, to see a pasture flowing with the blood of mangled corpses!" Over his thick breast, Chester pulled a tunic of green wool, decorated with red stags leaping among brown trees. "This is a first rate garment!"

"You admire Gerta's needlework." It would not do for the jongleurs to announce that I had gifted him with embroidery from my own hand.

"It is almost as excellent as the one Maud presented to me."

I sank onto a bench, feeling almost sure that he would not accost me. "Do not mention that Jezebel."

The earl gave me a long look. "Her Majesty was in a fine tizzy at the last peace talks."

I tried to keep my expression neutral. "I had barely a glimpse of the harlot. I was busy negotiating with the Count of Boulogne."

Ranulf's face revealed nothing. "Your rival drank her full of the sight of you."

"Capricious, jealous tantrums must surely repel her husband."

"The king still names her his darling mistress." Dressed, Chester strode toward my seat. "I thank you for your attentions, and would kiss you to mark my fealty."

I lifted my arm up in the air, willing to accept his ritual show of partiality.

The earl pressed his wet mouth into the back of my hand.

I arose to depart.

He blocked my path with his large figure. "Let us seal our mutual alliance, so that I can be sure of your loyalty to me." Chester lowered his lips onto mine and took a short, clammy kiss.

†

Spring

IN JOY, THE VERY earth throws off winter's persecution. The birds twitter; the worms disinter themselves from the soil. At Devizes, we exchange the stuffy air of the keep for fresh gusts of rain and wind. I am ready to plot and plan, to be done with inertia.

My thoughts revolve to my son Gervase, lately appointed abbot of the monastery at Westminster. Although only eighteen, he is most prudent, scholarly, and religious, quite fit for the post. It has been several years since I have had any contact with the abbess of Jumièges; the Count of Boulogne saw to all of the arrangements. Some must suspect the young man is the pretender's illegitimate offspring, but no one bothers to name his mother.

I grieve to find that I can barely recall the child that I held in my arms. I should not have been content to grow a stranger to the first fruit of my grand passion.

Just yesterday, from London, I received a description from the usurper himself.

> There is no real resemblance between us; the colorful locks of his infancy have deepened to an indiscriminate shade of brown. His dark eyes remind me of a lover I once had, and would have still, if it were not for her refusal. But my gaze is not in his face. His piety and sobriety are as foreign to me as his looks. Perhaps he is a changeling, not mine at all? Did the devil steal my son from the convent sisters? In fear and trembling, did they substitute this prig in his place?
>
> Gervase, steady and upright, seemed deeply suspicious of my interest. I passed off my visit as a courtesy call upon the head of his religious house. I asked him about his background, as if I were alien to it. He spoke of a mother who was lovely and kind, with black hair and noble manners. I believe that he is ignorant of his real condition and eager to remain so. He seems to sense that some stain attended his birth.
>
> Ah, my comely pet, so many years ago it was that I was Adam in the garden and you were my Eve. Though the Lord forbade us to eat the apple, in contempt we plucked and tasted it for ourselves. In our cupidity,

we denied that there was any authority greater than our own. Together,
equally to blame, we found bliss in rapacious sin.

Rolled up within the letter was a sprig of white flowers, shriveled
and wilted. Crushing the petals between my fingers, I inhaled a memory,
savoring its flavor. With a sharp, searing pain in my chest, I let the vision
evaporate around me, so that I stood once more outside the tower of love.

†

Summer

ALMOST FIFTEEN, THE LAWFUL heir comes back among us. Staking his
claim, the Plantagenet marches at the head of a small army of friends,
youthful Norman knights, and a larger group of hardy English
mercenaries, recently hired on credit at Wareham. I hear it recited, by
naive or conniving troubadours, that his saddlebags are stuffed with gold
and gems, the better to reward his regiments. Yet the boy writes to me,
asking for money with which to facilitate his offensive. Impressed with
his bravado, Duke Geoffrey allows Henry to undertake this escapade
across the Channel, but sends him off empty-handed. Such meaningless
permission is yet enough for the prince's green ambition.

I do not know what makes my blood churn more, my husband's
ambivalence, and his sly transferal of the child's safety to my oversight,
or the shameful impulsiveness that my son exhibits, without thought
for the risks of his enterprise. The Plantagenet dreams of rescuing me,
of winning the crown, of plundering booty, but he lacks judgment and
foresight. I cling to my only security, the belief, deep within me, that no
man on this island will dare lay a violent hand on the legitimate claimant
to his grandfather's empire.

The minstrels call him a beacon, marshaling us to safety, as we float,
rudderless, in an obscure sea. Indeed. Those about me begin to raise
their heads, suddenly awash in a rosier light.

†

THIS EVENING, AT COMPLINE, when the sun had finally begun to set on the long, hot day, I slunk out to a remote corner of the kitchen garden. A large terrier, usually employed to hunt down rats in the storerooms, trotted eagerly at my heels. He could smell the slab of meat hidden within my basket, next to a spool of twine and a sharp knife. I found the aromatic plant for which I had come, the pungent mandrake, and knotted one end of rope around its bushy leaves. The other I tied to the collar of the dog. I tossed his viands, some feet away, and the hound leapt to his dinner, exhuming my prize. The poor animal did not seem to mind that I had diverted the vengeance of the mandrake onto his narrow canine shoulders. Crushed, the root dresses the worst war wounds; we may soon rely on its curative powers.

Although Chester and I make ready for the upheaval to come, and husband our stores, my insipid courtiers while away the hours in scuttlebutt and calumny. They are all agog over the Plantagenet's misadventures in Wiltshire. Despite his bloodline, Henry fails to conquer even one village. At Cricklade, Stephen's garrison put his force to flight; three miles south, at the royal fortress of Purton, the prince and his men were routed from the field and retreated, desperate and terrified. His small, inexperienced band, lacking suitable armor and weapons and not particularly loyal to our cause, cannot triumph.

The boy has no coin to pay the incompetent army with which he surrounds himself. There are no battle spoils to requite its service. The child must be in a fine bind. I hear that his adherents idle about the countryside, drinking and fucking, waiting for the restitution that must come from some quarter. Some of the more cowardly Norman striplings run off home. A few of the British mercenaries, a rough lot, threaten my heir. He pacifies them with empty assurances.

Denise's son, Hamelin, is among Henry's entourage. I fear his influence. Landless and penniless, Hamelin schemes to make his fortune. His brother's safety will not be foremost among his concerns.

†

THIS AFTERNOON, RANULF LOWERED the gangplank over our moat, admitting my brother into Devizes. Gloucester had arrived to discuss the Plantagenet's frantic entreaties for funds, delivered to every one of our circle who might be inclined to underwrite his mishaps. Gore-stained couriers hand over these solicitations, describing his efforts on our behalf, and the ignominy of being unable to support men employed to fight in his name.

In the great hall of the palace, Robert discounted his nephew's plea. "Unfortunately, the boy is not ready to be our figurehead. His mistakes jeopardize our plans, so many years in the making. We should not allow his blunders to alter what has gone before."

Chester shrugged. "If you withhold your aid, he does not have the capacity to succeed where you have failed."

A mother's heart beat in me still. "While the prince remains in England, he is every moment in danger of being killed or captured."

My brother waved his elegant hand. He did not meet my eyes. "Given the impoverished state of our coffers, our remaining money is best spent buttressing Devizes or sponsoring defensive garrisons at our other strongholds."

Ranulf clutched Gloucester's forearm. "Your castles are all held in trust for the Plantagenet; he is here now to take what is his. Yet you will not help him? For what else do you sit and wait, but for him?"

The tone of Robert's rebuff was quiet, measured. "We should not enable the child to prosecute his intention too soon."

Chester scoffed, but said no more.

I did not like to hear my commanders at odds. "I am anguished for him, the infant whom I swaddled up to shield, and rocked in a crib to soothe. Someday soon, I intend to bequeath the Plantagenet with my father's throne. For now, I would end his distress if I were able. But our gold would dwindle to nothing in his hands."

†

Unsuccessful in his attempts to pick my pocket, my son has the audacity to submit an appeal to the Count of Boulogne, who forward his letter to me. Has young Henry discovered our secret?

> *Sire, you must remember me and pity me, for I am overcome with calamitous distress. You, who are placed so high on your throne of gold — could you, would you, rescue me from my weighty financial difficulties? It pains me as a knight and a prince to earn the opprobrium of a wastrel and a beggar. From the majesty of your heart, and in consideration of the nearness of our relation, might you aid me?*
>
> *I think of you warmly, in so far as it relates to my own honor, and would hope that you recollect the mistakes of your own early life, and put yourself in my place.*

Holding the parchment, my hands shook. For some moments, I was speechless, but with what emotion? Dismay, envy, fury?

Stephen boasts of the boy's diplomacy and of the boldness of his petition.

> *The lad hints at the mystery without betraying it. I admire his dash and his discretion, and would have him think me chivalrous in my turn. Although the young man is my rival, and would usurp my sovereignty, and beseeches me to pay off men who have fought to overthrow me, I would not have the country think that such a headstrong stripling challenges my divine authority. Without coin, he and his insolent bunch will continue to aggravate my barons, but my contribution enables him to hasten back to his father's duchy. Such noblesse oblige does not lessen me, but he who stoops to receive alms.*

The knave! The pretender will not name his true heir, nor apportion to the true prince all that is his by right, but allots him only an infinitesimal piece of it, calling it charity!

Father and son, the two halves of my heart: shall they do evil unto one another, or good? Which one of them shall come to atone? They are two of a kind, both full of conceit, taking and taking, trading between them what is mine. Someday, the Plantagenet will perceive how cheaply men rate their vows to one another, and how expensive is the gift of heaven's grace.

†

Fall

FLUSH WITH HIS HANDOUT from the royal treasury, Henry compensates his mercenaries and tears home, to Normandy. My son finds nothing in this escapade to humble him, treating it as a grand adventure that begins to make his name as a man of action. Descending upon the convent of Bec-Hellouin, where Marie finishes her education, he basks in a hero's greeting. The smitten girl measures him a gallant soldier, devoted and puissant enough to defy her parents, and his own.

Marie heaps praise upon him, her Messiah Prince. The Plantagenet encloses her paeans in his dispatches to me.

> *All shall pay you homage, strewing posies of myrrh and frankincense at your feet. Already, a great king could not avert his face, to deny you. The very Lord anoints you.*

I am asked to trust that the two do not lie together.

> *There is no longer any tomfoolery between us, no lewdness, now that she has had her flowers. In the past, I have wrongly courted my sister, beguiling her with sweet speeches and gifting her with affectionate tokens. But in this I take your Christian advice, and resolve to be chaste in her presence.*

†

HOW I ABHOR THE inveterate, intemperate, insinuating jongleurs! I cannot escape their outrageous verses. The newest arrivals to our court narrate a splendid dubbing ceremony, orchestrated by the Count of Boulogne to emboss Eustace's status. The pretender girded his nineteen-year-old son with the belt of knighthood, at the same time generously endowing him with territories, manors, and a numerous entourage of warriors, lifting his dignity to the rank of count. Finally, Stephen presented his own sword to that runt of a boy, lacking even the beard of a man.

My household avidly debates Eustace's merits, and the significance of his enhanced position. I imagine it cost the usurper a small fortune to bribe the minstrels, whose songs deem Eustace worthy of his elevation. They elaborate upon his "soul of steel," his "heart, so buttressed with courage that it cannot flail," wildly overstating the accomplishments and courtesy of Maud's uncivilized brat.

My cousin must be anxious about Eustace's hunger for fame and power, if he attempts to sate it. It is said that he pressures the archbishop of Canterbury to crown the false prince as the next king, while the pretender yet lives. This is a French idea, to be sure, alien to our notion of the accession. If only my father, the Lion of England, had organized my coronation before his own death! No upstart would have been able to steal the throne from the declared heir.

Praise be to Mother Mary, who stays the archbishop's hand in this matter. His Grace refuses to act hastily, and wishes to think long upon it before performing an indelible unction.

†

TODAY, AN ITINERANT PEDDLER accosted Gerta in a neighboring village, waved a stained, folded parchment, declaring it a missive for the empress, and offered to sell it to her for one piece of silver. My maid, suspicious of forgery and extortion, haggled him down to a copper.

We are nonplussed to find that the dirty paper delivers tidings from Avera.

> *Most Gracious Highness, I have had a vision, a revelation, that concerns you and yours. I have seen three horses stampede across a field, waving with green stalks of golden corn. The first steed is black; its rider carries a set of scales. In his wake gallops the second, bright red. Its rider brandishes an enormous sword. The third stallion is white. Its rider holds a bow, and wears the laurel of victory.*

The ambiguous omen of the three crowns is here repeated, and obscure to us no more. The three kings are all English. My father, evenhanded and just, rides the black animal. My cousin, redheaded and war mongering, sits atop the second mount. My son, the white prince, sure to hit his mark, will make all right before him.

†

I AM CRIPPLED WITH despair and stagger under the weight of my pain. Robert, Earl of Gloucester, worthy son of King Henry I, dies suddenly of some foul rot, without being shriven, without asking the Lord's forgiveness. How much this must be mourned!

Such a deficit to our cause cannot be tabulated, even by the troubadours who compose hymns to the earl's days. Their words only weakly memorialize he who was my first, my most preeminent, illustrious vassal. On this occasion, they cannot overemphasize the significance of Robert's guidance, or the value of his deeds done in fealty to me. My brother had a general's military talent and the mercy, circumspection, and learning of a sovereign. His manners and beneficence were such as even his foes should emulate. Knights on both sides of the Channel revere him, as a great example of pure nobility. Their squires yearn to hear and to repeat the tales of Gloucester's exploits and the refinements of his courtliness.

Surely, he was blessed. God preserves him now among the angels, in service to Christ. Heaven opens its gates to the Earl of Gloucester; it must be so. He desired wrongly, but understandably, in thrall to the beauties of the Creation. It was the Lord himself who fashioned the female body, from the rib of Adam, so that the pair, man and woman, mirrored the divine harmony. In my wisdom, I held my brother back from the abyss. Uncorrupted, he bloomed still, despite the weeds of temptation that wound around his stalk.

†

IN HER TERRIBLE GRIEF, Amabel interred her husband immediately, so that I might have no excuse to descend upon her castle. The countess sends me an intemperate, scathing scrawl, dispensing with the need for my presence at Bristol.

> *You are a pagan trollop who plotted against him. For you, bitch, he attempted, again and again, to exhume disorder and unrest. He was a fanatic in your ignoble cause. Enchanted by your unholy alliance, he would take no sage counsel against your perverse demands.*
>
> *May you be consumed, as a log within the blaze of a chimney. May you evaporate, as water in a trough. May you shrivel up, into dust, for me to trod underfoot.*

Oh, my brother, you have deserted my side and defected from my cause, but I would welcome you back, to solace you! My stomach aches and my breast tightens, as if I were some disappointed lover. How shall I fight on, without you to safeguard my offensive? How shall I reign, without you to ornament my court?

I shall inflict your memory upon the realm!

†

HERE IN BRITAIN, MY most talented commander sleeps in a cold crypt. Across the Channel, my beloved son abides without my supervision. Everywhere, I am alike apart from the one whom I both love and despise. Does it matter where I lodge my disappointment and my emptiness? The waterfowl begin their migration south, crying out some alarum. Perhaps I too shall be refreshed under a new sky, in Normandy.

The Mirror of the Plantagenet

Scroll Nineteen: 1148

Unable to stand fast and dry against the tempest of her own conjuring, the malevolent princess returned across the water to her husband's custody, where she found herself once more supplanted in his affection. Reflect: this was Matilda's destiny, always to be second. Her son drew ever closer to his wide fortune, while she sinned in obscurity, upsetting common decency, caballing with a witch. She assumed that the Virgin would consent to restore her to shimmering integrity. But the Holy Mother could measure the meager glimmer of the empress's faith, still pale beside heaven's vivid light.

†

Winter

DESPITE ALL OF OUR efforts to prepare Devizes to resist an onslaught of violence, I spare it the ravages of a siege, gifting it away. The Church accedes immediately to all of the surrounding manors at Canning. At the palace itself, I retain the right to lodge the loyal garrison chosen and trained by Chester, but only until such time as Prince Henry shall have returned safely to England and been anointed. The pope will possess Devizes entire at the pleasure of King Henry II.

I could no longer ignore the pontiff's threats. For seven long, frigid evenings, I prayed and slept, prostrate, on the stone floor of my chapel. When each sorrowful night evaporated into an icy dawn, I arose, stiff and sore, teeth chattering, to the blessings of the morning. But, in the quiet, solitary dark, I hearkened to my heart, and seven times heard the clarion call: "Who are you to molest the house of the Lord?"

Holy Mary stretches out her hands to reclaim what I unjustly appropriated. I am Her wayward child, lost amid some dense, wild wood, cowering and despairing, then finally stumbling across my mother's path. Running into Her skirts, I am indifferent to the menace and confusions that plagued me moments before.

Already, my bequest lessens my tribulation, as the Virgin promises. In return for my sacrifice of Devizes, I bask in Our Lady's pity. I had fallen from Her grace, but I shall redeem it in everlasting paradise. The Queen of Heaven showers down the rays of Her bliss, illuminating me.

Perhaps the troubadours shall defame my defection from my own war, my refusal to finish what I have begun, but the wandering rascals never appreciate me.

†

IT IS STULTIFYING WORK to pack my trunks with mantles and bliauts, corsages and slippers, cloaks and girdles. We fold and refold articles of clothing still likely to wrinkle despite our best attempts to store them properly. Gerta carefully seals her vials of herbs with sturdy stoppers and binds up my needlework with ribbons. I roll up my voluminous writings, attaching my seals. My maid nags me to do everything at once, and discounts the importance of my parchments.

Today, I have been distracted from my tasks by the arrival of FitzCount. Hearing a commotion in the bailey, I thought Chester had begun to load up the baggage mules. I was startled to see Brian at the entrance to my solar.

He bowed down very low before me, perhaps unwilling that I should see the emotion distorting his features.

"FitzCount, you take me quite unawares." Out of politeness, I ceased to sort my letters, although my fingers tickled to continue.

My vassal looked very much aged, with shadowed eyes and pasty skin. "Does my visit bewilder you, Empress?"

"I assume, sir, that you no longer wish to be actively in my service. It was more than three years ago that you left me to return to your domestic obligations."

Brian took small steps forward, almost broaching a respectful distance. "I have always been ready to fight for you, if need be. I refuse to acknowledge that you discard me. I have not perpetrated some great crime against you."

I smiled ruefully. "You do not find it possible to admire Basilia?"

FitzCount's expression deadened into sullenness. "That sorceress? At the crossroads between Wallingford and Oxford, she buries a bone from one of our unbaptized babies, born dead from her poisoned womb. For all her exorcisms, she does not have the power to eradicate my mania for you. I loiter at her hearth without one moment of harmony, counting out the turgid hours of each day. And the memory of you does not sustain me. Oh, my dark angel! The thought of your noble forehead beneath the black stream of your hair torments me, so that I toss about each night in sleepless anguish."

This was worse than I had imagined. "Your unseemly torpor does you no credit. Keep five leaves of the nettle upon your person, and be made safe from fear and fantasy."

My knight stepped up to my side. "Am I to have no true welcome?"

I tried to recall his vanished charms. "I advise you to be comforted by Basilia's veneration or Christ's compassion."

FitzCount laid his palms on my shoulders. "If you revolt against my amour, you sound my death knell. Laid to rest among my ancestors, I shall no longer trouble you with buffoonish complaints."

Was he bluffing? I shook off his grip. "I am grateful for your esteem and your fealty, but I cannot grant you your desire. I cannot show mercy where I have found none."

FitzCount stood his ground. "I shall gouge out my eyes, hack off my nose, shatter my fingers, and slice out my tongue! Then I will shove my wood into Basilia without regret, for I will be unable to compare her to your translucent flesh, to your honied scent and taste, to your firm and pliable form."

My blood stirred within me, but to embrace him would do neither of us any good. Pushing past, I sat down next to the fire, smoldering and smoky from inattention. "No, no! Damn up your river of love; permit it to eddy into a reservoir of religious devotion, as I have done. Repent. Wring out your soul, exhaust your spirit, give all of your passion to the Lord."

Brian knelt before me. "Empress, your chastity does not bar you from glory. You shine all the brighter, for husbanding your flame. But heaven has no such bargain to strike with me."

My patience had run out. "Boil forty ants in daffodil juice, sir. Drink it hot, burn your mouth on it, and your lusts will cool into impotence."

"You, whom I love, do me the most harm, as if you were my greatest enemy. I have been your champion on the field, and yet am not your chosen hero. You order me to decamp your presence, and to forget what came before, but it is my courtly obligation to remember. Even though you are fickle, I will rest stalwart and sure."

I stood up. "I am off, over the water."

He had no choice but to quit my chamber.

†

I FIND THAT MY maid attempts to adulterate FitzCount's suffering. This morning, when the bells rang out prime, she was nowhere to be seen. Disheveled and wan, reeking of sex, she finally made a belated appearance in my solar.

I had been scowling at my copper mirror, inspecting the ridges on my forehead, the brown spots on my nose, and the yellow tinge of my teeth. "Harlot! Whose prick was so hard that you could not leave his pallet to do your duty to me?"

Gerta reddened. "I caressed a baron sorely in need of affection."

At once, I intuited that she had lain with Brian. I was in no mood to be fair. "Why did you mingle your sweat with his tears?"

Gerta sighed. "Madam, why should I resist a knight wielding a stiff weapon, and in sore need of a conquest?"

Already I regretted my petulance. "More than once, I have asked you to lie with a lesser man for my sake." I held out my hand to her. "Forgive my tongue lashing. I am lonely and aggrieved."

Gerta ignored me, and began to make up my bed. "FitzCount was embarrassed to awaken in my arms, and bustled out from under my big bones as fast as any knave I have known. My complexion, ashen and gaunt, could not tempt him to dally away the morning."

I watched her smooth my coverlets and tuck them under the rush mattress.

My maid straightened up. "Sir Brian was in his cups; I sated his need. But I was no substitute for a queen."

"I begrudge you nothing that assuages your spirit. You have always been my steadfast helpmeet."

Gerta put her hands on her hips. "The ass asked me to procure some token garment of yours. I refused, of course, but he would have fought all the more bravely for your son if he had your malodorous nightdress stuffed under his mail, or nailed to his shield."

I snorted and picked up my looking glass. "His fidelity flatters me. The woman in this mirror remains vain, lascivious, and disturbed. When will she be completely liberated from the sin and misery that ails her?"

†

Spring

IN THE MILDNESS OF the new season, as the orchard begins to sprout and the birds to trill, I set out for the continent, at the head of a long train of carts and soldiers. I have been here, among my English people, for eight and one half years. I have little to show for it, leaving without the throne I came to claim. And yet, despite the failure of my ambition and the attendant burdens of travel, I rejoice to survey my native land, abundant in regrowth. Basking in the warm air, I spend a pleasant, almost leisurely month on the road, distributing pennies and blessings upon the crowds of pilgrims, clerks, paupers, squires, knights, and ladies that we come across. I exult in their accolades and well-wishes.

Whenever our route winds through a village or town, I step into its small church. The bells ring out my presence, as I grace its austere doorstep. Inside, the local householders and serfs reach out to touch or kiss the hem of my robes; my heart warms to see fidelity and confidence shining in their faces. Their honest gratitude, for the trouble I have taken, and their simple prayers on my behalf cleanse my spirit.

We spent last night encamped under the stars. Within my capacious, silken tent, a troubadour in our entourage, that sniping Bernard de Ventadour, unspooled the tragedy of a negligent king, indifferent sovereign of a fertile land. While he looked to his pleasures, a thick haze choked the sky and destroyed all the wheat and corn to be harvested. His Majesty, indecisive and indolent, did nothing to combat this misfortune, and there ensued an onslaught of inky ravens who clawed apart all the oxen and sheep in the fields. Still the king refused to save his realm, against the advice of the wiser men in his retinue.

I pretended to believe that Bernard painted a picture of my foe, and clapped with all my might at the end of his performance. For good measure, I paid him the compliment of a pair of scarlet shoes. But I suspect his aspersions, and wonder whether his barbs are aimed at me, and my line.

Oh Henry! When you are king, you must never shift your eyes from the changeable political landscape.

†

IN NORMANDY, ESTABLISHED AT Rouen Castle, I find my husband more finely lined, yet still striking a heroic figure. His pale eyes and sharp gaze retain their allure. Altogether, age and power complement his wiry face and well-preserved form. To mark my arrival, he presents me with an elaborate gift, an artificial tree fashioned entirely of bronze. Small squirrels, modeled from cabochon opals set in silver, perch upon its branches.

Denise is almost as exquisite as she once was. As they did in her youth, the fiery hair and pouting mouth enchant the duke, who remains smitten. Indeed, the leman rules beside him, as Duchess of Normandy in fact. I infer that the small, thin stripe her mouth became at my reappearance was the first frown she has worn in the nine years of my absence. Despite this small indiscretion, his mistress wears her frustration well, for she has little to fear. She has displaced me, in Geoffrey's soul and at his court.

I cannot hope to supplant her, and do not wish to do so.

†

TODAY DAWNED WARM AND clear. My husband and I, and the three sons of our house, along with Denise and Hamelin, met on a wide plain below the keep, in order to try out the handiwork of a new fletcher. His elegant bows prove extraordinarily light and sturdy, and his glorious arrows are feathered with the plumage of only the swiftest, rarest fowl. Delighted with our new weapons, we challenged each other to a match.

I wore a yellow bliaut that does not complement my skin tone. Denise, resplendent in a gray corsage laced up at the sides with green ribbons, easily monopolized Geoffrey's notice, although I shot at his side, and my aim was sure. I rolled my eyes at his slights, until finally the Angevin remembered what honorable attention was due to me.

He sighed. "If I am feared as a general, it is my beloved to whom I owe my martial will to conquer; if I am admired as a poet, it is she to whom I owe the polished style of my courtly compositions."

The strumpet strode over to us, tossing her bow aside. "I am done with archery. I mark at joy."

Hamelin scoffed. "Mother, when we are under bombardment, amour will not suffice."

Prince Henry laughed. "If we did not flirt and dilly-dally away the days and nights of a long siege, the investiture of a castle would be an unbearable ordeal."

Denise smiled upon the Plantagenet's insouciance. I do not perceive that she harbors my son any ill will, or intrigues to raise a question about his paternity, so as to impede his inheritance. Perhaps it is enough that she likes him.

My husband put his arm around his paramour's waist. "Despite the passage of time, my heart lightens whenever I see my favorite."

The slut slipped the string of the duke's bow off his shoulder and put her red head in its stead. "My interest in you has never waned, nor am I the trifling sort."

There was silence. Had they all heard the exaggerated rumors of my innumerable affairs: Stephen, Brian, Robert, Ranulf?

My younger boys continued to shoot at the targets, replenishing their quivers with boastful hoots.

William, almost twelve, cared nothing for romance and did not heed the conversation.

But boorish Geoffrey, over fourteen and a picture of his father in his youth, listened while staring down the shaft of his arrows. Into the hush that had fallen among the adults, he interjected: "Lady, we have been felicitous here without you; why do you come among us now?"

The Plantagenet cuffed his sibling on the arm. "Cad! The empress is no cloud to smother the sun, but our mother, returned to us after too many years spent fighting for my English throne."

Irate at the smart to his limb and the bruise to his dignity, Geoffrey whined. "Pardon me, Your Grace of Normandy."

My husband's voice deepened with annoyance. "Namesake, do not resent your own brother's magnificence. You will possess more than enough splendor for such an oaf as you are."

Geoffrey, canny in his belligerence, recovered his composure. "Your patrimony was not sufficient for you. You put ardor aside, when your squires dressed you in your armor."

Would Henry be able to renounce Marie, when the time came? "A knight is not always free to pursue his fancies."

Geoffrey's antagonism was undampened. "When I seduce a woman, it will not be in admiration or in lust, but for the benefit that I might obtain from her."

To find this Angevin son so unlike me in every way was mortifying. "Where is the honor in that? Such indecent talk will never merit a lady's trust."

Hamelin spoke up for Geoffrey, estimating as he did. "A feverish heart is a prison; women, swindlers all, are the jailors. Thinking too long on a girl is like repeatedly burning your tongue on the same scalding tankard of mead."

Denise looked surprised to hear him admit to a man's feelings. "A noble relationship, with all its courtesies, embellishes us. Love wisely and you will not regret it."

Only William still essayed to improve his skill with his bow. "Cease your commentary; hoist your arrows!"

†

ROUEN IS THE ADMINISTRATIVE and commercial center of the duchy. From the slit windows in our stone keep, and from the corridor along our battlements, I canvass our crowded, wealthy municipality. The burghers live in spacious mansions; the churches erect steep spires. The river Seine guides heavily stocked trading ships into port. The market squares throng with merchants and traders, hawking wares of every description, and ruddy peasants seeking work from the citizens. My nose tingles with the aroma of the public cookshops. Regardless of the noise and bustle, I sometimes even ramble incognito through the city's littered lanes.

The vibrant town is surrounded on all sides by cascading streams and gently rolling pastures, gracious hills and thick glades. The great hall in our stronghold overflows with mounted stags that the duke and his escort bag in the vicinity. To the west of the town, along the Seine, well-stocked fisheries supply our table. To the east of it, cloth manufactures run their water mills, operating a steady business. I have paid a dignified visit to both of these worthy concerns, for I would promote such prosperity in England, when Henry shall rule.

There is so much success at hand, so much new money in Rouen, that Duke Geoffrey takes out large loans from his rich subjects. I disapprove of these financial arrangements, but my opinion of them is not asked.

I myself generously pledge to construct two stone bridges, one between the town and the isle in the middle of the Seine and another connecting the isle to Saint-Sever, on the south side of the river. The extant wooden walkways, spindly and easily damaged by fire or brawling, do not assure safe passage between the castle and suburb, where sits the priory of Notre-Dame-du-Pré, built by my father in his royal park of Quévilly.

Lately, I prefer the priory guest quarters to the inconvenient, unwelcoming solar that I have been assigned in my husband's tower. Geoffrey is grateful for my protracted absences from his hearth, and for my willingness to permit Denise to manage his household in my rightful place. At my request, and in my name, the Angevin grants the priory a bonus, revenue from market tolls levied in its neighborhood.

†

SUSTAINED AND REFRESHED AT the priory, I refuse to see Avera, who sends a messenger all the way from her hovel in Angers, requesting to wait upon me in Rouen. Loathsome pagan, oracle of nothing; what has she to tell me that I do not already know?

Crossing herself at the mere mention of Avera's name, Gerta persists until I swallow gobs of rosemary butter, which she churns from the milk of a completely white cow, while she waves a baton inscribed with some Latin incantation. She thinks to protect me from the witch's elf-shot, the contagion of her magic, now that I am almost healed, almost reborn.

Through prayer, and self-abnegation, I ascend to wisdom. My transcendent fate unfolds before me. I lose what is dearest to me on this earth, in exchange for the keys to heaven.

†

Summer

SITTING IDLE IN NORMANDY, I imagine Stephen's supremacy in England, unburdened by a rival. But I am disabused of this misconception by the prating, ingratiating minstrels, spewing out their political verse. My darling, as always, is unable to preside uncontested.

Maud schemes to have the archbishop of Canterbury anoint Eustace as king. But public sentiment tilts toward the Angevin party. Tales of Eustace's sadism are legion. One ill-favored member of his circle was recently buried alive for some small infraction, a perceived lack of deference toward the false prince. On the whole, it is felt by most Englishmen that Henry Plantagenet is the lawful heir to his grandfather's realm.

†

Fall

THE LEAVES CASCADE DOWN from the trees, but such unwelcome changes in the scenery are nothing to me now. I am suffused with sobriety, and would not wish to be surrounded by lavish foliage and a luminous sky. Once again, my heroic son, my prized beneficiary, abandons his studies to take up arms in our cause.

He is not yet sixteen, but he is full of this, his second journey home, to be knighted by his great uncle, King David of Scotland. The Plantagenet will receive the grand emblems of the warrior's rank, and enter into his new dignity. He is to be dubbed by a ruling sovereign, as is right and fitting to his station.

The Earl of Chester undertakes to meet Prince Henry's landing, and to escort him northward, guarding and guiding him until they reach the castle of Carlisle. Both my heir and my ally promise me that they do not intend to stir up revolt along their way. Nothing must invite a battle between father and son before the boy knows what he is about, and can win. But can I be secure in the support of the notoriously capricious Chester?

Under one corner of the interior lining of my son's shield, I tuck a scrap of parchment, on which I have copied a bold prayer to my lady: "Oh, Holy Mother, freeze my heart into ice. Let no tears etch their tracks on my cheeks, for you have already cried a river, and its currents wash away the pain of all the world. My son must be as yours, the wind that blows the waters into waves and inundates the land, guaranteeing its rebirth."

Concurrently, Duke Geoffrey rides off from Rouen to put down an insurrection in Anjou, a siege that may last several months. With both men departing from these precincts, Matilda Empress rules Normandy. I recross the Seine and reinstate myself at Rouen Castle, quite prepared to take up my administrative duties.

†

LAST EVENING, A JONGLEUR, hoping to garner goodwill, heaped me with praises. "I am confounded by you, as fetching and radiant as a snowdrop. Who is not mesmerized by your mouth, so pink and plump; who can withstand your gaze, so mournful and clear?"

Expecting more talk of crowns and armies, history and kingdoms, I was touched to be styled a captivating female. In recompense for his compliments, I offered him a fine cloak, not much worn, and without holes or fleas.

Gerta laughs at my gullibility. She is sure that the panegyric was written for another patroness, decades younger. "Do not be his dupe,

Empress. Adulation is meant only to deceive us. If they laud you now, it is only to belittle you later."

I sigh, forlorn to be past my prime. The minstrels flatter me merely because there can be no more aspersions cast upon my house. The rightful prince sets off on his quest to fulfill his destiny as the legitimate sovereign above us all.

†

LETTERS FROM ENGLAND COME thick and fast, so that I hear of Henry's adventures almost as they unfold.

At the court of Carlisle, magnates loyal to me, including Brian, congregate to reconnoiter the Plantagenet and be recognized by him as early adherents. Robert's heir, William Earl of Gloucester, bends his knee to his cousin, despite the influence of Amabel's corrosive hate. The prince distrusts the effeminate William, and declines to strike up a personal friendship. My boy's chosen companions dream of war.

Overall, the ceremony devolves into a general rally in support of our party. The Earl of Chester, now my mainstay, organizes our resistance against the usurper in the Midlands, in Wales and the west, and in the north. All the barons who surface to honor Henry are crucial to our ultimate success. We do not shun the embrace of any vassal, however tardy his allegiance.

†

YESTERDAY, A SQUALID, HAGGARD Avera materialized at the portcullis to our keep. She had traveled from Angers by foot, mule, and cart. Her tatty garments emitted a swinish stench. I allotted her a solar far greater than her station and urged a bath upon her. She accepted with more alacrity than I expected. I dispensed my servants to wash her clothes, overlooking their squeamish groans and superstitious invective.

At supper, I was taken aback to see Avera's clean face beneath her brash blond locks, brushed and silky. Her laundered bliaut, threadbare but decent, sufficed under a patched but ornately embroidered corsage, clearly of luxurious provenance.

The seer retains a verdant beauty of Maud's sort, profusely inviting. Many of the courtiers, both women and men, were agog at the identity of my guest and aroused by the tempting enchantress. They imagined her to be the mistress of every sort of erotic pleasure, demonic or no. They outdid themselves, essaying to impress her with their wit and braggadocio.

Avera had no use for their posing, and devoted herself with gusto to a dish of young goose, stuffed with herbs, quinces, pears, grapes, and garlic, larded and roasted with ginger. She then polished off heaps of duck hotchpotch, stewed with pepper and cumin, burnt bread, minced onions, boiled blood, and ale. Jugs of sweet wine were emptied at a vulgar pace. I overlooked her gluttony, for I doubted that she had eaten so well in many a season.

When her hunger was sated, I invited her to take a seat beside me, and dismissed the higher-ranking members of my retinue, insisting that they dance and carouse. The mystic and I were left alone at the high dais.

After a pause, she spoke her purpose. "You rebuff me, but I will not be gagged. Although you are a queen, you must open your ears. If you would be staunch rather than feeble, set aside your pride."

I considered her abundant comeliness, straining at her clothes, and her heavy, limpid eyes. "I demean myself only before heaven. The mortification of my spirit, and the denial of my desire, primes me to receive the Virgin's light. I do not need you to teach me humility, or constrain my will." My mouth quivered.

Avera noticed the flutter of my lips. She regarded me full in the face. "Hearken to whoever has moved you, whoever calls forth your trembling."

To gain time, I drained my goblet of its liquor. The last of my food had congealed upon my trencher of bread. Why was I slow to react to her sallies? "Do not think to perturb me. I reject your revelations; they have always been unholy and base."

The witch bit her lip. "You are condemned to ride at the head of a troop of the dead. You sit astride a saddle emblazoned with red-hot nails, your feet in fiery spurs."

Was my majesty of no account to her? "Miserable wretch! Heretic!"

Avera spat onto the table. "How many is the number of your crimes? How many years are left to you, to atone?"

How dare she act as my confessor? "Incubus, of what do you accuse me?"

Her voice rose, but no one heard us over the music, stomping, and clapping coming from the other end of the great hall. "You take unrighteous pleasure in the awe and dread of your citizens. But understand: your power over them, your divinity, does not stem from your native distinction, your grasping ambition, your fluctuating wealth, or your pyrrhic conquests."

My ears pounded. "You are Denise's creature, here to flout me, here where I am the rightful duchess by birth and now again by marriage."

Avera barked out a laugh. "Geoffrey, so puissant a prince, but yet her humble page! In courtliness, the duke loads her with prestige. He would marry his whore and elevate her, if you were no more."

I sneered. "Do you threaten me? The laws of the church forbid marriage to men who have killed or have colluded in the murder of their wives. Are you their accomplice?" I pushed back my seat and stood, sending a flurry of pages scurrying in our direction.

Red spots mottled Avera's fleshy cheeks. "You misunderstand me, Empress. Denise gives me her custom; I sell her my aphrodisiacs. It is you who has my fidelity." The serf grabbed my hand, then kissed my palm. "Pax, pix, abyra, syth, samasic."

Twaddle! Would the peasant cast some spell on me? Now I knew what she wanted of me, what she longed to gift me with.

So often of late, I have thrown off my lusts, holding myself aloof from Brian, from Robert, from Stephen himself, in order to serve my son and the Virgin. But last night I dabbled in obscenity, lame before temptation, unworthy of my recent piety and self-control. Today, to atone for my pointless licentiousness, I abstain from food and drink.

†

FOR ALL THE OATHS that the Plantagenet and Chester swore, for all that
they vowed not to lure the pretender into a military engagement, it is
clear that they yearned to fight. Uncle David and his battalion of Scots,
Ranulf and my boy, along with all the knights friendly to the Angevin
cause assembled at Carlisle, set off to find the enemy. The Count of
Boulogne and his force of English warriors, up north to defend against
any such invasion, were just as willing to engage. When the burghers of
York appealed to the usurper to hurry to their city, in case my supporters
should strike there, both armies simultaneously approached the town.

Miraculously, a pitched confrontation between father and son was
avoided. The troubadours proclaim that the country folk sabotaged the
battle. I employ my own spy, a monk planted within Henry's retinue,
who witnesses and records what he can. It is his opinion that Stephen
and David secretly colluded, agreeing not to meet on the field. My uncle,
outnumbered, wished to avoid a rout. My source cannot fathom why the
false king hung back. The Plantagenet and the Earl of Chester seemed
vastly disappointed and a bit puzzled to be denied their blood sport.

Then the prince buoyantly decamped to Bristol, negligently
separating himself from Ranulf, his guide and protector, thus inviting
capture or worse. At least he had the prudence to choose unfrequented
byways, abandoned and forgotten roads unknown by his foes. Enemy
search parties attempted to waylay him, hoping to make a fortune in
ransom, but my heir escaped their ambushes.

At one point, his antagonists did spot him at a distance. Only by
dint of good horsemanship and amenable terrain did he manage to
elude Eustace himself. Outraged, Stephen's son plagues Oxford,
devastating the landscape, and mounts raids against all of our garrisons
in Gloucestershire. Poets in Eustace's pay opine that his rival, in grave
peril, has been driven out of the north.

Henry's jongleurs sing of the resplendent dubbing and his
spectacular escapes.

†

THE COUNT OF BOULOGNE and his armies stampede through Britain, bent on destruction. The harlot Maud, anxiously comparing her own puling son to my brave boy, orders her husband to eradicate the Angevin forces, once and for all. With that bitch's invocation ringing in his ears, he attacks everywhere, pillaging noble treasures, razing houses of worship, scattering the dwellings and food stores of the peasantry. Reducing his own subjects to extreme destitution, starving them, he hopes to guarantee their surrender. I hear tell that ravenous, homeless hordes barge into their own holy churches to wolf down the heavenly host. Verily, the usurper transforms his realm into a barren desert, incapable of sustaining life. Everything of mine that is fair and fine is forfeited to my cousin's brutality.

The pretender's depredations have been especially severe at my city of Devizes, where he burns down the town, entrapping my garrison in the palace. In revenge, and to draw him away, the Earl of Chester assaults Lincoln, maneuvering to retake the keep. The burghers of Lincoln defend their walls, awaiting royal aid. Stephen appears; a stalemate ensues. Although the local people suffer every imaginable injury, the possession of Lincoln tower remains unresolved.

†

HENRY MAKES FOR THE shires of Devon and Cornwall, aspiring to clear them of the usurper's partisans. Capable and cocksure, my heir invests the strategic fortress of Bridport, winning the loyalty of its castellan. I count this his first victory.

Sagely, the Plantagenet invites the advice of new, more experienced and prudent friends. They favor a mobilized truce, counseling him to dispense, for now, with the unending, hazardous cycle of raids and counter raids. His supporters need some respite from the pretender's battalions. They urge the prince to desist from further exploits, and to set off for the continent.

I concur. Despite this first military success, Henry remains unready for the decisive and fatal battle that must come between the illegitimate king and the lawful heir. In Normandy, he shall build up his resources among his continental allies, and wait until such time as he shall be, unquestionably, a man of eminence, able to guarantee a great and lasting peace.

†

SPURRED ON BY THE Plantagenet's imminent return, Marie flees her convent and journeys though icy snow and thick mud to Rouen. The runaway, pretty, red-haired, and refined, ensconces herself at my court. I often invite her to sit with me in my solar, a politeness that I do not extend to her mother.

Today, some prankster attempted to amuse us with his tricks, as if I could not guess that his apple, "possessed by the devil, Your Grace," had a beetle, stuffed inside its core, trying to creep out of its prison.

Marie would not laugh, even when the fool transformed a white rose into a pink one.

Gerta and I snickered in derision, smelling the vinegar whose vapors had dyed the petals. I dismissed the jester, dispatching him to con the naifs of the scullery or the stable.

I wondered at the girl's severity. "How you have grown to womanhood, while I have been away!"

She looked at her hands, clutched together in her lap. "I am contrite, madame, to think of my own stupidity, which threatens the future of a young man of immaculate ancestry, great high-mindedness, and deserved repute."

"You are sweet, well-bred, as noble and talented as your father. Another knight will find his joy fashioned in you."

Now Marie regarded me coldly. "I am a poor, fragile creature."

I grieved to find her still steeped in bitterness. "My son has spoken of your tribulations. I was pained to hear of them."

"When I writhed under the influence of my ill star, the prince's kiss upon my brow cooled my fervor. Sacks of French lavender under my pillow cannot soothe me to the same degree."

Gerta shook her head and muttered. "French lavender is bound to excite your passions, not curb them."

The girl blushed. "Alas! How shall I regain his affection, when even the highest falter and stammer before the risen Son?"

Did she speak of my boy or Mary's? "Your illness is mere longing, thwarted and festering. I give you my leave to love the Plantagenet, but chastely, and from afar. Pure devotion, a flowering virtue, puts him in no danger, and leaves you inviolate."

"Oh, Mother of Mercy!" Marie flung herself at my feet, and embraced my boots. "I am called celibate, but I am guilty of great hypocrisy. Cure me with your holy fire!" She began to weep, and almost to wail. "Touch me, heal me."

My maid drew her away, and hushed her up with an infusion of vervain.

†

GEOFFREY'S DAUGHTER UNSETTLES ME, and reminds me that I too have been mocked and deceived by Lady Love.

Never again will I see the one whom it has been my misfortune to adore. Never again shall I shiver under his flinty glance, raking over me with indifferent ardor. Never again will I boil at his arrogant excuses.

I refuse to relish his memory, to wallow in it. I must put my heart to sleep, forevermore. For it has gone on long enough! I give the scoundrel up; I execute him, jettisoning his corpse from my soul.

O Holy Virgin! Fasten me to the continent; bind me here, Mother, where I have only you to worship. Though he ransacks England, you must keep me here, across the Channel.

The Mirror of the Plantagenet

Scroll Twenty: 1151

The empress struggled to foreswear her lust. Yet, if she prostrated herself before the holy altar, still she swathed herself in a mantle of flesh and blood, and threw her head back to swallow a vicious tincture of ashes and honey. Matilda knew all the time that she could never elude the hour of her reckoning. But she lingered in a purgatory of her own making, powerless to rise above the iniquity of her hopes. Subject to the insanity of her passion, sovereign of nothing, she floundered.

†

Spring

MY HUSBAND RETURNED, AND supplanted me on the ducal throne. I have spent the last two years living quietly, passing my time in regular devotions, avid reading, and extensive self-communion. At times, I feel stagnated and resentful. But, for the most part, I am relieved to couch my strength.

Geoffrey soon dispensed with the supposed continental authority of the French king, declaring the sixteen-year-old Plantagenet of age. In a newly rebuilt section of Rouen Cathedral, surrounded by noble supporters, he invested the boy as Duke of Normandy in his own right. During the ritual, my husband bellowed out his superior pleasure in the prince's manner: "He has proved himself a warrior and a leader of men; he is daring, adventurous, and courtly!" Everyone present cheered in true faith except a jealous Geoffrey the Younger, who had nothing to gain from his brother's ascension. I rejoiced aloud to see my son kneeling before my spouse, then standing, elevated, at his side.

I insisted that the Plantagenet place his ceremonial sword before the high altar, and solemnly vow to be a true knight of the Church and of Our Lady. He did so, with a serious grace, reassuring to our entire retinue of magnates, and the crowds of burghers and prelates that had pressed into the cathedral behind our procession. The sword itself, a gift from the Angevin, had a pommel of gold, inlaid with blue cloisonné enamel, and a golden hilt, decorated with cabochon sapphires and pearls.

We feasted all the rest of the afternoon. Graciously, my husband allowed his minstrels to proclaim that both duke and duchess bequeathed Henry his province, through his mother's inheritance and his father's military conquests. Bernard de Ventadour, in particular, outdid himself. His inflated, complimentary rhymes grated on my ear, but satisfied the boisterous jubilance of our party.

The following day, the two Dukes of Normandy held a tournament in celebration of their puissance and prosperity. For the games, father and son wore matching tabards, silk tunics displaying their heraldic insignia, which I had fashioned for them. They rode similar white chargers, lately imported from Spain. The various prizes, announced in advance, included a lion, a pig, and a bear.

The rules were those of the melée. Two opposing units of warriors had been assembled with great tact, so that each team was equal in size and strength, and so that traditional enemies were not expected to fight alongside each other, as allies. Weapons were blunted with care. Safety zones were established, just within the boundaries of the city, although the skirmishing was to take place outside the walls, encompassing and trampling many of our most fertile hectares.

At dawn, hundreds of mounted men presented themselves in the fields, eager to acquit themselves to their honor. They split into two massed formations, awaiting the sounding of the trumpet and direction from their nominal overlord.

Noble ladies and elderly male courtiers observed and supported the proceedings from the crenellated battlements of Rouen Castle. The local burghers and their wives clustered along the walkways of the city walls, or climbed to the top of steeples and bell towers, in order to cheer and marvel at the sight.

Standing among the royal party, on the ramparts, Marie's breaths were shallow, for she perceived Henry to be at risk. She ripped off a brooch from the neck of her corsage, and thrust it to a page. "Deliver this unto the young Duke of Normandy, with the compliments of Marie of France. If he is to endure any blow, he must suffer the hurt for my sake."

This would not do. Who was she to order my servants to do her bidding? "Halt! There has been some small mistake. Present the brooch to the elder duke, with his daughter's compliments. Bear the same message, if you will. But the jewel is for her father."

Marie stood silent, flushing with some mixture of shame, frustration, and worry.

The tournament was relatively short-lived, and never at a standstill. Geoffrey and Henry, together leading one of the two armies, effectively smashed their force into the ranks of their adversary, less able to stay tightly arranged. At terce, Henry led a turnabout charge, from the rear, and an unambiguous victory was theirs within three hours.

In spite of the quick triumph of our two dukes, Hamelin had been able to unseat a great number of soldiers, and imprison them for the ransom of their armor and horse. Once one had pledged his surety, the boy was off to attack another victim, and increase his spoils. Sometimes he could be seen snatching the bridle of an animal, and dragging the steed out from under its rider.

Denise laughed and clapped at each of his sallies, but frowned at the hasty conclusion to the tumult, which served to limit his gains.

Her greed rankled Gerta. "Empress, your prince looks like an angel, shining, radiant, in his armor. His splendid chivalry earns everyone's esteem. He fights not for profit, but for glory."

Denise's mouth twisted, and the successful conclusion of the celebratory games was marred by pettiness.

†

MY HAND QUIVERS, AND my handwriting suffers, for I have just heard tell of Adeliza's death at Arundel. Her earl, still Stephen's man, transmits the woeful news, and imparts a lock of her golden hair, in honor of my once sacred friendship with his wife. Of late, she preferred her husband's handsome face to my claims upon her, yet I grieve the loss of the confidante of my youth.

Bernard now lodges continually among us, haunting my fireside, eating my victuals, and drinking my mead. In exchange, he dogs me with poetry and flattery, attempting to extenuate my sorrow. Although his banter and songs are unlikely to resurrect Adeliza from her crypt, or even to assuage the ache in my heart, he reminds me that life unspools itself, ever unwinding, and that the harsh north wind of winter is always supplanted by the mellow, balmy breeze of spring.

Would that this wisdom were enough. Adeliza, forty-eight, shrugs off her earthly cares, yet I, forty-nine, continue vibrant, ambitious, unhappy under restraint. Despite all that I give up, I am not resigned from life.

†

THE PLANTAGENET IS EIGHTEEN now, and the two Dukes of Normandy reign jointly. Suddenly impatient to do away with any lingering uncertainty over Henry's pretensions, Geoffrey determines that my son should pay homage to the Frankish sovereign. He will not tolerate any whispered claim that the boy's position remains illegitimate until he kisses Louis VII in fealty. How can he doubt that my magnificent prince holds my father's territory aloof from any overlord, giving precedence only to God?

King Louis, however, responds favorably to my husband's overtures, agreeing to unite with us, in amity. And so the Plantagenet travels to Paris to swear allegiance to him, in return for French recognition. Henry consents to be Louis's vassal, dispensing with some part of his pride, in exchange for a continental peace that will allow him to focus his resources on the war to come in England.

†

Summer

ROUEN CASTLE FAIRLY THROBS with the upheaval of preparation.

With some trepidation, I announce that I intend to make one of the party, to participate, as is proper, in the feudal rites. I hanker to spend long days in the saddle, my skin and hair refreshed in the pristine air. I am eager to survey the great city of Paris, so famed for its elegance, learning, and decadence. I look forward to taking the measure of Eleanor, its renowned queen.

My husband amicably permits me to join the ducal entourage, and does not interfere when I pack my red silk tent, Brian's gift, so as to be assured of some dignity and repose along the route. The Angevin amiably overlooks the two extra carts in our train, which convey its rolls of fabric, long cypress poles, and the tools necessary to erect it.

Of course, Denise accompanies us. Gerta's presence is deemed necessary to the women's comfort. De Ventadour shall entertain us upon the road. We will be quite a big company around the campfire.

Yet Marie is not to go, and grows despondent. Pallid, she mopes about the keep, trailing Henry's footsteps. The prince is more than fond of the dour girl, but tires of her idolatry. Fortunate in his personal favors, and utterly artless, he discounts the sting of unrequited love. In accordance with my wishes, the Plantagenet's marital ambitions far outstrip this incestuous affair. Precocious Marie sees clearly that their relationship is at an end, but wallows in her melancholy. While she suffers, my son, blithe and abandoned, carouses with innumerable willing companions, who throw their virtue at the new duke- and king -to-be. In this, he has the Angevin's blessing.

Neither is Geoffrey the Younger to travel in our caravan, for the rancor between my heir and his sibling grows to such proportions that my husband can no longer tolerate the younger brother's hate. Geoffrey's bitter outrage at his omission is ugly to behold, only strengthening his father's wish to exclude him from the imminent adventure.

I still find it odd that the Angevin prefers Stephen's son to his two legitimate offspring. The Plantagenet is a finer specimen of knight, more refined and courtly than the others, but any other man would cleave to his own blood. Can Geoffrey not smell it?

†

EIGHT DAYS AGO, WE set off from Rouen. Thus far, the road has been easy, dry and wide. Yesterday, we crossed the border into the Vexin, a small county southeast of us, lodged between Normandy and the Isle de France. It has long been a sort of buffer zone between unfriendly territories, but on this journey we admire its fruitful serenity. Henry tallies its prosperous beauties.

Just now I have a blaring headache, the effect of last night's excessive carnival. At dusk, I was apart from our campsite, alone in a meadow, making use of a field privy. Hearing the pounding of hooves, I crouched low to conceal myself. I hurried back and found my family and attendants crowded around a courier dressed in Stephen's colors. Expecting something terrible, I found to my delight that it was the best possible news.

Maud, the thieving, whorish, false queen, is dead! She expired at Heningham Castle and has already been buried before the high altar at the abbey of Faversham, in her loyal county of Kent. Faversham is a fitting resting place for that strumpet, for it is a decadent house, filled to the brim with treasures stripped from my subjects during the Count of Boulogne's endless wars.

The herald described the usurper, at first beside himself in despair, then frantic with arrangements for his wife's interment. In very little time, craftsmen carved Maud a lavish tomb of marble. The royal messenger insisted that God's hand must have been upon the work, speeding its completion. I laughed aloud at such a miracle, for it is the miracle of my revenge. Everyone in our train was jubilant to hear of the harlot's demise, and showered our enemy's envoy with liquor and kisses.

As Henry reveled with me in the death of our foe, I shared my scorn and exultation. "Imagine her at the pearly gates, demanding entrance! Maud, aflame with promiscuous fever, flaunting herself, but denied passage into paradise! Heaven measures her presumption."

The Plantagenet laughed. "She would toy with the Lord Jesus Christ, and lead him to her chamber, and take communion with him, eating and drinking of his body and blood."

I could not grimace at his obscenities, in the face of Maud's greater heresies. "She is blind to His divinity, too enormous, too precious for her to apprehend."

My son and I strayed closer to the great bonfire that blazed in the center of our encampment and partook of the drink being doled out to the celebrants. Before I thought the better of it, I gulped down more than was prudent. As I quenched a thirst that had already been extinguished, my gaze wandered to my husband, so handsome and yet not my heart. He stood with his hands on Denise, who gave herself liberally, out under the open sky.

Numb, I thought of Stephen, free at last, and of my own perpetual bondage. But what does it matter? My soul is too deeply wounded, my inner light is too dim, to rebound in love.

The prince sensed that my happiness was not unalloyed. He loitered near me. "I have heard, Mother, that Queen Eleanor of France is both exquisitely attractive and much discontented. Her husband holds himself like a monk, humble before his abbot, or a boy not yet grown to his full height, who still fears a beating from his father. It is said that he squirms aside, effacing himself, to allow priests to pass him by in the corridors of his own palace! Shackled to such a spouse, Eleanor chafes at the dull round of her existence."

How well I could imagine the weight of her chains, the bonds of an ill-assorted marriage. "The queen's court abounds in chivalry and corruption, for in such does she drown her ennui and distress."

The young duke perked up, grinning in anticipation. "Her possessions stretch from the Loire to the Pyrenees, from the central mountains to the western coast."

To me, Eleanor seemed the victim of her wonderful circumstances. "She must miss the southern light under the gray northern skies of Paris. She surrounds herself with mercenary wits, in an attempt to illumine her damp and gloomy castle."

Dizziness and a growing nausea sent me into my red pavilion. While the others still wassailed, I lay down upon the bed of aromatic leaves that Gerta had readied. I smelled the odor of roasting meat, and thought of Maud's corpse. I yearned for a pound of her flesh, to cure and treasure. I heard a lovely melody, played upon a zither and a harp, and my strength ebbed away from me. The rumpus continued unabated, but I fell into a troubled sleep.

†

Fall

PARIS IS A WONDROUS and aggravating place, for its antiquity breeds austerity and piety on the one hand, licentiousness and folly on the other.

Yesterday, we attended the sumptuous banquet that paid tribute to our arrival. The great hall of the French royal palace was hung with damask tapestries. The most beautiful among them depicted the colorful birds and varied beasts of a lush forest. Attached to the borders of the weaving were small silver bells, which jingled elegantly whenever ruffled. On the dais, thick carpets were spread underfoot, and scattered with rose petals. The high table was cluttered with candelabra; a profusion of costly wax candles burned down, only to be immediately replaced by a chamberlain.

I was introduced to the king, whose abstemious appearance much intrigues me. Louis, slender and wan, almost fades into insignificance. He adorns himself too simply, in vestments more appropriate to a cleric. It is said that Louis is all meekness, but I suspect his quietude to be a pose.

He was very courteous to the Normans and especially to me, placed beside him. With spindly arms, he doled out my portions of food.

All the viands were drenched in sauces of sugar, pepper, and cinnamon. I sampled many unknown luxuries: the eggs of fish, called "caviar," and a bitter, soothing drink, known as "tea." The very water we rinsed our mouths with was scented with lime, to hide its impurities.

Throughout the feast, His Majesty's azure eyes looked mildly upon me, but I saw his soft glance intensify into a cold glare when it rested on his wife.

On my other side reposed a boisterous Eleanor, not yet thirty years old, with lustrous black eyes and extravagant red hair. She is too tall, but has a superbly toned figure and a strong constitution. She wore a rich silk dress, gold in color, embroidered all over with priceless gems. She had paint upon her eyes and lips, although she did not need it, dazzling as she was. She was loaded down with glinting jewelry, also superfluous, given her immoderate gown and flamboyant natural charms. How Maud would have hated her!

Eleanor paid much heed to me, beginning with a jest. "Do you think, Empress, that my costume is worth the lifelong toil of the worms who made it?" The queen tossed her hair, so that her diamond earrings shook.

The French king answered in my stead. "You are decorated like a pagan temple, not so much ornamented as laden down with precious metals and stones."

Eleanor cackled and turned to my husband, on her other side. "What say you to my indecent finery, Your Grace?"

Geoffrey unsheathed his flattery. "Your very bracelets, your brocade, your golden circlet: none of these do your loveliness any justice, for what nature gave you far outweighs the contributions of the arts."

Several troubadours who stood behind the queen's place mumbled their appreciation of the Angevin's wit. I guessed that Eleanor's suggestive remarks were usually lobbed at them.

The queen swerved back to me. "I have quite the reputation for opulence and frivolity. Is it not so, Empress?" She rolled my title off her plump, carmine lips.

Did she test me, before my two dukes? "I would not repeat a slur against one of my cousins, madame. I believe that we are related through Robert the Pious, king of France at the time of the Millennium. His son Robert, Duke of Burgundy, was your great-great-grandfather and his daughter Adela was my great-grandmother."

Eleanor decided to be kind. "Looking at your comely face, I would never have known that we were not of age."

Louis tapped the table with his thin fingers. "I am also your cousin, for the eldest son of Robert the Pious was King Henri I, my great-grandfather."

The Plantagenet spoke up, from the other side of the French sovereign. "Family trees are a bit confining."

The queen smiled briefly at the prince, then resumed her chatter. "Paris can be stifling to the imagination."

Henry did not want to be a mere listener at the board. Her Majesty's obliviousness to his merit inflamed his cheeks. "It is a fantasy land and you are its ruling principle."

Eleanor gave the young duke a longer look, from head to waist. "I am almost what the jongleurs proclaim me to be."

Bernard piped up, from his spot at my back, presumably presenting some nonsense prepared just for this occasion. "If queens did not exist, the poets would have had to invent them, so necessary as they are to a nation's glory."

Her Majesty giggled. "France can refuse none of my demands. I commanded Louis to ransack a nearby shrine, to procure me the slipper of the Holy Virgin, credited with one hundred and three miraculous cures."

Denise, on the far side of my husband, and at the fringe of the baldachin placed above the high table, had been waiting for her chance. "Did Our Lady wear slippers? I would think that she wore sandals. And if she did wear slippers, their delicate fabric could not have survived the ravages of time." She blushed, perspiring under her nose, seemingly relieved to have declared herself immune to the glamour of the queen. The leman's pulchritude, so invincible in Rouen, appeared as watered down as the wine one serves to children and the elderly.

Eleanor grew serious at this aspersion cast upon her powers of logic. "May the righteous souls in heaven shrivel up your tongue! May it remain useless and desiccated, until such time as you kiss the Virgin's shoe, and renounce your apostasy."

Her Majesty noticed her husband, nodding and smiling. Seeing his approbation, she remembered herself and tried to plague him anew. "I would not have the churches of Paris be lackluster, empty of glittering reliquaries. We have the reputation of our court to think of."

The French sovereign hung his head at his wife's profession of hypocrisy and avarice.

Dismissively, the queen held out her goblet to Duke Geoffrey, whose manly beauties she apparently appreciated. While he drank from her wine, she stroked his arm, as if to assure herself of his lean strength.

Sternly, Louis examined the Angevin. "I regret that Her Majesty attends only to what dazzles her eye."

Denise's expression was dismal, her envy incompatible with decorum. "Perhaps the queen chases after refinement, and is a student of taste, instead of its master."

Eleanor's cherry mouth sneered. "Who is this person at my table? What is her name? I cannot recall it."

I winced for Denise, and for my husband, who had brought such a rude wench to the royal notice. I enunciated carefully. "A queen's humility is her most glorious attribute."

Geoffrey looked grateful for my intervention.

Eleanor nodded, acknowledging my chastisement.

The French king's interest in me enlarged, but I found myself famished, and busied myself with the culinary delights.

Louis sighed, then clapped his hands to initiate the entertainments. Thirty musicians, fiddlers, pipers, and drummers, filed into the hall, and began to tune their instruments. Just as many Saracen dancing girls, shapely and scantily clad, began to assemble in front of the dais. When the music commenced, they balanced themselves upon large balls. Swinging their arms and twisting at the waist, so as to move them along the smooth floor. All the while, they snapped their fingers and hooted.

I found it amusing to watch Denise endeavor to feign indifference to this riveting display.

The queen shrugged. "This spectacle surely will banish our dark humor."

His Majesty slammed his spare fist down on the board. "Perverse and profane! This dance is all innuendo, and no grace."

Eleanor clenched her teethed, and made as if to rise from the table, until Louis's demeanor suddenly changed, from one of authority to one of submission.

She resettled herself upon the dais. The French queen would not be cowed.

The lewd acrobatics continued and we ceased to talk.

†

DISCONCERTINGLY, DUKE GEOFFREY SUCCUMBS to the charisma of the Frankish queen, who encourages his suit. Fascinated, he composes odes in her honor. Today, he has been invited to her solar to recite them. Gerta, having flirted assiduously in the kitchens, snidely confides that my husband has been practicing a few simple magic tricks, natural experiments devised by King Solomon himself to court the love of a princess. He has perfected a small explosion of fire in the palm of his hand. Will this seduce Eleanor out of her bliaut?

At the same time, Her Majesty enchants Henry, although the Plantagenet is less successful in his addresses to the royal lady. Marie's name, once so dangerous to him, becomes an empty byword. The prince dreams only of the jaded Southerner, lively and stubborn. My splendid young duke values her regal cunning, perceiving that it could complement his capabilities. Thus, he bemoans his youth, for she is his elder. He disparages his robust and manly form, for he fears that she judges him thickset. He discovers that he lacks what the troubadours term "imperial legs," thin and well molded at the thigh and calf.

Woebegone Denise! It falls to me both to admonish her and to essay to dissipate her wretchedness. This afternoon, I walked with her in the palace garden, surveying the wilting, emaciated remains of the season's blooms.

She paced silently beside me, scrutinizing the ground.

I huffed at the absurdity of cheering up my husband's discarded mistress. "Cease this unmannerly sobriety! We are here to celebrate the Plantagenet's ascension to grace."

The leman started to cry. "He has nothing to smirk over, for his father purloins his prize."

I groaned. "Neither duke presumes to woo the married queen with anything more than empty courtesies."

Insolent Denise had not forgotten her old grievances. "Men took liberties with you, Empress, who were as willing as this slut."

I stopped my promenade, forcing her to halt as well, for she could not go before me. "This is not the time for you to vex me, who attempts to ease your burden."

Tears rolled down her chin. "Her Majesty embraces Geoffrey in lust. Yet she teases Henry out of ambition. Your little prince plots to betray his French overlord, to whom he has not yet even sworn."

I picked out wrinkles on Denise's face that had not been there in the spring. I did feel for her. "Who is not base?"

She trembled with impotent fury; her cheeks burned as fiery as her hair. "Frog bitch! Did you see her sharp, white teeth rip the meat from the roast? She could maim a man with those fangs."

I cradled the leman's shoulders. "Eleanor's heart aches. Deserving of a robust, virile husband, she finds herself espoused to a prim monk. Yet, she must bear this finicky, unsexed man a son. Her two daughters, one six and one lately born, shall not suffice. For two centuries, every king of the Capetian dynasty has sired an heir; the French succession has been uncontested. Louis is no romantic knight, but it is his consort who is the culprit."

I had shocked the wench, who followed my reasoning further. "You wish both your dukes to bed this woman, so that she can birth a boy for Louis? What do you care for the tribulation of your enemy?"

Vehemently, I denied it. "I did not mean to suggest that one of my house should come to rule here. I was merely explaining Her Majesty's motivation to you. France will never let her go. It thinks of her dowry, the entire southwestern Mediterranean basin. She is doomed to live here, without love. Under these circumstances, the lady amuses herself at our expense. She understands that one of our Normans is too old for her, and one is too young."

My rival could not lay aside her unhappiness. "Queens freely spend other people's treasure!"

†

ON THREE SUCCESSIVE DAYS, Denise called upon the good angels, Gabriel, Michael, and Raphael, to rekindle Geoffrey's preference for her. She fasted throughout, bathed in scalding water, and dressed herself all in white, so as to purify her body to receive divine intervention. Gerta sniggers that the necessity for celibacy did not present a problem to our would-be necromancer. Despite his leman's pious arrangements and Latin invocations, my husband continues to tangle the coverlets of the queen.

Last night, my maid heard high-pitched shrieks and the Angevin's angry recriminations. She crept near the duke's private quarters, where Denise knelt before the barred entrance to her lover's chamber. The naïve fool called on her sweetheart, pleading for his forbearance and affection. Finally, His Grace stormed out of the door, dragged his sobbing mistress back to her own room, and bound her to her bedposts.

I can still remember the feel of the back of his hand.

†

YESTERDAY, DENISE AND I were taking in our stockings, which hang too loosely around our ankles. They are nowhere near as stylish as the tightly fitting hose that the women wear at the French court.

Making himself at home in my solar, Bernard de Ventadour settled himself on an elaborately cushioned divan, primed to divert us with gossip.

The wench sniffed, peering at her stitches, and pouted becomingly.

Bernard gaped at her, and his palm drifted, coming to rest upon his member.

My husband's mistress blushed deeply, and inched her bench away from the knave. Despite her carnal nature and rampant appetite for evil tidings, her idol worship of Geoffrey does not abate.

Finding Denise unreceptive to his suggestive advances, Ventadour began to flatter me. "Empress, your wit is the boast of the English and the Normans. You have besotted the Frankish courtiers, who praise your talents and, of course, your fine face."

I discounted the cad's remarks, focusing instead upon my altered stockings. They were finely remade and would accentuate my still slender limbs. "How can the dogs see anyone else beside their radiant queen? We are all cast in her shadow."

Slighted a second time, Bernard straightened his posture. "The French king is surely obsessed by her. He would idealize her, the way a small boy venerates his illustrious mother, but he cannot do so in the face of her trifling, her wantonness, and her cynicism." Here the troubadour paused, waiting for us to exclaim at his deft metaphor. Neither of us was in the mood to stroke his ego.

The jongleur resumed his prattle. "Eavesdroppers are privy to Louis's violent outbursts and Eleanor's devious explanations. Somehow, under the spell of her manipulation, His Majesty ends every marital argument by apologizing for his own abuse."

What could the queen of France teach me?

Denise considered her adversary's stratagems. "He knows she is culpable, but the witch will not toss away her crown."

De Ventadour smirked, quick to flaunt his clerical education. "A wife's adultery destroys the marital union of the flesh."

I dropped my work onto my lap. Did the minstrel credit every rumor that circulated above my own head?

†

DESPITE MY RESOLUTIONS TO transform myself into a votive of the sacred, I husband the flame of the profane. Unable to withstand the pervading atmosphere of Eleanor's decadence, my shallow piety is no match for the troubadour's unrelenting cajolements. Surely, he is some hellish succubus, luring me into the abyss of fire.

More vain, now that my prettiness wanes, I respond when Bernard serenades me, calling me his "magnet, " or naming me "Beautiful Glance."

Gerta shakes her head, and stamps her feet. "How can you bed the spawn of a kitchen wench? He is hardly worthy of my notice, and should be entirely invisible to you. His love songs were written for the ears of common prostitutes."

Perhaps it is so, but having a jongleur at my beck and call has its benefits. I set de Ventadour the arduous task of making a horoscope for the Plantagenet. He rises to the occasion, with more discretion than I had supposed him to possess, drawing "a figure for the arrival of a certain person in England." Gerta rolls her eyes at the number of questions about Henry's birth that Bernard puts to me, and points out that I deserve most of the accolades for the document he produces. Not every biographical detail remained at the forefront of my mind; I could not assure him with absolute certainty that a star had fallen into my mouth at the moment of the prince's conception. But we agreed that it must have done so, for who was delivered into the world on that day but England's Messiah?

Tonight, I have been on my knees in the rushes, praying to the Holy Mother. Seeing through me, unveiling my secrets, Mary does not answer my petition. I need Her intercession, for I cannot hold myself aloof from the devil's enticements. No matter that I belittle my love for Stephen, clambering up into the hills of faith. Here, in France, my foot has slipped upon the twisting path, and I stumble back and down, collapsing into a cesspit of sin.

†

TODAY, MY YOUNG DUKE did homage to the French king. Now, without question, all the territory of Anjou, Maine, and Normandy falls to my family. It is almost incredible, verily a miracle. Anjou and Normandy have been enemies for the last two hundred years, but in the Plantagenet they are united as one. In return, Henry regretfully acknowledges that the coveted Vexin belongs to France.

This morning, we gathered in the church dedicated to the Virgin, on the eastern tip of the Island of the City. Once sacked, the building has been stupendously restored. Still, I measure it too small for a royal cathedral. I have heard that Louis intends, on this same foundation, to build a great house of God, dedicated to Our Lady.

First, the French sovereign demanded of the prince: "Do you wish, without reserve, to become my vassal?"

Henry firmly declared: "I wish it," thereby engaging himself.

They two great men clasped hands. My heir swore faithfully to defend his liege lord and to protect him from all comers. Louis bequeathed him a kiss of peace.

To end the service, a choir of monks performed some extremely captivating chant, written by a celebrated abbess, praising the vast wheel of the cosmos, encompassing all the Lord's creation, encircling all that He has given life. This type of music, another of Eleanor's new fashions, has a refrain that repeats itself, over and over, low and grave, while higher voices sing a melody above it. This polyphony, born in the south with the queen, is like my best embroidery, winding fine, luxurious filaments into coarser, hardier fabric.

At none, on a wide, open meadow just over the Seine to the south, there was a ceremonial performance of martial skill, in single combat. The two dukes had agreed to tilt against one another, so that the French should not have cause to mock Norman horsemanship. Henry was eager to increase his fame, and Geoffrey to reestablish his importance in the eyes of the world.

The Angevin displayed a new shield, the gift of the French queen. In comparison to the Plantagenet's heavier and broader one, his was somewhat petite, less convex, almost triangular. Its inside panel was painted, and depicted two figures wrapped in an embrace. I doubted that this fancy love token would protect my husband as well as Henry's apparently obsolete weaponry.

A pained Denise whined. "Why does a knight joust, other than to win the adulation of whores?"

Wound around the Angevin's lance was a plait of narrow ribbon, in the queen's heraldic colors, blue and gold. Henry's spear bore a twisted knot of my red and gold. He did not seem satisfied with his equipment, and the two men faced each other with a worrisome lack of amity.

The ritual began with the ordeal of the lance. Both of my dukes sat atop their steeds with upright poise; neither posture could be faulted. Both spears were couched at perfectly right angles. When they galloped toward one another, I could see my husband's thighs flexing. My son relied more on his spurs. Both charged at a leisurely pace, with loose reins but enormous control, so as to strike at each other with restrained force. Both of their shields, old and new, withstood the collision, which splintered and shattered their lances. Neither man was unhorsed.

I exhaled. The large Parisian crowd clapped politely, but did not seem overwhelmed by their composed performance. Were they waiting for blood?

After acknowledging the applause, Geoffrey and Henry trotted off to receive the attentions of their squires. Dismounting with care, they handed off their broken weapons, and strode toward one another with their swords at the ready. The Angevin's insouciance was met with the prince's grim annoyance.

I closed my eyes, as their blades clashed together, and let the clanging din wash over me.

Gerta pinched me. "What a racket they make! Watch the sparks fly, Empress!"

When the noise had lessened, I looked again, and discovered my dukes bowing to each other's closed faces, before moving off in opposite directions.

The French queen made her way to my side. "The brave lord of Normandy is noble of bearing and virtuous of heart."

"My son is a true prince."

Eleanor smiled opaquely, not bothering to correct my interpretation of her remark.

To conclude the day, His Majesty dispersed munificent gifts of Hungarian stallions and Arabian spices to all the chamberlains, stewards, impresarios, philosophers, and minstrels who organized or ornamented the proceedings. His munificence ensures that the troubadours and historians will broadcast the details of the festivities, and his royal largesse.

The Mirror of the Plantagenet

Scroll Twenty-One: 1152

A s it is ever so, the empress's second husband came to the end of his earthly sojourn. Rapidly, her son ascended to greatness, according to the awesome judgment of God. This prince was blessed in everything: in the bride of his choosing and in his command over her. There were those who begrudged him so many favors, but he trod upon their envy with his heel. His mother, once the subject of our story, and of history, stepped aside, committing herself, at long last, to the pure and the true.

†

Winter

ON THE FRIGID JOURNEY home, far less pleasant than our coming hither in the summer, I am not consumed by the promise of a new amour. Before we left Paris, I gave Bernard the boot, forbidding him my private company. Whenever we coupled, it was the poet who panted and swooned, and sang to me of his intense delight. My tepid avowals dismayed him; my rejection humiliated him. For several days, he brooded and expostulated, insisting that a wise man such as himself well knew how to conceal an affair.

Exasperated by his stubbornness, Gerta called the fool to my solar, and flourished one of my rings, set with a superb emerald, placing it in a silver bowl. I spit on the stone and induced the poet to mingle his saliva with mine. My gem glistened before us, as if stimulated by our commingled fluids. My maid then rinsed it clean with a draught of wine. Turning to de Ventadour, she demanded that he set his sights instead on Eleanor's beauty and generosity. Cowed, the disappointed sycophant agreed to exchange one queen for another.

My latest affair was a newly sprouted seedling, exposed too early to the frost, dying overnight. At my advanced age, I am still capable of laughter and elation, but Bernard could not stir me to my core. I see how far I have come. Even my perfidious cousin, once my secret treasure, cannot exhume my heart.

†

THE ALLIANCE OF INTEREST between my two dukes unravels under the spell of the queen of France. Some of our party speculate that Eleanor gave herself both to the father and to the son, while others dispute the likelihood of Henry's success with his sire's conquest. Either way, the trollop frays the accord that had grown up between the Plantagenet and the Angevin.

Yesterday, the two Graces rode alongside one another in a narrow ravine. My destrier ambled directly behind the pair, and we three were some distance ahead of our retinue. The creaking of our leather saddles and the huffing of our horses in the icy air muffled our conversation.

Geoffrey's tone was acid. "I forbid you to correspond with Her Majesty. As I have known her, so any relation between you two would be incestuous."

Henry looked over his shoulder at me, shrouded up against the weather in a thick wool mantle, trimmed with ermine. "You dishonorably slight your duchess, an empress, before all the world, and cruelly supplant your court favorite, all to fornicate with a woman for whom you can have no real use."

My husband snorted. "The queen is the wife of your liege lord. To sully her would be treason."

The prince shook his head. "I shall not touch the lady before she is mine."

I was bemused to hear my son turn his failed seduction into respectable circumspection.

Geoffrey raised his eyebrows at the Plantagenet's ambition. "She is all licentiousness, without any propriety. Your wife should possess an unanswerable dignity."

Dispersing a shower of small stones, Denise's stallion caught up with our mounts.

Looking displeased, her lover straightened his back. But he took his spleen out on my boy. "Eleanor would never consent to such a union. Look in your mother's mirror. You are short and broad, fat, I tell you. She, with her gleaming white skin that glows like the moon, could never give herself to you."

Of course, the leman encouraged Henry's suit. "I think the two would be well matched, with their red hair, noble foreheads, and eyes that burn brightly, like the night stars."

The Angevin refuted his strumpet's tactics. "The queen's curls cascade like molten gold, giving radiance to her whole face. They cannot be compared to his carrot tufts."

My throat tightened at this aspersion. Would jealousy undo all that had been done?

Now Geoffrey was lost in a reverie. "Her ivory throat, her snowy bosom: these were charms out of legend."

I had no patience for my husband's mania. "Her sumptuous garments blinded you. At the welcoming banquet, they were worth a castle."

Denise's eyes went dark. Her mouth looked wan above the folds of her rough cloth veil. "The only robe that matters is the cloak of our good deeds."

This exalted piety was new to her and not at all credible. None of the three spoke sensibly, warped as they all were by Eleanor's poisonous influence.

What could I say to combat her appeal? "Her Majesty is descended from heretics. Her grandfather kidnapped her grandmother and made her his concubine. The old man died excommunicate from the Church, cursed by a hermit who swore that no one of the house of Aquitaine would ever know happiness. Both parents were also buried without the promise of redemption. Would either of Your Graces risk an eternity of damnation to be with such a one, a sprig of a house of infamy?"

My husband spurred his charger, cantering away from us.

†

TWO DAYS AGO, WE stopped to rest at the fortress of Le Lude, near Le Mans. Hamelin and a party of relatively green knights join us here, traveling from Rouen. My other sons do not take the trouble to be among the first to welcome us back to Normandy. Yesterday, Henry and a cadre of younger men from our expanded entourage set off into the forest, on an extended excursion to hunt fresh game. I hope that this small separation will allow the two dukes to cool their tempers.

But the Angevin, always so vigorous and facile, falls ill. After a short spurt of falconry near the keep, Geoffrey felt heated and plunged into a freezing stream. Before sext, he returned to Le Lude, to read in its great library. Soon the duke was beset by chills, although he burns with a high fever.

Today, Denise is beside herself with anxiety. With an ashen face, she paces distractedly through the baileys. Forcing her way past his attendants, and into his solar, she strews her lover's sheets with dracontinium, an herb said to counteract infection. She smears the walls of Geoffrey's room with the entrails of a catfish, dragged out of the moat, so as to ward off any bewitchment. The idle pages and mystified medical men at my husband's bedside cross themselves before abusing her nonsensical incantations of "cuma, cucuma ucuma cuma uma maa."

My maid takes the matter into her own, more capable hands, and with the cooperation of a mendicant friar, inscribes several sugar wafers with healing prayers, transcribed in the most austere and authorized Latin. Gerta hand-delivers them to the duke's chamber, and places them under his tongue.

I too begin to fear the likelihood of some catastrophe. I add together the number eight (for there are eight letters to Geoffrey) and the number six (for there are six letters in Le Lude). Conjoined, they are fourteen, and even; His Grace will not escape his fate.

†

I HAVE JUST RETURNED from my husband's solar, where his steward and I witnessed the last will and testament of Geoffrey Duke of Normandy, Count of Anjou and Maine. The Angevin bequeaths to the Plantagenet all three of his territories, almost disinheriting Geoffrey the Younger, save for a gift of three important strongholds: Chinon, Mirabeau, Loudon. His Grace bestows nothing upon William; he is to be provided for out of the largesse of his eldest brother. I blush to think of the coming impoverishment of my lesser sons.

Always leery of Geoffrey's intentions toward Henry, I am shocked at this unexpected favoritism. My husband cannot resist the allure of passing down a great realm, stretching from the Channel to the southern tip of Anjou. He cannot bring himself to split up the enormous dominion that he has spent his whole life piecing together. He comprehends that the Plantagenet needs all of our continental possessions to generate enough manpower and revenue to win England from the Count of Boulogne.

Yet the Angevin offers his namesake some hope of preferment. If Henry invades Britain successfully, gaining the English throne, then his younger brother shall be enfoeffed with the Counties of Maine and Anjou. Such an arrangement guarantees that the second son will fight bravely for the betterment of the first.

Denise's settlement amounts to three manor houses and their adjoining land. She will be able to live out her life in ease and to transmit a petty nobleman's legacy to Hamelin, often in debt to moneylenders. Perhaps her son will no longer need to resort to pawn shops in order to keep himself in horse and armor. Marie receives a small dowry. Overall, the leman's endowment bears no resemblance to her rich position as the substitute Duchess of Normandy, but it is more in keeping with her native social status. Again Geoffrey puzzles me, for what he imparts to his mistress is no more than what is right.

†

UNCOMFORTABLY PASSIVE IN MY strange bedchamber, and uneasy in the eerie silence of the keep, I ventured back to my husband's side and dismissed a retinue of squires and priests. Vacant, the duke's solar resounded with his labored breathing.

The Angevin lay awake, between this world and the next. To my confusion, he asked my pardon. "Do you forgive my violence, Empress? Our marriage, lately chaste, achieves a perfect, unsullied dignity. We stand side by side, not hand in hand, but joined none the less, according to the will of heaven."

I regarded his perfect features, unchanged in extremity. "I do absolve you, Your Grace, from your crimes against me."

Geoffrey smiled thinly. "You are gracious and clement, Holy Queen. You are sweetness and mercy."

"I regret to not have inspired more of your poetry."

"I repent of any shame that I have brought upon you; I was often blind to your value. You are as white as the moon, and as bright as the sun, as high as the mountains, as unyielding as the currents of the sea. The dawning glory of the Plantagenet proves your worth and virtue."

I trembled at his praise, almost unable to believe in his approbation.

"You must vow, wife, to leave me unburied, until such time as the young duke shall return. He must swear, upon my corpse, agreement to the terms of my dispensation."

I pondered this last request and nodded my head. I felt generous. "Husband, do you have anything that you wish to ask me? In all justice, I will answer."

Geoffrey considered me for a moment, and I him. "It is no matter; the law unites us, and we are reconciled. You did not present me with a son beneath my notice. History names him mine." Suddenly anxious, the Angevin struggled to take in air. "I would say my adieus to one who was long my solace, if you will permit me this final insult."

I summoned a page, sending for Denise.

Very soon the distraught mistress burst in upon us, showering her caresses upon the recumbent duke. Her voice was too choked with sobs for her words to have any clarity.

My husband placed a hand over his paramour's wet mouth. "You will no longer have the luxury of behaving with abandon."

Dismayed, Denise stopped her fawning. "For years, we explored together the kingdom of the senses. Your household always wondered whether you were prompted by more than lust."

His Grace grunted. "For many years, my courtly heart belonged to you."

She still worshipped her knight, but his recent offenses had hardened her. "Now I measure the scope of your attachment."

The duke looked bewildered. He touched her red curls.

Denise backed away from him, although I could imagine what such a sacrifice cost her. "I have already lost what I value most, above everything else." The wronged woman devolved into another paroxysm of sobs, distorting her loveliness. "Of all the hateful whores, I am the most despised, and the unhappiest. I was dignified on high, preferred to all others. When you tossed me aside, I suffered deeply over my long and hard fall."

I sighed at her sordid lack of tact. "Be consoled by His Grace's willingness to see you now."

My husband stared with glassy eyes.

For some minutes, the leman cried heatedly, still at a distance from her erstwhile favorite.

As Geoffrey's inhalations became more ragged, he remembered her, who mourned him more than any other. "For the space of many, many years, you were enough for me. You were my bliss, and my hallelujah."

But for Denise, his false heart would no longer suffice. "Will I be recompensed?"

"May Jesus Christ grant you what you desire. I cannot." The words petered out and he closed his eyes.

With a short gasp, the wench gathered him up. Then my husband died, in her arms, with their argument ringing in our ears. She screamed out her guilt and sorrow.

Cringing, I pried Denise away from the duke's body. Humbled by her misfortune, she was beneath my notice. Yet I knew the tribulation of her coming solitude. I could not withhold my prayers, either for the false knight who had wounded us both, or for the fate of all women no longer relevant to the affairs of the world.

†

AWAITING PRINCE HENRY'S RETURN to Le Lude, my mind stalls, awash in perplexity. For a second time, I am widowed. Shall my life revolve, now that Stephen and I are both free? Shall I fight for him, as I have fought against him?

Tied to Geoffrey, I set myself apart, independent, and regarded not my marriage vow. I copulated with knaves, soiling myself. Body and soul, I am unclean and unworthy, even of my cousin.

I stand now at a crossroads. I see before me the route to virtue, at an intersection with the route to love. Do I step to the left or the right, to the wrong or the right? My foot wavers in the air; where shall I set it down?

I lower my shoe upon the golden way, toward paradise. Refusing to look behind me, I give him up.

†

HENRY IS SHOCKED, OF course, to apprehend what has transpired in his absence, but by no means distraught to find himself the sole Duke of Normandy, Count of Anjou and Maine.

The Plantagenet's face is inscrutable as he views the mummified body of his titular father. Encased in a linen shroud, Geoffrey lies in state, in a chamber draped with black wool. The pale figure illuminates the somber room, as a feeble taper penetrates a vast darkness.

†

YESTERDAY, WE LISTENED TO my husband's steward intone the particulars of the Angevin's testament. The prince drummed his fingers in impatience, then smacked his leg at the caveat favoring his antagonistic brother.

At first, Henry declined to take an oath to obey his father's wishes. "Why should I not rule the world from Scotland to Anjou? Why should I be less than I might be? I am being asked to cede half of my portion. What do I owe young Geoffrey, who hates me, and whom our late father mistrusted and feared?"

I beseeched him to honor His Grace's decision, for the sake of peace and amity, but it was not until this morning that he finally pledged to accede to the Angevin's plans. I shiver to recollect that his voice wavered and his eyes were slit small as he agreed to follow the will's directives. Although he vowed to enrich his foe, it was clear that he remained disgruntled at the injustice.

Due to the delay in negotiating Henry's acquiescence, Geoffrey's corpse has begun to decompose, and exudes a most foul smell. Gerta informs me that some of our hypocritical courtiers whisper that the prince's greed is indecent. The point is moot, for the usurper sits astride the English throne.

†

ACCORDING TO HIS WISHES, we inter Geoffrey the Fair at the cathedral of Saint Julian in Le Mans; he is entombed where we were married, where he was first elevated to a great station. There he lies in effigy, a handsome knight, carved from white, translucent alabaster, illustrious and lustrous, both. In contrast, his blue shield, with its golden lions, glitters in colored enamel. A record of his significant military campaigns is engraved into the smooth marble base of his sarcophagus. In death, the duke is distilled to his essential nature: inanimate, cold, martial.

This morning, the family and courtiers froze through an interminable Mass. Pinching my chattering teeth together, twisting my numb fingers, I ruminated upon Geoffrey's bier. I glanced over at Henry, whose face was tight, almost disdainful. Marie's despondence was evident; I remembered that the bond between her and her father was once uppermost.

To my ears, the music sung at the service was not nearly as moving as what we had recently heard in Paris. During the mourning office, a large incensoir swung above us, imbuing us with the divine musk, particularly jarring in our frigid nostrils. It seemed impossible to find my faith under my furs, and I mumbled the Lord's Prayer. At long last, the bishop pronounced the Angevin's absolution from the final judgment.

Leaving the cathedral, passing through its enormous portals, our retinue swelled. A large cortege of the poor, paid alms to carry candles in the procession, attached themselves to our party.

Only Denise tarried, loitering by the final resting place of her beloved.

Curious, I melted away from my son and our barons to return to the apse.

The leman acknowledged my presence with a curtsy. "I was a lady capable of discriminating among men, and so gave myself to the model among them. Finding him so worthy, I dared to adore him openly. Why should I not have the world's esteem?"

Some monks wandered forth from the shadowy recesses of the choir and started to chant the seven penitential palms, praying for the soul of Denise's hero.

She unearthed some gold from her purse and pressed it upon one of the brothers. "You must report to me any miracles that you witness here. I will pay you well for your evidence."

I took her hand. "I would be your benefactress."

The mistress blushed. "You are the grandest of women, encircled by vagabonds and thieves. I was another pretender, another foe who wrongly usurped what was yours, the seat of power at your husband's side."

†

Spring

HAMELIN JOINS DUKE HENRY'S court in Angers, so as to abet His Grace's schemes to cement control of Anjou and Maine. Denise immures herself in one of her manors, but I remain at the head of my son's entourage.

All the talk in the new season concerns the termination of the French royal marriage. The divorce has everyone's disapproval, including my own, although I once dreamed of the same. Separated from Geoffrey, and burning to dispose of him, eager to be at liberty to wed my cousin, I was unable to implement my plans. How is it that Louis's queen smashes her way through all the rules and forms, into happiness?

Somehow, the world engages to please Eleanor, who renounces the king as "feckless," "rotten," worthless to her. Her husband withdraws his garrisons from Aquitaine, declaring her a "strumpet," undeserving of his throne. A church synod decrees that the crown union is dissolved on the grounds of consanguinity, the Frankish sovereigns being related to one another within a forbidden degree. Only divorce can save their souls from jeopardy and restore the king to true religion.

Their two daughters are declared legitimate princesses of France. Their custody is awarded to His Majesty. Eleanor's titles and territories are restored to her, as she possessed them from her father. Her Majesty becomes once more Duchess of Aquitaine and Countess of Poitou. Both spouses shall wed again freely, as long as the duchess respects her vassalage to Louis.

Why was I, Holy Roman empress, unable to rewrite history according to my desire? I was hung upon the rood of my passion, but she employs hers as a battering ram.

†

DOFFING HER ROYAL RANK, the heiress departed homeward, south through Blois. Lovely, vastly wealthy, she was tempting prey to a slew of adventurers. On the first day of her journey, Count Theobald of Blois, Stephen's nephew, attempted to waylay her. Acting quickly, Eleanor jumped onto a barge on the Loire and floated down into the town of Tours. On the frontier of Touraine, my son Geoffrey unsuccessfully tried to ambush her, thinking to violate her and force a marriage. Her Grace outfoxed him, taking another road to safety. Lately, she has arrived in her own provinces, residing now at her castle in Poitou.

If the Angevin were alive among us, I would be suspicious of his own plots, given the likelihood that the duchess would agree willingly to ally herself to him. As it is, the Plantagenet quits our circle, without notice.

†

I HAVE NO NEED of Avera. The heralds' cries echo my predictions. Only weeks after the erstwhile queen's break from the Frankish king, Duke Henry united himself to the duchess, in the cathedral church of Saint Pierre, in Poitiers. My vehement prince and that immoderate harpy wed hastily, shiftily, but although they shirked the proper protocol, the deed is done.

The Plantagenet might better have given his name and hand to the elder of her girls, Princess Marie. Louis would have consented to the match; Henry was the most eligible bachelor in Europe. But the young duke charts his own course.

I have a letter from him, in which he neglects to hang his head before me.

> *Eleanor brings me Aquitaine and Gascony, which I proudly add to my Normandy, my Anjou, my Maine. I control the Atlantic to the Mediterranean, from the Pyrenees to the Channel. All that remains is our England. But were the whole universe mine, I would throw it all over to lie down beside her.*
>
> *I know that you will be the only one to agree that she is not too old for me. At almost twenty, I am quite experienced, and thirty years sit lightly*

upon her glorious face. The marriage is very like your own to my father. You too were a queen who condescended to marry a promising Angevin, transferring to him your own inheritance.

Do not blame me for avoiding any display of regal pomp. For I wished to hurry the ceremony before any meddling clerk should proffer dry parchments to prove that the blood connections between me and my bride were no less incestuous than those which so recently gained Eleanor her freedom from her sniveling, sexless monk of a husband.

God will forgive me, if it can be said that I sin, for it is He who graces my angel with perfection, and sets her down amongst us.

My annoyance is not assuaged by my son's self-satisfaction, but my feelings are nothing to Louis's ire at the two ingrates who have seen fit to combine themselves without his prior and formal consent as their overlord. The king is livid that this sudden and unexpected aggrandizement of the duke denies his two daughters any hope of inheriting Aquitaine from their mother.

In retaliation, Louis calls upon Eustace. They are joined by my young Geoffrey. Indeed, all who are, or who would be, in league against the newlyweds meet at the castle of Montsoreau on the Loire. They would, if they could, seize all of Henry's territories, dividing Normandy, Anjou, and Aquitaine into so many parcels to distribute among themselves.

The Plantagenet had intended to set off for England in the near future. To this end, he had begun to assemble a fleet at Barfleur. In the face of such protest, he stays to defeat his foes on the continent, perhaps to besiege all these antagonists altogether, in one keep. He races to meet them, before they move on. From Poitiers, he charges furiously northward, riding several horses to their deaths.

With such news as seems forever disturbing my calm, I sleep little.

†

I HEAR TELL OF Denise, both from the ill-natured rumors that circulate here, and from her own letters, one of which I receive this morning.

I regularly visit His Grace's tomb, to indulge in my memories. It irritates me to find pushing crowds of fat matrons demanding cures and scores of pimpled novices beseeching my beloved's intercession with the angels. The simpletons have made his bier into their shrine, when it is properly only yours, and mine.

I have some of his jewels and some of his girdles and arms; you do not begrudge me his chattel, I suppose? Before his sarcophagus, I touch a ring to the hand of his stone effigy, but no demon appears to reanimate his corpse. I put it upon my own finger, but I do not faint away dead, as I might prefer.

At home in my petty manor, I trace a circle on the ground with his knife, and then place the dagger in the center, beside jars of ashes, flour, and salt. And yet, no matter my rhymes or mathematical equations, my master does not arise from his grave, resuscitated.

Is it any great riddle that I do not essay to concern myself with the local affairs of my little estate?

For my part, I collect my second widow's dower. Almost all are well-tenanted properties. Flush with riches, I arrange to disburse much of my good fortune.

But to whom? The Angevin endowed Henry with the whole world. Stephen has provided for Gervase. Young Geoffrey casts his lot with our antagonists. William poses a problem. I would marry the boy to Marie if they were not half-siblings. I have no insight, yet, into the true nature of his character. Will he merit a sizeable bequest?

I put aside a small token for Denise's girl, to add to my husband's donation. Her marital prospects thus improve; this increased fortune should tempt a baron, at the very least. But Marie thwarts every plan, and hints that she will permanently immure herself in a convent. The monies set aside for her will be swallowed up by the sisterhood. Will she be able to stifle her fervid lust, under a habit?

A gratuity to Bernard seems to be in order, although Gerta marvels that I would pay him for the honor of bedding me. "He who sticks his nose into everyone else's business, and then sells his scandal, is ill-deserving of your esteem or your patronage. He trades his honor for a few gold coins."

It comes as little surprise to either of us that de Ventadour accepts the stuffed purse without transmitting any expression of thanks, not even the most formulaic one.

By messenger, I convey a small treasure to Avera, but my man returns from her hovel, his task undone. He finds no sign of the enchantress. Her nearest neighbors claim that she deserted Anjou some months ago. Gerta engages to discover what has become of her. We pray that she has not fallen victim to local superstition.

I can never adequately repay my maid for her long-term fealty. Exiled from her native land, she has seen me through war and villainy, siege and strife. So often, I scandalize her with my ungovernable desires and considerable hatreds. Yet Gerta rebuffs the very mention of an annuity, preferring to continue her service and share my portion, until the end of our days.

†

Summer

ELEANOR MAKES ONE OF our household in Angers, while Duke Henry fights the evil alliance to which their match has given birth. Situated halfway between my north and her south, neither one of us feels much at home. Which is to be queen here, the duchess or the dowager?

Our relationship stiffens. I blame the capricious wench for dabbling with my husband mere months before wedding my son. I appraise her too great a harlot to wear my English crown.

Every day we sit together, the two Graces, without the companionship of our bright boy. I demonstrate my growing negation of life and joy, in the face of her wholehearted acceptance of them. We have few conversations that do not end in open or silent disagreement.

Even in the absence of most of the knights, Eleanor bedaubs herself with paint. Yesterday, I watched it melt in the midday heat. "Is that cuttlefish powder or flour on your cheeks? They are both most unsuitable to the weather."

"Hah! I am no lyre to respond to the picking of your nails." But my daughter-in-law could not resist an argument. "I know far more of the womanly arts than you do."

"Of course you do, for they were exactly what your first husband disliked."

The duchess spouted her tinkling laugh. "You are right there, Empress. Louis thought that it was not at all in keeping for his consort to have knowledge of medicaments and poultices, tisanes and tinctures. Common herbs are the resort of the poor; quack's nostrums are the placebos of the merchants. The pious leave healing to God."

My mind wandered over Gerta's canny tricks, and my own.

The insufferable whore had a stash of insults ready for me. "Mother, you should swallow an infusion of dill to offset your damp temperament. Dill is a wonderful restorative for the elderly, especially northerners. If dill does not suffice, perhaps your maid could brew you leeks in honey, or boil the juice of beets. Either will warm the blood of a person known to suffer from a cold-hearted disposition."

Gerta, attending upon our needs, could not remain quiet. "Beet water eliminates dandruff, of which the empress has none. Did Your Grace not think to provide long and dark turnips, twice stewed, to your Frankish lord, to increase his seed? Such a pity that you did not have the expertise to bear him a son."

Fortunately, the duchess did not consider my waiting woman's abrasive words to be insubordinate enough to punish.

†

BERNARD SLINKS INTO OUR castle, for he is now an established member of Eleanor's circle, and necessary to her vanity. Although Gerta occasionally catches him staring at me, he never meets my eyes. I pretend not to notice him, any more than I do the other entertainers in our midst.

Today, I could not resist teasing my daughter-in-law about her supposed subjugation of the troubadour. "How he hurries here to make you a present of his adulation! If his hounding disconcerts you, I would be happy to exile him from the county. For what does he tarry, if not to realize his joy in your embrace?"

Pleased, the duchess made a bow of her lips. "He claims that he is a man in the sway of a mad passion. He calls me his 'Beautiful Hope.'"

Gerta snorted. "He has quite a reputation for swordsmanship."

Eleanor frowned. "Your foolery annoys me, woman. Bernard's adoration remains platonic, as is appropriate to our respective stations. His unrequited flirtation amuses me, and helps to pass the time in this backwater, devoid of our barons and my prince."

†

OUR HENRY BURNS AND invests castles throughout the Vexin. His siege of Montsoreau, well directed and thoroughly prosecuted, establishes his complete superiority. Young Geoffrey is forced to submit to his elder brother's conditions. The Plantagenet strips his sibling of the three Angevin keeps bequeathed by their father. King Louis signs a truce with his vassal the duke, slithering back to Paris to avoid further military engagement. Eustace had never answered the Frankish king's call for help, preferring to remain abroad, the better to wrap himself up in his father's stolen glory.

†

GERTA'S CONSIDERABLE NETWORK OF informants unearths the details of Avera's awful demise. The Church's position on witchcraft has always been clear; in theory, anyone caught practicing sorcery shall be executed. But, in practice, one hears of lighter punishments dispersed for benign spells, useful potions, and questionably accurate divination. Priests caught indulging in necromancy, even of the malevolent sort, are considered cleansed by a three-year fast of bread and water.

Talented Avera, hardly infernal, but certainly a tormented soul, was slain by an angry mob in Rouen. Perhaps she infuriated an elderly, well-connected burgess, by promoting an affair between her husband and some other, younger woman. Whatever the cause, she was whipped in the public square, eviscerated, then hurled from the city walls. Her stomach was paraded through the streets, to the jeers of her customers.

†

THE PLANTAGENET IS RETURNED to us. Eleanor organizes a progress through Aquitaine, so that her husband might survey her massive domain, and remember to appreciate the enormity of her dowry. The duke happily complies, eager to witness the harvest of her vintage and sample her Bordeaux. But such a honeymoon will have to wait. A travel-stained herald brings us a message from Brian, despairing of the security of Wallingford Castle, under attack by the usurper.

The courier barely touched the roasted beaver's tail we presented to him, for he was too busy exhorting the Plantagenet to attend to FitzCount's letter.

Henry's mouth was stuffed full of saffron pottage, and he waved his fingers, permitting the man to read the scroll aloud.

> *If you have any regard for your adherents, or any wish to win back your realm, you must return over the Channel as soon as possible. On your eastern flank, Wallingford is in extreme distress. Bestir yourself, for you are the Savior!*

Henry shrugged. "Let my English vassals mortify Stephen themselves. I have just now quit the field of battle." The prince stretched a thick arm over his wife, to grab at a dish of fish, mint, and parsley, steamed in ale.

The duchess grinned. "The king's constant assaults upon his people are nothing out of the ordinary. What is your urgency?"

The herald brushed off her input. "Your husband's allies can no longer support the notion of civil war. If Wallingford falls, the empress's party will disintegrate."

I thought of Brian's will to serve me. "Why should the Count of Boulogne's success be assured? He has never held FitzCount's fortress, although it has long menaced his position at Oxford."

The courier spoke in earnest. "For this latest bombardment, His Majesty recruits the ragged citizens of London. In addition, scores of noblemen ride to his aid, more than in any recent time. Over the last month, Stephen's forces have constructed an elaborate and ingenious wooden edifice, which will probably mean the downfall of the castle. The battalion within the tower no longer braves nightly sorties. Wallingford begins to fear starvation."

The time had come for my heir to recover what was once mine and was now to be his. I met the duke's eyes. "It is likely then that the garrison will submit to the pretender and turn over the keys to the keep."

Eleanor tried to tempt her husband, who had been briefly her slave, but was already her master. "You grow too serious, my sweet. Gratify your whims today; seek power tomorrow."

The messenger pursed his lips at the duchess's indifference to the fate of our friends. "Sir Brian entrusted me to seek out England's true king."

FitzCount was ever our most faithful adherent. "Henry, do not lay waste your strength in idleness or sloth."

His Grace took a swig of wine.

Bernard spoke up, without anyone's leave. "Who is the most estimable among the noble assembly of knights, he who feasts upon the most succulent morsels at the high table, or he who turns the table over, and sets off on a Christian quest to liberate a kingdom?" Clearly, it would suit him to console the lonely Eleanor, when deprived of her handsome spouse.

My son's wife tried one more time to beguile him. "My love, you must travel south to drink the juice of my grapes, and soon, before it sours."

But the Plantagenet was my heir, above all. "Your claret may be as brash or as subtle as your French logic, but I will not taste it this year."

†

THE HERALD HAD ANOTHER delivery to make, from Sir Brian to me. As I unrolled the scroll, my heart thumped in my chest. Would he expiate my crimes against him, or unleash further rage and misery in my direction?

O Mistress Love, I inhale deeply, and exhale stale air, but it cannot be said that I live. My heart is full of adoration for you, but there is no enjoyment or succor for me in the world. I continue to serve you, despite the pains that I have taken to overcome my weakness, to eject your image from my mind and my soul. I am still your obedient slave, for your worth has not dimmed in my eyes.

I do not truly atone. God cannot be fooled; I will never be redeemed. My existence is one of continual torment; I am entrapped, irrevocably. O Lady Love, to know you is to err in word and deed.

I hope for death, but it does not come. Your cousin, my rival in everything, stalks my keep. I sit upon my battlements, in defiance of his bowmen; their arrows rain down to my left and right. Perhaps he pardons me, knowing that I twist in the wind, miserable without you. His mercy is nothing to me, for yours is withheld.

†

THE PRINCE CONVENES A council of advisors to strategize the coming conquest of England. An armada of thirty-six ships rests at Barfleur. The continental magnates provide one hundred and forty knights and three thousand foot soldiers, mostly mercenaries, for the invasion army. There has been some talk of landing our forces at Bristol, despite the unpropitious season, for it remains the headquarters of our faction on the island. However, Wareham, our only secure port on the southern coast, is once more to be our chosen destination.

†

LAST NIGHT I TOSSED about until dawn, in the thrall of a gruesome vision, in which the Holy Virgin underscores the vile negligence with which I have left so much unsaid to my son.

I lay in a trodden battleground, polluted with the carnage of a recent engagement. When I arose, I saw the spires of a distant, glittering city. Tramping with difficulty through the muck and gore, seeking something of great consequence, I wandered toward its shimmering gate and discovered it to be entirely constructed of gleaming gold and silver. Every wall, building, and tower was fashioned from a precious metal. I searched broad, deserted streets, running with rivulets of blood, until I reached the white crystal castle at the heart of the town. Its outer bailey was a cesspool of refuse, mutilated corpses, and discarded military equipment. Stumbling across it, I realized that my skirts were soaked through, red to my knees.

Stepping over several prone guards, perhaps dead or merely enchanted, I entered the sparkling keep. In its innermost chamber, resplendently lit by candlelight, I saw a sleeping knight whom I knew to be Stephen, resting whole and safe. I covered him with kisses, so that he awoke and embraced me. He entrusted his sword to me, in return for my vow that none should ever wield it but our son.

Waking, clammy and anxious, I understood Mother Mary's directive. At first light, I hurried, disheveled and frantic, to Henry's solar.

Despite the hour, he was awake, sitting before a cold hearth in the dim room.

I hastened out with my telling, sick to death of my secret. "I have come to reveal what may surprise you, concerning your birthright. The usurper sired you, while the Angevin and I were separated and considering the annulment of our marriage."

The duke did not respond, but in confusion or consternation? Had he already guessed his identity?

My voice shook. "Do not think that I wish you to spare his life. On the contrary, you must slay him."

The prince dropped his face in his hands, rubbing his temples. He hummed a bit, off tune, through his teeth. Did he await further explanation?

I reached out my arms, although he did not see the gesture. "Vainglorious, I did not watch my steps, and so fell from my dignity. Many have trod upon my name, trampled it in the dirt. I paid a high tax for the privilege of an imperfect bliss. Now I have repented, and reclaimed the soul that I pawned into my cousin's keeping. Cut him down! Defend my honor and the renewed purity of my spirit."

The Plantagenet did not alter his posture. "I am somewhat jolted, Mother, to hear this news of my paternity, although not by your history, which bears the mark of a splendid stamp. It is a relief to be freed from certain obligations to the late Duke of Normandy, now that he is little more to me than a guardian."

I hugged my shoulders, clad only in a thin linen chainse. "If you wish to signal to the Count of Boulogne that you are aware of the relationship, you need only call him 'Arthur,' once his alias."

Henry nodded. I squinted, essaying to commit his face and form to memory before he departs on this last, great escapade, to win or lose all. Thickset, unlike slender Stephen, he is shorter than he should be, but puissant, hale.

His Grace interrupted my study. "Nothing will content me, Mother, but the king's defeated heart. I am off, to action!" He rose, striding to exit the solar.

A small scuffling outside revealed Eleanor, listening at the door.

The Mirror of the Plantagenet

Scroll Twenty-Two: 1152

*A*s it was to be, the Lord in His mercy swept Duke Henry into England. The Plantagenet's foes ceased their resistance, quaking and receding before his victorious spirit. The voices of Matilda's enemies warbled in fear; her allies sang of the coming of their righteous prince. Delivered from exile, the empress resigned herself to the loss of her own importance and stood ready to submit to a greater glory. Her own star had fallen, but behold the Lord's grace and His miracle: in her acquiescence, in her abdication, the flower of her grace did not wither.

†

Fall

HENRY DECAMPS TO BARFLEUR. Eleanor, half swollen with child, pines for the privileges of a royal court, to divert her from physical discomfort and loneliness. Angers bustles with pilgrims, clerics, and clerks, no fit companions for the once proud Lady of France, now the lovelorn duchess. Bernard's position strengthens, as his compliments become more and more indispensable to her leisure.

My company also suits Eleanor's frustrated temper. Today, while the bright days endure, we strolled among the castle fields, admiring the reds and golds of the ripening landscape. She seemed to walk upon her heels, more than her toes, a sure sign that she carries a boy. To keep the duchess's dullness at bay, we set ourselves to word games.

All her brilliance settled upon her idol. "Henry: the 'H' is his High Valor, the 'E' is his Energy, the 'N' signifies his Nobility, the 'R' is his Royalty and the 'Y' is his Youth."

Stepping through the rustling, crackling leaves, I marveled at how swiftly my boy had demolished her pride. "He is no king yet, but you have already been a queen!"

The duchess tinkled her laugh, unlike anyone else's. "That pitiful land of yours, smoldering in its own ashes, moldering no doubt, is reborn by his coming."

Suddenly, Eleanor shuddered, then pressed her palm against her belly. Seeing my wince, she said, "It is nothing, Empress, just the babe wrestling with my innards. A strong son for his sovereign sire."

I frowned. "You are sick with fondness, as you have been before, with other men."

The duchess steadied herself, straightening her expensive drapery. "You, of all other women, should understand my complaint."

My empathy withered my dislike. "You gasp for breath, you drown, in an oozing swamp of want."

Gerta wandered some paces behind us, but now kicked savagely at the dry ground.

Lady Eleanor scoffed. "Your heartless maid comprehends only the sin of it!"

It was sweet to talk as I had with Adeliza, unburdening myself to another princess. "I have been hungry for love, as if yearning for a sugary treat that melts away on the tongue the moment it is popped into the mouth. But the confection is expensive, and when we sample it again and again, unthinking of its price, we accrue a great debt. The pleasures of love are brief, and its delights fade, almost immediately. What lasts, its sordid aftertaste, is rue."

We stood silent for some moments.

The duchess took my hands. "Lady Love deserves our tributes. We fight in her column; if we sustain casualties, if we are routed, if we prevail, it is no matter, for it is all miraculous."

Gerta would not be catechized by an argument such as this one. "The empress lost the very essence of herself, in the service of her beloved; she gifted him with all that she was."

In everything, Eleanor venerates excess. "I undertake the most horrible quest, when sublime Lady Love commands it of me. I am her most courageous vassal."

I squeezed the girl's palms, my daughter's palms, to dissuade her from my own folly. "Alas, how much we have in common."

†

As THE WEATHER GETS colder, Eleanor makes do with fireside frivolity. She has not had one message from her departed husband, so instead takes solace in trivialities. Trained dogs walk on their hind feet for her; monkeys march in formation; gymnasts form enormous pyramids. She justifies her liberal tips and constant feasting by asserting that her husband's knights are likely engaged in greater feats of gluttony on their campaign, and will surely return draped in booty, vessels of gold and silver, garments of silk, and mantles of sable and ermine.

Bernard passes so much time in my daughter's company that I see her less than before. Eleanor reserves her most salacious humor and her keenest insights for her new favorite. They play round after round of "The King Who Does Not Lie," taking turns as the monarch who must test his wit against the inane questions posed by the other players. In the today's game, the duchess wore the paper crown, and debated which was to be preferred, a young, handsome, vicious paramour or an old, desiccated, virtuous one. Surprisingly, she argued in favor of the elder, good man, much to the hilarity of me and Gerta, who heard the story secondhand.

My maid suspects that my daughter, in defiance of her rounded belly, lies abed with the versemaker. Her eyes glinted. "No two thoughts about it, she wants to punish the duke for his neglect."

I remembered pining for Stephen, in the arms of Brian FitzCount. "She is no better than a widow. The Plantagenet is thoughtless and disrespectful to keep her in suspense, and deny her the satisfaction of a word. How she would swell and swoon, to welcome a courier, dispatched by her hero on the battlefield! If only Henry would take the trouble to return a piece of himself to her."

Gerta rolled her eyes. "If your son were here, in the ardent clutch of his new bride, I am certain that you would still have to evade a constant volley of de Ventadour's compliments. He may deceive the erstwhile queen of France, but I judge his devotion for her to be coldly mechanical."

I sighed to think that I might have to subvert further advances from the minstrel. Did I prefer my son to be a cuckold?

†

THE PRINCE RECEIVES INFORMATION, for all that he forgets to transmit it. Just yesterday a messenger galloped into the inner bailey with my heir's orders for his household. The duke banishes from Angers all "ill-assorted riff-raff," and specifically decrees that Bernard shall accompany the Norman invasion, in order to record its martial exploits. The ages to come must know of the Plantagenet's elevation to eminence.

In addition, the duchess has a letter, but it is not the sort she yearns for. His Grace disparages his wife's companion and pointedly demeans her wit. She thrusts the note at me, as if daring me to defend my son's irascible insults.

> *Are you simple or conceited enough to fall prey to the man's trite, mercenary adoration? When he compliments your unfathomable comeliness and your inestimable purity, and licks his lips, he is dreaming only of my gold and his position at the center of my court.*

Tonight, as we sat among a numerous assembly, a subdued Bernard offered up his farewells directly before Eleanor's chair, although he looked down at his own boots, and not into the hot gaze of his reputed idol.

The duchess, irate at her favorite's coming deportation, spoke her mind indiscreetly, ignoring my pointed coughs. "The selfish duke does not allow me to have the slightest enjoyment! Would that I were an albatross, to swoop after you across the Channel. You might stand at the prow of your boat, and watch me bathe in the ocean." She cackled at the shocked tittering of our guests.

The expression on her troubadour's even features turned sly. "I am away, to England, yet to be separated from its two queens. Whether the island sky is blue or gray, alight with sun or obscure with rain, its gardens shall bloom with your flowers: crimson, yellow, and white."

Eleanor frowned and I sighed, for I am done with flirtation and vanity. Despite all my vainglory, my purported loveliness has been put to no service. My handsome face could not guarantee men's allegiance, for all that it attracted their regard. I carried my comeliness on my shoulders, a cross of temptation and delinquency.

†

THE PLANTAGENET AND ALL his ships successfully crossed the Channel into England. With his troops at his back, Henry arrived safely at Wallingford, and there discovered what had been well hidden. My vassal's castle rots from within. Its garrison defends a keep peopled only with Brian and Basilia's two sons, both lepers, tragic figures sent among us by the Lord, so that we might see how malformed our souls appear before the Heavenly Host. Aware of Henry's imminent arrival, both husband and wife had fled, sequestering themselves in separate religious houses.

I would never have foretold it, that charming FitzCount would bring forth such mutilated creatures, such warnings. "The Lord works what He will," says my prince, in a letter. And so it is, that heaven endows Brian's perverted marriage with deformed offspring, blistered and cracked; the children suffer for their parents' sins. Leprosy is an incurable disease, save by witchcraft. Were her children too misshapen, too deformed, for Basilia's skill? Did she lack the courage or the wherewithal to procure the fat of a stillborn infant or the mortal blood of an innocent youth?

I have been no real friend or patron to the knight who served me with the utmost fidelity, so caught up was I in my own tribulations and delights. Likewise, my son turns his back on Wallingford in order to address other, more pressing situations. I have his justification, excusing himself from the siege.

> *I have determined not to march to the relief of the fortress, for it is an isolated Angevin outpost, sitting well within the royalist Thames Valley. Instead, I shall begin our fight for Britain in the west and the north, where our allies still have the upper hand.*

I bear witness to FitzCount's fealty, surrounded by his neighbors' treason. Yet, his patient, faithful adherence is nothing, in the end, to our Messiah, whose plans are for England entire.

> *My arrival home is as momentous for my subjects as Jesus's own coming among them would be. I do nothing but repeat the priests' assertions when I tell you this. At the mass held to commemorate my landing on native soil, the bishops said: "Behold, the Lord, the ruler, is come; the kingdom is in His hand."*
>
> *Bernard earns his keep; his verses embellish me among the barons, although no more than I deserve. He reminds them that I am heir to my grandsire's name, high renown, and empire. He paints a harsh picture of your Eden, your Fair England, now fallen into gloomy desolation and lurid ruin, but promises that I am its solitary hope, its Savior, its dawn.*

Who is de Ventadour, but some French serf grown bold with his tongue? Who licensed him to ignore my history and my claims? If my people rejoice, it is because the son of their mother, their true queen, comes among them, to deliver them from the tyrant who has stolen their prosperity and peace. Duke Henry shall liberate the land and reestablish England's glory.

†

WITH THE ONSET OF truly foul weather, Eleanor resumes her reliance on my company. Together, we dissect each of the Plantagenet's occasional briefings, when messages arrive addressed to either of us. I attempt to decipher whether Henry values my legacy and sacrifice. She essays to take the temperature of his ardor or disillusionment. We both want to know whether His Grace's need for us waxes or wanes.

Lately, heralds apprise us that the prince marshaled his forces and marched to the city of Malmesbury, wedged between our strongholds of Bristol and Gloucester, but still loyal to Stephen. The burghers climbed atop their defensive walls to hinder my son's approach to the town. Our archers mowed many of them down from their perch, allowing our foot soldiers to scale the stone perimeter. Our battalions eagerly burned and pillaged until all the residents sought sanctuary in the local monastery. Unfortunately, Malmesbury keep continues to hold for the pretender.

Today, I disparaged my son's savagery. "The end is near. We cannot now risk the profound sympathy that the English feel for their prince."

Eleanor rested her head upon my shoulder. "I will reign alongside the Plantagenet, in the land of his father and grandfather. I freely admit to you that I wish to place another crown upon my curls." She picked herself up and shook out the red tresses, as if to evidence their impoverishment.

Oh, my daughter, do not forsake me, when our duke returns to us. Who else is left to me?

†

EVER THE DISREPUTABLE, SECRETIVE, two-faced lout, Bernard writes privately to the duchess.

Thus, it is Eleanor who first informs me of the meeting between father and son. As soon as she received his scratchings, she whirled through the tower, bursting in on my solar.

I sat among charcoal and parchment, devising scenes and tracing designs for a great tapestry to celebrate the second Norman invasion. We shall weave it together, in honor of our beloved boy.

My daughter slammed the door with the force of her girth. "King Stephen and Prince Eustace, along with a whole host of armed followers, came to defend Malmesbury Castle from the Angevins."

My heart skipped a beat. My sketches were at my feet, unattended. "For the love of Christ, did they clash?"

"Wait, wait. On a stormy day, the two enemies faced each other across the River Avon. The waterway, swollen by rain, ice, and snow, roared, clearly impassable. English and Norman banners flapped in a stiff, cold wind. Splendid equipment rusted under the onslaught of the weather."

I stood up, creasing my parchments. "Spare me your troubadour's details! Was there a pitched skirmish?"

"The usurper declined to put his life and the Plantagenet's on the line. Your cousin refused the fray, apparently squandering his opportunity to end the civil war. His soldiers withdrew from the riverbank."

Now I could breathe. "Conditions must have favored us, so that the Count of Boulogne feared another Battle of Lincoln. Who could cross against a strong current? Who could wield a slippery lance, or protect themselves with a slick shield?"

Eleanor strode over to me, lifted the hem of my kirtle and considered a drawing of the young duke astride a mighty steed, in the midst of slaying his foes. "If peace comes, it will be without a magnificent conflict. Your lover will never consent to Henry's death. Pray to the Virgin; give Her mercy your thanks."

I glanced down. "Your husband aches to spill his father's blood in a decisive contest. And that viper Eustace, son of the sorceress Maud, stands between the prince and what is rightfully ours. He burns to establish his prowess and eliminate his rival for the throne."

Heedlessly, the duchess crumpled my sketch with her foot. "The English people wish, above all, for an end to unrest and destruction. King Stephen must understand this. His maleficent wife rots in her tomb. Before him stands the son born of his true love, the rightful heiress to Britain. He can no longer deny the will of heaven."

"The pretender has plotted, again and again, for his bishops to anoint Eustace."

"But they have refused; he could not persuade the church to crown another usurper. Stephen retreats to London. Malmesbury is ours."

I exhaled, surprised to discover that neither rage nor joy roiled my once tempestuous soul.

†

BERNARD STEADFASTLY PESTERS AND flatters the duchess.

His perseverance irks me, for it threatens the peace of my house. I encourage my daughter to toss her admirer's insipid, aggravating nonsense into the moat. His poems are inelegantly styled, his diction is flawed, and his subject is sure to be considered treasonous the moment two bejeweled crowns are lowered onto two red heads.

An inveterate blockhead, of dubious tact, Bernard tattles on the Plantagenet's latest romantic dalliance, an entanglement with the Countess of Warwick, whose decrepit earl stands with the Count of Boulogne. In a fit of extreme jealousy, Eleanor takes to her bed, complaining of a burning in her womb and something wrong with the child. She prays to Saint Anne, patroness of difficult deliveries, and bemoans her husband's devious inclinations, apparently forgetting her own.

Gerta is suspicious, and immediately imagines that the duchess is sterile, too old to bear us an heir. She measures my daughter's rotundity with a critical eye, as if to ascertain whether it is a cushion worn to simulate pregnancy. Forgetting her place, she demands that Eleanor hand over a flask of her urine, so that we might steep it in bran overnight and count the number of worms that flock to the pot. She marvels at my daughter's supposed scheme and our own gullibility, and wonders whether the duchess intended to substitute another baby for her supposed fetus, or would now pretend to endure a late miscarriage.

Sometimes, even my trusted maid goes too far. The Frankish queen is reborn as our English hope; she is the vessel for the fruit of our vine. I send her a message, urging her to step three times over a grave, while beseeching the Holy Virgin's intercession against the evils of a strangled, lame, or stillborn birth.

†

TODAY, I TRIED TO comfort Eleanor, still interred in her private chamber under the pall of her embarrassment.

I found her much humbled, ready to blame her own past doctrines for her present mortification. Tears ran down her lovely features, for once unadorned with cosmetics. "My first husband's somber temper and rigidity repulsed me, and so I was ever blithe, loose, and cavalier, despite the necessities of my position."

"None of your vassals thought you pious, but nor were they honoring all the commandments, for they were too busy estimating the cost of your entertainments and the value of your furs."

"I should have wrapped myself up in a woolen mantle, the better to cloak my sins."

"If you had put up your hood, then you might not have captured my son's attention." I stroked her hair.

She was full of his merits. "He can converse in every known tongue, between the North Sea and the River Jordan."

This was too much, even for me. "The Plantagenet's excellences are so astonishing, so diverse, that they must not be exactly specified, lest a comprehensive account exhaust the resources of our memory."

"Would that I could deserve his perfection!"

I smiled, but without mirth. "Only insofar as you consider his lineage, beauty, wisdom, and good conduct, as it is defined by the law and noble practice. Regrettably, adultery is a sin only in a woman."

†

ELEANOR AND I DISTRACT ourselves with the dicing games of hazard and queek, and, most obsessively, with draughts and chess, competing to capture each other's kings, queens, bishops, and knights. With gusto, we sweep the pieces off the illuminated boards. Full of strategy and bravado, we clamor to defeat one another, again and again, sublimating both our strangled aspirations and unlucky romances.

Perhaps it should have been obvious to me all along that only a man could regain what a man had stolen. My son, my amber knight, strives eagerly and pointedly; he does not blunder. Glory and triumph shall be his rewards.

†

I LISTEN TO THE jongleurs' accounts of the Plantagenet and his defense, at last, of Wallingford. His adherents have become more plentiful, as word of his successes disseminate across the island, and His Grace now rides at the head of an enormous assortment of three hundred knights and foot soldiers. They assault the new-fangled siege machine that the pretender's troops erect outside FitzCount's keep. Our battalions are repulsed, but persist in troubling our adversaries. The Count of Boulogne and his brat, Eustace, should arrive shortly.

The versemakers debate among themselves: who shall be the master of the castle?

Fools! Is it not as clear as a penitent's tear?

†

HOLY MOTHER MARY ENTRUSTS to me the Plantagenet's own recollections, so that I might be privy to what actually happened at Wallingford, when he and his true father came face-to-face. A fatigued courier warned me that His Grace's invisible ink had been whipped from of the fat of an entirely white hen, but Gerta and I easily discolored and darkened it with a salt rub. For added security, the prince had abbreviated many key names and descriptive adjectives, but his chilling account was easily decipherable.

> *Our armies were within sight of one another, Mother, with only the River Thames to separate us. It was an awesome thing to witness a thousand Britons with a thousand well-wrought swords, hanging back above a rushing stream. It was a moment of expectation before the*

onslaught of hell. I could sense in the air the fury about to be born; I could feel the general wish to slay, no matter if it were their own brothers.

My units were fewer, but we had better discipline and the men were willing to keep to their line, the better to outmaneuver Stephen's rabble. The thief-king perceived my tactical advantage and attempted at the last minute to rearrange his formation. In his haste to be everywhere at once, he was thrice thrown from his destrier. These mishaps could not improve his chances.

I had taken special care of my own appearance. My pages had spent the entire night polishing my armor. It shone like the sun. In my spectacular garb, I was the illustrious duke, the noble prince, among the warring bands.

The Earl of Sussex, Adeliza's widowed William, stood with our cousin. In the pregnant pause, he called out his hopes, thundering, so that we all should hear him above the gushing river. "Let us stop here, men of England, and substitute heroic pity for heroic action. For what purpose are kinsmen pitted against kinsmen? This is abominable madness! We should not permit it on our beautiful island. Let us now declare a truce between relations."

There were cheers on all sides, especially from the mouths of the earls and mounted men, for whom a ceasefire meant further months of anarchy in which to strengthen their own positions at the expense of my throne.

But my stomach churned in anger, for although I was sick of the discord that robbed me of my realm, I wished for a complete victory. I would reign as my parents have never done, but in the image of my grandfather, whose royal authority was but infrequently thwarted.

Yet the shouts grew and grew in favor of the Earl of Sussex's proposal, so that both the pretender and I were forced to submit to the general clamor for delay. Two weeks without hostility was the demand.

That night, cloudless, was made to fit our purpose. In certain places, the Thames recedes until it is just a mere rivulet. Here we met, without witnesses. The sky was black like tar. We stood in silence, lending an ear to the whistling wind.

I said, "There is a man called 'Arthur,' to a lady who remembers what they did create together."

It was pitch, Mother, but I do think that he blushed.

Then I was ashamed of this feminine show from the creature who had stolen my inheritance. I regretted that I had brought on his flush with my softness. "What will you say to your God when he accuses you?"

The usurper seemed taken aback by my virulence, coming as it did upon the heels of my generosity. "You have become a man, and a soldier, when I was not watching."

I continued to be harsh, for that was the way to win him over. He is an old goat now. "I arrive, sir, a duke and a prince. As such, I come to lift the siege between us. I come to do what my mother, my uncle, and even my grandfather could not, to establish the rightful succession."

As we parlayed, the night deepened. His famous red hair was as invisible in the dark as every other claim that he may once have had to the world's notice. His small, thin voice was all that was left of him. "My battle engines have won much acclaim; they are still trained upon the keep. But I am through with fighting. Let us exchange our hostages. Let no knight complain that he was imprisoned because of our family dispute."

"I want Wallingford Castle; it is in the empress's gift."

I could hear my father's deep sigh. I waited for his capitulation, and not in vain.

"These terms are most favorable to the Angevin rebels, but I submit to such a peace."

By morning the various troops and all the freed captives had begun to disperse.

Eustace was beside himself. Several of my escort heard his raving against this improperly tame conclusion to the investiture of Wallingford. In desperation, he shrieked against the Fates and pummeled two of his own pages. Time is his foe. He begins to suspect that his father plots to lay down his arms for good, in favor of "the traitor."

✝

FULL OF IRE AND disgust, Eustace departed from Wallingford into Cambridgeshire, where he proceeded to ravage the countryside, in the hopes of provoking the duke to nullify the détente. Maud's brat quickly ran out of coin with which to pay his hordes, so he led his marauding army to Bury St. Edmunds, one of England's greatest monasteries. The brotherhood received him with dignity and circumspection, feasting him with all that they had, but refused to hand over their treasury. Eustace repaid their hospitality and sanctuary by razing their store of crops, already harvested.

But vengeance is already ours. At a crude encampment, among his own rough companions, Eustace rapaciously stuffed himself full of freshly slaughtered game. Immediately, he was overtaken by a criminal madness, ending with his mortal throes.

The news arrived this very evening, at dusk, just as the duchess felt her first pains. Full of the herald's message, I hurried to her rooms.

Even in the first moments of her confinement, Eleanor looked as if she could not bear her ordeal. "There is word of His Grace?"

"No, my dear, but there are wonderful tidings, nonetheless. Eustace is dead. The false courage of those oafs who oppose the duke will falter. You shall be their true queen."

The duchess groaned, twisting about on her mattress.

I grabbed her hand, so that she might squeeze mine while her movement lasted. "It is a day of woe for our enemies. With the loss of his bestial spawn, the Count of Boulogne will designate Henry his heir, in name and truth."

Eleanor calmed herself, optimistic about the sudden boost to her ambitions. "Verily, it is the Lord who anoints the Plantagenet."

The duchess had chosen Gerta to be her midwife, for she had four times brought me to bed of a living boy. Other competent crones shuffled in and out of the chamber with fresh linen and water, as my maid directed.

Now I invoked a prayer. "Hail Mary, full of grace, mild Virgin of virgins, merciful Mother of the greatest Son, let your blessing bring forth another son, of holy issue, to the honor of Thy holy name."

To my surprise, my daughter underwent less travail than most. In four hours, she pushed forth a fine son.

Eleanor looked radiant; her own blood became her. "He shall be the future Count of Poitou and Duke of Aquitaine; he shall have, therefore, the name of my father, William."

I felt a great burden lifting from my own breast. "You give him the moniker of the conqueror, fulfilling your obligations to our royal house. I have no objection to your choice."

As one of the waiting women warmed and cleaned the loudly wailing infant, the duchess grinned at the cacophony. The she yawned. "Such a fine gift to present to a husband."

Gerta compressed her belly, still bloated with fluids. "If the sex act is an expression of cherishing love, then a knight releases an especially potent juice and a male child sprouts inside his wise and pure lady."

I kissed the once and future queen. "Henry's seed is as vigorous as he is; the son that is come to him shall be the king of England."

†

EUSTACE HAS BEEN BURIED at Faversham Abbey in Kent, beside the bitch who bore him. The monks there had little to say in his praise, so settled on a paean to his soldierly abilities, although the predatory, black-hearted warrior was constantly engaged in projects displeasing to almighty heaven.

His timely passing removes the most significant obstacle to a settlement between the Angevins and Stephen's party. Now all future violence may be evaded.

The archbishop of Canterbury serves as the chief negotiant between the pretender and the Plantagenet. We trust the Church to unravel their rivalry. It is God's providence to make peace; his delegate lifts the scourge of civil war, bestowing the Lord's prosperity in its place.

†

HIS GRACE RETURNS TO Normandy; we are all met in Rouen. The duke, delighted with his legitimate heir, dotes on the swaddled prince.

Bernard usually avoids me, and trails after the duchess, much as before.

Gerta reports that de Ventadour complains to the castle steward of winter flies in his dark and inconvenient chamber. The kitchen staff accommodates his request for dried bunches of shredded fern. If he would wake at prime with the sun, he might easily toss the loaded trap into his smoldering grate. But the sop lies abed until well past terce, long after the flies have resumed their position upon his ceiling.

This morning, we happened upon one another in a constricted stairwell. Likely not to be overheard, he hissed: "Virago!"

I was so taken aback by his forwardness, and his disrespect, that I allowed him to scuffle off to his hidey-hole without imprecation.

†

TONIGHT, WE HELD A dance of celebration, alongside our Norman friends. My son took many turns with me around the great hall of the castle. We stomped our feet and swung ourselves about to the raucous tunes of the players, until, sweating and laughing, we had to retreat to a cool antechamber behind the royal dais.

I had forgotten what it was like to fall down against a man's body, hot with exertion. "For a moment, I am young again."

Henry panted, much as I did. "I do battle, astride a warhorse, with less effort."

I giggled, open-mouthed.

We looked out into the enormous chamber. Eleanor flounced by, hand in hand with Bernard.

The duke's high humor deflated. His still shortened breaths were audible. "That man has a way with his pen, but he is a dunce, pandering to the whims of every grand lady he meets. He had better limit himself to courting the favor of our female parasites, our vacuous crowd of handmaidens, no better than village busybodies. He should have the good sense to withdraw his compliments from a person of such stature as my wife."

I shrugged, essaying to soothe his temper. "You are too mighty to heed petty scandal; you are a peacock in the chicken coop."

"Mother Hen, do not cluck at me." His Grace resumed his equanimity. "Are you prepared to meet your nemesis within your own household?"

I was stunned out of my giddiness. Did he mean my once beloved, my own demon, he who had made my life a living hell?

"Tomorrow, the bishop of Winchester arrives in Rouen, to discuss the terms of our amity. He assists the archbishop of Canterbury with the Church's diplomacy." The duke rearranged his red silk tunic, richly embroidered with pennants and unicorns. Eleanor was an able seamstress, but she had had my help with this complicated craftsmanship.

I tasted the bile rising in my throat. "His Grace despises us and perhaps plots to undermine you."

Henry flapped at the neck of his shirt. Rivulets of perspiration traveled down his cheeks. "Again, you speak like an old woman. The bishop admits that his past conduct has been unworthy, a stimulus to enduring conflict. He repents of his interference."

I ground my teeth together, to think of that withered incubus. "He repents of the result."

The prince took my hand. "He discovers that we are kin; after all, he is my uncle."

I shook my head. My hair, loose to my waist and wound with ribbons, fanned out over our joined fingers. "His Grace, however obsequious, does not act out of sentiment. He looks to the future, under your reign, maneuvering to be your Primate."

My son squeezed my upper arms.

I envisioned Stephen, drugging the guests and attendants at his own feast, so that we might lie together.

Now Henry held me under the chin. "I met Winchester and spoke to him at length. We were of one mind."

How I ached to hear it. "There can be no commonality, nor any brotherhood between you."

The duke lifted my jaw, so that I might not miss his severity. "I believe that His Grace loves me now."

I brushed the boy's fingers from my face. "You have the look of the usurper, to whom Winchester has always given way. You conduct yourself with honor; he trusts your word, although Stephen repeatedly swore falsely to uphold him. He should pledge himself our vassal, but do not deem him sure."

"I will be his overlord, and the source of his aggrandizement. Where else should any man place his faith, but with me, the king to come?"

†

THE WEATHER IS SO biting that we spend the brunt of everyday at the blaze in the keep's great hall. The wily bishop is fond of the fire. I am required by etiquette to cede the warmest seat to my most distinguished guest, but I do so with ill will.

Today, over steaming goblets of fragrant rose liquor, Winchester's tone was especially patronizing. "It is a fine thing to be at rest after the exhaustion of eternal strife! Let us bow our heads in thanksgiving."

I could not bear his hypocrisy. "We rejoice, for the seditious, illegitimate pretender no longer ferments civil disturbance."

The Plantagenet looked annoyed to hear us wrangle, but Eleanor interjected. "We all exult in the deliverance from chaos, most especially my husband, who is the true prince of the people."

His Grace was careful to flatter his next benefactress. "A queen well measures the price of war, but tranquility is the gift of the Lord." A scrap of macerated flower petal clung to Winchester's lip.

That rogue Hamelin clustered with us at the hearth. "I pray that His Majesty and my brother continue to toss the royal scepter back and forth between them, so that the threat of turbulence persists. In troubled times, the overlords have no choice but to make much of their brave warriors, and share their spoils with a greater evenhandedness. God may spread concord down upon England, but not until men-at-arms such as myself open the gates to walled towns and lower the drawbridges of fortified castles."

Henry was roused into enthusiasm. "Well might we heap rewards upon gallant men, wielding their weapons in our glorious cause!"

Denise's son was as brutal and narrow as he had seemed as a boy. I tried to cow him. "Your suit of mail, in which you strut so proudly, will serve no purpose in paradise."

But Hamelin flourished his mother's talent for seduction, endeavoring to lure his half-sibling from his holy purpose. "What care I for heaven? Whom should I meet therein? Aged abbots and skeletal friars, risen from their putrefying crypts? Crippled beggars, barefoot clerks, tattered pilgrims, plague-ridden orphans, awakened from a communal pauper's grave? Look for me in purgatory, among the fierce pirates, painted whores, gouty earls, and jaded minstrels. I will drink to the health of my fellows there, all the brutal knights and their licentious, noble ladies."

The bishop coughed; the sacs under his eyes wiggled. "You are most unwise, when you neglect to draw a veil over the viciousness that defiles your belt of knighthood. If you cannot restrain yourself from bad conduct, if you insist upon following the well-worn path to ruin, keep your failure of courtliness to yourself. You pollute our ears with your degenerate talk."

I turned to Hamelin. "Permit me to speak as your father, who is no longer with us to guide you. You must go, with humility, to confession, and be given a penance; you must fulfill its terms with obedience, and be washed clean of your misdeeds."

Hamelin sulked, but did not refute my advice.

The acrimonious bishop blinked his eyelids and smiled.

†

ALL THE PARTIES CONCERNED agree to the major terms of Henry's accession. The Count of Boulogne adopts the Plantagenet as his successor, but continues to reign unto death. The prince regains what is his mother's rightful inheritance and his true father's conquest. At the coronation to come, all may cheer, without reservation. History is to legitimate all that I have done.

This contract essentially replicates the one that was proposed and accepted by me in the year of Our Lord 1141, before the dishonest knave of a usurper refused it. Seventeen years of anarchy must be laid at my cousin's feet. I blame my once beloved's imbecility and the greed of his strumpet Maud for the tragedy of upheaval.

The duke returns to England for the royal Christmas Court, where he and Stephen will sign their accord. I would witness the rites, but neither empress nor duchesses is invited on the journey. How then shall I protect my son from the dangers that still surround him?

Today, regardless of the sleet and mud, the household rode out in the fields, in order to exercise the horses. Henry was oblivious to the ugliness of the world. "Now that I am no longer his enemy, it is senseless to rebel against the pretender, even in my mind." The duke kicked his heels into his destrier's flanks and cantered past me.

I spurred my mare on, so that I could catch up.

Unwilling to be hounded, Henry picked up his steed's pace, galloping even further away. Over his shoulder, he shouted, "The king is fifty-eight years old, not immortal!"

We approached the apex of a large hill, giving out onto a view of Rouen. From our saddles, we looked at the snowy rooftops of the growing town and the busy manufactures in its outskirts. I patted the steaming neck of my mount. "He cedes you nothing that was not already yours."

The Plantagenet scraped some dirt off his stirrups. Then he looked me over. "Mother, I little thought that your bitterness would outlast our civil war. Your disappointment grows rancid. If you are at all anxious to reward me, the knight who has fulfilled your quest, you must excise the putrefaction. Heartache is futile. Concern yourself, nourish yourself, with my greatness or with your own goodness. Perhaps, Empress, you were specifically chosen by Christ to be sacrificed." The duke nodded at me, no more than an elderly dowager.

Overwhelmed, I could not reply. Tears poured down my cheeks, like icicles under the eaves of my eyelashes.

"Behold your child, with one foot on your throne. Behold his devotion to his mother, whose great seat he yearns to fill. Gladden your spirit, for he shall wear the mantle of your greatness, with your name on his lips." After all, it is my son who reminds me of my duty.

†

I HAVE SPENT THE night in prayer to Our Lady. Her intervention has brought forth a miracle. "Hail Mary, blessed among women. Blessed is the fruit of your womb, Thy Son." I too am chosen, from among other queens, to be a holy vessel for the heir to the world, to bring forth the Messiah.

†

HENRY WRITES TO US of the grand ceremony of reconciliation at the Christmas Court in Winchester.

> *When the king progressed with me through the streets of the town, there was such joy among the folk that they could not contain their adulation, but continually burst out into singing and cheering. Lovely young maidens wept and tossed bouquets at my feet. Stephen and I were attended by throngs of dignified clerics and rich magnates, who all exclaimed at this stupendous welcome from the people, their willingness to declare their new fidelity.*
>
> *Inside the cathedral, Henry of Blois placed me upon his own episcopal throne. A great assembly of distinguished persons commingled. We could hear the shouting crowds outside the church, as my father acknowledged my hereditary right to his kingdom and confirmed his gift to me of its honors. In return, I allowed him control, if he wanted it, over the realm for all his life, and did him homage.*
>
> *Then His Majesty, and all the archbishops, bishops, earls, barons, justiciars, and sheriffs who were present, each took an oath. They swore that, after the death of the present sovereign, I should come into Britain and have it as my own, without opposition.*
>
> *I received all their kisses, embracing them as their liege lord.*

Eleanor prizes this communiqué as an inestimable treasure. She cherishes the fold of parchment, as if she could take communion from it.

I blush now to think how I worshipped at the false altar of desire, before I came to the notice of the Virgin.

A royal courier took me quite by surprise. He had a document for the Lady Dameta, if she still lived, from the Lord Arthur. To my relief, it was not a love letter.

> *I have bequeathed my most opulent sword to my most valiant son. And I have made him a greater present, the grant of my whole fief. In all my affairs, I have promised, as is fitting, not to act without his advice and counsel. If any man shall infringe upon my rights, as they still are, our Henry shall be the first to punish them.*

The Mirror of the Plantagenet

Scroll Twenty-Three: 1154

I have sung unto you a prolonged cycle of the empress's love and strife. If I have any supporters among discriminating men, I shall be esteemed by them all the more for bringing her chronicle to its conclusion. Thus, be it known, that after the long winter of his war, the pretender met his earthly end. The Plantagenet wore the English crown and his sovereignty was much applauded for the good peace that it promised. As for Matilda, she thrust her rebellious mind and wicked body away from her newborn soul. The Virgin was merciful to the princess who had persisted in indecency year after year, acknowledging her calamity and accepting her remorse. In the depths of her conversion, the empress marveled at heaven's strength and pity. In displeasure, the Almighty had destroyed the land of her father; in compassion, He exalted the realm of her son. He who created the queen of resignation was the king of kings.

†

Winter

HENRY RETURNS TO NORMANDY in order to escape the difficulties that plague England in the aftermath of his adoption, primarily due to the multiple claimants to each parcel of property, whether great or small. Some judge must determine between them: often a deposed earl who stands for me, a resident baron of Stephen's and some mercenary knight who has managed to build a fortified tower during the recent years of mayhem. How shall all these rivals be appeased? There are not enough castles, manors, fiefs, or titles to satisfy all of them. Surely, many of the nobles will refuse to make expensive sacrifices merely to assure the tranquility of our throne.

The Plantagenet intends to restore territory and honors to all those who lawfully possessed it in my father's time. The recent elevations and newly written deeds he deems fraudulent. But he wishes to announce this verdict after his coronation, when the power of enforcing it shall also rest with him. In the meantime, until the demise of the pretender, his word is not yet the law.

On the other side of the Channel, the Count of Boulogne sets out on a progress, to display himself before the British people as the gallant champion who dissolves their dissension and abolishes their discord. Will my England fete and please him? Declining to follow in the usurper's train, refusing to loaf about without total authority or complete dignity, the prince returns across the water, to address himself to his duchy.

†

THE PLANTAGENET LANDS ON the continent, but does not appear among us in Rouen, for some fool, refusing to accept the new political realities, revolts against his name at the castle of Torigny. Henry proceeds to invest the disloyal keep, with the aid of his youngest brother. William, now seventeen, is ready to prove himself a worthy ally, and is eager to be knighted by the sword of his illustrious sibling. My heart lightens; William has none of young Geoffrey's poisonous enmity.

Agitated by the disharmony in Normandy, I endeavor to remain stoic. I have paid a high price for my prize, stripping my soul of its pride and greed and fantasy. In exchange, my heir shall bless the world. I am content with the bargain, an old woman's settlement, to be sure. But the Virgin is my model; I am privileged to play Her part.

The duchess fidgets, wheedling Gerta for love charms and beauty potions. My maid winds massive, lustrous auburn wigs into Eleanor's own hair, to thicken her tresses. Local women profit from their lovely curls, hacking them off in exchange for a clinking purse. I frown at the duchess's borrowed splendor, the fortune on her head. It is the province of heaven to glorify us with comeliness. A woman's face is the handiwork of the angels. I am ashamed at how often I permitted Gerta to overstep, in my own futile scramble to preserve and magnify my beauty.

Yet I do not speak out against my daughter, for she has given my son her true heart. Her maneuvers beseech his desire and devotion. How can I scold her, or teach her that these things do not endure? I was guilty of the same vanity, in the service of the same cause. For too long, I struggled to abate my own feverish excitements.

How sweet it is to have finally mastered my own debased passions. My infatuation is extinguished. But I do not rest secure in this victory over myself. I pray daily, almost hourly, perpetually on my guard, continually besieging my own self-fortress. I have eradicated all my defenses; I have decimated the garrison fighting on the behalf of what was forbidden. My soul submits. But still I stand guard upon my engines of warfare, ready to take up my arms against temptation.

It was my fate to be a golden pyrite, a burning rock, sequestered on the arid pinnacle of the highest mountain. Stephen was just such another, and in the same place. We emitted great heat, scorching the flesh of any creature that ventured too near. If we two had incinerated only ourselves, no harm would have come from our incendiary natures. Hot and indifferent, we rolled toward one another, so that a blaze erupted that consumed everything of value, all the good things that Christ and his saints had bequeathed upon the world.

Consorting together, my cousin and I were ever surrounded by a ring of flames. Upon this fire, I have poured a cold torrent of rebuke. The Count of Boulogne lit an evil candle within me, but I am now formidable enough to snuff him out. I am wholly chaste. The deep waters of heaven flow through me, cold and pure.

Again and again, I adore and give homage to Mother Mary. With continual vehemence, I bestow myself in vassalage to Her; ardently, repeatedly, I give myself in fealty to Her. I escape from the Iower of Love, where I was a cramped prisoner of war, and set off on a voyage to the island of the Word.

†

Spring

THE PRETENDER LIES DYING; a cryptic herald does not explicate further. All my muscles tingle to hasten over the sea. At his side, I will have nothing to fear, for I have found my lady's grace. I shall take leave of my knight, here on earth, before we rise to paradise, for there I shall not know him.

Henry, home among us, refuses to hurry a departure, for he would put every Norman affair in order before taking up his throne. The duchess, concerned for my equanimity, tries to rush his preparations. But the Plantagenet will not be unseemly, and would show that he trusts in England to endure and abide. He measures its faith and tests its promises.

Eager for physical exertion, His Grace organizes a hunting expedition. Our castle seethes with personnel dedicated to ensuring the success of his sport. Numerous knight-huntsmen and their various servants swarm through the keep, reviewing and packing up their particular gear. My son lends an ear to flunkies who forecast the weather, predict the location of herds, and suggest the surest equipment. The prince invites some of the leading men of the duchy to accompany him; they begin to arrive here with all of their squires and baggage, further swelling our numbers and straining the resources of our hospitality.

Today, I had to waylay the Plantagenet in the muck of the stables, where I found him inspecting his mounts. A nervous page twisted his cap in a far corner, but I was unlikely to find my son so nearly alone any time soon.

I swallowed my pride. "Appoint your brother William to look after our affairs here on the continent. Start off for your English future, with me at your side." The sun was too weak to have penetrated the barn, and I huddled into my cloak for warmth.

"I will train him in my methods, after I return from the chase. He remains a wee bit naïve, and needs my firmness." The duke squatted beside a magnificent racer, and inspected his forelegs. The animal whinnied its approval of his sure touch.

I huffed at my his obstinacy. "When you were seventeen, you thought yourself quite fit to rule. William is able enough to be your regent."

Henry stood upright, and smiled thinly. "To direct the affairs of the world is no easy adventure. I myself have been asking the advice of assorted chiefs and sages about the matter of Britain. They all agree: right now, contrary winds blow in the Channel. To cross would be very unwise."

"Your ministers are no geographers."

The Plantagenet walked away from me, and out into the bailey. Now there were many loitering nearby who might hear us. He seemed to speak to them, and not to his interfering mother. "I wish England to be without its sovereign and yet, in fear and in love, at peace."

I darted after him, as he stepped off. How much longer would he have any use for me? "I shall come with you, to witness your coronation, as is right and fitting and praiseworthy."

His Grace spun around, and placed his rough hands upon the shoulders of my thick mantle. "I assume that you are not determined to toss aside decorum. I would have no whispers against my mother's conduct, for the sake of some hopeless fixation."

I dared not blink. "I no longer care for Boulogne; I do not intend to salute him."

The prince guffawed. "Drivel! What courtly lady braves a sea voyage to visit her lover's deathbed, merely to renounce her feelings for him?"

I knew that my cheeks flushed pink. When had I ceased to be an empress? "I would show myself inviolate to him."

"I shall forbid you to visit him, if you persist in troubling me. He wronged you many times over, but you must no longer concern yourself with what is long past."

Shameful tears ran down into my mouth. "I wish to demonstrate to him that I have found what I have been seeking, a reconciliation with Our Lady."

The duke could still be moved by a woman's imprecations. He kissed me hard on the mouth. "Together, we flower in the garden. But you are the stem, the stalk, humbly rooted to the earth. I am the blossom. My scent is glorious, and wafts over England."

I pursed my lips, and swallowed hard, for I could taste the sour truth. "I am the royal way, the road you and Stephen both trampled."

†

As THE DAYS PASS, the bells chime out the Lord's hours. Still, I am over the water, far from my declining cousin, at the port of Barfleur. Supposedly, we are impeded by the currents, although each day dawns fair. Eleanor is inclined to credit her husband's caution, but I find it unlikely that more than one White Ship can dampen the fates of a family. Heaven is on my side now—this I forefeel. The duke and duchess and their heir will be in Mary's hands on the crossing—this I foreknow. The time is come.

Today is Whitsunday, the Feast of the Pentecost, when the Holy Spirit descends into the Apostles, miraculously endowing them with understanding. Blooms decorate the facades of all the churches in the town. Parades of children sing anthems in the streets. Gerta submerges herself in the kitchens of our inn, and alludes to carrot soup, roast veal, pigeon pies, and gooseberry tarts to come. Tonight, we feast to celebrate our own hard-won wisdom, and to pray that favorable winds blow.

†

ʃ*ummer*

AT LAST, WE TRAVERSED the Channel, and with God speed. Midway through the journey, the fears of our entourage were excited by a dense fog that separated the crown ship from the others of our fleet. For a spate of time, we could not see the flares or hear the drums of the other boats, nor they ours. Yet despite the eerie spell of isolation, every one of our vessels came safely ashore. The ducal family landed at the port of Southampton. The other crafts made for various harbors along the coast. All our party shall reconvene on the highway to London.

†

ALONG THE WAY, THROUGHOUT the countryside, our cortege swells with noblemen and prelates eager to welcome their Messiah and accompany his caravan. Many of the villagers and farmers cheer our passage. It is well known that the pretender will soon pay his due to death. As we march by their fortresses, the barons loyal to the Count of Boulogne shiver in doubt over the security of their land and positions. But no knights block our path or threaten our well-being. All is tranquil, for the archbishop of Canterbury awaits the Plantagenet with open arms.

The usurper beleaguered my realm with iniquity and destruction; the land that had been the mirror of religion in the time of my father has long reflected a picture of impious disruption. Now, my son's righteous peace begins to heal and uplift all of us.

†

AS SOON AS MY horse plodded through the stone courtyard of Westminster Palace, I tossed the reins to the nearest page. With some agitation, I skittered to my assigned room to wash off the dirt of the road. My hands trembled, yet I managed to wipe my chin and cheeks and replace my riding headdress with a fresh veil. The tremors in my fingers echoed the palpitations of my heart, pounding in my chest. I lacked the composure to await Gerta's assistance, and a complete change of garments, and so dispensed with any sartorial splendor.

On my walk to the Count of Boulogne's solar, I had the corridors to myself, for every household attendant was busy facilitating the arrival of our large party to the castle. Having grown up in this keep, I easily found Stephen within the royal chamber that my father set aside for his own use.

My knight-errant still lives, although his appearance is macabre. His skin fades to the color of chalk. Illness pares down his face, so that his skeletal features, his high brow and pointed chin, jut out of his thin flesh. His flinty eyes sink into his skull. His famous red hair bleaches ashen. Dark red fever spots mar his cheeks, dashing garish color upon them.

When I entered his presence, the pretender smiled an occult grin and dismissed his entourage. "I knew that you would come, for who else remains?"

I recognized the leering conceit of my handsome chevalier. He looked obscene, yet I was drawn to him, as my familiar.

I caught myself wishing that I had not bound up the remnants of my own beauty. But as soon as I became conscious of the urge to tempt him, I knew that I had been right to swaddle my physical fairness, still an open wound upon my soul. I have made this pilgrimage to pledge farewell to carnal love.

I had not noticed it at first, so intent was I upon his cadaverous mien, but now I smelled the horrible odor of disease. Apparently, the usurper is much discomfited from a terrible and chronic diarrhea. It is to be hoped that such a mortification of the flesh serves as a penance, and warrants his salvation.

He grimaced, but greeted me with a chivalrous tribute. "Hark! My mistress knocks on my door, and comes forth to waken my sleeping heart and water my arid soul." As was his wont, he lived in the moment.

Mute, I stood before him, awash in memories.

Despite my silence, Stephen's eyes brightened. "Love is as strong as Death. How this consoles me, and reminds me that I need not evade what is to follow. There will be further solace for me, among the angels."

My cousin was ever optimistic, even now. "Matilda, if the land were mine again, it would be no more wonderful than my imminent ascent to paradise, when I shall bask in the Lord's glory."

Had he discovered that faith was our only true comfort? Could we stand together, in joint service to heaven? I approached his bed, taking his bony hand in my soft palm. "You should be despairing, yet you are certain. You slip away, yet for Christ's sake you remain rooted to the truth. You are surrounded by eternal silence, yet you hear the sublime melody."

The Count of Boulogne gave me his other hand. "I remember the moment I first beheld you, that elegant girl, her eyes shining with the will to rule, her face beaming with the hunger to please. From the beginning, you were my shining star."

I held his fingers tightly, to impress upon him our mutual atonement. "But you repent of our relationship, and of all your other amorous intrigues."

He would not succumb to my suggestion. "Touching you, I recall every one of our secret embraces, and all the other private dalliances that enriched my years. I regret none of the kisses that I showered upon comely maidens, nor any of the caresses that I received. They say that females are the source of our depravity, but debauchery was my own compulsion. Still, I shall pass through the pearly gates, for I was a godly king."

I despaired that I had misunderstood him. "Now, you must choose betwixt your gallantry and your piety."

The pretender's words drew me in. "I once betrayed you; I know it well. I was not enough of a general to win the war that I declared upon you."

We were intimates, despite his sacrilege. "You were too courageous when you plotted the theft of my inheritance. You have the blood of your grandfather, the conqueror."

For a moment, he competed with me to be the most noble and courteous. "I was a usurper. You were the Lady of the English."

"Our son is to reign; I bemoan nothing on that score."

There was a pause. Verily, we had more complaints to make than encomiums to lavish.

A small wheeze escaped Stephen's chapped lips. "It came to pass that I was inconvenienced on your account. Maud suffered a thousand pains, knowing what had transpired between us, and she made sure that I repaid her for my lack of fealty."

My heart burned at that name. "I do not wish to avenge myself upon you, although I myself have agonized immeasurably. Now that you are stripped of your strength and resources, you still have me to lean on. I will not abandon you. You have recognized our boy at last, and I exult to see justice done. "

"I do not marvel at your compassion and charity. You are merciful to me today; the saints shall be mild tomorrow. So I was lenient, and loath to enforce crown liberties, when it was my turn to arbitrate men's fates." As his stomach cramped, the knave's voice cracked.

I glimpsed his agony, etched in the twist of his lips and the beads of sweat on his brow. I reached over to smooth his brittle hair, feeling him once more beneath my fingers. "Do you wish me to call your physicians?"

He groaned. "They cannot help me. My end will come when it will. But do you remember me to the Holy Virgin." Stephen's eyes met mine. "Be careful, Matilda; do not allow my passing to injure you too greatly. See that I am buried beside my family, resting alongside Queen Maud and Prince Eustace at the abbey of Faversham in Kent. Go in peace from thence to your son's coronation."

His countenance swam before me, and I fell from Her grace. "Nothing is as it was. Nothing is as it should have been."

"My wife has prepared our nuptial couch, among the thick grasses, under the shade of the tree of knowledge."

Stricken, I cried out. "I bore you your heir!" My cheeks flared red at my failure to forswear what had been.

My cousin winced. "You are one island; I am another."

Keening, ashamed, I flung myself away from him, but stopped at the door of the chamber. "I begged you so many times for clemency, but found you hard-hearted. The benevolent Mother Mary blessed me when you cursed me, succored me when you stripped me of all that I had."

Stephen understood that I was ready to desert him. "Hallowed be Her name. She is light and life, in the face of temptation and death. Let us praise Her, and Her son, and yours, and sing songs to them."

I would not be cheated again, turned hot and cold by his facile, lying tongue and my broken heart. "Farewell. You are no more vanquished than I."

I ran off to my solar, where I fell to my knees. Have I passed through my last ordeal? Will I be resurrected, whole and pure?

I disown, forgo, gainsay, and withhold myself from him, body and soul. I choose, admit, affirm, and grant myself to Mary. He shall not rob me of eternal serenity, for I am nothing but the vessel of a Mother's love.

But I hear the bells tolling; my cousin has died this night.

†

THREE SUNS HAVE SET on a world without him.

Today, a subdued archbishop of Canterbury anointed King Henry II. Westminster Abbey itself is ill kept and in need of repair, for my cousin's coffers, always depleted by warring, were not at the Church's disposal. The rites of accession felt somewhat improvised, for the duke and duchess had accelerated their coronation plans, having found with their wedding that a less than sumptuous show matters not.

At least the Plantagenet had attired himself with opulence. I insisted on splendor, and he acceded with nonchalance to my proffered silks and ermines. He looked the very portrait of a sovereign, but belittled my fanfare: "These vestments do not shine more than my armor. My subjects should see my lively expression, my robust body, my dignified carriage. They may have confidence in my valiant energy, my princely poise, and my vital determination. It is not necessary that they think highly of my tailor."

For all his bluster, Henry II held his head high beneath his crown of solid gold, a priceless treasure that had been among my trunks when I departed from Germany. Embossed with roods of opal, it weighs so much that it had to be bolstered up by two long silver rods, held in the hands of his attendants. Over his head, other pages waved pennants that displayed the shield of the Plantagenet: three golden lions facing forward, charging across a red field. He embellishes Henry I's motif, for his arms declare his three-fold inheritance, through his grandfather, his father, and me.

Marooned on the continent, I had prepared my own ceremonial costume. Today, I officially adopted new colors, those of the Virgin. My pleated linen bliaut, white as the lily, set off my flowing silk jacket, red as the rose. I left my hair unbound, in Her holy image. I eschewed costly jewels. In my right hand, I carried a wooden staff; I positioned my left hand upon my breast. I adorned myself in Her placidity, amidst constant upheaval, and in Her incorruptibility, among the pernicious.

A magnificent assembly of vassals thronged the gloom of the ancient cathedral. The crowd sparkled with assorted brilliants, as bright as the stars in the night sky. Faces radiated relief at the evasion of death and suffering. It seemed to me that our courtiers basked in the glow of the wonderful age to come. I recognized many of my former enemies and others who had once, twice, thrice sworn to serve me.

A choir of young boys welcomed the arrival of their Messiah, chanting: "Lord, now we are yours! Command us! Employ us! We shall live in you!"

The archbishop raised his hand, assuring all our silence. From the regalia displayed upon the altar, he held aloft a golden eagle. "The consecration of a king is a sacrament; the sacred oil is an indelible balm. Neither water from a stagnant wayside pool nor the crashing waves of the ocean can wash the unction from an anointed sovereign." The archbishop tipped the bird forward, so that oil flowed through its beak, and he dripped it in the shape of a cross onto my son's red hair. "Many have been the atrocious evils wrought upon us. Never have a people endured more ruination or greater sorrow. And so I pray to the Lord that His light shall banish the darkness of hell, and that His love shall subdue the devil."

His Majesty pledged his oath to the church. "I shall be the guardian of heaven's abundant gifts and Christ's illumination." He turned to the congregation of barons and earls, friends and foes. "I will insist upon your fidelity and your counsel, in return for the privilege of your fiefs. I will not forfeit your life, lay claim to your forests and keeps, or deprive you of your titles and honors without just cause."

How well it behooved him to address his vassals directly, the very moment he had gained his crown!

The archbishop next anointed the duchess. Her pink face looked charming under a short veil, held in place by a diadem furnished all over with solid gold flowers. This tiara had also been mine. My coronation gift well became her remarkable head of curls. And so Eleanor became queen, sharing the throne, with specified powers as consort. "When King Henry is absent from England, Your Majesty shall issue his writs in your own name and under your own seal."

Finally, His Grace made the sign of the rood over my head. "Hail Mother! Blessed is the treasured infant of your womb. You were chosen to bring forth the Prince of Glory. Forgive us our doubts and mistakes."

Despite the dictates of protocol, there was scattered applause. I listened, numb, to the rest of the Mass, steeped in joy and surrender, washed of resentment and agitation. I prayed for the wisdom to understand my fate. I am renounced, I am sacrificed, but I am reborn. I still have a place among the English; I remain their Mother. But they petition me for compassion, and look for justice from my son.

When the royal party departed the abbey, a throng of local burghers, merchants, guild masters, and moneylenders roared their shrill approval, as they had robustly cheered our illegitimate predecessors. London is their capital of profit and ease, and their ignoble prosperity still galls me. They worshipped Boulogne and his slut of a wife, and would have none of me. I never took my brother's advice and learned to conciliate them. Gusts of wind were pungent with the teeming Thames and the acrid scents of wool and beer. I held my nose, for I am replete with what is ill-favored and vexatious.

†

AT TONIGHT'S CORONATION FEAST, each magnate and bishop present paid his respects to the new king with an honest heartiness. Regardless of his age or agility, every man bent his knees to the boy of twenty-two.

During the copious meal, companies of pages cut the viands up into bite-sized pieces, so that we, at the high table, were not put to the trouble of using our cutlery. Blaring trumpets heralded the arrival of each new course. Our washbasin was fashioned in the shape of a swan. We wiped our fingers on squares of silk, red and gold in honor of the occasion.

Jongleurs performed bawdy songs, and then were succeeded by the tomfoolery of acrobats, jugglers, and conjurers. Late in the evening, Bernard materialized at the dais to recount a long historical poem, whose subject was the return of the irreproachable Greek hero, Ulysses. A harpist accompanied his recitation.

Henry yawned throughout this muted performance, and waved over an elaborate, boat-shaped flagon of wine.

I noticed that he was still sober, although most of our guests had slipped onto the floor rushes or away to their pallets.

A replenished drink loosened the archbishop's tongue. "Your Majesty rules an empire that stretches from the Scottish border to the Pyrenees. You are more than a Holy Roman emperor. You are such a one as Charlemagne."

†

LAST EVENING, AS THE bells struck compline, I took a circuitous, discreet walk through the lesser-used corridors of the palace, so as to exit the bailey near the maze, where I once trysted with my cousin. My veils were as opaque as fashion allows, to stymie the curiosity of the gardeners, or any courtiers out for a stroll.

Meeting no one, I wandered, fascinated, among the verdant paths of the labyrinth, relishing their austerity and their circuitry, as cold and cyclic as the movement of time. It felt right to be trapped in a tangle of inextricable cause and effect, as cruelly rhythmic as nature, indifferent to the bliss and woe of the sinner.

As I roamed, I communed with Lady Mary. She thinned out the foliage, and lightened my tread. With Her guidance, it became simple to find my way to the center. I could rove, letting the Virgin direct me to the heart of the enigma. There, I flung myself in the dirt before my Holy Mother, and mingled my tears with Her own.

Without question, everywhere, and in everything, I must follow Her winding course, for it leads straight to heaven.

†

I NEED HER INTERCESSION, for I could not forgo the road to Kent, and a visit to the pretender's grave. I wanted to renounce my cousin again, for repudiation purifies me. It settles me to sacrifice Stephen, to suffer denial, as I would the sharp needles of a hair shirt or the hot whips of a lash.

Henry refused to travel with me to Faversham Abbey, preferring my journey to go unremarked by the gossips. His Majesty cares nothing for the mausoleum of the House of Boulogne.

And so, alone, amazed, I lingered before the usurper's massive stone tomb, inlaid with bands of precious metals and blanketed with a silk coverlet embroidered with colossal gems. I stood transfixed by the profusion of emeralds, topazes, sapphires, jasper, and onyx. Twenty candles burned at the sides, feet, and head of the sarcophagi. An amethyst censer swung nearby, heavily perfuming the extravagant display. Entombed within so much vulgarity, my once beloved rested, at peace, for all time. No business of state, nor female recriminations roused him from the luxury of his bed.

My cousin never ascertained that desire cannot damn the river it erodes within the soul. His external comeliness withered, yet he never redeemed his inward ugliness. He was my courtly lover, but he did not deserve my surety. His treated promises and sworn kisses were mere figments of my imagination. The English were likewise ill-used by his hollow affection. A third of the British populace perished while the knave sat upon my throne.

†

OUR SON BEGINS TO rule, issuing a conservative charter of which I well approve, confirming all the concessions that his grandfather had given and granted, outlawing all the evil customs that his grandfather had abolished. There is none of Stephen's mind in it, for Henry II erases the usurper's governance, resuming the protocols of Henry I.

The Plantagenet dismisses a flock of coarse, frivolous friends such as Hamelin, appointing in their stead somber and well-respected deputies. He ignores the old allegiances and the old affiliations, choosing practical men who will help him to create a centralized state, loyal only to the party of the king. But, primarily, he forges his own way, attending busily to his subjects' complaints and rivalries, hearing their cases and pleas at all hours of the day and night. He struggles to reestablish public order and to strengthen the right and might of the courts and of the law, balancing, in all cases, justice with prudence.

The island is rife with dispute and competition for honors or fiefs, yet the feuding melts away like the steam above a boiling cauldron. The well-armed barons seek compromises or settlements, so that they may lay down their weapons and demolish their strongholds, in subservience to His Majesty's authority and in fear lest the others move more quickly to gain his confidence. The earls surrender all the towers that have ever been crown properties and cease to occupy any manor within the royal demesne. The kingdom is returned to its expansive estate, as Henry I held it, entire, for our heirs to come.

The peasants gloat, for the Plantagenet banishes the pretender's mercenaries, the standing army that was vainly devoted to reinforcing my cousin's preeminence. I pray to the Virgin that my son will not need to impose his will upon the English. Henry appears sanguine, and secure, although I recollect the hatred of his brother Geoffrey and the ill will of Louis of France. But, for now, on this side of the Channel, my son gleefully accepts the embrace of gratified people, yearning for the restoration of amity and affluence.

Henry II declines to repeat my mistakes, and is leery, lest he be considered a tyrant. By the time that his dominance over the realm is absolute, it shall be with his subjects' full concurrence. Under the guise of slow and thoughtful action, he persuades the English that it is for the best that he alone controls the empire.

I do not need it spelled out for me. He is the future; I am the past.

†

Fall

WITH THEIR MAJESTIES, I dawdle in England, at the royal manor of Bermondsey, in the east end of London. They could not long reside at Westminster Palace, quite decrepit, due to the sloth of Maud's housekeeping, and the paltriness of the crown treasury. I was loath to dally where I was once so brutally deposed, and so followed in my son's wake.

That snake, Henry of Blois, again proves himself disloyal. His Grace has long delayed the return of his palaces to the crown. Now, when veritably forced to relinquish the castle of Winchester, he flees abroad to France. The old man, maker of princes and almost a prince himself, does not dare to defy Henry, but obeys His Majesty's commands without due fealty.

And now he writes to Bernard, and commissions an epic poem! Our minstrel, agape with delight at the bishop's unlooked for generosity, will not specify the composition's subject. I suspect Winchester's patronage guarantees political verse complimentary to my foes and disparaging of me, hence pure calumny, neither useful nor agreeable. I am uneasy, and rather dread the publication of his inevitably false, exaggerated, and malicious account. De Ventadour actually packs his meager bags, and slinks off to settle down in some monastery hereabouts, so as to invent his insulting, misleading tale in seclusion, far from the noisy distractions and perpetual demands of court life, not to mention my pointed stares.

Oddly, the bishop's herald also transmits a small parcel addressed to me, a most gorgeous book, a *Mariales*, recounting the life and miracles of the Virgin, paying homage to Her power and mercy. When I unwrapped it, my breath caught in my throat to perceive what a treasure he had made over to me. Under its cover, I discovered a letter.

> *O empress, Greetings! I have had a vision of the most gentle Holy Mother, radiating goodness, lit from within by the eternal flame. She commands me to carry you in my heart, for you too have given forth a Son, ennobled by the Spirit of God.*
>
> *It was, for many years, my deeply held belief that you were a mediocrity, not fashioned to rule over men. I admit that I audaciously stole from you the right of succession. Perhaps it was not for me alone to determine whether there should be peace or war, quiet or storm.*
>
> *For my brother's sake, I denounced you and your dark lusts. I always made it my business to limit Stephen's follies, and your raven charms unmanned his body and troubled his mind. It was you who made him less of a king than he might have been.*

The snake still speaks with seven tongues, and his corroded heart still pumps with venom.

†

WE ENDURE AT BERMONDSEY. The worsening weather dampens our mood, and my household is given to bickering. I do my best not to notice.

Eleanor talks incessantly of her coming child, convinced it is another boy. The queen would have a second prince, this one born in the purple. Rather fat now, she still accepts the effusions of the minstrels. She is found handsome by those who think more of her largesse than of her person. Much is made of her "goodly reign."

His Majesty praises the awkward proportions of his bride. He presents her with a brooch, inscribed to his darling. Gerta smirks, thinking the king prefers his sultry, careless wife to fasten her mantle more closely about her shoulders.

Eleanor's distrust of her spouse grows apace. My maid ferrets out a royal bastard, sired upon a tavern whore in Normandy, who dares to name her boy "Geoffrey Plantagenet."

Today, we gathered in the queen's solar, for it has a splendid view of the river and a commodious hearth. Her Majesty attempted to interest her husband. "I hear that Louis has given your brother Geoffrey an audience. The topic was the last will and testament of the late Duke of Normandy. Geoffrey insisted that he had a right to be Count of Anjou, now that you have risen to sovereignty in England."

The Plantagenet sat unmoving before the blaze, staring into its orange glare. "Bah! Louis dismissed the pathetic oaf, for he would respect the claims of a king before those of a landless knight."

Eleanor tapped her ringed fingers upon the armrest of her wooden seat. "You should not discount my experience in these continental matters. I know Louis's policy well. He recognizes the shortcomings of the French military, the laziness of his soldiers, and the ineptitude of his generals. He always prefers to parley with the powerful, rather than to fight them. Thus he retains his nominal authority and receives the willing oaths of stronger neighbors. You have no need to secede from Anjou, for Louis will never force you to do so. Besides, Anjou connects your Normandy to my vast territories."

His Majesty's expression softened at this display of political prowess on his wife's part.

I spoke, although the king had not given me permission to interfere. "You might consider, sire, the possibility of paying your brother an income; his vitriol must stem from his poverty. There is no question of granting him the Angevin fief. The vow that you took on the corpse of your father is invalid, for it was sworn under duress and in ignorance of its eventual repercussions. The pope will certainly agree to annul it."

Eleanor reached out her hand, and ran it along her beloved's sleeve. "Perhaps I have some troublesome nobleman in Touraine or Poitou, whose fidelity is suspect. Invest his castle, and give his liberties and titles to your degenerate brother."

I have no pride in my Henry's disloyal sibling. "You have received an appeal for help from the citizens of Nantes, who wish to be free from the cruel overlordship of the Duke of Brittany. You might make your brother the Count of Nantes. Without any warring, you placate an intemperate foe and infiltrate another province. Gift Geoffrey the County of Nantes!"

The Plantagenet stood up, and admonished us all. "I have waited all my life to be great; I find that I am greater even than my dreams. Worthily, I shall steer the ship of state with a firm grasp on the rudder. I shall not be any woman's creature, nor any puffed up historian's. I shall see everything, hear everything, and be master of it all, by right and justice."

There was a brief spell of silence. Then Eleanor essayed to beguile her husband. "Your Majesty, I take my only joy from you. I would have it mixed less with consternation. I would love more lightly."

The king relented. "Mother, did you hear my siren's call?"

I sighed. Once I was a young swallow, pulsing wings a blur in the morning sky, whistling sweetly from my vibrating throat. Now I am an old crow, idly circling in the dusky void, mute before the dying day.

†

PASSIONATE MARIE PLEDGES HERSELF to the convent of Shaftesbury in Dorset. Trailing her idol to Britain, but finding him lifted so far above her, and herself unremembered, she sequesters all her unrequited emotions in a nunnery.

A provincial clerk, attached to her sisterhood, shuffles into my presence with an elegantly inscribed note.

> *My private distress subsides, and I do not wish to turn my back on every past tie. I hope that we may correspond in the years to come, when both of us shall be at a remove from the ostentatious hub of civic affairs.*
>
> *For too long, I grieved too pointedly, and groaned aloud with longing, and clutched my breast, and found nothing worth the wretched trouble of arising from my bed, but now my heart gladdens to think myself engaged*

to be a bride of Christ. With patience and forethought, I await the day when I shall make my vow.

There is no more perfect groom than the martyred Son of the Eternal King. If I am not to wed your Henry, then I am satisfied. I shall rest forevermore untouched, and love purely.

Will Marie profit from her seclusion, and fill as many parchment scrolls as I have? The Lord gifted her with a quick wit and a silver tongue, the better to voice his Holy wisdom. I predict that she will come to be known as a troubadour, or rise to the rank of abbess.

It would console unseemly, depraved Denise to retreat from the pestilence of the world, but she declines to do so. As the proverb says: "A woman must have a husband, or a wall."

†

RESIGNED TO THE COURSE of events, and pleased by my son's preeminence, I have arranged to retire with Gerta to the monastery of Notre-Dame-du-Pré, outside Rouen. I rise up from the gaming board of life, tossing aside my dice, prepared to devote the rest of my earthly time to the sacred way. The cloister shall be my framework, as if I were a cramped creature carved and docked into the stone lintel of a church portal. Yet, so circumscribed, my soul will expand, until it is immense and harmonious.

Gerta does not sink into dejection. She is mollified to quit trouble, worry, and intrigue for the tranquility of the priory and its royal park. She predicts that the Lord will hear the plea of a suppliant handmaiden, and, in His wisdom, will pardon her multitude of offences. She names her art "natural magic," feats in keeping with His commandments, pious miracles welcome to his notice. She denies having practiced any criminal, demonic sorcery, capable of perverting heaven's will. Too old to change her ways, she wraps a clump of heliotrope and a wolf's tooth in laurel leaves, and stuffs the twisted bundle under her girdle. For the most part, she trusts that God will not strike her down with wrathful affliction, but prefer to take her as on as His servant, thus preserving her soul. She will be redeemed alongside me, not tested.

I am satisfied that Mother Mary, who joined us together throughout our lives, does not think to part us now. One must seek to be always in the company of those whose merit is tried and true. I have Gerta and she has me; of this we shall be possessed.

King Henry approves of my plans, for I shall function as his regent in Normandy, allowing him to prevent the rise in status of any one vassal in the duchy. He fears his brother Geoffrey too much to trust William with authority over the province. Henry plans, instead, to grant his youngest brother the island of Ireland, once it should be conquered for Christendom.

And so it is. In my abdication, I will not be completely the nun, but rather the sometime duchess, a person of consequence. If His Majesty is not to do it, then I shall see that it is done.

†

ENRAPTURED, WE CANNOT FULLY comprehend the Plantagenet; he is too awesome, amazing, inexplicable. His Majesty is already a figure of the minstrels' fables, already a legend. They call him a panther, strong and lithe; he snarls, poised and primed to pounce, but exudes some alluring, mesmerizing fragrance.

As she who begot him, I am famed for my potent beauty and my masculine spirit. The jongleurs insist that I am fortitude itself, that my spirit is all vigor, without weakness. They misunderstand me, a princess made entirely of love. I sing to you my entire history, and it is the work of love, first of a perfidious love and then of an authentic one.

At the end of a broken, divided life, all I yearn for is a unified soul. In prayer to the Virgin, I remake myself whole and undefiled, as everything divine is stable and entire. Am I not greater now than I was before? The three kings were my framework, and held me in place. But you who have read or listened to my true account can acknowledge my own claims. I, too, was a king, courtly, good, and wise, somehow refuted by naysayers and rebuffed by betrayal.

I was nailed upon a cross until I undertook a great forsaking, two resignations, of passion and ambition. It comes to pass that the only throne I shall ever see is the shining seat in paradise, the perennial chair before the hearth of the perpetual fire. Yet, in this seat, as Mary's first and highest acolyte, I am at my zenith, towering above the complacent princes, bombastic knights, supercilious barons, obsequious minstrels, and slavish priests who promised me power or snatched it away from me.

You, chivalrous, noble, discerning, generous listeners, have unspooled my epic story of sin and atonement, resurrection and coronation. You have appraised the worth of my treasure stores, and counted the tolls and fees that I have paid. You, who have looked deep into my mirror, will not forget to hail and salute the Holy Mother.

Some Notes on Matilda Empress

Many of the events depicted herein actually occurred, particularly those of historical significance. Taking artistic license, I have tampered a bit with chronology, conflated some secondary characters, invented a few minor players, and completely imagined all the private moments unlikely to have been recorded for posterity. This is a novel, not a history textbook, and the "true story" is still somewhat obscured by gaps in the historical record and centuries of conflicting interpretations of the surviving documents. Overall, I have used the most interesting "facts" to construct a solid framework for my house of fiction, then fashioned its more fluid walls with a tangled thatch of love, ambition, honor, duty, resignation, and faith.

Matilda, a real person and a real empress, inherited a great realm from her father, King Henry I, but struggled and failed to attain her rightful throne. Her disloyal cousin Stephen, who stole her crown, had been her childhood playmate, and sworn to her service. At the time, there was idle curiosity and a hint of gossip about the complex nature of the relationship between these two, and a few historians, from the thirteenth-century onward, have debated the question, wondering if they were lovers, but only in the time before Matilda's marriage to Geoffrey of Anjou. Most academics discount the idea that Henry II could possibly have had *every* right to be King Stephen's heir, and insist that the usurper's "adoption" of his successor at the end of the civil war was merely formulaic. Henry II is never spoken of as "illegitimate," and, if Matilda and her cousin were perhaps briefly entangled, the idea of a life-long love affair between the antagonists in a great civil war is a fabrication of my own.

I have read widely in my attempt to absorb and recreate the atmosphere that set the stage for the adventures of Matilda and her circle of friends and foes. Contemporary letters, annals, chronicles, epics, liturgies, memoirs, poems, and romances have stimulated my flights of fancy. Among the many modern titles that I have consulted, I am most indebted to Marjorie Chibnall's thorough, scholarly *The Empress Matilda: Queen Consort, Queen Mother and Lady of the English* (1991), Nesta Pain's engaging *Empress Matilda: Uncrowned Queen of England* (1978), Joachim Bumke's comprehensive, absorbing *Courtly Culture* (1991), Madeleine Pelner Cosman's inspiring *Fabulous Feasts: Medieval Cookery and Ceremony* (1999), and Richard Kieckhefer's fascinating *Magic in the Middle Ages* (1989). I am grateful for their research and analysis, their anecdotes and data, their maps and footnotes. All errors of understanding and perspective are my own.

Acknowledgments

atilda Empress has been my hobby for more than twenty years, starting with my first early draft in 1996 through its countless revisions. I always intended the story to be more than just a private exercise, so finally sending it out into the world brings me enormous satisfaction.

I could not have spent so much time living in the twelfth century without the patience and support of my family. My husband's firm conviction that the novel would appear someday in a bookstore, if I just kept at it, sustained me when my own assurance flagged. My children, for their part, put up with stacks of research, piled high, even in their bedrooms, and often discovered that I had poached their private stash of post-it notes or red pens. All of their delight in *Matilda Empress*'s publication, after so many years of working and waiting, magnifies my own.

I would also like to thank my earliest readers: Amanda Brainerd and Kristin Hohmann. They graciously implied that I was a real writer before I could rightfully claim the title. Stephanie Cabot's insights and suggestions made the novel stronger, and the heroine more accessible. Melissa Barrett Rhodes and Ivan Shaw went out of their way to help me secure a beautiful cover image. Eric Brown has been a wise counselor, especially given my status as an absolute beginner. And Jesseca Salky made the introduction that has made all the difference.

I'd still be daydreaming about this career were it not for the good faith and enthusiasm of her friends at Archer Lit. Tyson Cornell, Lisa Weinert and the Archer/Rare Bird team, notably Alice Elmer, Julia Callahan, Hailie Johnson, and Andrew Hungate, have returned Empress Matilda to the public stage, smoothed her rough edges, talked her up, and made her timely. I am very grateful for their offer to take me on, and for their belief both in the project and in me.